Filthy Lucre

FILTHY LUCRE

Simon Rose

SIMON & SCHUSTER

LONDON • SYDNEY • NEW YORK • TOKYO • TORONTO

First published in Great Britain by
Simon & Schuster Ltd in 1990

Simon & Schuster Ltd
West Garden Place
Kendal Street
London W2 2AQ

Simon & Schuster of Australia Pty Ltd
Sydney

British Library Cataloguing-in-Publication Data available
ISBN 0–671–71701–4

Typeset in 10/12pt Sabon by Selectmove Ltd, London
Printed and bound in Great Britain by
Billing & Sons Ltd, Worcester

To the memory
of Sid Chaplin,
who was always so encouraging

Filthy Lucre

∗ ∗ ∗ 1 ∗ ∗ ∗

UP, DOWN. Up, down. Up, down. He was exhausted. In his younger days he had been able to manage it easily and even rather enjoyed it. But at his age, it tired him out so quickly.

It wasn't only the exhaustion that got to him. It was the sheer, bloody monotony. Up, down. Up, down. Up, down. Over and over again. He wondered idly if there were any way of working out roughly how many ups and downs there had been in his life?

He realised with a start that his attention was wandering. That would not do at all. He risked a quick glance down to check how things were going. Up, down. Up, down. Up, down. Perhaps just a bit lower. He adjusted his position. Up, down. Up, down. Up, down.

He looked down again and grunted with satisfaction at what lay beneath him. Shouldn't be too long now. Up, down. Up, down. Up, down.

When you thought about it, it was a pretty stupid thing to be doing at his age. No sooner had you recovered from doing it one way than you had to do it all over again back to front. Up, down. Up, down. Up, down. True, winter in West Africa was lovely, but was it really worth the effort? Two thousand miles really took it out of you, whatever your age. Up, down. Up, down. Up, down. Boy, how his wings hurt.

He could smell London now. He always could smell it before he could see it. Not a particularly pleasant aroma, but it was to be home for the summer, as for every summer before it. Up, down. Up, down. Up, down.

There was his marker. The big chap on top of the pole with the dead lions down below. The place was full of those common noisy starlings as usual. He flew on, adjusting his course slightly. Not long now. Trafalgar Square was no place to bring young house martins into the world.

9

He preferred a bit of peace and quiet and, as far as he was concerned, Gilbert Square had it all. Solid, dependable buildings crammed with roomy perches. Trees and grass in the middle. Lots of good, nest-building material within easy reach. What more could you ask?

He flew lower and circled the familiar square, pleased to be back again, before heading for number seventeen. He pulled up sharply. That couldn't be right. That wasn't number seventeen. It was the wrong height, the wrong shape, the wrong colour. What was going on? He hovered, bewildered. He was sure he was in the right place. He recognised the buildings on either side, lovely cream-coloured old structures with plenty of snug nooks and crannies. This giant thing was all hard and nasty. What had happened to his perch?

Birds were coming in to land all around him. If he didn't do something quickly, there wouldn't be anywhere left. He laid claim to a narrow ledge with an overhang under which he could build a nest, but he wasn't happy.

Oh shit, he thought grumpily.

Had he looked down, it might have cheered him a little to see that his expression of disgust had landed right in a human's eye.

With his other, Jeremy tried to look on the bright side. Perhaps it was a sign from the heavens, a harbinger of good luck. Although not a superstitious type, on the following morning he was due to start work at British Industrial Group, the latest graduate intake to one of the most successful companies in the land, and he had been feeling uncommonly nervous. To forestall any mishaps on the morrow, he was indulging in a dry run, taking himself and a stop watch on the Underground from his flat in Sussex Gardens in Paddington to Russell Square.

He clicked the stopwatch. Twenty-eight minutes and fifty-five seconds door to door. Nineteen minutes thirteen seconds on the Underground and nine minutes forty-two seconds' walking at both ends. He jotted it down. He would allow another five minutes for unforeseen eventualities, just to be sure. It was his ability to master even the tiniest detail, he felt, that would soon mark him out as a young man going places, a chap to watch out for, a rising star.

Wiping the good luck from his eye, Jeremy crossed the road and entered the park to get a better view of British Industrial's new headquarters, passing as he did Major Peregrine, the man who had done more than anyone else to challenge their construction.

The Major was out walking his dog, Rommel. As he was only too willing to tell anybody who would listen, the Major had been instrumental in bringing Rommel to heel in North Africa in the Second World War and he kept his hand in against a fresh bout of Hunnish belligerence by bringing to heel a succession of dachshunds bearing the Field-Marshal's name. The current Rommel was the fifth.

Major Peregrine was but a pale shadow of his former self. A Gilbert Square resident of thirty years standing, he had been bitterly opposed to the plans to tear down a perfectly sound Georgian town house and replace it with a fourteen-storey office block. As chairman of the residents' committee, he had gathered seven thousand signatures on a petition, the majority of them genuine. His confidence that they could keep intact a square which had survived the attentions of Goering's bombers and the aspirations of more than one set of property developers had been justified. Reluctantly, the planners had rejected the proposals they privately considered brave and innovative and Gilbert Square, a fine example of the work of Thomas Cubitt, was saved. The bunting had gone up in the Square and the residents, most of whom made it a habit never to speak to any of the others, were sufficiently elated to clink a glass or two together.

The Major's mood of elation and triumph had lasted just two days, snuffed out by the fire that swept through number seventeen Gilbert Square, leaving behind an empty shell. As the planners delighted in pointing out, it would be impossibly expensive to rebuild the house to its original specifications. How fortuitous, therefore, that it was on the site of number seventeen that British Industrial wanted to build their new headquarters. What a catastrophe it would have been if number fifteen or nineteen had been gutted instead. To lessen the danger of the house collapsing of its own accord, thereby putting the lives of the Square's residents at risk, the planners had considerately rushed through planning permission. The bulldozers were in operation within days.

The other residents of the Square were only too quick to remind Major Peregrine that he had sworn that the bloody building would go up only over his dead body. As one aged dowager, coming across Rommel being taken for his constitutional in the park, remarked

11

loudly, since both building site and Major were visible at the same time, one of them must be a mirage. Lashing out with her walking stick, she was able to prove to her satisfaction that whatever else the Major might be, he was certainly no optical illusion.

As he limped back to his basement flat, Major Peregrine reflected that even a man of his word should occasionally be allowed to use a figure of speech. His only consolation came when, for the sake of appearances, he made a big show of trying to hold his breath at the opening ceremony of BIG House. The violent coughing fit this set off had sent his dentures flying, embedding themselves in the neck of one of the British Industrial's directors. But it was a pyrrhic victory. The building had still opened. For the first time in years, the Major learnt what it was to face defeat. He also learnt that they do not make dentures like they used to. His new pair was giving him hell.

Today, as on every other day, he refused to allow Rommel to pause until they crossed the road and reached the monstrosity. Only there was the dog permitted to cock its leg. The Major had been experimenting with Rommel's diet for the past three months, but although the concrete was beginning to turn a satisfyingly disgusting shade of green, nothing that passed through the dachshund's digestive system seemed capable of rotting it. It needed something stronger, thought the Major. Something much stronger.

He thought about what he had just thought. Then he thought some more. For the first time since the bulldozers had begun work on BIG House, the Major straightened up to his full height. He smiled. 'No use whimpering in a foxhole. Eh, Rommel? What's the best form of defence? Attack, that's what,' he barked. 'After all, what goes up must come down, don't yer know.' The dachshund did not answer. It was having enough trouble ensuring that what had gone down came out the other end.

With a spring in his step, the Major yanked the dog away in mid-ablution. There were plans to be laid.

On the other side of the square, Jeremy gazed admiringly up at BIG House. What a magnificent building. The architect had obviously intended the headquarters of British Industrial Group to be a vigorous statement of the rôle business played in modern society. Its height clearly demonstrated the way business towered head and shoulders above the rest of the community's concerns. Its sheer brutality presumably symbolised the survival of the fittest. The concrete cladding was undoubtedly there to make the point that fancy decoration and fripperies were uncalled for in a lean, modern company while the pipes that ran in all directions over the face of the building were surely the architectural equivalent of the handshake, showing that nothing was being concealed. The triangular BIG logo was amusingly woven into the fabric, showing the human face of the company, with triangular windows on some floors and a triangular entrance porch. It was, Jeremy reflected, an honest building and one that told the onlooker a great deal about the enterprise it housed.

To say that Jeremy was keen on his new job would be an understatement. His admiration for the company and its boss, Alexander Prosser, amounted almost to idolatry. He devoured every scrap of information on both that appeared and knew the article from *Business* magazine which he carried around in his wallet off by heart. He mumbled it under his breath, like a litany, as he stared at BIG House.

'There are those who say that credit for the extraordinary revival of British business fortunes should be given to this one company and, in particular, to the man who has made it what it is today, Alexander Charles Prosser. Like some giant, omniscient eagle the larger-than-life mercurial tycoon controls the vast British Industrial Group empire from his penthouse eyrie. Prosser's bull-at-the-gate business methods brook no opposition. Anyone or anything that stands in his way is simply floored by this human dynamo. There seems no business activity that Prosser is incapable of understanding intuitively.

'While others stick to their dull, traditional, lasts, BIG's activities are many and varied, ranging from engineering in the form of the original company, British Iron Girders, through leisure, restaurants, hotels, tobacco, brewing, car parks, housebuilding, property and food retailing. BIG has bought up sixty different companies in the ten years since Prosser took the helm. As he himself says, "0–60 in ten years isn't bad going, and we're still accelerating." In short, whatever the flavour of the pie, if it looks tasty enough Prosser is likely to have his finger well and truly stuck into it.'

Jeremy's lips stopped moving.

Dusk was settling over London. The noise level, at a peak since eight that morning, was beginning to subside. The birds, clearing the carbon monoxide from their throats, were able to make their voices heard once more. As Jeremy gazed up at the thirteenth floor, where he knew Prosser's office was located, the lights went on. Excited, he realised that the chairman must still be working. What energy the man must have.

Jeremy stepped backwards on to a tramp lying in the doorway behind him.

Had he been able to levitate himself thirteen storeys, Jeremy would have seen that Alexander Prosser, chairman and chief executive of British Industrial Group, was indeed working flat out. Lying on his back on the couch in his office, his face would have been invisible to anybody gazing through the window, obscured as it was by the naked back of one of his personal assistants, Lorraine Summers. Astride her employer, Lorraine was doing her bit for Britain and for British Industrial, keeping alive the memory of Saint George.

Neither mind, however, was concentrating wholeheartedly on the matter in hand. As she rocked from side to side and up and down, Lorraine was trying to sneak a look at her watch, wondering if she would still have time to meet Janice at the CineCentre in Tottenham Court Road, where they had arranged to see the latest Burt Reynolds film.

And while Prosser absent-mindedly massaged Lorraine's breasts, inwardly he was congratulating himself. His application for membership of Bart's was coming before the committee tomorrow. It was about bloody time that he belonged to the club whose membership was restricted to the inner circle of British businessmen. After all, was he not helmsman of the fastest-growing conglomerate in the land, one of the wealthiest men in Britain, a confidant of the Prime Minister and widely tipped for a knighthood in the next Honours List? He could not understand why it had taken him so long to be accepted by his peers. True, he had had to step on a few toes in his time. But which of those stuck-up old farts who had founded the club had not crushed a few tootsies or clipped the odd corner in his time? That ridiculous comment of Sir Jocelyn Pardoe's which had found its way into the papers had not helped, of course. 'Jumped-up little barrow boy' indeed! The patronising, aristocratic sod would have to eat his words when he learned of the latest member to enter his club's hallowed halls.

To Lorraine's consternation, Prosser's own member, having entered her hallowed halls, showed little sign of wanting to leave. As she looked into his face, simulating frenzied passion while trying to

14

avoid those cold eyes of his, she wondered why it was always the short, balding, slobs who were so successful. For if she was Saint George, he was most definitely the dragon, with all the attendant skin problems those beasts must have suffered from.

She accelerated her actions in the hope that she could finish him off quickly and depart, to be seduced by the more attractive charms of Bert Reynolds. It did not take long before Lorraine's prowess got the better of Prosser's preoccupation. She made to uncouple herself.

'Where do you think you're going?' snapped Prosser.

'I thought. . .'

'Letters,' he ordered.

'Yes, Mr Prosser.' Dutifully, Lorraine remained astride her boss. His working practices took some getting used to. She hoped it wouldn't take too long, or he would have time to recover himself. If that happened, they could be there all night, as she knew from bitter and sore experience.

'To Harry Shepherd, managing director, Prosser's Exhaust Centres,' he dictated. 'Dear Harry, I have received a letter from a grateful customer, delighted that the exhaust with which your chaps fitted his car lasted for nearly three years and comparing us favourably with our competitors.

'New para. What the hell is going, Harry? Those frigging lumps of metal are supposed to last only as long as the one-year guarantee. If they all survive to see their second or third birthdays, turnover is going to take a nosedive. You know that it is my policy never to interfere with the running of BIG's subsidiaries, but I strongly suggest that you find a new supplier better able to meet our specifications before I have to find a new managing director. Take care you don't exhaust my patience. Open brackets. Ha ha, joke. Close brackets. Yours et cetera.'

Prosser's index finger wandered up his right nostril to do a little excavation work. Locating something of interest, it brought it out into the daylight, showed it off to its owner then flicked it away. Prosser glanced at his notes. Lorraine's pencil halted and then began racing across the page again. 'To Jamieson at the Newcastle brewery. . .'

Jeremy disentangled himself from the blaspheming, spitting tramp and backed off with profuse apologies. He moved further up the pavement, there to resume his vigil. Thin and somewhat gangling, Jeremy wore about him at all times a wary, hunted look which was the inevitable result of having been the butt of other people's jokes for much of his twenty-four years.

His bright red hair alone would have been enough to ensure a fair degree of teasing over the years. But it was Jeremy's misfortune to suffer from two other, rather more troublesome curses.

The first was to have been presented by his parents with a surname that was considered downright hilarious by almost everybody he met. When he wasn't being regaled by quips that revolved around carrots or traffic lights, he was having to face variations on the 'Bet you're troubled by wet dreams' theme.

Jeremy could only suppose that his father had never had to suffer this type of ridicule in his youth. Otherwise, surely nothing on earth would have possessed him to settle in the particular part of West London that accounted for the third of the trinity of afflictions facing his son. Try as he might to pretend that he really hailed from Egham or Sunbury, the truth always seemed to out sooner or later, forcing him to admit that yes, ha ha ha, he really was, guffaw guffaw, Jeremy Seaman from Staines.

'Dear Bob,' continued Prosser to his accommodating personal assistant, 'Thank you for your letter, concerning the board's decision to seek 350 redundancies at your plant. I can understand your concern that the workforce is being cut back slightly at the same time as output targets are being increased. I note that you, quote, won't stay and see a third of the workforce made redundant, unquote.

'New para. I am sad that after so many years you should choose to leave us over so trivial a matter, particularly as by resigning in this abrupt way you are breaking the terms of your service contract and forfeiting your compensation rights. However, I am sure that, at 57, you will welcome the opportunity to move on to pastures new. Yours et cetera. P.S. Love to Doreen and the kids.'

Prosser snatched at the phone burbling by his ear. 'What the fuck is it? I thought I said I wasn't to be disturbed. It's who? Good God. Well, what the hell are you waiting for? Put him on. . . Well, well. Jack Butterley, as I live and breathe. It's been a long time. How is Nostrum and the world of soft drinks?'

'A damn sight more relaxing than working for a bastard like you, Alex.' The voice was West Country, full of good humour, in marked contrast to Prosser's sharp, rasping tones. 'How are you, you old rogue?'

'I try not to let things get on top of me,' said Prosser, leering at Lorraine. 'Hang on a moment, would you?' He clamped his hand over the mouthpiece and waved her away. 'We can finish this in the morning.'

She detached herself. As she collected her clothes and made for the door, he caught her rump a glancing blow. 'And we can polish off the letters at the same time.'

Lorraine could still hear him guffawing loudly as she closed the door behind her. She looked at her watch. Damn! The film would already have started. She made for the lift, zipping up her skirt and buttoning her blouse as she went. What a job.

'So, to what do I owe this considerable honour?' asked Prosser.

'You're talking a bit flowery these days, Alex. Whatever happened to that beautifully terse Geordie brogue of yours?'

'It got lost somewhere along the way. Like you, Jack. It's ten years since you walked out on me, remember, and we hardly parted on the best of terms. I seem to recall you calling me an evil, callous, robber-baron who would sell his own grandmother if she had any assets left worth stripping.'

The earpiece boomed with Butterley's laughter. 'I'm sure you took it as the compliment it was meant to be.' The voice became serious. 'Alex, I may have an interesting proposition for you. I think we should talk.'

'So talk.'

'It might not be such a good idea to have this particular chat over the phone, if you know what I mean. I'm in a phone box just round the corner.'

'All right. Come straight round. I can give you half an hour. I'll ring down to tell them to expect you,' said Prosser, his nostrils curling slightly. He was intrigued. 'No. On second thoughts, perhaps it would be better if you avoided the main entrance. Use the garage.'

The Major glared at his kitchen wall with disgust. By day it was a perfectly acceptable shade of yellow. By night, together with the walls of his bedroom and living room, it was transformed into a deep shade of purple.

It was that bloody building. Monstrous enough in the daylight, some cretin had had the bright idea that it should be illuminated

17

at night by a powerful purple light located on the roof of one of the buildings opposite. Not content with indecently exposing the front of BIG House, the vulgar violet rays bounced off the building and sought out the hidden corners of Gilbert Square. The Major's basement flat was one such corner. By day, he had to stand on a chair and crane his neck in order to be irritated by the building. By night, he did not even need to move from his armchair.

It was from this recumbent position that the Major outlined the situation, as he saw it, to Rommel, lying stretched out in front of the fire. 'The situation, as I see it, is that these chaps have effectively declared war by constructin' that thing. It's the Falklands all over again. Our territorial rights have been infringed and it's up to us to defend them.'

The Major, craggy-faced with a bushy white moustache, short back and sides, bald front and top and a fondness for tweed, was the very epitome of the military officer as seen by countless cinema-goers over the years. There was a good reason for that. The Major had learnt everything he knew about soldiering from the silver screen. He had left school to go not into the Army but into insurance. He had not even seen National Service, finding it necessary to visit Australia at just the time that his contemporaries were being called up.

Plain Ronald Peregrine had returned from the Antipodes as Major Ronnie Peregrine. The title was a boon to his business, in more ways than one. Should any client show an inclination to read the small print, the Major would launch into a well-honed litany of the many ways of disembowelling a German with a bayonet. Clients would sign almost anything to get out of earshot. Although now retired, the Major had seen no reason to abandon such a useful title.

Much as he might bluster about mounting an assault on BIG House, however, the Major had not the slightest idea how to go about it. If he had actually served in the Army, he might at least have an old service revolver lying about. He rummaged through the kitchen drawers, searching for suitable weapons. But the most lethal thing he possessed was a bread knife and he couldn't see it having much impact on a fourteen-storey office block. Gloomily, he opened a tin of dog meat for Rommel, placing the bowl in front of the fire. Just as gloomily, Rommel inspected it, wondering what effect it would have on his digestion.

* * *

18

Prosser waited for Jack Butterley impatiently. It *had* been a long time. Butterley and he had run British Iron Girders for almost two years, even though old man Sanderson had still owned the company then. Butterley had been a damn good manager, Prosser reflected, if a bit too straight for his own good. He was also a touch soft when it came to handling the workforce. That was what their final quarrel had been about, although they had been getting on each other's nerves for some time, fretting that old Sanderson would live for ever, denying them the free hand for expansion they so desperately craved.

It had been fun working with Butterley in the beginning. Prosser still remembered how shocked he had been when his colleague had announced he was leaving, since when he had hopped from company to company until ending up as finance director at Nostrum a few years back. Butterley had left just too soon. Only four weeks after his departure, old man Sanderson had died in a tragic accident, leaving Prosser in sole control. The building of the British Industrial empire had begun.

Prosser walked over to the lift as the doors opened, welcoming Butterley with a bearhug. A stocky man, Prosser's arms still had some of their strength from the days when he had boxed for money in the clubs of Byker.

'Steady on, Alex. If that's the welcome you give people you don't like, God knows how your nearest and dearest survive your affections.' Butterley shook himself free. Ten years had changed his old friend. He had put on a stone or two, was balding and seemed even shorter than he remembered. 'You haven't changed a bit, Alex,' Butterley said politely. 'Well maybe a little stockier perhaps, and the forehead's a touch higher than it used to be. But otherwise you're just the same.'

Prosser frowned. Over the past few years, he had grown unused to people speaking their mind. Butterley always had been bloody insubordinate. 'And you, Jack, still look as though you're auditioning for a place in Burton's window.' He led the way, keen to show off the fruits of his success. 'Like the new building?'

'Outside, it has all the charm and elegance of its owner,' Butterley said dryly as he entered Prosser's luxurious office. He looked around him at the massive wooden desk that dominated the room, the raft of video monitors, the Persian rugs on the polished wooden floor and the host of original paintings adorning the walls; he spotted a Lowry, a Sutherland, a couple of Hockneys and even, if he was not mistaken, a Cézanne and a Monet. 'But this is. . .' he hesitated, refusing to let Prosser know he was envious '. . .not bad. It's certainly a step up from that draughty prefab behind the foundry, Alex.'

'You're not kidding. I live above the shop these days,' said Prosser, indicating a circular staircase. 'Most of the next floor is mine. I've a swimming pool directly above, a gymnasium, sauna, even a pad for the chopper on the roof.'

'All mod cons,' said Butterley. 'You've not done badly for yourself.'

Prosser was disappointed his old colleague didn't seem more impressed. He shot his left wrist forward. 'Not done badly? You don't know the half of it. What about this watch, Jack? Red Gold. Only two like it ever made. The other is in white gold.' As he spoke, he pulled back the cuff on his other wrist, revealing another, almost identical, watch. 'Guess how much they cost?' he said, laughing at the startled look on Butterley's face.

'I've no idea.'

'Fifteen grand apiece, give or take a few bob. This suit wouldn't give you much change from a grand. The shoes were three hundred. Even the socks cost twenty quid. Each. I've probably got forty grand's worth of clobber on right now. You're right. I've not done too badly for myself in just ten years.'

'Still the same modest chap you always were, Alex,' said Butterley, as he wandered around the room looking more closely at Prosser's exhibits, which most of them undoubtedly were. This was less an office, more a gallery exhibiting Prosser's wealth. 'But are you truly happy, Alex?'

'What sort of bloody fool question is that?' Butterley hadn't changed much, thought Prosser. It was still impossible to tell when he was being serious or not. And he was still several inches taller than Prosser. He did not like other people being taller than him, which meant that he disliked practically everyone he met. He particularly detested it when smart aleck journalists referred to him as 'larger-than-life'. He knew it was their way of saying 'short'. It was only mildly better than 'confirmed bachelor'.

Butterley was in a reminiscent mood. 'Do you remember when we both went to be measured up for our first proper suits? The tailor asked whether you dressed to the left or the right and you'd no idea what he meant. When I explained, you barked at him: "Upwards. What bloody business is it of yours, mush?"'

Prosser laughed politely, but did not care to be reminded of the days before he knew how to behave as a gentleman. 'The tailors come to me now, Jack. I'm far too busy to go to them.'

'What are they doing here?' asked Butterley, indicating some surprisingly poorly-executed busts of Napoleon, Churchill and Alexander the Great.

'My inspiration. You'd be amazed how much we can learn from great military leaders of the past. These days the great wars are fought in the boardroom, not on the battlefield.'

As Prosser strutted round the room showing off, Butterley noticed he had his right hand jammed firmly inside his jacket. With his prize-fighter's nose, broken twice in his short career in the ring and at least once outside it to Butterley's knowledge, he looked like a comic-book version of Napoleon. The resemblance to the bust of the emperor was remarkable. And to that of Churchill and Alexander as well, now that he looked more closely. With a start, Butterley realised that the busts weren't badly done at all. They were designed to make the great leaders look like Prosser. Good grief, what had happened to the man? He had become pompous almost beyond belief.

Butterley wandered over to the window to conceal his amused expression. 'It's a fantastic view. You must have a good head for heights. . .unlike poor old man Sanderson,' he added quietly.

'He was getting on,' Prosser said sharply. 'Doddery old fool. Why he went up to the foundry gallery on his own at his age is beyond me. He must have lost his balance, I suppose.'

'Can't have been very nice, falling into molten iron.'

'We didn't find out where he'd gone for over a week. By then he was holding up that new bridge over the Tyne. We held the funeral there. I think it's what he would have wanted. He always said iron flowed through his veins.'

'How very fortunate that you were there, ready and willing to step into his shoes.'

'I'm forgetting my manners, Jack. Sit down,' said Prosser coldly, anxious to steer the conversation away from that particular subject. He indicated a table, around which several abundantly upholstered armchairs were ranged, checking to make sure that no sensitive documents were lying around before seating himself. He picked up a device like a television remote control unit and pressed a button. 'Ron, sandwiches and beers for two,' he said into thin air. 'Great device this, Jack. Watch.' He pressed another button, and the curtains drew together. Another, and all the lights in the room dimmed except those above their heads. Prosser settled back into his chair. 'So, how are things at Nostrum? Are you still producing that dreadful dandelion and burdock stuff we used to make ourselves sick with when we were kids?'

'Sadly, yes. It's our loss-leader. Hardly anybody drinks it now. Even Noah thought it was old hat, but you wouldn't think so if you could hear the bloody Westbury clan rant on about how marvellous their products are.'

He broke off as the door opened. A giant of a man shuffled in, dressed in white boxer's shorts and singlet, carrying a tray of beer and sandwiches. A little more hair on the face and he would not have looked out of place behind the bars in the gorillas' cage at London zoo. The table shook as he placed the tray on it. When he straightened up, his hands came down almost to his knees, adding to the impression that here, at last, was the much sought after missing link.

'You remember Ron Niblo, my old boxing coach?' Butterley stood to shake hands. 'He's my gentleman's gentleman, now,' said Prosser, economically cramming two lies into two words. 'He looks after me, don't you, Ron?'

Ron grunted, presumably indicating a reply in the affirmative.

Nursing his crushed fingers, Butterley watched Ron shamble from the room presumably to shake a few more bananas down from a tree. His attention distracted, Butterley did not notice Prosser pressing another button on his box of tricks.

'I thought he was in. . .'

'He came out two years ago,' said Prosser indistinctly, his mouth crammed full of cheese and pickle. 'He's a reformed character. You won't catch Ron dropping a lump of concrete on anybody's head now. He's learnt his lesson. It's "Don't get caught".' Prosser laughed at his own joke, spraying his half-chewed food into Butterley's lap. He stopped laughing just as abruptly as he had started. 'Right. Enough of the polite chat. What do you want?'

Tomorrow, Jeremy felt, was going to be a turning point in his life. He was well aware of his own failings, regretting that he was not one of those who, through sheer necessity, learns to give as good as they get. He had never mastered the art of badinage. Jeremy got, but for twenty-four years he had never given his tormentors anything stronger than a nervous smile in return.

All that was going to change. From the moment he walked through the doors of BIG House, Jeremy Seaman nice guy would disappear, to be replaced by Jeremy Seaman, tough, ruthless, ambitious executive. If Alexander Prosser could do it, so could he. It was all just a matter of adapting the right attitude.

He was intelligent enough to do well, he knew that. He had always been the perfect, if pedantic pupil, seeking refuge from the barrage of teasing in his studies. The more he was ridiculed the harder he worked. His was a solitary existence, not only at school, but also at Cambridge where, to his bitter disappintment, he had found no shortage of wags among the elite of British youth trying to prove themselves the heirs to Oscar Wilde by bouncing their witticisms off Jeremy.

But he suffered, as he knew only too well, from extreme diffidence, a problem if you wanted to be a tough, ruthless, ambitious executive. This appalling shyness was a result not only of the incessant teasing but also of the efforts his fervently devout parents had made to protect Jeremy from the real world, which they saw as being almost unremittingly evil. Nobody asked Mr or Mrs Seaman more than once whether Jeremy could come out to play.

And if they were reluctant to let their son mix with other boys, they were adamant that he have no dealings at all with members of the opposite sex, all of whom were agents of the devil ready, if the opportunity were granted them, to lead him down a path of dishonour, degredation and damnation.

Such were the visions of hell conjured up by his parents that Jeremy grew up with a terror of the opposite sex and a complete ignorance of the mysteries of procreation. Love was something else, though. And at Cambridge, in the arms of the chairs of the Arts Cinema he fell head over heels for a woman of breathtaking beauty, a woman of wit and sophistication who had no need to stoop to making low remarks about carrots. After seeing her star in My Man Godfrey, there was no doubt in Jeremy's mind that Carole Lombard was the most wonderful woman in the entire world. His discovery soon afterwards that she had been killed in a plane crash in 1942 devastated him. He had worn a black armband for weeks.

23

* * *

'When I arrived at Nostrum, Alex, I was really on a high. I was going to be the new broom, sweeping the cobwebs away from a stuffy old family firm still stuck in the nineteenth century. It didn't take me long to realise that they didn't really want a modern finance director, good at juggling money around, using it to make more money. The family would probably be happier with a whiskered chap with a quill pen and a ledger, sitting on a high stool all day adding up numbers and saying "Yes, Mr Westbury. No, Mr Westbury." I think I was just brought in to placate the City. Unfortunately, I have three per cent of Nostrum's shares, which I foolishly bought when I joined. I had no idea then, of course, that trying to get anything radical through at a Nostrum board meeting would be like swimming through treacle. There have been times, I don't mind telling you, when I would happily have pushed David Westbury, brother Michael and uncle Timothy into their own vats.

'The only bright spot was when I stuck my neck out a couple of years ago and said I would resign if they didn't dedicate more money to research. It worked. Put together a smashing R&D team, Alex. Really bright chaps. But whenever we tried out some new concoction on the Westburys, you'd have thought we'd farted in their faces. If they'd turned their noses up any more, they'd have broken their flaming necks. Nothing we showed them would persuade them to alter grandfather's formulas one tiny bit, not by so much as the addition of even one extra dandelion leaf to the pot.'

'I hope you didn't come here just to cry on my shoulder, Jack,' said Prosser, ripping open a can of beer. 'I really am a very busy man.'

'You'll never make a hundred, Alex. Your strenuous efforts to be diplomatic and charming will give you a heart attack long before then. Of course I'm not wasting your precious time. Do you have any idea how big the soft drinks market is? Over three billion pounds a year in Britain alone. That's real money, Alex.'

'So?'

'So when was the last time anybody came up with a really exciting new product? Coca-cola is over a century old, for heaven's sake.'

'And you, I take it, have a new product?'

'Not just a new drink, Alex. A cast-iron racing certainty of a drink. With a good wind behind it, it could be the next Pepsi or Coke, although I doubt if the Westburys have ever heard of either.

They certainly didn't go for this stuff. They took one taste, spat it out and told us their forefathers would not have approved.' Butterley paused, waiting for Prosser to say something, but his mouth was wrestling with a sandwich. 'I know you have as little to do with the outside world as you can these days, but did you ever come across a sweet for kids, a sort of powder, which started fizzing and popping when it got inside the mouth?'

Prosser nodded.

'Well, we've come up with something similar in a way, except in the form of a drink. Take a swig and it explodes into every nook and cranny of your mouth. It's like having a firework display go off inside. It thrashes around so much it would wake a corpse.' Butterley took a sip of beer, taking the chance to glance carefully at Prosser's nose. Nothing. 'We've also bunged in quite a few nutrients and calories so that we can claim it's a great antidote for all that junk food kids shovel down their throats. And we've also stuffed it full of caffeine, 200 milligrams per litre, the maximum allowed by law. Not only does that enhance the impression that it revitalises your system and gets you going, but it also means that Fizzical – that's our name for it – could become just the teensiest bit addictive with some people.'

'Let me get this straight. You've produced a drink that could become addictive?' Butterley nodded. 'I do believe you're losing some of your scruples at last, Jack.'

'Coke would never have got off the ground if it hadn't been for the cocaine in the original recipe. Fizzical's a darn sight less harmful than other things the brats are probably trying.' Butterley looked at Prosser's nose again. It was twitching slightly. He had for to force himself not to smile. At least one thing about Alexander Charles Prosser had not changed. His nose had always been the giveaway in the old days when he thought he was on to something good. Prosser had never understood why his humbler second in command had always beaten him at poker.

Butterley reckoned he had caught his fish. Now he just had to reel him in. Carefully.

Jeremy had made only one job application, the successful outcome of which was undeniably helped by a glowing reference from his tutor, whose fear that Jeremy might stay on as a postgraduate left him no qualms about committing the most appalling perjury.

The self-confidence which the job offer from BIG had given Jeremy was further bolstered by a six months business studies course. For the first time in his life he had found himself the object not of ridicule but of envy. Other students were due to work for dull metal-bashers, supermarket chains or City securities houses. But Jeremy already had his foot on the bottom rung of the most glittering ladder in the business firmament.

By way of dress rehearsal for the following day, Jeremy had donned his new work clothes. Unlike the others on his course who had aped the fashions of the flash youngsters in the City, Jeremy had shrewdly emulated the dress sense of his favourite lecturer, a man with considerably greater experience of the business world. He felt splendid in his new attire, a brown single-breasted suit, crisp beige polyester shirt, subtly-striped chocolate tie and the suede brogues which, so the salesman had persuasively assured him, were what all the best-dressed young executives were wearing these days. He had been receiving admiring glances from passers-by all day.

Butterley chomped reflectively on his sandwich.

'All right, Jack,' said Prosser. 'I'll bite. What's the pitch? Why are you telling me all this?'

'The dummies that make up Nostrum's board won't touch Fizzical with a ten-foot bargepole. I don't give a bugger about them, but I'm damned if I'll let the opportunity of a lifetime slip through my fingers. The only way I can be certain it gets produced with the proper backing is if someone like you takes over the company and kicks out the existing board. . . with one exception, of course.'

'I see. And in addition to becoming chief executive of Nostrum, which I assume is your aim, what else are you after?'

'Complete operational and financial autonomy. No meddling from you. A five-year service contract at £150,000 a year. Oh, and an itsy-witsy royalty from the sales of Fizzical to see me through nicely to my old age. Say one per cent of turnover?'

'One per cent?' Prosser spluttered. 'What a good job you're not greedy, Jack. But tell me, just to satisfy my curiosity, what is there to stop someone getting hold of this stuff, having it analysed and then producing it themselves, leaving you out of the picture altogether?'

'While I'm sure that a man of your integrity would never dream of doing such a thing, I suppose it is possible that other people might not be quite so scrupulous. So I have taken one or two elementary precautions, such as letting our lawyers tie the whole thing up with oodles of lovely patents and licences.' Prosser grunted involuntarily as Butterley continued. 'It's not that I don't trust you, of course, but I knew that you would want to be certain that by buying Nostrum, you buy Fizzical as well.' The fish was practically out of the water, thought Butterley. One more sharp tug should do it. Time to tell a little white lie or two. 'The trouble is that if you're interested, we may have to move fast. The family is keeping pretty quiet about it, but I'm fairly certain they've had an approach from somebody wanting to buy the company.'

'I don't like the sound of that, Jack.' Prosser picked up his glass and took a substantial swig of beer.

'If rumour's to be believed, it's Sir Jocelyn Pardoe.' Butterley moved quickly, but not quickly enough to avoid the beer spewed out by Prosser. It mingled with the coagulating cheese and pickle in his lap. Butterley left it alone. The last thing he wanted to do was distract Prosser, whose nose was quivering wildly now.

'Pardoe? Does he know about the new drink?'

'I don't see how he can. He must just have decided that he can do more with Nostrum than the existing management. But then there are creatures living underneath stones at the bottom of my garden pond that could do a better job than that shower. The place is ripe for rationalisation. And it would fit in neatly with Pardoe's existing drinks operations, of course. He's already got pop coming out of his ears. If he got hold of Nostrum and discovered Fizzical, he could start producing it almost immediately.

'From what I can tell, though, it looks as though the family have decided to tell Sir Jocelyn to take a running jump. I hope so. I've worked bloody hard on Fizzical and I reckon it could catapult Nostrum into the big league. I don't want a toffee-nosed gentleman bastard like Pardoe taking all the credit. I'd much rather have a working-class bastard like you in charge.'

'You flatter me, Jack.'

'Of course, if you aren't interested,' Butterley said disingenuously, 'I suppose I could always chance my arm with Pardoe. If I told him about Fizzical, he might be sufficiently grateful to meet my terms. Yes, not a bad idea now that I come to think about it. After all, it was you who always told me not to let friendship interfere with business.'

'There's no need to be hasty, Jack. I'm sure we can work something out. After all, Nostrum's not ICI, is it? What's it worth? Forty million?'

'Fifty, though you'd need to offer something around sixty-five to get control.'

Prosser thought aloud. 'And you've got three per cent of the company. If it's taken out at that price, you'd stand to make four hundred and fifty thousand smackers overnight.'

'A man has to eat, Alex.'

'I'll have to tot up a few numbers and see where we stand. I can't imagine it'll be too great a problem. Oh, and I think it might be sensible for me to try some of this stuff for myself before we go much further.'

'I can arrange that.' An idea flashed into Butterley's mind and he struggled to keep himself from smiling. 'I've taken a big enough risk in coming here tonight. I can pass this off as an old boys' reunion, but it's better if from now on we aren't seen together. I'll be in touch when I've made the arrangements for you to pick a sample up.'

'You could always come and work directly for me, Jack. You know that.'

'Strange though it may seem, Alex, not everybody thrives knowing that at any moment the sword of Prosser suspended above their heads could come crashing down.'

'Incentive, Jack. That's all these buggers understand if you want to get them off their arses and do a bit of honest graft.'

The two men rose and shook hands. Prosser noticed with disgust that Butterley's crotch was covered with a sludge of food and drink. The man really ought to learn some table manners.

'Of course strictly speaking,' said Butterley, 'what we are cooking up is not terribly legal.'

'Don't worry, Jack. I won't tell on you if you don't tell on me.' As Prosser led Butterley to the lift, he asked casually, 'Just to satisfy my curiosity, Jack, what the hell is in this potion of yours?'

'You'll find out about the chemicals that give it its fizz when you take control of Nostrum and not before. As for the drink itself, it's quite old hat really: dandelion and burdock.' Prosser guffawed loudly.

As Butterley entered the lift, he turned to look back at his former colleague. 'I see you're still up to your old tricks, Alex.'

'What do you mean?'

'Your flies are undone, you dog.'

At ground level, Jeremy limped across the square to get a closer view of BIG House. His ankle throbbed. He had escaped from the foul language of the tramp, only to be attacked, for no apparent reason, by a man walking a dachshund through the park who had lashed out at him with a stick, obscurely snarling: 'Bloody mirage.' Londoners certainly knew how to make newcomers feel at home.

His bewilderment evaporated as he approached the entrance of BIG House. He knew that once he passed through those doors each day he would feel safe and secure. As he approached, the revolving doors began turning of their own accord. Startled, Jeremy drew back and the doors stopped. His heart sank a little. He had never had a very good relationship with mechanical objects. They and he just didn't seem to get along. If he was going to have to manoeuvre through these things every day, perhaps it would be a good idea to get in a little practice.

He moved forward again. The doors turned. He stepped back. They stopped. He looked around quickly to see if anyone was looking, then ran towards them. Just as he got to them, the doors started moving.

Noticing the brass nameplate to one side reading 'British Industrial Group', Jeremy stroked it for luck. This was his home now.

Jeremy's antics with the doors were watched on a monitor by Mr Bennett, the head of security at British Industrial. Mr Bennett was nothing if not a conscientious man. He put down his copy of *Men Only* and studied the screen closely. Looked harmless enough, but you never could tell. Mr Bennett made certain that he would know him if he saw him again then, when he was satisfied Jeremy posed no danger to anyone but himself, he put his hand back in his pocket and returned to studying, in rather more satisfying detail, Avril from Aylesbury.

The purple building glared at the Major and the Major, standing on a chair in his kitchen, glared back. The walk in the open air had done nothing to clear his mind. He had yet to come up with any constructive ideas. The evening peace of the square was broken by a street-cleaning lorry, redistributing the dirt and watering it to keep it in place for an hour or two.

Major Peregrine felt the first faint stirrings of an idea. . .

* * *

On the thirteenth floor, Prosser felt some faint stirrings of his own. They would have to wait. He was engrossed in a study of his computer screen, calling up data on Nostrum and examining the latest cash-flow projections for British Industrial Group. While he concentrated, nose aquiver, his left hand was also hard at work, grabbing the remaining sandwiches, picking his nose, rubbing his crotch, opening and pouring cans of beer into his gaping mouth.

As he assessed the financial position of Nostrum, the germ of an idea lodged in his brain and began to grow. What was it Butterley had said? If Pardoe got hold of Nostrum, he could begin producing the drink almost immediately. . . Most interesting. It opened a whole new train of thought.

Prosser opened the two top buttons of his shirt and reached inside, pulling out a three-and-a-half inch computer disc attached to a chain around his neck. Force of habit made him look round to check he was unobserved. Satisfied, he unclipped the chain and inserted the disc into the machine. He tapped in the necessary passwords and searched for the information he needed.

So Sir Jocelyn Pardoe wanted Nostrum, did he? Well, it would not do to disappoint Sir Jocelyn.

The only fly in the ointment was Jack Butterley who had walked out on him ten years ago. Prosser could not forgive him for that, even though having him around at the time might have meant a delay in arranging old man Sanderson's accident. Butterley was a competent enough manager, but Prosser was damned if he was going to give away one per cent of a goldmine like Fizzical. But then, as Jack himself had said, you should not let friendship interfere with business. It was not as if there was anything setting out their deal in writing. Butterley really was too old-fashioned for his own good.

Prosser took the tape of their conversation out of the recorder, marked the label, and locked it in the bottom drawer of his desk. You never knew when things like that might come in useful.

He pressed a button on the speakerphone on his desk. 'Ron, who's on duty tonight?'

'Jacqui, boss.'

'Tell her I'll be up in a minute. In both senses of the word.' Prosser grinned. Of all his personal assistants, Jacqui was perhaps his favourite. It was extraordinary how innovative she could be at times. This was turning into quite a pleasant evening.

After six cans of beer, nature caught up with Prosser. Ignoring the sumptuous washroom adjoining his office, he pulled back a curtain, threw open one of the thirteenth-floor windows and looked out over the lights of London. Somewhere out there were those supercilious bastards who refused to accept that he was now a gentleman. Chief of all the bastards was Sir Jocelyn frigging Pardoe. Well, Sir Jocelyn had it coming to him.

Prosser pulled a chair up to the window and lowered his zip.

Down below, Jeremy Seaman clicked his stopwatch to begin the journey back to his flat. Not before time. Despite the clear sky, it appeared to have begun to rain.

* * * 2 * * *

JEREMY had planned his first morning at British Industrial with mind-numbing precision. He would rise, spend a calm five minutes on the lavatory before brushing and flossing his teeth, steep himself in a hot bath for ten minutes and then climb into his clothes, already waiting neatly for him by the bed. Beside them was his combination lock imitation leather briefcase, proudly boasting his initials and containing a pad of paper, some pencils and spare pens, an A-Z of Business Terms, two rounds of salmon paste sandwiches, a copy of the *Sunday Times* in all its constituent parts and the much-read, much-creased letter telling him to present himself at BIG House on the first of April at nine-thirty.

He had it all planned precisely and had set the alarm clock for seven-thirty, secure in the knowledge gathered from his reconnaissance yesterday that it took twenty-eight minutes and fifty-five seconds from door to door.

At seven-thirty, Jeremy's alarm clock failed to go off.

At nine forty-six, the door to Jeremy's flat flew open and a flustered, unwashed, unkempt young man in brown hurtled down the three flights of stairs. On reaching the bottom, he raced back up them again, letting himself into the flat and snatching up his forgotten briefcase before rushing out again. It was only then that Jeremy noticed the rather strange smell. He made a mental note to put some of his first pay packet towards having the carpet cleaned.

'It's not too bad today, Mr Prosser. You're going out to view the new development at Windsor this morning. Harvey will meet you there. The helicopter is due to pick you up in five minutes. You have to be at L'Escargot for lunch at one with the City editor of *The Times*, which means being back here no later than twelve-forty. The car will pick you up downstairs at twelve forty-five.'

Sally looked up, to find the tycoon staring unashamedly at her legs. God, he was a lecherous sod. Was there ever a moment in the day when he wasn't feeling horny? She crossed her legs, making sure that her skirt rode further up her thighs. That should get him nice and hot under the collar. And under the belt too. If he had to be on the roof in less than five minutes, there would be damn all he could do about it. She was safe to tease him with impunity. It would do him good to get frustrated with no prospect of being able to alleviate the condition. Serve the dirty bugger right!

Getting Prosser steamed up was one of the things Sally enjoyed most about her job. As she continued her summary of the day's appointments, she rested her right ankle on her left knee. Very slowly she let her right knee drop lower and lower, giving him an ever-widening glimpse of the flesh that lay above the black stockings. She was delighted to see it was having the desired effect. He was adjusting his position, not only to get a better view but also to ease the discomfort caused by his burgeoning appreciation of the sight on which his eyes feasted.

'Come here,' he ordered.

'But Mr Prosser,' Sally said innocently, 'you have to be on the roof in just five minutes.'

'If you think I'm walking up there with a massive hard-on waving in front of me like a flagpole, you've got another thing coming, little lady. Come here.'

Shit. Why couldn't she have waited? Just the thought of his disgusting stubby hands touching her made Sally shiver.

The phone rang. She snatched at it, and listened for a moment. 'It's for you, Sir,' she said with relief.

'Yes, what is it?' barked Prosser. His mood suddenly altered. He was pleasant, almost obsequious now. 'My application for Bart's? It had gone clean from my mind. Of course, the committee must be meeting about now. . .They have? Splendid. What did they decide?. . . Oh, I see. Well, thank you for telling me. . . It's very good of you to have gone to so much trouble. Yes, we must have lunch some time. Goodbye.'

Prosser's face had turned a deep shade of red. He stood up and spoke very quietly, sounding all the more menacing for not raising his voice.

'The bastards. The filthy, rotten, stinking bastards! How dare they! Don't they know who I am? I'll bet that conniving, low down git Jocelyn Pardoe is behind it.'

Furious, he picked up the bust of Napoleon and flung it at the wall. It shattered into a thousand pieces.

Sally stayed as still as a rock. She had no wish for his anger to be turned on her.

Prosser's outward rage evaporated as quickly as it had arisen. 'I'd better get off to Windsor. Have you got the papers?' He snatched the attaché case from her and headed for the circular stairs.

Just before he disappeared from sight, he stopped and turned. 'Sally, if a Jack Butterley calls, put him straight on to me. No matter what time of day it is or where I am. Put him through immediately. Understand?'

'Yes, Mr Prosser. Whatever you say.' She was sorry to see that his erection had disappeared.

Prosser continued through the fourteenth floor and out on to the roof. He glanced up at the sky, which threatened rain. Typical.

The sight of the helicopter, an Aerospatiale Dauphin 2, waiting for him with its rotor turning, cheered him a little. He had never quite got over the thrill of riding in them and this one, his fifth, was his pride and joy. The twin-engined machine, with its call sign G-BIGE, could take up to thirteen passengers, but he had had it adapted to a layout more appropriate to a man of his standing, with just three comfortable armchairs and the invaluable couch. Just feeling the force of the wind generated by the blades invigorated him. There were only three other businessmen in London allowed to land helicopters on their buildings, he thought smugly.

Prosser ducked as he headed towards it, carrying his case. He waved at Biddle, the pilot, as he entered the cabin and closed the door behind him. Strapping himself in, he selected a compact disc from the rack beside him and slipped it into the player.

The helicopter lifted, tilted forwards and banked to the west as it climbed.

He turned the volume full up. The cabin filled with the sounds of the Band of the Blues and Royals playing a Sousa march. The time had come to do something about Pardoe. He glanced at the label to see what he was listening to. It was 'The Invincible Eagle'. Prosser snorted. Nobody was invincible, not even Sir Jocelyn Pardoe. Once his wings were clipped, he'd plummet to earth like a stone.

On the thirteenth floor, Sally swept up the pieces of the bust and threw them in the bin. She opened a cupboard to reveal rows upon rows of Napoleons, Alexanders and Churchills. She selected a particularly villainous-looking Bonaparte and set it out.

Butterley? Hadn't Lorraine mentioned somebody of that name ringing up last night and being sent away while Prosser talked to him? She went over to the bookshelf and took out the *Directory of Directors*. There it was. 'Butterley, Jack Horace. Finance director, Nostrum plc.' She read on.

When Jeremy entered BIG House a little after half-past ten, he felt none of the elation he had anticipated the evening before. The journey on the underground had been hell. Far from taking twenty-eight minutes fifty-five seconds to get to work, it had taken him considerably longer than that. Although there were far more people using the Tube than on Sunday, there seemed to be fewer trains. It didn't make sense. Jeremy did not care for being packed into a poorly ventilated box in close proximity to so many other people, particularly as someone nearby was suffering from a terrible personal hygiene problem. He had not been able to identify the source, but it was similar to the odour present in his flat. It really was most unsavoury. And to cap it all, he realised, to his increasing discomfort, that in his rush to leave he had forgotten to go to the lavatory.

He was so agitated that he did not even have time to worry about the revolving doors at the entrance to BIG House. He paid them no heed as they ferried him through. As he approached the triangular reception desk, he cursed himself for hurrying so much. If he had taken it just a little slower he would not have started sweating so heavily.

The receptionist, striking in her long Livid Lemon fingernails and Palpitating Primrose eye make-up, was on the phone, her loud London accent owing more to East Enders than the pearly kings and queens. Breathing heavily, Jeremy positioned himself directly in front of her, trying to look like someone it was worth finishing a call in order to attend to.

Finally, she put down the phone and turned her false eyelashes in his direction. 'Can I 'elp yer?' Her bored tone of voice firmly implied that he had come to the wrong place.

'My name is Seaman. I believe you are expecting me,' he said, keeping his arms close to his sides.

She consulted her papers. 'I ain't got nuffin' down 'ere about no Seaman. Salesman, are yer?'

Jeremy drew himself up. 'Certainly not. I am due to start work here today. I have a letter telling me to be here at. . .this morning.' He put his briefcase on the counter, spun the locks to the date of his birthday and then spun them again after remembering that he had changed the combination from his birthday to that day's date, the beginning of the new era. The letter had worked its way in between the pages of one of the many sections of the newspaper and by the time he retrieved it, the girl was on the phone again. He pushed it at her, ignoring the scattered sheets of the *Sunday Times* on the floor.

Only when she had finished her call, a long-winded discussion of which wine bar she and someone called Tracey should favour with their presence in their lunch hour, did she turn her attention to Jeremy once more. She took the proffered letter and studied it, her Saucy Citron-shaded lips moving as she read.

'It's signed by Mr Nettle,' she announced triumphantly. 'He's the head of Human Resources. That's who you should see.'

'Human what?'

'Resources. It's like Personnel really, only we have to say Human Resources instead. It's more caring and considerate.'

'I see. Well, perhaps you would be so caring and considerate as to tell him I am here.'

'Oh, I don't fink you'll catch Mr Nettle in at this time of the morning.'

'Perhaps you could try. He will be expecting me.'

Somewhat huffily, another phone call was made.

'Mr Nettle isn't in yet, I'm afraid. Perhaps you'd like to take a seat and I'll call you when he arrives,' she said adding 'Sir' very much as an afterthought.

'Thank you.'

As he turned away, a man wearing a dark suit and sunglasses approached the desk, flashing some form of identification.

'Luncheon Vouchers, love.'

'Again? We've only just had a delivery.'

'I know. Bit of a cock-up, I'm afraid.'

'You want Human Resources,' she said, attaching a badge to

36

his lapel and rewarding him with a broad smile. 'Just go straight through. Fourth floor. Turn left when you come out of the lifts.'

In designing the interior of BIG House, the architects had not stinted when it came to flora and foliage. The entrance lobby resembled one of the glasshouses at Kew, not only in appearance but in ambient temperature as well. Steam was piped in to keep the plants happy. Jeremy, hot and sweaty from his dash to work, was soon sweltering. The three-legged chair on which he perched, triangular to match the BIG logo like so much else in the reception area, was curiously unstable. Yet although Jeremy was just twenty feet away from the reception desk, it was still only by sitting right on the edge of the chair and leaning to one side that he could see it from behind a plantation of yuccas. By keeping himself in view of the receptionist, he hoped to remind her of his presence. His uncomfortable position was rendered still more uncomfortable by his ever more pressing need to visit the lavatory, a need exacerbated by the incessant noise of a fountain nearby. He also felt hungry, but thought it would look bad if he took out his sandwiches.

The Major usually found shopping a tedious chore, but this morning was different.

The shop assistant returned and put the colander on the counter, next to the wire-cutters, heavy-duty pliers, glass-cutter, torch, boot polish and batteries.

'Also lookin' for some artificial flowers,' said the Major. 'To go in the colander, don't yer know.'

The young man's mouth dropped open. The old chap was mad, barking mad. Still, it was his money. He brought over a selection of flowers.

The Major examined them, took a handful and ripped the petals from them, leaving just the stalks and leaves. 'These are splendid. I'll take 'em.' He already had a decent pair of binoculars, so that only left the duffel bag, balaclava, donkey jacket and air rifle.

Trying to keep his balance, Jeremy looked around him, observing for the first time that there were several fully-grown trees in the lobby. About forty feet tall, they extended to the upper reaches of the atrium. It seemed a terrible waste. All that money spent on the flora and yet they couldn't be looking after it all properly. The plants gave off a most disgusting odour.

37

The entrance was busy with people going about their business. Motorbike messengers arrived every few minutes to drop packages at the reception desk or to pick them up, their radios crackling helmet inside. You couldn't tell if they were black, white, male or female, human or Martian.

Once past the reception area, there was a desk manned by a tough-looking security guard. Just behind him a few stairs led to the Paternoster lifts, a type Jeremy had never come across before. There were two openings, but they had no doors. Inside the holes, cages appeared and disappeared on an ever-moving conveyor belt. He watched in fascination. As the cages came level with the floor, people would step in or out of them, those on the left being carried skyward and those on the right vanishing downwards.

After a while, even this novelty palled. Jeremy's discomfort was increased by the security guard, who never took his eyes off him. The receptionist, on the other hand, absorbed in slapping polish on her nails, had barely given him another glance since despatching him into the forest, not even when he had leaned a little too far and sent the chair and himself crashing to the ground.

Why should that creature, a slip of a girl with only the most tentative grasp of the English language, be permitted to spoil his great day? After all, he was prospective management and she was – well, she wasn't prospective anything. Perhaps if he had another, rather stronger, word with her? At the very least, walking about would help to relieve the pressure on his bladder and get him away from that repulsive odour.

He weaved his way back through the prickly yuccas, noticing guiltily as he approached the desk that the pages of the *Sunday Times* were still strewn about the floor. He gathered as many as he could into his arms and faced the receptionist, who was examining her inch-long nails closely, wondering whether she had done the right thing in toning them down from Livid Lemon to Mellow Mustard. She trilled 'Ta-ra' to the Luncheon Vouchers' man as he handed back his badge and gave her a thumbs-up sign, then turned reluctantly to Jeremy.

'I, uh, wondered if by any chance, Mr Nettle was back yet.'

'Back from where?'

'From wherever he has been.'

'Far as I know, he hasn't even got here yet. So he can't very well have gone anywhere to be back from, can he?'

38

'I, uh, suppose not. Perhaps you could try his office again.'

She did, putting the phone down harder than she needed when she got an unexpected answer.

'It seems Mr Nettle did turn up in his office for a moment or two,' but he has gawn away agin.' She regarded Jeremy suspiciously, as if he was privy to knowledge of the movements of the man that were being concealed from her. He was now moving from foot to foot rapidly in an effort to stave off the evil moment.

'Where?' he said, with panic in his voice.

'I couldn't say. Perhaps if I paged him for you?'

'No, not Nettle,' Jeremy said desperately. 'The lavatories.'

'Is this chap bothering you, Charmaine?' The security guard materialised by Jeremy's elbow.

'Sez he was told to come 'ere this morning, Mr Bennett. But he's not on my list.' The security chief had no need to enquire any further. This was definitely the chap who had been playing silly buggers outside last night. Close to, he looked even more suspicious. Mr Bennett had never liked red hair. It was well known that most communists had red hair, though some used dye to conceal the fact.

'Not on your list, eh? I wonder if you'd mind opening your briefcase, Sir?'

'My briefcase. Why?' What was it about people in uniforms wearing peaked caps that always made him feel guilty.

'Security, Sir. Can't be too careful these days.'

Pages of the newspaper were scattered again as Jeremy struggled with the locks on his case. He was getting flustered. He really had to go to the lavatory soon. Very soon. Almost immediately. He got the case open.

Mr Bennett looked inside. Slowly he took out each object in turn, examining it carefully. First the pad of paper, then the pencils and the pens, and then the book. He came to a tupperware container through the lid of which he could see something wrapped in silver foil. 'Perhaps you had better open that for me, Sir.'

Over the guard's shoulder, Jeremy glimpsed a door bearing a person's silhouette. The time had definitely come. He made a run for it, scattering the pages of his *Sunday Times* in his wake.

'Oi. Stop,' came a shout from behind him, but Jeremy was past caring now. He dashed inside. He couldn't find the urinals. He darted into the only open cubicle, just as the door beside it opened. There was a scream.

'A man!'

The yell was accompanied by shrieks from the other cubicles, which rapidly cleared. Jeremy barely noticed. He was having the pee of his life.

Only when he had spent his penny's worth did it dawn on him that he must have gone through the wrong door. To his surprise, he did not feel in the slightest bit embarrassed. His need had been great. To have hesitated any longer would have been disastrous. Therefore he had done the right thing. QED.

However, now that his need had been satisfied, he was not sure of the best thing to do next. If he went straight out, somebody might see him. If he stayed where he was, someone might come in and find him there. Either course of action could cause terrible complications. A glance in the mirror decided him. He looked awful. He could hardly start work looking like that.

He wedged the bin against the outside door. He might as well take the opportunity and make himself presentable. Perhaps by the time he had finished, Nettle would have made an appearance. As he washed his hands, his nostrils picked up that appallingly pungent smell again. It finally occurred to Jeremy that it might in some way be connected with him.

He sniffed at the underside of his shoes. He sniffed under his arms. He sniffed his jacket. He even bent down and sniffed. But he couldn't locate the source of the smell. He must be mistaken.

He washed his face, and felt better for it. But when he tried to comb his hair, the comb got caught in something sticky. He had found the source of the pong. He filled a basin and put his head under the water.

It is not the easiest task in the world to dry yourself using a roller towel whose roller refuses to roll. With his hair still soaking wet, Jeremy combed it into place.

He looked at his watch. Just gone eleven. He should have started work an hour and a half ago. This time he would not take no for an answer from that chit of a girl. She really was a disgrace to the company. When he ran the place, the receptionists would be required to have a minimum of two A-levels.

Jeremy removed the bin and gingerly pushed the lavatory door open an inch or two. He could not hear anyone. If he just strolled out nonchalantly, no-one would be any the wiser.

He opened the door and took a step.

'Freeze right there, carrot-top! Armed Police.'

* * * 3 * * *

JEREMY was only too happy to freeze. If the two heavily-built, ugly-looking gentlemen in flak jackets carrying even uglier-looking machine pistols had asked him to strip naked and dance a hornpipe with chrysanthemums in his hair, he would have done it unquestioningly. He knew nothing of firearms, but even he could appreciate that the weapons were aimed straight at him.

One of the men inched forwards, his stern, unblinking gaze fixed firmly on Jeremy's face. Jeremy raised his hands as high as he could, but it didn't do anything to placate the gunmen.

He tried closing his eyes. That helped considerably. Things looked much brighter, so to speak, with his eyes shut. Perhaps he was just having a rather vivid nightmare. He hadn't really woken that morning yet. At any moment the alarm clock would go off and he would wake, go to the lavatory, brush and floss his teeth, take a nice hot bath, get dressed, pick up his briefcase and head for work just as planned.

He was spun round viciously to face the wall. The gun barrel, surprisingly cold, was pressed against his temple and his legs were spread apart by the gunman's boots, rudely shattering his daydream. Rudely was putting it mildly. A hand roamed all over him, prodding and probing places even Jeremy felt reticent about exploring.

A voice from some distance away called out loudly: 'It's all right, lads. It's not a bomb.'

'Not a bomb?' The voice behind Jeremy sounded disappointed.

'No. More what you'd call sandwiches.'

'Sandwiches?'

'Yup. Salmon paste, it smells like. . . Yes. Definitely salmon paste. Quite tasty, but he's used brown bread. Prefer white myself. Don't hold with this health kick lark.'

'Shit,' said the man, his roaming hand clenching tightly with frustration.

Jeremy doubled up in agony.

Obviously still a little miffed, he kicked Jeremy's ankle, hard, by sheer coincidence landing on exactly the same spot as that targeted by the Major's stick the previous evening. Jeremy, slumped on the floor, was past caring. His eyes were still closed. He had no wish to open them. Goodness knows what further horror awaited him.

When he eventually decided it was safe to look about him, he could see more men in flak jackets, preparing to leave. One of them had a remote control unit. With one hand he was controlling a green Meccano-like machine on wheels. With the other he was tucking into Jeremy's sandwiches.

The popular notion that red-headed people have ferocious tempers was not one that anybody would have applied to Jeremy. For twenty-four years he had displayed the equable temperament of a placid pig. But he had not had a good morning. He had woken late on the most important day in his life, arrived at work in a dishevelled state, been fobbed off for half an hour by a girl with an IQ too low to be recorded, gone into a ladies' lavatory by mistake, discovered something unpleasant in his hair, been menaced by two men with guns and assaulted viciously by one of them. And now, to top it all, someone was eating his lunch.

Something snapped inside him. He limped across to the reception desk and snatched the remnants of his sandwiches back from the flak-jacket.

'Mine, I think.' He turned his attention to the security chief standing nearby, regarding him with undisguised loathing. 'And I strongly suggest that in future you temper your zealousness with just a smidgeon of common sense.'

The lobby was filling up with evacuated staff returning to their desks. Charmaine the receptionist had returned to her station. She could hardly wait to get Tracey on the phone. This was better even than the time when Princess Anne had visited BIG House. What had he been doing in the ladies' loo? She'd have to nip over as soon as the coast was clear and have a good look around.

But Jeremy had not finished yet. His wet hair dripping on to the reception desk, he turned his wrath on her. 'And as for you, young lady, if you spent less time on the phone discussing the deeper meaning of life with your friend Tracey and a little more on the job for which you are being paid, perhaps none of this would have happened.

'Now, if you don't have anything more important to do, I wonder if it might not be asking too much for you to get hold of Mr Nettle for me. Not this afternoon, not tomorrow or next week, but at once. Immediately. Tout de suite.'

'Certainly, Sir. Right away. I'm sorry, Sir.'

But before she could pick up the phone, Jeremy was tapped on the shoulder. 'I'm Nettle.'

Jeremy spun round. His spring had still not quite unwound. 'About time too. Do you have any idea how long I've been waiting?'

Nettle was taken back. He was used to a more servile attitude from graduate trainees on their first day of work. He was a rotund man with sparse, slicked-down hair and a pencil-thin moustache. His round face shone oilily and his manner was similarly obsequious. If you could have melted Nettle down you could have cooked with him.

'Dreadfully sorry, not around. Things to do, things to do. Here now though. What a morning, eh? Still, all sorted out in the end.' His words came out like short strings of sausages. 'Charmaine looking after you properly?' he asked, indicating the receptionist, but not waiting for a reply. 'Splendid, splendid. Expecting you of course. Welcome to British Industrial Group.' He grabbed Jeremy by the hand and shook it vigorously.

Jeremy was still holding what was left of his salmon paste sandwich. Nettle wiped his hand clean again with his handkerchief. 'Follow me. Show you to your office.'

This was more like it, thought Jeremy. An office. He picked up his briefcase, but left the remnants of his sandwich with Charmaine. It was no longer terribly appetising.

To his surprise, Nettle led him down the stairs.

'What a day. What a day,' he continued. 'Evacuating seven hundred and fifty people. Bomb disposal chappies. All over sandwiches. What a to-do. My word, yes. Still, good practice.

'Luncheon Vouchers, as well. Most unfortunately. Scam, of course,' he said mysteriously, opening a door and leading Jeremy into a dingy corridor. This had none of the opulence of the reception area, with its plants and thick carpet. Here the floor was laid with peeling linoleum squares, the walls painted a dirt-disguising shade of brown. The lighting was dim. All most unprepossessing.

'Got delivery this morning. Ordinary way. Pound a day for every-one. Seven hundred and fifty staff. Three months at once. Fifty-one thousand, seven hundred and fifty pounds worth. Lot of Luncheon Vouchers. Lot of money.

'Delivery men hardly gone. Chap turns up. Spins his yarn. Awful mistake. Faulty batch. Very sorry. Shouldn't be used. Take them away. Delivery chaps bring more later. I wasn't there. Girl not to know. Chap went off with vouchers. I came back. Thought, hello Nettle, bit odd. Checked. No problem with vouchers at all. Rang down. Missed him on way out. Then bomb scare. Guv'nor won't be pleased. Won't be pleased at all.'

He stopped half way down the corridor. Jeremy picked up the smell of what he took to be the canteen, unpleasantly reminiscent of his old school dining hall.

Nettle was still talking. 'Here we are. Office. All mod cons. Afraid not much light. Architects intended it storage space. Got to leave you now. Pop back later. Explain the set up. Get you sorted out. Better ring Police. Fifty-one thousand, seven hundred and fifty one-pounds Luncheon Vouchers gone missing. Looking for fat thief. Eh? Get it?' As he laughed, his whole frame shook, sending waves of fat rolling up and down his body.

Unwilling to shake hands in case Jeremy's palm concealed further horrors, Nettle gave a weak wave and disappeared down the corridor.

It was spartan as offices go. Just a desk with a phone, a cupboard and a small bookcase, on which stood a petrified plant. The one tiny window was set high in the wall. Through it, Jeremy could see the feet of passing pedestrians. The only other light came from a flickering neon strip in the ceiling.

Still, only a bad workman blames his tools. He was here to work, and he could work just as well here as anywhere. Jeremy went to close the door, which he was glad to see already had his name on it. In large, white letters, it read: 'Jeffrey Simpson. Graduate Trainee.'

Mr Bennett stared at Jeremy's retreating back with unadulterated hatred. There was nothing unusual in this. Mr Bennett hated most people, particularly his father, who had thought it highly amusing to christen his unwanted son Gordon, after the well-known expletive.

The misfortune of his name was where all similarity with Jeremy ended. Unlike him, Mr Bennett had not retreated into a shell but wreaked his revenge on the human race through his work. He had toyed with the idea of various professions. At one time, he had longed to be a policeman, at another, a traffic warden. Both occupations offered enormous scope for being rude and aggressive. But he opted in the end for a career with Customs and Excise and had spent six happy years at Gatwick Airport doing his best to wipe the smile off the faces of happy passengers returning from two weeks in the sun. His methods of humiliating both male and female travellers had soon earned him the admiration of his colleagues and the plaudits of his bosses.

Finally, however, his superiors' belated realisation that Mr Bennett had found the very same packet of cannabis resin during five separate illegal strip searches on female passengers led to his seeking alternative employment. Landing the job of BIG House's chief security officer, Mr Bennett had found his earthly paradise. Here there were no petty regulations to tell him what he could and could not do. The staff of BIG House were entirely at his mercy and Mr Bennett had none.

Taking the field every weekend for his local rugby club enabled him to kick, hit, gouge, scratch and sit on people a great deal in the name of sport, but even that did not give him the same warm glow as did stopping a senior executive of five years' standing from entering the building when he had left his identification card at home. The smart bottle-green uniform with its peaked cap was just the icing on the cake. Mr Bennett did not cultivate friendships so there was no one close or brave enough to risk taking him on one side to tell him that the uniform did nothing to disguise his appearance of being a vulgar, beer–swilling sleazeball with a virulent dandruff problem.

Mr Bennett could not think of a moment in his life he had enjoyed more than picking up the phone that morning to inform the Police that a man asked to open a package in his briefcase had done a runner. At long last a real terrorist attack, something Mr Bennett had planned for, nay longed for, these many years.

That red-haired chap had made him look a proper charlie and Mr Bennett did not like that. He did not like it one little bit. But the chance would come for him to get his own back, or his name was not Gordon Bennett.

Still fuming, he left one of his staff in charge and sought some fresh air.

'Having trouble?' asked the Major. He and Rommel were making another urinary assault on the concrete of BIG House. Mr Bennett had seen this bloke around often enough to be on nodding terms with him.

'You could say that. Some idiot started off a bomb scare. Turned out to be sandwiches.'

The Major would not normally have countenanced fraternising with the enemy, but information was a valuable commodity. 'Sandwiches, eh? Still, can't be too careful, I always say.'

Mr Bennett brightened at this bit of common sense. 'That's my motto too. Never know when some crackpot isn't going to let rip.'

'These pinko commie agitators are everywhere, you mark my words. Just because the government's done the unions down don't mean the trouble-makers have all gone back to Moscow. Gone to ground, more likely. Bidin' their moment. Sometimes wonder why we bothered fightin' the war.'

A military past always impressed Mr Bennett. 'Army?'

'That's right. El Alamein, Tobruk, you name it. Seventh Armoured Division. Rank of Major. Special Operations. Can't say more.' He tapped his nose with the end of his index finger, looking Mr Bennett up and down. What a slob. 'Smart uniform, that. Very well turned out. Credit to your profession.'

Mr Bennett's chest puffed with pride, taking his enormous belly with it and forcing his straining belt even lower. He hauled it back up in vain attempt to keep his paunch under control. 'Thank you, Sir. I believe in looking my best.'

He decided to confide in the Major, who appeared to be a kindred soul. 'It's very odd, though. The chap who started it all, a red-head, was hanging round last night, acting very suspiciously. I thought it strange at the time. Now he turns up, cocky as you please, a new employee, turning the place upside down.'

'A red-head, eh? Saw a red-head hangin' round for hours yester-day. Could be an infiltrator, a fifth-columnist, set upon evil deeds. Basic military principle. Attack from inside. Thought of that?'

'No.'

'You should. Just because a cove don't turn out to be a terrorist today don't mean he ain't going to be a terrorist tomorrow. He might just be bidin' his time. Can't be too careful these days.'

'That's him. Look,' said Mr Bennett in a hushed voice.

47

Jeremy's face was visible at pavement level. He was standing on a chair, trying unsuccessfully to open the window. Rommel cocked his leg against it, blurring Jeremy's limited view still further.

'Splendid animal you've got there, Major.'

A bright yellow Rolls-Royce Silver Spur emerged from the basement garage and took up station outside BIG House.

'Better disappear. The guv'nor must be coming out.' Mr Bennett hurried back inside.

The Major walked briskly back to his flat. He knew enough about Rolls-Royces to know that jacking one of the monsters up to change a tyre was as devil of a job. Of course, such emperors of the road didn't get flat tyres very often.

He opened his kitchen window and steadied the barrel of his newly-acquired air rifle on the sill. This was going to be one of those rare occasions.

Let battle commence.

He squeezed the trigger.

* * * 4 * * *

'SORRY to keep you, Mr Simpson.' Nettle returned to find Jeremy struggling with the window. 'Ah, settling in I see. Good, good.'

'I'm afraid there seems to have been some sort of mistake,' Jeremy said.

'Nettle was needled to find him still harping on about the morning's events. 'Said sorry. Can't do more. What's happened has happened, Mr Simpson.'

'But that's just it,' protested Jeremy, climbing down from the chair. 'My name isn't Simpson.'

'Not Simpson? Of course you're Simpson. Says so on the door,' said Nettle conclusively.

'I know what it says on the door, but that isn't my name. There must have been some mistake.'

'Mistake?' said Nettle, affronted. 'Don't make mistakes. Human Resources. Fully computerised.' He opened a folder he had brought with him. 'Cambridge, yes?'

'Yes,' replied Jeremy.

'Good. Peterhouse?'

'No.'

'No?'

'No. Sidney Sussex.'

'Oh. Maths?' asked Nettle, a little of the confidence disappearing from his voice.

'No.'

'No?'

'No. Economics.'

'Oh,' said Nettle, thoroughly confused. How could his files possibly be wrong? His system was computerised and quite, quite infallible. He was beginning to find this young man irksome.

'Not Jeffrey Simpson then?'

'No. My name's Jeremy Seaman.' Why was it taking the silly man so long to understand? 'Look. Here's the letter you sent me telling me I was to start work today.' Nettle studied it closely.

'But this is addressed to Jeremy Seaman,' he said at last.

'Yes. That's me.'

The message finally sunk in. 'Must have been some mistake,' said Nettle sadly. 'Better go check files. Seaman, you say?' He turned at the door. 'Shouldn't bother with window. Doesn't open. Air conditioning. Only thirteenth and fourteenth floor windows open.'

Sally ducked. Alexander the Great flew over her head and hit the wall, narrowly missing the Lowry.

'How long can it take to change a fucking tyre, for Chrissake? And could I get a bloody taxi while that idiot chauffeur played about? Could I hell! I had to walk half way there. Me, Alexander Prosser, walk. And by the time I got there, that hack from *The Times* was completely pissed. Thought the whole thing hilariously funny and threatened to use it as a diary piece.

'Then I get back to find there's been a bomb scare and that some con-man has waltzed off with fifty thousand quids' worth of Luncheon Vouchers. Who handed them over?'

'Just a young girl. Only started the other week. She wasn't to know.'

'Sack her.'

'But, Mr Prosser. . .'

'Sack her. And get Nettle to cut the pay of his entire department by twenty-five per cent this month. That includes him. That should teach them to be a bit more careful in future.'

'Yes, Mr Prosser,' said Sally disapprovingly.

'They should think themselves lucky I'm not asking them to pay me back the money.' He wandered over to the window and stared out. 'No call from Butterley?'

'No, Mr Prosser.'

What was the man playing at? Surely he didn't need this long to make some simple arrangements?

'Get Daniels up here and give him this.' Prosser tore a sheet with a dozen or so names on it from a pad on his desk and thrust it at Sally. 'I want his people to do the usual run-downs on these companies and I want them fast. Make sure he also asks Butler's to get us the latest shareholder lists. Get those flash Harry merchant bankers off their butts and doing something to earn their astronomical fees. If I'm needed, I'll be up on the roof with Maggie. I owe myself a little relaxation.'

Sally shivered. Relaxation? With Maggie? Uggh.

She left the room to call Daniels, head of British Industrial's Marketing Intelligence department. As she waited for him to arrive, she glanced down the list. Nostrum was one of the companies on it. So was the hated Pardoe Trust. Interesting. Something was most definitely going on.

A buzzer sounded on her desk. She glanced up at the monitor to see Daniels waiting outside.

She pressed the button to let him in. Prosser was obsessed with security. Even relatively senior personnel, including Daniels, were not given the combination to the door. Marketing Intelligence reported on British Industrial's competitors, assessing their strengths and weaknesses, warning of hostile moves they might be planning, studying their business methods and practices and, most importantly of all, hunting out possible acquisitions for the company. Even though its activities were kept well under wraps, it was generally known in BIG House as the 'dirty tricks department'. It could hardly be a coincidence that the doors to the offices of Daniels and his assistant were marked 'MI6' and 'MI5' respectively.

Daniels himself was in his mid-thirties. A former corporate stockbroker who had irritated the regulatory authorities with what he termed a minor breach of some piddling little rule or other, he was a snappy dresser of the old City sort. A tall and distinguished man, he wore his conservative clothes as if he was modelling them. He was another one who thought himself God's gift to women, though Sally disliked him intensely. He would never look you directly in the eye and his face was cavernous, with hollowed out cheeks, as if somebody had stuck the nozzle of a vacuum cleaner inside his mouth and it had stayed like that.

Daniels planted himself in front of her desk. 'Hello, gorgeous.'

'Are you talking to me, or looking in the mirror?'

'Touché. So, what's so important that one of the trolley men can't take it?' he said, using the nickname given to the firm's messengers.

Sally handed over the paper, together with Prosser's message.

'Funny chap, the guv'nor,' said Daniels, studying the list. 'Doesn't even trust his own people. Always adds red herrings. His usual ratio is six to one. Twelve firms here. So he's probably only really interested in two. Pound gets you a penny I know which two, my lovely.'

'Which?' asked Sally innocently.

'No, no. Not even to please you, my delightful creature, will I risk the wrath of our lord and master for speaking out of turn. Unless, of course, you want to do yourself a favour and come out to dinner with me tonight.'

'You know as well as I do, Mr Daniels,' she said pointedly, 'that Mr Prosser has a rule against thirteenth-floor staff fraternising with other members of the firm.'

'Hmm. If you mixed with we proles below stairs, you would hear some outrageous rumours about what really goes on, and comes off, up here.'

'I have better things to do than gossip all day, Mr Daniels.'

She pressed the button to let him out and then returned to Prosser's empty office to clear up the pieces of the latest bust bust. As she opened the cupboard, she noticed that they were running low on Alexanders. She had better order some more.

The Major checked his duffel bag. Donkey jacket, torch, spare batteries, binoculars, wire-cutters, colander, artificial flowers, boot polish and a copy of the *Sun*. All present and correct. He opened the door to the flat an inch or two to see if anybody was around. When the coast seemed clear, he slipped out.

'Here we are again.'

Nettle was back. Jeremy had been waiting for over an hour and was ravenous. The smells from the canteen wafting down the corridor were driving him mad. The sooner they got this business sorted out the better.

Nettle was in a black mood. He didn't mind sacking people, even though the new girl had been quite a pretty thing. But he wasn't so enthusiastic about cutting his own salary. He opened the file he had brought with him. 'You did say Seaman, didn't you?'

'That's right,' said Jeremy, brightening.

'Oh,' said Nettle, rather as if he had hoped for a different answer. He consulted his papers. 'Jeremy Seaman?'

'Yes.'

'Economics?'

'Yes.'

'Sidney Sussex?'

'Yes.'

'Ah.' Why was this turning into such a bitch of a day? This chap wasn't even on the short list. The psychological profile was startling to say the least. Definitely not the sort of person British Industrial was after. Could he get rid of him without a fuss, he wondered? 'Of course. Seaman. Jeremy Seaman. As I thought. All clear now. Look,' he said sympathetically, 'been bad day. Why not go home? I'll sort it out. Start again fresh tomorrow. New leaf.'

High in the branches of a sycamore in the centre of the square, a blue tit chirruped away happily, content with its lot.

Its call turned to one of alarm as a large shadow fell over it.

But the bird was too late. It managed no more than two loud squeals before it was still, its skull crushed swiftly and violently.

* * * 5 * * *

RON NIBLO, in his habitual singlet and shorts, threw open the curtains to Prosser's bedroom. As the light poured across the bed, Prosser groaned. Not the usual early morning groan, but one of pure pleasure.

A large mound under the bedclothes indicated the source of this. With an alarm clock as sophisticated as Jacqui, Prosser rarely had any problems in getting up in the morning.

'Rise and shine, boss.' Ron placed the newspapers and overnight faxes and telexes on the bedside table.

'How can I help rising, when Jacqui's doing the shining?' said Prosser, propping himself up against the bedhead. 'You certainly picked a good one there, Ron.' Oblivious to the ministrations of Jacqui's tongue, he picked up the *Financial Times* and flicked through its pages.

It was one of Ron's jobs to provide Prosser with his bevy of personal assistants. It was no easy task. There were plenty of available girls who could type at eighty words a minute and take shorthand at a hundred and twenty, but there were relatively few who combined such premium secretarial skills with those of a high-class hooker.

Jacqui had been on the staff for nine months. She seemed to relish the work, claiming it preferable to being the best typist in Shepherd Market. Her habit of chewing gum constantly irritated Niblo, but it didn't seem to bother Prosser, except for that notably stormy occasion when she had forgotten to take it out before 'waking' the boss one morning. The fuss he'd made, you'd have thought he'd caught some anti-social disease, not just a bit of chewing gum in his pubic hairs. Lorraine and Lucinda were both old hands now and although not strictly professionals in the same way as Jacqui, both had been satisfactorily serving, and servicing, the boss for over a year.

Only Sally was causing problems. She had been here less than six months, replacing a girl stupid enough to get herself pregnant. At first she had seemed ideal. She was certainly a looker. Even Ron, whose predilections lay in another direction entirely, had to admit that. Lush, auburn hair. Green eyes. A peaches and cream complexion. Great figure. Stunning legs. And, like all the girls Prosser picked, at least a head taller than him. The boss adored tall girls.

After years with Prosser, Ron had guessed he would go for Sally and he had, picking her out straight away, without even waiting for the final, most important test of all. If Ron hadn't known him better, he would have said that he was in love. Prosser claimed her nose, which turned up at the end, was one of the sexiest things he had ever seen. She was certainly different from the others. For a start, she wasn't subservient. They all knew their place, but Sally kept making wisecrack comments and coming out with her own opinions. She didn't mix much with the other girls either. They found her stand-offish and superior. Even Lucinda, daughter of a civil servant high up in the Treasury and the ultimate pearl-bedecked Sloane Ranger, with all the arrogance of the breed and the usual quota of brain cells, seemed a little in awe of her.

Sally's biggest drawback was her refusal to play ball when it came to the extra-curricular activities. A year ago, Prosser had decided that, as a believer in the free market, he should subject the girls to the forces of competition, giving them each marks which determined the size of a bonus they received each month. He claimed it was the most brilliant worker incentive scheme ever dreamt up, raising both productivity and quality as the girls vied with each other to increase their pay cheques, though with the one drawback that the healthy competition between his personal assistants now made threesomes a little too rigorous for safety.

Ron kept his eye on the bonuses. There had not been one entry against Sally's name. It couldn't be long before he was looking for her replacement.

He went through to the kitchen to prepare Prosser's breakfast. The phone rang as he was squeezing the life out of an orange. It was Jack Butterley. Ron buzzed through to the bedroom, but didn't replace the receiver. Loyal to Prosser though he might be, it didn't do any harm to keep abreast of events. You never knew when you might pick up a good tip for the market.

'Morning, Jack. You're up bright and early.'

'Hi, Alex. I can't talk for long, but I've managed to arrange a drop for you.' He gave Prosser the details.

'I appreciate the need for secrecy, but is it really necessary to make it into something out of a James Bond film?'

'It's the only safe way, Alex.'

'All right. I'll come,' said Prosser.

And, thanks to the expert probing of Jacqui's tongue, he did.

After Prosser replaced the phone, a broad grin spread across Jack Butterley's face. It was true that he needed Prosser. But there were a few old scores to be settled and there was no reason why he couldn't combine the two. He had a feeling he was going to enjoy himself enormously tonight, which was more than he could say for Alex Prosser.

Terrified of oversleeping again, Jeremy had hardly had a wink of sleep all night. When his new alarm clock went off promptly at six-thirty, he had already been up for half an hour. He was washed and dressed by seven, and at Gilbert Square before eight. It would look just as bad to arrive early as late, he felt, so he walked into the park.

That choleric man with the stick was there again, walking his dachshund. In stepping to one side to avoid him, Jeremy had stepped straight onto one of Rommel's turds, conveniently arranged at strategic locations across the grass.

After scraping his shoe, Jeremy wandered round the park and square until nine, reading. He read the *Financial Times*, he read the plinth of the statue of political reformer, John Cartwright, the plaque on the house boasting that Sir Roland Hill had lived there from 1837–1839 and the notice on a sad-looking copper beech proclaiming that it had been planted by President Nehru in 1953. He gave a wide berth to the tramp he had trodden on the day before, still huddling in the same doorway across the square from BIG House.

Finally it was time to clock on for work. But this time, because he was concentrating on them, Jeremy found the automatic revolving doors took some getting used to. You had to get your speed and rhythm just right. Twice he found himself back outside on the pavement.

Once inside the jungle of the atrium, he faced another obstacle: Mr Bennett.

'It's all right. I know my way. Mr Nettle took me to my office yesterday.'

'No-one gets through without an identification card. I'm sorry, but rules is rules,' said Mr Bennett with sadistic pleasure, ramming his short stubby fingers into Jeremy's chest.

At the reception desk, Charmaine, resplendent in Passion Pink lips, Vampy Vermilion eyes and Sexy Salmon pink nails, brightened up on seeing Jeremy. Perhaps he would provide her with some more good gossip with which to overawe her friend at lunch. Tracey's employment in the typing pool put her at the centre of BIG's grapevine. But since this chap's arrival, it had been Charmaine who had been the one with all the news. It was really getting Tracey's knickers in a twist.

'Mr Nettle isn't in yet,' she said, replacing the receiver, 'and I'm afraid Human Resources have no record of a Jeremy Seaman. Perhaps you would like to wait?' she added sweetly.

Cast off into the forest of yuccas again, Jeremy was kept under close observation not only by the hopeful Charmaine, but also by the suspicious Mr Bennett. It was as he was sitting there, in the steaming heat of the BIG jungle, that his nostrils signalled to him that he hadn't spent quite enough time wiping his feet on the grass. There were still definitely traces of the dachshund on his shoes.

Perhaps if he sloped off to the lavatory? No, perhaps not.

It was nearly a quarter to ten when Charmaine waved him over.

'Mr Nettle sent vis dahn wiv his apologies. He's tied up nah, but he'll try to pop along to see you later.'

Jeremy thrust the card in Mr Bennett's face as he passed saying, louder than necessary, 'Are you sure you wouldn't like to search my briefcase today?'

Mr Bennett breathed deeply. 'I'm sure that won't be necessary, Mr Simpson.' There would be plenty of time to get even later.

Outside the house martin was hard at work gathering material for his nest. Others went in search of their mate first but years of experience had taught him that if you already had a well-appointed nest ready to move into, you could have your pick of the possible mates. You couldn't beat a nice cosy nest when it came to pulling the birds.

Sally was running through Prosser's appointments diary. He seemed in a much better mood today, almost jovial.

'Anything on this evening?' he asked.

'Dinner with one of your tame MPs. Junkin.'

'Get me out of it. Something more important has cropped up. Better make sure the car will be ready at seven-thirty. And tell Roach I want to have a long meeting with him tomorrow morning.'

Sally made a note of it. Roach was British Industrial's finance director, Prosser's right-hand man, and one of the few people the boss had any time for.

Curious, she tried a little fishing. 'What about Mr Butterley? Are you still expecting him to call?'

'No. You can forget all about that now,' he snapped. She was right. It *had* got something to do with Butterley.

When Sally left the office, Prosser thought back to that early morning phone call. He wondered if Butterley were deliberately having fun with him. If so, two could play that game and it was not one which Butterley would win.

Sally's voice came through on the speakerphone. 'I've arranged another date for Junkin, Mr Prosser. But he said you would want to know there's a whisper on the grapevine that you're to be in the next list. He said you would know what he meant.'

Prosser swung his chair from side to side, barely able to conceal his delight. This was it at long last. A sword on the shoulder job. Sir Alexander Prosser. Acknowledgement not only of his sterling contribution to the country but also of his Sterling contribution to Conservative Party funds, with British Industrial pouring a hundred thousand pounds into the coffers last year. It was only fair that he, as the head of the company, should receive something in return for being so generous with shareholders' money.

Prosser had become something of an expert on the Honours system, having waited in vain for his recognition on previous occasions. The next Honours List would be announced in mid-June, so he ought to be getting the letter offering him his knighthood early in May. Just a few weeks to wait. How he would love to see Sir Jocelyn Pardoe's face when he read the news. His nose would be put so far out of joint, it would dislocate itself.

It wasn't turning into a bad day. Not a bad day at all. And if tonight went well, a new chapter could be beginning in the glorious history of British Industrial. Tonight? Damn. He'd nearly forgotten. He buzzed Sally and made a rather unusual request.

* * *

58

Nettle claimed to sympathise with Jeremy's predicament and promised him that everything that could be done was being done. But it appeared that the computer was no more able to comprehend the startling proposition that Jeffrey Simpson was really Jeremy Seaman than Nettle was.

In the meantime, he was advised to be patient. But Jeremy was bored with being patient. He wanted some work to do.

He shut his increasingly repellent shoes in the cupboard until lunchtime, read the newspaper, put his *A–Z of Business Terms* on the bookcase, watered the dead ivy, read the contract and terms of employment at British Industrial Group, studied the internal telephone list he had found in one of the drawers of the desk and then, exhausted and somewhat disillusioned, fell asleep with his head on the desk.

The Major was feeling pleased with himself. His reconnaissance of the previous evening had gone well. Wearing the donkey jacket and carrying a copy of the *Sun*, he had been able to wander at will around the council depot without being challenged.

After dark had fallen, he had crouched in nearby bushes with the binoculars, watching the depot intently. Thanks to his skilful camouflage, he had remained unobserved.

It was only when he had arrived back at his flat that the Major realised he had forgotten to change back into his ordinary clothes. He had wandered two miles through the streets of London with bootblack on his face and a colander stuffed full of artificial leaves on his head, and nobody had paid the blindest bit of notice.

The fruits of his expedition could not be picked for a day or two yet and the Major needed something to keep the spark of battle alive until then. He glared across the square from his kitchen window. The yellow Rolls stood outside BIG House again. Yesterday, it had developed a puncture. Such an occurrence happened only rarely. The chauffeur had probably never had to deal with such a thing before. The Major reasoned that the chances were that he had not yet bothered to have the old tyre repaired.

He decided to test this hypothesis. He rested the air rifle on the window frame and took aim.

* * * 6 * * *

JEREMY was woken by the phone.

'Hello?' he said, his voice blurry with sleep.

'This is Sally Fluke, Mr Prosser's assistant. I wonder if you would have time to run a small errand for Mr Prosser? Come to the twelfth floor, walk up the stairs to the thirteenth and announce yourself.'

Jeremy could hardly contain himself. An errand? For Mr Prosser himself? He checked he had his notebook and pen, dashed to the lavatory, peed, washed his hands, straightened his tie and flattened his hair.

His shoes. He had forgotten his shoes. He raced back to his office, took them from the cupboard and hared back to the lavatory. Turning the taps full on, he held them underneath, sole upwards.

Although they were a little damp when he put them back on, what was a minor inconvenience at a moment like this?

He stood in front of the left hand Paternoster, watching first one, and then another, compartment rise out of the earth and disappear upwards. It didn't look the sort of thing he could master on his own. No-one was around so he dashed up the stairs to the ground floor, where it was busier. He watched a few people entering on the up side. The trick seemed to be to walk forward just before the bottom of the cage came level with the floor. It looked simple enough.

Jeremy stepped forward a little too early and fell against Tracey, teasing terror of the typing pool and lunchtime companion of Charmaine on reception.

'Ohh. We're a bit forward, aren't we?' she teased.

Jeremy was mortified. Surely she didn't think he had done it on purpose? 'No, no. You don't understand. I haven't ever done it before.'

The girl emitted a loud, raucous, braying noise which Jeremy could only suppose to be laughter. 'A virgin!' she screamed. 'I'm flattered you picked me to be the first.'

Jeremy went the colour of ripe beetroot. 'No. I mean. . .that is to say. . .I've never been up in one of these before.'

He had to endure her teasing and hyena-like laughter all the way to the ninth floor. 'I'm sure we can arrange something if you've the inclination. See you around,' she said, blowing him a kiss as she stepped out.

Jeremy had been so flustered he hadn't paid attention to the girl's exit.

He waited his moment. The tenth floor appeared and then disappeared below him. The eleventh floor appeared and disappeared. This was his floor. Blast. He moved too early and stubbed his toe. The twelfth floor disappeared. It was the last floor. The compartment was going up into the roof, preparing to drop down the other side. Jeremy panicked. Did the cages turn upside down as they went over the top? He braced himself.

The cage disengaged the runners, swung easily across to the other side, and re-engaged, starting its trip down. Jeremy was so relieved he hadn't been tipped on to his head that he missed the twelfth floor on the way down, too. It wasn't until the seventh floor that he plucked up the courage to jump out.

He decided to stick to the stairs. His shoes squelched and squished noisily as he climbed. From the twelfth floor, a carpeted stairway led to a thick security door with a keypad beside it and an intercom. A closed-circuit camera was mounted above the door.

Jeremy pressed the intercom button.

'You must be Mr Simpson,' said a disembodied female voice. 'Come in.' A buzzing noise sounded as the lock was thrown.

'No,' said Jeremy, into the microphone, eager to correct the misapprehension. 'There's been a mix-up. My name is Jeremy Seaman.'

There was no response, so he pushed the door. It did not move. The buzzing noise had stopped. He pressed the button again.

'If you push the door now, you will find it will open, Mr Simpson,' said the gently mocking voice.

Jeremy pushed. It would be easier to explain inside.

'Hello. I'm Sally Fluke, one of Mr Prosser's assistants.'

'Wow.' Jeremy marvelled at the opulence of the surroundings.

Sally marvelled at Jeremy. She had asked Nettle for someone who wouldn't be missed for a few hours. He certainly seemed to have come up trumps. This chap was behaving like an out of town hick let loose in the big, bad City for the first time. Look at his clothes. What did he think he looked like? That terrible brown suit and the ghastly matching tie.

She looked down. Brown suede shoes, for goodness sake! And they appeared to be soaking wet.

Jeremy, for his part, kept telling himself that he had arrived. Only his second day at work and he was finally here, where his idol worked and lived. Prosser himself would have walked on the carpet underneath Jeremy's feet. If he'd been on his own, he might have knelt and kissed it.

He followed Sally's gaze and noticed his shoes.

'They're wet,' said Jeremy, unnecessarily.

'But it's a lovely day outside.'

'Would you mind terribly if I didn't explain? It is just a little embarrassing.'

He looked so miserable and uncomfortable that Sally simply shook her head and smiled at him.

It was the first friendly gesture shown towards Jeremy since he had arrived at British Industrial. He smiled back. After all, here he was, on the thirteenth floor, hand-picked to perform an important task for Mr Prosser himself. Things were really beginning to look up.

He realised with a start that Sally had been talking to him.

'I beg your pardon?'

'I said a tramp's costume. Mr Prosser is going to a fancy dress party and has decided to go as a tramp.' Jeremy looked so crest-fallen at the banality of the task set him that she played it up a bit. 'He particularly stressed that someone trustworthy be sent out to get it. That's why you were chosen.' That was certainly one way of interpreting Prosser's command to 'Find me the latest frigging graduate trainee and tell him to pull his finger out of his arse. I've got something worthy of his talents.' Prosser, who had never enjoyed the benefits of higher education, if indeed he had enjoyed any education at all, hated graduates with a vengeance and loved humiliating them.

Sally felt guilty. This one seemed so keen and eager to please. He had even taken his notebook out and was writing it down.

'You'll find a few fancy dress hire places in the Yellow Pages. Use a taxi if necessary. You'll be reimbursed later, unless you need an advance.'

'Oh no. That's all right,' replied Jeremy, even though it wasn't. His bank was grumbling about the size of his overdraft, even though he kept telling them his first salary cheque was due soon. But he didn't want to give the impression he was short of funds. He could take the money from a dispenser and have it back into the bank before they even noticed.

She showed him to the door. 'If you could have the costume here by five-thirty at the latest, Mr Simpson.'

'It's Seaman, Miss Fluke.'

Sally looked down at her skirt, puzzled. There *was* a small stain. But surely not? It was clean on that morning.

'Coffee, I should think,' she replied, thoroughly confusing Jeremy.

It didn't make sense, Sally thought after she had let Jeremy out. Prosser *never* went to parties if he could avoid them. He was the most misanthropic person she had ever come across. And any arrangements like that would surely have been made through her. And come to think of it, what bloody business was it of Simpson's what she had on her skirt?

Jeremy missed the ground floor, was carried into the basement, round the bottom and up the other side, eventually managing to escape on the third floor. He squelched down to his office, took the Yellow Pages from the cupboard, and began dialling.

'Problem. What do you mean problem?' barked Prosser into the speakerphone.

Daniels hated breaking bad news to Prosser. There are those who believe that there is nothing to be gained by punishing the bearer of bad tidings. Prosser was one of them. There was nothing to be gained, but he frequently did it anyway because he enjoyed it. 'You know that new hypermarket in Sheffield we've had all the problems with over planning permission, simply because there's an old cinema on the site? Well, we did the usual thing. Spread the green stuff around. Got a few local councillors in our pocket. No trouble. Now it seems some local nutter went over their heads and got directly in touch with the Department of the Environment. We didn't get wind of it in time to head it off. Word has it that the cinema is about to be listed. Fine example of Art Deco architecture and all that crap. If that happens, we won't be able to touch it.'

'Can't we fire off one of our double-barrelled lawyers at them?'

'Too late for that, I'm afraid.'

'You worry too much, Godfrey. I think you'll find this is one problem that will simply go away of its own accord. Send me up a copy of the plans and leave the whole thing to me.' Christ Almighty! Had his staff no initiative of their own? Prosser pressed another button. 'Ron, get in here would you?'

A faint hissing noise was heard. Prosser walked over to the other side of the room and opened the lid of the Tube, a computerised update of the old fashioned pneumatic message system so popular in department stores. He took out the plans and spread them out on his desk.

'Ah, Ron. Come in. How's your map reading these days?'

Jeremy was beginning to panic. Only one of the nine shops he had rung said they had a tramp's costume in stock. He had rushed straight round in a taxi, stopping to extract five twenty pound notes from a cash dispenser, only to find that they had rented it out in the intervening quarter of an hour.

He had no choice but to order the taxi back to Gilbert Square. In the safety of the cab, Jeremy had removed his damp shoes and was wriggling his socks in front of the heating grille. He was sure he could still smell that blasted Dachshund's business.

Where on the earth was he going to get a tramp's outfit? He could hardly go back to Miss Fluke to suggest that Mr Prosser might prefer to be a pirate or a Roundhead instead.

The answer came to him as they turned into Gilbert Square. Why hadn't he thought of it before?

'No, not here. The other side of the square please,' he told the driver.

The meter said five pounds forty pence. Jeremy got out and opened his wallet. He had no idea how much he should tip the cabbie. He handed a twenty pound note through the window. 'Keep whatever you think appropriate,' said Jeremy.

'Thanks, guv. That's very generous of you.' The cabbie gunned the accelerator and drove off without a backward glance.

Jeremy was aghast. How could he possibly explain that it had cost him twenty pounds just to get to the other side of Gilbert Square? He hadn't even asked for a receipt.

Fortunately the tramp he had stepped on on Sunday was still there, tightly clutching a brown paper bag. Jeremy tried not to breathe in too deeply. 'Excuse me.'

'The moon's not made of green cheese, you know,' said the tramp accusingly.

'Eh?'

'No. It's the earth that's made of green cheese.' The tramp took a swig from his bottle. 'The elves told me, so it must be true. Got any carrier bags?'

'No, I. . .'

'Git-face. Bat's droppings make you blind, you know.'

'No, I didn't know. . .Look, I wonder if. . .Um, do you think I might borrow your clothes for a while?'

The tramp screamed out loudly: 'Rape!'

'Shhh!' Jeremy looked around him nervously. 'I mean, how much money do you want to lend me your clothes till tomorrow?'

'Money?' The tramp's craziness was abruptly replaced by a sly craftiness. 'For my clothes?'

'Yes.'

'For the clothes off me very back?'

'Yes.'

'For these glorious vestments, handed down in my family from generation to generation.'

'Yes.'

'These heirlooms? These priceless heirlooms?'

'Yes, yes. Look, they really are very beautiful. How much to borrow them for a day?'

'How much you got?'

'Eighty. . . Never you mind how much I've got.'

'What a coincidence. That's exactly how much it'll cost you. Eighty nicker.'

'Eighty pounds! Just to borrow those rags for a few hours?'

'They may be rags to you, but they're home to me and a few thousand fleas. Eighty quid it is. Take it or leave it.'

Jeremy looked at his watch. It was gone half-past three. He only had two hours left and he was still going to have to get the clothes cleaned. 'Okay. Eighty pounds it is.'

'Shake on it,' said the tramp.

Jeremy shuddered at the idea of such close contact with the derelict. 'I am quite happy to take your word as a. . . as a gentleman,' he said magnanimously, handing over four twenty-pound notes.

The tramp counted the money out slowly, then stuffed it into some recess deep in his garments. 'Well, if you won't shake hands, have a drink,' he said, grinning broadly.

'I don't drink,' said Jeremy truthfully.

'I insist.' The tramp held out the brown bag.

Jeremy wanted to take out his handkerchief and wipe the neck of the bottle, but couldn't risk causing offence. He shut his eyes and took a quick gulp.

'It's mineral water,' he said, surprised.

'That's right, me old cock. Perrier, wiv a twist of lemon. We aren't all alcoholics, you know.' The tramp sniffed loudly, then spat on the pavement, narrowly missing Jeremy. 'Here, what am I going to wear if I give my clothes to you?'

'I hadn't thought of that.'

'If you leave me in me undies, I might die of exposure. Just another cruel statistic. You'll have to get me some new togs.' The tramp stood up and put his arm around Jeremy's shoulder. 'So where's it to be, me old China? Oxford Street, Bond Street or Knightsbridge.'

It was the mention of Bond Street that made Jeremy aware just what it was about the tramp he found so peculiar. Even though much of what he said was in the vernacular, the man spoke with one of the poshest accents Jeremy had ever encountered. If it is wasn't for the fact that he was sleeping rough, one could have taken him for a BBC newsreader.

'You call the taxi while I nip back into the doorway. It has to be a cab because I get travel-sickness something rotten on the Underground or buses. You get the door open and I'll hop in before the cabbie's got the time to stop me. You wouldn't believe how these taxi-drivers discriminate against we gentlemen of the road.'

He pinched Jeremy's cheek. 'Do cheer up, mate. Put on your party face. Tell you what, while we're shopping, why don't we get you some shoes? You'll catch your death walking round like that all day.'

Jeremy looked down and saw his brown socks. He had left his new shoes in the taxi. It was uncharitable, he knew, but he hoped he hadn't managed to get rid of all that dog muck.

* * *

Prosser jabbed a finger at the speakerphone. 'Sally, some bastard is putting a wheel clamp on my Roller.'

'Oh dear, Mr Prosser,' she said, sticking out her tongue at the loudspeaker.

'Oh dear? Is that all you can say? Tell that fucking chauffeur that unless the car is ready to move by seven o'clock, he is going to be looking for a new employer. Get him to check the paintwork too. If there's one scratch on it, I'll sue the bastards. Then tell Nettle to find me another chauffeur.'

'Yes, Mr Prosser.' This chauffeur was the fifth in the six months she had been there. Usually it was Prosser's Choice that got them. Either exceed the speed limit or lose your job. It wasn't long before they were out of work, one way or another.

'Are those clothes here yet?'

'No, Mr Prosser. They'll be here by five-thirty.'

'Those graduate trainees are bloody parasites. One second late and he's out on his arse, too. I'm going up to see Maggie. She must think I've forgotten her.'

Sally grimaced. Just thinking of that terrible Maggie made her feel sick.

'Which do you think suits me best, the grey flannel or the Prince of Wales' check, Jeremy?'

The tramp had insisted on knowing Jeremy's name. 'The Prince of Wales check is very nice,' he said miserably, looking pointedly at his watch.

'Very nice, *Sebastian,*' admonished the tramp.

'Very nice, Sebastian. Look, do you think we might hurry this up? Why not try it on?'

It can't be every day that someone wanders in off the street with a tramp to buy him a new set of clothes. Yet the assistant had not batted an eyelid and was looking after Sebastian with considerably greater attention and servility than Jeremy was usually afforded.

'You know, I think I will. Hold these for me, would you?' He handed Jeremy several heavy Sainsbury's carrier bags. 'Why don't you pick out a pair of shoes for yourself while I change? Take my advice, get yourself something nice and traditional. Nothing fancy. Something like these,' advised Sebastian, indicating his own footwear.

67

He disappeared into the changing room, leaving Jeremy goggling. Instead of the tattered and worn shoes held together with string he might have expected, Sebastian was wearing immaculate black brogues, beautifully polished. Come to think of it, there was something else odd about Sebastian. He didn't smell. Or, if he did, the faint scent was more like after-shave than the rank stench of a man who had slept rough for weeks.

Jeremy sneaked a look inside the carrier bags he had been given to hold. What on earth was a tramp doing with a cellular telephone, a camera with zoom lens, a miniature cassette recorder and a pair of binoculars?

*** 7 ***

IT WAS NEARLY five-thirty, the time of day Mr Bennett liked least, when the tide changed and the stream of employees flowed out of BIG House. Much as he disliked people entering his precious building, he recognised that unless they did so he would not have the pleasure of being able to stand in their way. It depressed him that he could produce no good reason to prevent them returning to the streets in the evening unchallenged.

Charmaine was ignoring him, pretending still to be cross about the trivial little episode that lunchtime when he had put his hand up her skirt under the pub table and refused to take it away when she had asked him. Such a tease, Charmaine. Her and her friend Tracey. Always saying no when they really meant yes.

Mr Bennett affected not to care less, sitting behind his desk with a scowl on his face, dreaming of glory on the rugby field. Glory and the Lewisham Leopards were not natural bedfellows. Thanks in no small part to Mr Bennett's own contribution, the Leopards were renowned throughout South-east London as the most vicious group of fifteen individuals you could gather in one place without the riot squad being called out. Those foolhardy enough to take the field against the Leopards found skill and prowess with foot and ball little defence against the unfortunate and frequent accidents with which the game was littered. Whereas the opposition saw only one ball on the field to grab, kick, punch and pummel, the Leopards saw thirty-one or, if the referee was proving difficult, thirty-three.

Mr Bennett's daydreams took him not to Lewisham, but to Cardiff Arms Park. It was the deciding match for the Triple Crown, the score was level and only five minutes of play remained. One of the Scottish wing three-quarters had broken loose with the ball and was running it up the field, with the Welsh defence falling into disarray as he swept through them. Nothing stood between him and a certain try except Bennett, the wizard Welsh full-back. Bennett positioned himself, ready to make the most important tackle of his career.

It was unfortunate for Jeremy that he should have chosen this particular moment to enter BIG House at the run with Sebastian's clothes bundled in his arms.

If he rushed, he reckoned he could just make it. It had been half-past four before Sebastian had been kitted out to his satisfaction. The bill, including that for Jeremy's new shoes, had come to nearly three hundred pounds and the assistant would not take Jeremy's cheque. It had been the surprising Sebastian who had saved the day, handing over a credit card. Jeremy hoped his bank would not bounce the cheque he had made out to Sebastian. Ethically, he should have warned him of this possibility, but he was too concerned to find a laundrette and get back before the deadline.

He entered BIG House, the clothes still slightly damp but with five minutes to spare. Once again his knack of failing to contemplate the difficulties of revolving doors got him through them with ease.

It was as Jeremy sprinted to the lifts that the world seemed to crash in around him. His legs were pinioned together and he was brought to the ground by the full force of the sixteen-stone bulk of Mr Bennett, in whose ears rang the cheers of the delirious crowd of Cardiff Arms Park. Although Jeremy was halted dead in his tracks, the clothes were not. They shot out of his arms and into a compartment of the Paternoster lift. Jeremy lifted his head just in time to see them disappear upwards.

He tried talking, but with most of the wind knocked out of him speech was difficult.

'Whaasgoingon?' he croaked.

'Just where do you think you're going, me lad?' demanded Mr Bennett, now firmly back in Gilbert Square, if a little unclear as to why he and the saboteur were lying together on the ground, providing free entertainment for the amused homeward-bound employees of British Industrial Group.

'Clothes,' gasped Jeremy. 'Prosser. . .wants. . .clothes.' He must only have about four minutes by now.

'What clothes?' asked Mr Bennett, not unreasonably.

By now the clothes would be halfway up BIG House. Mr Bennett stood up to dust off his precious uniform.

Jeremy took advantage of this, rolling forward into an ascending cage just coming into view, oblivious to the four foot he fell and to the two shrieking secretaries upon whom he landed.

'Do you make a habit of dropping on defenceless girls?' demanded Tracey from the typing pool.

Jeremy ignored her. He had more important things on his mind. He reckoned that Sebastian's clothes must be about six cages ahead. If he got out at the ninth floor, he should be in time to stop them on their way back down. He staggered out of the cage and crossed to the descending lift. Jeremy grabbed the clothes as they came into view and sprinted up the stairs, pushing the entry buzzer to the thirteenth floor. Sally pressed the button and Jeremy fell through the door.

After six months at British Industrial, Sally reckoned that she was no longer easily surprised by anything, but the sight of Jeremy, his face already bruised from its recent contact with the reception area floor, one trouser leg ripped below the knee, leaning against the wall gasping for breath sent even her normally immobile eyebrow up a notch.

She fetched the first-aid kit and began dabbing his face.

'I'm glad to see you're punctual. No problems, I hope?'

Jeremy's speech was erratic, interrupted not only by his attempts to get his breath back, but by little whimpers as the cotton wool touched the more sensitive parts of his face. 'Nothing. . .I. . .couldn't handle.'

'I like the new shoes. They look so much drier than the old pair.'

'Left. . . old. . . pair. . . in. . . taxi,' he gasped.

'Of course you did. It's the sort of thing that happens every day.' As she attended to his injuries, Sally wormed the story of Jeremy's day from him. He was only too glad to share his horrendous experiences, although he thought it judicious to leave out some of the details of Sebastian's eccentricities.

As she listened Sally found, to her surprise, that she was developing a soft spot for Jeremy. Everyone else she came into contact with in British Industrial was so self-confident, so sure of themselves. This chump, on the other hand, seemed so vulnerable and helpless. He was surely too nice to survive for long in the shark-infested waters of British Industrial.

She prised his fingers away from his precious burden. One day, if she was feeling particularly cruel, she would tell Prosser about the

71

night he wore real tramp's clothes. It was a pity that Jeremy had had time to wash them.

She opened the door to let him out. 'You can't have had your first pay packet yet. Have you any money left?'

He shook his head. He had been planning to walk home.

Sally opened her bag, took out twenty pounds and thrust it into his hands, ignoring his protests. As he shambled out, she said 'Good night, Mr Simpson.'

'Seaman,' said Jeremy weakly.

In the centre of the square, a sparrow rested contentedly on a branch of the copper beech planted by Nehru, a contribution to world peace and harmony. In the last minute of its all too brief life, the bird snapped up a convenient grub from the branch on which it stood, wolfed it down and began to preen the feathers on its chest.

Years of comfortable town dwelling had slowed the sparrow's reactions. The blow that killed it took it completely unawares, snapping its neck with terrifying force.

*** 8 ***

NOSTRUM's factory was a long, low brick building on the outskirts of Reading. Constructed at the height of the Industrial Revolution it was considered, even then, to embody few of the latest innovations in style or technology. The Westbury family's dedication to the recipes of their forebears was matched by an equal devotion to their work conditions and practices. Apart from those alterations forced upon them by the mollycoddling laws enacted by interfering politicians, little had been done to rid the place of its similarity to a workhouse. Even the Victorian Society had little love for the place, dubbing its distinctive architectural design 'Gloomy Gothic'.

Ernie Beamish usually hated doing night duty at the Nostrum plant, stuck for twelve hours at a stretch in the draughty Port-acabin grandiosely known as the 'Security Wing', with nothing but eight black and white closed circuit monitors and non-stop Radio Two for company and only a one-bar electric fire to keep him warm.

Tonight, though, he also had Janice, from Sterile Bottle Inspection, who was not only keeping him company but also doing a splendid job in staving off the cold. Janice had sat down opposite him in the canteen before his shift started and asked him a few desultory questions about his job.

'It's the pits,' Ernie had replied truthfully, shovelling in his egg, sausage, tomato, bacon and chips. 'It'd bore the pants off you.'

'Well, I'm always game for something new,' she said slyly. 'I've had them taken off in a good many ways before, but never by boring. Why don't I pop in later.'

She tottered in a little after nine, having exchanged her overalls for her formal evening wear, a boob tube, mini-skirt and high heels. Considering her reputation at Nostrum, Ernie was surprised it had taken her so long to get round to him. If only half of what his colleagues said was true, she had spent almost as much time in the security hut as he had.

Janice was a direct girl, with no time for the traditional niceties and prevarications of courtship. She locked the door and sat straightaway in Ernie's lap, attaching her mouth to his with all the tenacity of a limpet mine. Her tongue, playing an inverted game of tug of war with Ernie's, won easily, reaching the spot where his tonsils had been until the age of ten.

With one hand, she unzipped his flies and began massaging him. 'Not much in the way of security protecting that, is there?' she giggled, while Ernie struggled to get his breath back. With the other, she pulled her knickers down to her ankles.

Given a choice, Ernie would have liked a little more in the way of foreplay, but he was given no choice. Janice wrapped her legs together behind the chair, pinning him to it and forcing him inside her.

In the background Russ Conway ran his fingers over 'Tiptoe through the Tulips'.

It wasn't long before Janice discovered that boredom was not confined to the job but also extended to the man doing it. She spun the swivel chair round so that she faced the screens, hoping that they might provide a little diversion from the task in hand. The cameras sited within the factory itself held nothing of interest for her. The last thing she wanted was to look at the production line where she spent her working day.

But the monitor covering the area round the main gate showed signs of movement, a man shambling along rooting through the large bins there. She knew from her previous visits that the bins were popular with tramps who took cardboard boxes, paper and all manner of packaging to use as shelter.

Janice enjoyed watching these dregs of society from the safety of the security hut. It made the sex seem so much more exciting and decadent. She gripped the chair harder.

Ernie was not too happy about Janice staring over his shoulder in the midst of what ought to be their joint ecstasy. He swung the chair round so that he was facing the screens again, raising it slightly in the process. But Janice was not to be thwarted so easily. She swung the chair back again.

This tramp was a picky one. He didn't seem satisfied with anything he found. He was scattering boxes left, right and centre and throwing mounds of paper and other rubbish to the ground.

'What's he got there, Ernie?' she asked.

Ernie swung the chair round to look for himself.

He had found it at last. He'd murder that bloody man Butterley when he got his hands on him! In the bin by the gate, he had said. There were bins everywhere. Thank God they hadn't been emptied. They were very late, thanks to that idiot chauffeur. Yet another puncture *and* the dreaded clamp. It had taken hours to sort it out.

Prosser hadn't thought to bring any gloves. He hated to think what the evil-smelling sticky mess that he had burrowed through with his bare hands a couple of bins back might be. But this was definitely it, a bottle wrapped up in shredded paper. His initials, ACP, were scrawled on the label.

Prosser jumped down with the bottle, only to find himself face to face with a real gentleman of the road, whose own perfume blended subtly with that emanating from the surrounding bins.

'I'll 'ave that, mate,' he said, snatching it from Prosser's grasp before the great man had time to react.

Prosser could have flattened the newcomer with little difficulty, but that would put the bottle and its precious contents at risk. He tried another popular form of persuasion.

'I'll give you a hundred pounds for it.'

The tramp found this hilarious. He roared with laughter, exposing Prosser to the sight of a broken row of teeth and an onslaught of putrid breath that, bottled, would have made an efficient paint-stripper.

He peered closely at Prosser. 'A 'undred parnds? That's rich, that is. Wait till I tell the boys.' And, with the tears streaming down his face, he unscrewed the cap and took a swallow.

He spat it out, straight into Prosser's face. 'Aggh. It's poison.'

Prosser's reactions were just quick enough. He threw himself to the ground, getting his hands to the bottle just before it hit the pavement.

He scrabbled around and found the top, putting it back on again and jamming the bottle into his pocket.

Prosser stood up to find the tramp staring at him. 'You said you wus gonna give me 'undred parnds,' he said accusingly.

'When you had the bottle, it was worth a hundred pounds,' said Prosser. 'Now that I have the bottle, there's nothing to negotiate. You should learn about risk reward ratios.'

The tramp pushed past him in disgust, in search of saner and more intelligent company.

Janice watched this little drama with interest while Ernie wriggled and jiggled and tickled inside her. To her astonishment, the monitor showed what was clearly a Rolls-Royce drawing up a few yards beyond the bins. A uniformed chauffeur jumped out, walked round to the back door on the other side of the car and opened it. A well-endowed young woman, apparently wearing nothing more than a pair of shoes and earrings, emerged from the Rolls clutching a bottle of champagne. She waved the chauffeur away and beckoned to the tramp, who broke into a run.

Janice was finding this all terribly arousing. Ernie, building up his own head of steam by now, was also fascinated by events outside. Yet they could see the screen clearly only one at a time. As each struggled to turn the chair so as to face the monitor, the motion intensified their love-making.

The girl and the tramp got into the Rolls which moved off. Seconds later, it stopped abruptly. The back door burst open and the tramp was pushed out on to the road. The car reversed quickly. The girl climbed out again and walked back towards the factory, greeting the other tramp with outstretched arms.

The two walked together towards the car, climbing in. The Rolls drove off, stopping just a few yards beyond the first tramp. The door opened once more and something was thrown to him before the car sped off, out of sight of the camera.

The tramp walked back towards the factory gates bearing his trophy. He sought out a quiet spot. He had no wish to share this with any of his less refined acquaintances. It had been a long, long time since he had enjoyed a bottle of champagne.

Jack Butterley disentangled himself from the safety of a clump of bushes. A camera good enough to take photographs in this light had been expensive, but if the pictures came out properly, it would be the best insurance policy he had ever bought. Let Alex Prosser try to double-cross him now.

* * *

With the disappearance of the car, Janice and Ernie had lost interest in events outside the hut and were concentrating upon bringing their own proceedings to their natural conclusion. Janice was moaning. The noises from her throat grew louder and louder as her gyrations grew wilder and wilder.

Neither she nor Ernie saw the tramp shaking the champagne bottle, nor did they witness the moment when the cork flew out of its neck. They were not aware of it flying straight towards the camera, nor of the monitor going black as the glass in the lens was shattered.

They found it hard, however, to miss the earth-shattering screech of the alarm system which erupted in the hut just as Janice's screams peaked and Ernie erupted inside her.

Instinctively, he spun the chair round sharply to see what was happening. It was one spin too many. The swivel had been raised as high as it would go. It teetered for a moment at the top of its spindle and then the chair seat crashed to the floor.

Janice landed, as so often, on her back, with the man and the chair seat on top of her. Either the sex, the sirens or the sudden fall were too much for Ernie, whose heart promptly gave out.

Janice's screams turned from joy to horror as she realised that Ernie's really was a dead weight. She screamed and screamed and screamed while the sirens screeched and screeched and screeched, drowning out the strains of 'Tie a Yellow Ribbon Round the Old Oak Tree' on the radio.

Janice was still screaming when the police broke into the hut fifteen minutes later.

She was screaming again soon after that as she showed her gratitude to the two officers kind enough to rescue her from her predicament. Ernie and his chair had been returned to their spindle.

It was some time before the four long arms of the law finished rendering Janice assistance and the policemen turned their attention to the monitors. After all, alarms were always going off, but it wasn't every day you came across a sight like that which had greeted them when they burst into the Portacabin.

Constable Norris spotted the video machine with its never-ending half-hour spool of tape. He switched it off. As he was to find out later, the only thing of any interest on it was a recording of a tramp opening a bottle of champagne. Everything else that had taken place outside the gates had already been recorded over.

Had the policeman pressed the button just a minute earlier, the machine would still have carried the image of a departing Rolls-Royce, bearing the number plate BIG 1.

* * * 9 * * *

NOT ONLY was it nearly midnight, it was also nearly five years since the Major had last driven, parting company with his trusty Morris Minor, friend and servant for over a decade, just past the Cobham turn-off on the A3.

Reliable little runner though it had been, until the Major had introduced it to an oak tree, it had borne few resemblances to a street-cleaning wagon. It was fortunate, therefore, that there were few other vehicles abroad, for the Major's progress was a little erratic. He did not discriminate between the two sides of the road, utilising both with equal favour.

For most of the two-mile trip from the depot to BIG House the Major was stuck in first gear. By the time he rounded the corner into Gilbert Square, acrid black smoke was belching both from the exhaust and from beneath the bonnet.

He managed to stop the truck outside the garage entrance to BIG House. Leaving the engine running, he jammed a black balaclava over his head and jumped down from the cab. Unhooking one end of the hose he jammed it through the closed grille of the garage door. Returning to the side of the wagon, he pulled a lever and watched the water begin to gush from the hose.

Satisfied, the Major returned to the cab, took a hammer from his duffel bag and struck several blows at the keys in the ignition. Jumping down, he did the same to the lever controlling the water before heading home.

Back in his flat, the Major surveyed his handiwork through binoculars. The black plume from the exhaust confirmed that the engine was still running, but there was always the possibility the wagon would be discovered before its tank was empty. The Major hoisted his air rifle and shot out two of the tyres.

* * *

On the thirteenth floor of BIG House, Prosser unscrewed the cap of the bottle, poured a little of the liquid into a glass and held it up to the light. It was a murky, dark brown. Fizzing gently in the glass, it looked nothing out of the ordinary.

Could Butterley have been spinning him a yarn? Perhaps the frustration of life at Nostrum had sent him over the edge?

'Would you mind telling me what is going on?' asked Lorraine petulantly.

'Quiet,' snapped Prosser, breathing in the sickly sweet aroma as if it were a fine wine. 'Why don't you do something useful and get your clothes off?'

He took a sip. Long-forgotten memories of a pleasant taste from childhood came flooding back. Dandelion and burdock. Nothing more.

He took another swig and held it in his mouth. The gentle fizzing became more pronounced. Suddenly his whole mouth came alive as the bubbles furiously swelled and popped. Even when you had been told what to expect, it was unnerving. Then, as suddenly as it has started, the fireworks stopped. The abrupt stillness made him feel very calm and peaceful. He rolled the liquid around his mouth, but its force was spent.

The taste was pleasant enough, though. He let it flow down his throat. The fizzing enhanced the effect of the drink. Butterley was right. It really was tremendously refreshing. If this wasn't a winner, he didn't know what was.

To his surprise, he found himself reaching for the bottle to pour out another glass.

He noticed Lorraine, wearing only a lacy, red basque underneath her gaping fur coat, her hands impatiently planted on her hips. His desire, satisfied twice in the back of the Rolls, stiffened again. He took the fur coat from her shoulders and indicated with a nod of the head that she move on to the couch.

He turned back to pick up the glass. If the drink had such an extraordinary effect inside the mouth, might it not behave in a similar way in another warm, wet orifice?

Lorraine's frantic squeals a few minutes later indicated that it did.

* * * 10 * * *

'IT'S VERY ingenious, Alex. I'll grant you that. But it's also very complicated. And in my experience, the more complications there are, the more there is to go wrong.'

Prosser had just finished outlining his idea to Joe Roach, who listened, as was his wont, with his eyes closed as he assessed all the possible implications. This was how the two always worked. Prosser would set out the broad picture of what he wanted to achieve while Roach, an accountant by training, would work out the practicalities of his boss's ideas and see that they were implemented.

The two men could hardly have been more different, both in character and appearance. Where Prosser was audacious and daring, Roach was cautious and calculating. He was also, in contrast to his boss, lean, with a studious, unmemorable face. He wore glasses and blinked a lot. His chin was covered with stubble, not by design but because it grew so quickly that he needed to shave at least twice a day. He was, however, no taller than Prosser who, despite his preference for leggy females, took care not to be overshadowed by the males around him. Roach was also a family man, as the multitude of snapshots of his wife and daughters around his office testified. It seemed an unnecessary gesture to those who worked near him, as his wife was hardly ever off the telephone.

'Joe, you've tried the drink. You agree on its potential. We have got to have Nostrum.' Prosser, excited and impatient, paced around the room while he talked.

'I agree. But there are far simpler ways to get our hands on it. Nostrum's a pipsqueak of a company. We could snap it up just like that,' Roach said, clicking his fingers. 'Is it really necessary to involve Pardoe?'

'That supercilious bag of wind has been a thorn in my side for too long. I want him neutralised. And if something should go wrong, we can always buy Nostrum outright. Even at two or three times its current price, it would still be a snip.'

'I've no objection to that, it would be perfectly legal. But, Alex, doing it your way doesn't just bend the law of the land – it shatters it into little pieces. I am not too keen on doing a spell inside just to help you get even with Pardoe.'

Prosser stopped wandering around the room and stared straight at Roach. 'Are you saying you won't go along with it?' he asked belligerently. Prosser was not used to subordinates, however senior, expressing qualms about his proposals. Now that Butterley had reappeared on the scene, Roach, who was proving increasingly squeamish, might not be quite so indispensable as he had formerly appeared. True, he knew a great deal about Prosser that the tycoon would rather he did not bandy about. On the other hand, Roach featured prominently in the meticulous records which Prosser kept on the computer disc around his neck.

'Not at all, Alex,' said Roach hastily, only too well aware of the dangers of thwarting the boss. 'I just don't think it's worth our risking going to jail for.'

Prosser nodded. 'You're right, of course. We need someone else who will go to jail for us if the need arises. A patsy, a fall guy, somebody to take the rap. Well done, Joe. I'll get to work on it straight away. In the meantime, I'll ask Butterley to get us an up-to-date list of all the Nostrum shareholders. It'll be quicker than asking the company direct and this way we won't tip them off that something's in the wind.'

Roach slid a copy of that morning's *Telegraph* across the table. 'Have you seen the paper yet?' An item on page three was circled.

Prosser picked it up and skimmed through the two-paragraph piece under the headline: 'Runaway juggernaut demolishes cinema'. He tossed it back on to the desk and tutted. 'It's shocking, the way they allow those lorries on the road with faulty brakes.'

'Alex, that site is at the top of a hill. How could a lorry poss-ibly. . .' His cellular telephone burbled. 'Roach here. Yes, Desirée? How's my favourite wife?. . . Well, I'm sorry Jocasta has been sick, darling, but I don't see how I. . .In the washing machine? That's interesting. . .Sorry, darling. I didn't mean interesting exactly. . .'

While he was talking, his free hand tapped out a number on one of the two telephones on his desk. The bell on the other began ringing. 'Desirée, I have to go. This must be the important call I've been expecting. Goodbye.' The phone stopped ringing as he replaced the handset.

'I used to get the girls on the exchange to make sure she never got through to me. One night I left my briefcase unlocked and the crafty cow sneaked a look at the number of the cellular phone. Now she never gives me a moment's peace. Marriage is a bugger, Alex. Don't ever try it.'

When Prosser returned to his own office he found Lucinda at the window, staring intently at something through his binoculars; so intently that he was able to sneak up on her and goose her. She jumped a satisfying height into the air.

'You bloody moron! You nearly frightened the life out. . . oh, Mr Prosser. I didn't realise it was you. I was just. . . just. . . ' Unable to come up with a satisfactory explanation, Lucinda simply simpered.

'What's so fascinating?' he asked, pulling the binoculars from her grasp and adjusting the focus.

Lucinda backed away, trying to reach the door unobserved, but Prosser clicked his fingers loudly. 'Stay,' he ordered. 'Can you enlighten me as to why my chauffeur is at this moment scrabbling round inside my car with a hair-dryer?'

If there was an easy way to explain to a tycoon renowned for his quickness of temper that person or persons unknown have taken it upon themselves to empty a thousand gallons of water into the basement garage of an office block, it was not apparent to Lucinda. She did her best, but he did not take it well.

'Pass me Napoleon, please.' She flinched as she handed it to him. But she was safe. He opened a window and waited for the chauffeur to move away from the car. Then, taking account of wind direction, he dropped Emperor Napoleon Bonaparte.

'Shit.' The bust had fallen three feet short of the chauffeur, landing in the centre of the roof of his brand new Rolls-Royce Silver Spur. Even from the thirteenth floor and without the aid of binoculars, Prosser could see that the dent was more than a minor cosmetic blemish.

He stabbed out a number on his speakerphone. 'Mr Bennett?' he said, threat oozing from his voice like poisoned syrup, 'how nice to talk to you. I wonder if I might bring a matter or two to your attention? I was thinking of that minor problem we had with the police and the bomb disposal people, as well as that little mishap with over

83

fifty thousand pounds' worth of Luncheon Vouchers going astray. In addition, you will recall, my car was clamped, at considerable inconvenience to myself, despite the fact that your department is supposed, through the use of that lubricant known as money, to ensure that such things do not happen.' As Prosser spoke, his voice rose in a controlled crescendo of which Rossini himself would have been proud. The pianissimo had now given way to mezzo-forte. 'Our garage was, so I understand, flooded last night by a street cleaning machine – do not try to interrupt me, Mr Bennett, if you please. I don't care whether you were on duty or not. Now, on top of everything else, some vandal has just smashed the roof of my car while it has been standing under your very nose.' Prosser was now screaming into the loudspeaker at full fortissimo. 'I imagine you are attached to your nose, Mr Bennett. If you want it to remain attached to you, I strongly suggest that you pull your fucking finger out of whatever disgusting crevice it is currently occupying. Find out what is happening and stop it.'

Without waiting for a response, he switched the machine off.

'Lucinda, a graduate trainee ran an errand for me yesterday. Find out who he was and have him up here in ten minutes. Get Nettle to dig out his file for me. No, better make that fifteen minutes. There's a little something I want you to do for me first.'

Jeremy's morning had been fairly fruitless. Try as he might, he could not get Human Resources to recognise his existence. He needed them to refund the money he had spent yesterday, three hundred and sixty-five pounds ninety-seven pence if you included his shoes, which he had timidly suggested he was justified in claiming for as he had lost the other pair in the course of duty.

To Jeremy's surprise they had no quibble with the amount at all and were only too willing to reimburse him. But not as Jeremy Seaman. They still had no record of a Jeremy Seaman on the computer. As far as they were concerned, Jeremy Seaman did not exist. He could have a cheque made out to Jeffrey Simpson, in whose name an account had been opened at Jeremy's bank. But that would have brought him no nearer to getting the money because, as he told them over and over again, he was not Jeffrey bally Simpson.

Even before the cheque to Sebastian went through he was having trouble with his own bank account. In response to his claim that he was now a valued employee of British Industrial Group and would shortly be in receipt of a pay packet, the assistant manager Mr Cutpurse demanded some proof, in the form of a letter from BIG perhaps. Human Resources for their part, happily provided him with such a letter. But as it informed the reader of BIG's employment of a Mr Jeffrey Simpson, it got Jeremy no further. The vicious circle remained unbroken and Jeremy remained broke.

He was still trying to find a solution to this quandary when the phone rang, summoning him once more to the thirteenth floor, apparently to meet Mr Prosser in person.

Jeremy wisely shunned the lifts and walked up the stairs.

Miss Fluke was not around. This meant he could not thank her for the kindness she had shown him yesterday. It also meant he did not have to explain why he could not give back her twenty pounds yet. Jacqui, the busty personal assistant who opened the door to him, was remarkably uncivil and uncommunicative. As he was soon to learn, on those far from rare occasions when the sun did not shine in the heart, mind and mouth of Alexander Prosser, the chairman and chief executive of British Industrial Group made absolutely certain that the misery was spread around the entire thirteenth floor. Nervous almost to the point of incontinence, Jeremy followed her to the door of the great man's office. He could have accomplished this with his eyes closed, so strong was her scent. She opened the door for him and departed. She did not go in herself. She didn't fancy another tongue lashing.

Inside, Prosser was seated behind an enormous oak desk, loudly balling out somebody on the telephone. Jeremy, in his idol's presence at last, cowered near the door. Afraid he might blot his copybook if he was thought to be overhearing the conversation, he hummed to himself to drown it out. Prosser's office was already familiar from the countless articles Jeremy had cut from newspapers and magazines. From the windows down two sides of the room, the view over London was every bit as staggering as he had expected.

Prosser observed the gawky and unprepossessing young man hovering near the door. He certainly looked promising. Keen but naive was the tycoon's unerring first impression. But why was the idiot humming?

He watched Jeremy looking round the walls at his collection of pictures. If the young man knew anything at all about art, he ought to be bloody impressed. They were all labelled, not so much to show off but because Prosser had trouble remembering the names of most of the artists and their creations. He was assured by his advisers that they were all top-notch people. So they ought to be. He had forked out almost six million pounds for all the bits of framed canvas on the two floors of the building he occupied. Amazing, wasn't it? A few dabs with a paint brush and some of these artists could earn several hundred thousand quid. He had to slog his guts out for months to make that sort of money. Still, his collection had recently been valued at a little over ten million pounds, so he wasn't complaining.

Finally, Prosser put the phone down.

'You can go,' he barked.

Puzzled, Jeremy obediently turned and opened the door.

'Not you, you bozo,' he bellowed at Jeremy who turned back again to see a young lady emerge from underneath Prosser's desk.

'Lost my contact lens,' she said feebly to Jeremy as she passed him.

Lucinda straightened her pearls and walked out of the office. She didn't mind the odd bit of cock-sucking. It was all part of the job. But she hated Prosser's habit of bringing other people into the room. He loved humiliating her. She still recalled with horror the time he had called a meeting while she was seeing to him under the board-room table. The bastard had even threatened to get Daddy in for a chat sometime while she was at work. Lucinda would dearly love to quit BIG and the less than tender embraces of Prosser but he had made it abundantly clear that if she did, the press would get to hear of the time she had stupidly blurted out what Daddy had said was going to be in the Budget, information which had enabled Prosser to make yet another small fortune. If he did that, bang would go Daddy's pension.

Jeremy was so overawed by the great man striding towards him that he did not notice that while Prosser's right hand was greeting him, the left hand was zipping up his fly.

'You must be. . .' Prosser let Jeremy fill in the gap.

Jeremy hesitated. Was he supposed to be Jeremy Seaman or Jeffrey Simpson? If he got it wrong, he would be sent away and he would have lost his chance to prove his brilliance to the head of British Industrial Group.

Prosser waited. Anyone incapable of remembering his name ought to be perfect for the rôle he had in mind. Unlike Sally, Prosser did not take to Jeremy instantly. Apart from the fact that he had grave doubts about the young man's intelligence, the trainee also had the audacity to be at least nine inches taller than his chairman.

'It's Jeremy Seaman, Sir.' Hesitantly, he plumped for his own name.

'Welcome to British Industrial Group, Jeremy,' said Prosser, fixing him with his friendliest smile, usually reserved for cabinet ministers or businessmen whose companies were about to be swallowed up. 'Please sit down, won't you, Jeremy?' he said, indicating one of a pair of sofas and picking up the personnel file. 'You don't mind if I call you Jeremy, Jeremy?' Prosser sat down opposite him.

'How are you getting on at British Industrial, Jeremy. Everything up to your expectations?' He paused, but no words came from Jeremy's mouth. It is, after all, a little difficult to tell the chairman and chief executive of the company you have just joined that his Head of Human Resources is a mindless moron. 'Good, good. I like to see my staff happy. I don't hold with the old-fashioned way of doing things, Jeremy, where staff feel themselves cut off from the bosses. I put a great deal of BIG's success down to the management's willingness to listen to what its people have to say. I don't have all the graduate trainees up here, but I was very impressed by the way you tackled that job for me yesterday. Very impressed indeed.'

'Thank you, Sir,' gulped Jeremy

'I'm interested to know a little more about you. How about a quick resumé of your career to date?'

Jeremy stammered out the details of his qualifications, his college and business school course. Then suddenly, the dam of nervousness broke and he began gushing forth the full, the very full, story of how he came to want to work for British Industrial Group and for its brilliant entrepreneurial head. Seaman's puppy-like devotion convinced Prosser that he had struck pay dirt. He struggled to stop himself yawning.

'Reckon you can do my job, Jeremy?'

'No, Sir. Well, I mean, not yet, Sir. But I hope one day I might do well enough to. . . ' He shuddered to a halt.

'Good. I like to see a bit of drive and ambition. Economics and business studies, eh? So you know all about supply and demand, price elasticity and all that stuff, do you?'

'Yes, Sir,' said the eager Jeremy.

'More than I do. Can you read a balance sheet?'

'Yes, Sir.'

'Good for you. I can't make head nor tail of the bloody things.'

'But. . .'

'What about business plans? Know how to draw one of those up?' he said viciously.

'Yes, Sir.' Jeremy was thoroughly confused.

'I wouldn't even know where to start. I left school at fourteen. Never passed a ruddy exam in my life. I sometimes wonder where I might have got to if I had had the benefit of a proper education.' His sarcasm was wasted on Jeremy, who merely nodded sagely. 'Still, what do I need an education for when I've got all these educated people working for me, ready to show off their tricks at the click of my fingers?

'What I do have that most of you pen-pushers don't have is a feeling here,' he said, hammering himself where his heart ought to be, 'that tells me what will work and what won't. I buy and sell, Jeremy. I buy and sell companies, I buy and sell property and I buy and sell people. What's more, I am bloody good at it. I tell my minions what I want to do and they make sure my wishes are carried out. What's your speciality?'

'I've done a lot of work on business ethics.'

'Business ethics?' Prosser was taken aback. Wasn't that a contradiction in terms?

'Oh, yes. It's a fascinating subject.' Jeremy's enthusiasm was running away with him. 'Suppose, for instance, that you are faced with several candidates for a job. All of them are good, but one works for a competitor of yours and tells you that if you employ him he will give you comprehensive details of their client records. What do you do?'

'You tell me, Jeremy.'

'You don't give him the job, of course. If he's stolen information from his previous employer, he may also do it to you.'

'I'd like to see the bastard try it.' How much must this ridiculous education have cost? You'd be stupid not to employ the chap. The only sensible course of action was to give him the job, get the information from him and *then* give him the boot. 'That's fascinating, Jeremy. It's convinced me that you're the right person for a little job I need doing. I want to find out if you've got what it takes, or if you're going to be a graduate trainee for the rest of your life. Do you read books?'

'Oh yes, I'm a voracious reader.'

'Well, I've not got much time for that sort of thing. I've been asked by *Business* magazine to write a small piece about what I'm currently reading and I don't want to let them down. So I wondered if you could write the article for me, discussing those books you think I would be reading if I had the time.'

'Certainly, Mr Prosser. I would be honoured to do it.' Jeremy got out his notebook and began to scribble furiously.

'I rather thought you might.' Look at the sap, staring with those eager eyes, like a sheepdog ready for the next whistle. Except he wasn't a sheepdog. He was one of the sheep, eager not only to be fleeced but to lead the way into the slaughterhouse.

'What sort of books do you want me to put in?'

'I trust your judgement, Jeremy. Why not simply write about the books you're reading at the moment, pretending that you're me? Nothing too highbrow mind. I don't want to give people the idea that I read Shostakovich and all that stuff.'

Jeremy was still scribbling in his notebook. Prosser stood up, the interview over. 'If you could have it ready by the end of the week.'

'End of the week,' murmured Jeremy, jotting it down.

'Thank you, Jeremy,' said Prosser.

'Thank you, Jeremy,' said Jeremy, still writing.

'Goodbye, Jeremy.'

'Goodbye. . . Oh.' He stopped scribbling and stood up, towering above Prosser. 'Sorry, Sir. I got carried away. You can rely on me. Absolutely. Thank you very much for giving me this chance.'

'I am sure it's no more than you deserve,' said Prosser, as he showed him to the door. 'Jacqui will show you out. She's got that tramp's costume for you.'

'About the clothes, Sir. They took a bit of getting hold of and. . .'

'I've already said thank you.' Prosser's veneer of friendliness was beginning to crack. Being nice to people, particularly people whose wages he paid, was a great strain.

'It's not that, Sir. It's just that I had to use my own money.'

'Well, just pop along to personnel – I mean Human Resources. They'll sort it out for you. Goodbye,' Prosser said, virtually pushing Jeremy through the door. Graduates, eh. Who needed them?

The Major put down the scissors and admired his handiwork. 'What do you think to that, Rommel? Pretty impressive, eh?' If the dachshund had an opinion, it kept it to itself. But the Major was well pleased. He had created what was, if his memory of a brief spell working backstage in a theatre served him correctly, known as a gobo.

Carefully, he rolled the sheet of heat-resistant acetate, with the four letters cut out of it, and stuffed it into his duffel bag, along with the scissors and some heavy duty adhesive tape. Letting himself out of the flat, he wandered a little way down the side of Gilbert Square opposite BIG house, then climbed the steps of a house long ago turned, like his own building, into flats. He knew no-one listed on any of the buzzers, but pressed them all.

'Who is it?' demanded a disembodied voice from the entry-phone.

'Delivery,' lied the Major.

The lock buzzed. The Major pushed open the door and began climbing the stairs.

'Jack. How nice of you to call. I had meant to ring you, but it's been one of those days. You know what it's like.' Prosser had kept Butterley waiting for five minutes before deigning to speak to him.

'I know exactly what's it's like, Alex. What did you think of the drink?'

'The drink?' asked Prosser vaguely. 'Ah, yes. The drink. Very interesting. I've given it to a couple of people here to try and they agree that it is definitely interesting. But whether it's as exciting as you made out to me the other day is another matter.'

'Alex, you seem to forget that I know you. Stop pissing me about. Do you want the company or not? I can still talk to Pardoe.'

Prosser leaned back in his chair and smiled. If his plan worked out, Pardoe wouldn't be able to buy his way out of a biscuit barrel.

'It's a tough decision, Jack. The drink has possibilities, certainly. But it's far from being a cast-iron certainty and, without it, Nostrum's a bit of a dodo, isn't it?' Prosser refrained from mentioning the results of the researches by Godfrey Daniels and his department which showed that Nostrum could be dismembered and its land sold for at least as much as the company was likely to cost. 'On the other hand, you're an old friend, Jack, and I value your judgement. So I'll recommend we go ahead. But I should warn you it will take a little time to set up.'

'For some reason, my blood runs cold when you use the phrase "set up". Why taking over a company the size of Nostrum should pose any difficulties is beyond me, but I guess you know what you're doing.'

'Things would happen more quickly if you could get hold of an up-to-date shareholders' list.'

'Consider it done. Anything else?'

'I think it would be more sensible if you didn't come through the switchboard any more. Better call my Vodaphone instead.' He gave the number to Butterley.

'Okay. Good luck, Alex.'

'Don't worry, Jack. Luck won't have anything to do with it.'

Jeremy left his preliminary notes on his desk, took the clothes Prosser had returned to him and made his way out of the building. He was floating on cloud nine. Hadn't Mr Prosser himself entrusted him with two tasks of considerable responsibility almost as soon as he had arrived at the firm? He obviously recognised potential when he saw it. He was rather shorter than Jeremy had expected, only coming up to his neck. But then there had been plenty of short, great men in history.

Jeremy beamed as he passed through the foyer. The carefree attitude of his principal suspect was not appreciated by Mr Bennett, whose less than sunny disposition had been clouded still further by Prosser's phone call. One day soon, he promised himself, he would wipe that inane grin off that young man's face.

Jeremy negotiated the automatic revolving doors with few problems. He felt he had got the hang of them now. As long as you didn't think too much about what you were doing, getting through was a doddle. It surely couldn't be too long before he could cope with the lifts.

Jeremy crossed the Square. As he approached Sebastian, he noticed him staring at BIG House through binoculars. Jeremy stood directly in front of him, blocking the view.

'Cor, lumme, you gave me a fright, guv. Fort I'd gawn blind,' said Sebastian. 'Oh, it's only you, Jeremy. You know you really shouldn't sneak up on people like that. It isn't nice.'

Jeremy handed the bundle of clothes over, noticing that Sebastian was once more attired in rags.

'Thank you, Jeremy. You're a scholar and a gentleman.'

91

'What, er, happened to the clothes I bought you?'

'Sold them. Got a good price too. Over twenty quid. Now listen,' he said, ignoring Jeremy's outraged splutterings, 'you've done me a good turn, so I'll do you one. Stay away from the thirteenth floor if you know what's good for you.'

'How on earth did you know I was up there?'

'I know a lot of things, Jeremy. Take my advice and keep away from the thirteenth floor, and especially keep away from Prosser. It isn't good for your health, if you know what I mean.'

'No I don't. What do you mean?' But somebody was approaching along the pavement. Sebastian let out a burst of maniacal laughter. 'Pilbeam sank the Bismarck. Spare a penny for the gynaecologist,' he screamed. 'Scram, Jeremy,' he said more quietly. 'I've got a reputation to keep up here.'

Prosser inserted the computer disc and searched for the phone number he needed. Committing it to memory, he removed the disc and reattached it to the chain around his neck. Taking his a cellular telephone with him, he climbed the circular stairs from his office, past the fourteenth floor, emerging on the roof. Although his office was swept regularly for bugging devices and was in any case too high for anybody to use a directional listening device from any of the surrounding buildings, Prosser was not a man to take unnecessary chances where his own neck was concerned.

He might have been a little less relaxed had he realised that he was being closely watched through a pair of high-power binoculars from the shadowy recesses of a doorway on the opposite side of the square.

He stabbed out the number. The call was answered by an uninformative female voice. 'Yes?'

'Mr Fallas, please.'

'Who shall I say is calling?'

'A former client.' Prosser waited.

'Nicholai Fallas speaking.' The voice reflected the considerable variety of Eastern European countries whose citizens had come together over three generations to produce this mongrel offspring.

'Mr Fallas. I hope that you recognise my voice. You may recall that you last worked for me eight months ago on an investment project in danger of foundering.'

'Would I be correct in thinking that it was my firm's discovery of the sexual deviancies of a certain company chairman that assisted in a particular takeover battle?'

'Your memory does you credit, Mr Fallas,' said Prosser. 'That video was one of the most entertaining I have ever seen. I have need of your services again. I should like to be kept informed of the day-to-day activities of David Westbury, chairman of a drinks company called Nostrum. Should anything emerge about his brother Michael or uncle Timothy Westbury then so much the better. Has Sir Jocelyn Pardoe ever used your company?'

'I understand Sir Jocelyn does not approve of the activities of firms such as mine.'

'In that case, I'm sure you won't mind adding his name, and that of Lady Amanda Pardoe, to the list.'

'Of course not. But the manpower required will be considerably greater than for your last assignment.'

'I understand. Twenty thousand pounds will be deposited in your account as down-payment. I trust that will be satisfactory.'

'Will you require a meeting?'

'I think that might be unwise, Mr Fallas. Your reports can be sent through to my personal fax machine. If you need to contact me urgently, you can get me on this number.' He gave it, then broke the connection. He liked doing business with Fallas, renowned as being the best and, not entirely coincidentally, the least scrupulous financial investigator in the business world. If this went well he might suggest making Fallas's company part of British Industrial Group on a permanent basis.

Prosser's next call was to the number of a purposefully inconspicuous company he owned in the Cayman Islands. He had never seen the offices of the company, nor had he ever met its two 'directors'. As far as Prosser was concerned, the greater the arm's length at which they operated, the better. Identifying himself only as 'Big Boy', he gave an order to buy two hundred thousand Nostrum shares, the funds for which should be debited from a numbered Swiss bank account. Much as the Swiss might pretend to go along with the crackdown on securities fraud, the bank was unlikely ever to reveal who was behind the account. To protect against that unlikely event Prosser had installed several defensive layers of nominee companies between the bank and himself – rather like Russian dolls, one nestling incestuously inside the others – using such leading financial centres of the world as the Netherlands Antilles, the Turks and Caicos Islands, and the Cook Islands. No regulatory authorities could possibly unravel the tangled trail. Prosser was not one to take risks with his liberty unnecessarily.

He ordered two further purchases of Nostrum shares, for similar but not identical amounts, one backed by a bank in Bermuda and the other funded from Liberia, both countries with a relaxed view towards the regulation of their financial services. He then asked for two nominee companies to be set up, each for the purpose of buying small amounts of Nostrum shares.

When he had finished, Prosser remembered Maggie with a pang. He had been neglecting her recently. That wouldn't do at all. She would think he had forgotten her.

Mission accomplished, the Major celebrated his safe return to terra firma by taking Rommel for a stroll across the square to see at closer quarters the fire engine he had glimpsed from his vantage point on the rooftops. Mr Bennett was standing nearby.

'What on earth is transpirin'?' asked the Major.

'Somebody flooded the garage last night. Unloaded a thousand gallons from one of those street washing vans. Took hours to get it away; the bastard had punctured the tyres. The inside of the guvnor's car was under an inch of water. Didn't half make a mess. The Police thought the whole thing hilarious. Clamped the Roller, too, just to make it doubly difficult to get it off to the garage. And guess who gets the blame for it all?'

'Most unfortunate. Most unfortunate. You on duty last night?'

'No. But I'm responsible for the incompetence of my men. Of course, there's one less of them now. Goodness knows how we'll manage.'

'You should get somebody local,' suggested the Major. 'Someone who can keep an eye on the place even when not on duty.'

Mr Bennett's brain, never one of nature's finest, had been rendered still slower by years of rugby. The Major tried again.

'Somebody with military experience, perhaps. Someone in tune with your theory about that red-headed chap.'

At last the penny dropped into place.

'You don't mean you?'

'Bit long in the tooth, Mr Bennett, perhaps. But after a life in khaki I miss the uniform and discipline. I should welcome the chance. A military mind, that's what you need. It is obvious this is all part of some fiendish campaign. What's more, you can see this magnificent edifice from my flat, so I'd effectively be on duty twenty-four hours a day.'

'If you can start next week, then you've got a deal,' said Mr Bennett, delightedly.

They shook hands on it, oblivious to the sudden and gruesome demise of a large blackbird just a few yards away.

*** 11 ***

As FAR AS Alexander Prosser was concerned, a bedroom should be just that, a room for beds. His had three.

Tucked into one corner was a cot said to have been used by Napoleon on his Egyptian campaign, on which the Emperor had reclined comfortably while young locals were tethered naked nearby as distracting bait for the local insects. On the other side of the room was an eighteenth-century Balinese divan, adorned with intricate carvings of couples, trios and quartets illustrating different sure-fire methods of increasing the intensity of orgasms by accompanying them with hernias, strained ligaments and torn discs.

The main bed, a four-poster occupying much of the room, was said to have belonged at one time to Louis XIV. Spacious though it was by the standards of the time, Prosser had found it unduly restricting when he and his personal assistant of the time had first tested it. Despite the pleadings of the antique dealer who had brought it to his attention, Prosser had had the bed extended in several directions, had the ludicrously ornate canopy strengthened so that it would support the weight of a human body hanging from it, either way up, had a communications system installed in the bedhead and hi-fi speakers installed in all four posts.

The dealer had had a nervous breakdown.

Prosser had also had the four-poster made into a convertible, with cords that pulled the fabric above it aside. Otherwise there would have been little point in the ceiling mirrors. There were also a few placed at strategic positions on the walls, but most of the wall space bore those parts of Prosser's art collection which he preferred to keep for his eyes only. Even the most hardened vice-squad officer might have raised an eyebrow or two when faced with these lurid examples of obscenity and depravity. A selection of late-eighteenth and early-nineteenth-century Indian and Japanese woodcuts and water colours were mixed with Western erotica from the likes of Rowlandson, Georg Grosz, Henry Fuseli, Tom Wesselmann and even a pair of late and extremely suggestive Picassos.

Prosser was propped up against the pillows watching a giant television screen on which three women and two men were demonstrating an alternative use for a supermarket shopping trolley and the groceries it contained. Jacqui, always put out when Prosser watched porno movies in her presence, was trying to prove once again that there was nothing on screen that a professional like her could not match in real life. Prosser was on the point of capitulating when the phone rang.

He opened a small door in the bedhead and reached inside. 'What the fuck is it, Ron?. . . Can't it wait till the morning?. . . All right, all right, I'll come now.'

To his irritation, however, he wasn't quite ready to do so, so he had to shrug Jacqui off. With a rapidly flagging erection he pulled on a pair of trousers and a shirt and headed for the lift. Ron had stressed the urgency of his presence and he wasn't someone to be panicked easily.

Jacqui, fuming, lay back and studied the screen. Some ludicrous tale about the sexual shenanigans of supermarket checkout girls. It all looked surprisingly familiar. Of course. That was her with the cucumber. Now surely *that* would interest the little shit.

On the other side of Gilbert Square Prosser, with Ron Niblo and Mr Bennett, was staring up at BIG House, watched by the Major in his kitchen, jubilant at the success of his handiwork.

'The switchboard's been inundated with calls. You must be able to see the bloody thing half way across London.

'Gordon Bennett,' muttered Mr Bennett, using his eponymous expletive for the first and last time in his life.

'Yes. It is quite dramatic,' agreed Prosser. 'As chief security officer, at least for the time being, do you have an explanation for it?'

'Somebody seems to have got it in for us.'

At a signal from Prosser, Niblo grabbed Bennett's arms and pinned them behind his back. 'And I shall have it in for you if you don't put an end to it very soon.' Prosser spoke very softly, his smile made all the more menacing by the purple glow. 'I don't like my staff to let me down, do I, Ron?' So saying, he rammed his right fist into Bennett's swollen stomach, winding him. The left

97

swiftly followed with an agonising jab to the kidneys.

Mr Bennett's sixteen-stone bulk crashed to the floor. 'Get that light put out now and find out how they've done it. I don't want to hear of any more untoward happenings. Understand?'

The prostrate Bennett nodded. Niblo kicked him savagely as the two men turned away and strode back towards BIG House. Prosser glanced up as he re-entered the building. He had to admit that it really was a most ingenious act of vandalism.

High above his head, thanks to the sheet of acetate so lovingly cut by the Major and placed over the light, the word 'FUCK' shone out in purple letters ninety feet high.

* * * 12 * * *

THE NEWSPAPERS had a field day. Although that particular word was never permitted to grace their own prose, that did not stop the majority of them splashing a photograph of it over their front pages. Prosser, displaying an untypical reluctance to talk to the press, gave a short statement proclaiming his belief that it was the work of anti-capitalist cranks and refused to say anything more on the matter.

Jeremy, whose *Financial Times* had not thought fit to mention the appearance of the biggest piece of graffiti in the world, had to fight his way through a reception area teeming with shabby and excitable people laden with cameras, notebooks and tape recorders.

He was not particularly curious to know their business. He had work to do for Mr Prosser, and was raring to go.

To his horror he found his office empty. All the papers on his desk had gone, as had his copy of the *A-Z of Business Terms* and even the dead plant.

He rushed up to reception. But Mr Bennett and his colleagues, attempting to return several gentlemen of the press to the gutter from whence they had so obviously just crawled, showed no interest in the information that Jeremy had been robbed.

The noise from the reporters was so great that Charmaine could hardly make Tracey hear what she had to say.

'That's right. Hundreds of them,' she screamed into the phone, fluttering the false lashes of her Saucy Seaweed-coloured eyes at the pressmen and parting her Harrods' Green lips as sexily as she was able. 'The *Sun*, the *Star*, the *Mirror*, all of them. I've 'ad me picture took fowsands o' times already. It's great. Much better than the bomb squad. One of 'em offered me two 'undred quid if I'd pose topless. I mean I ask yer. Mind, two 'undred quid is a lorrof money. Whacha fink, Tracey?'

Jeremy threw himself into the mêlée and fought his way to the front. Charmaine put down the phone after promising to reveal all over a quiche and Bacardi at 12.30. Here was that red-headed chump who started the bomb scare. Maybe this was more of his doing.

'I've been robbed,' explained Jeremy, breathlessly 'My office. All the papers, everything, has gone.'

'Ooh dear,' sympathised Charmaine. 'What did you say yer name was?' she screamed, her fingers poised above the keyboard.

Jeremy did not want to give her or the computer the satisfaction of denying his existence again 'Simpson, Jeremy Simpson,' he said emphatically.

She tapped the keys. 'We ain't got no Jeremy Simpson.'

'Of course you have. He's been working here all week. He's got an office in the basement,' said Jeremy, uncertainly. Perhaps Nettle had wiped him from the computer completely. 'And his office has been robbed. . .I mean, my office has been robbed.'

'If you'd like to take a seat,' shouted Charmaine, 'I'll try to get somebody from Human Resources to come down.

Prosser sat and fumed. This *would* have to happen on the morning of a board meeting. In theory British Industrial Group was run, just like any other company, by its board of directors. Even Prosser had been unable to find any way around the regulations that compelled the board to meet from time to time.

So around the table sat seven gentlemen hand-picked for their outstanding ineffectiveness and spinelessness, seven superannuated deadbeats who could be relied upon not to interfere with his running the company the way he wanted. While it must have been obvious to anyone of the meanest intelligence that they had no real rôle to play, the vestiges of their pride still forced these wet blankets to pretend that they had something of value to contribute to the overall management of British Industrial. The real running of the companies within the group was in the hands of capable managers whom Prosser rewarded amply, while ensuring that they would never achieve the status of directors.

This morning all seven were keen to chip in their pennyworth about the disadvantages of being a director of a company which projected an infamous four-letter word onto the front of its head-quarters. For the money he paid them, mused Prosser, they should

100

be prepared to let him tattoo the word on their buttocks and thank him for it afterwards.

He treated them like the bunch of wet public schoolboys that they were, bringing them to heel with a humiliating roll call. 'Collingwood?'

'Here,' came the mumbled response.

'Armstrong.'

'Here.'

'Eldon. . . Bourne. . . Akenside. . . Stowell. . . Brand.' Each responded sheepishly to his name, although it took several attempts before Brand, hard of hearing, spoke up. Roach ought really to be there too, but Prosser and he had long ago agreed that there was no point in both of them wasting their time with this ridiculous charade.

'Gentleman, before we get down to the main business of the meeting, I have something of importance to tell you. As we have discussed to little effect on previous occasions, the return on capital at British Iron Girders, the founding company upon which our conglomerate is based, has fallen dangerously low and shows no sign of picking up. I am pleased to say we may now be able to repair this sorry state of affairs. A plan has been presented to me which would involve closing the foundry.' He ignored the murmurs of disquiet around the table and continued, 'There's a possibility of turning the site into a giant amusement park, based around the theme of our industrial past. Death-defying rides through the old coal mine, treasure-hunting on the slag heap, a monorail trip through an imaginary factory, that sort of thing. Not only is this an extremely innovative and exciting idea but the potential profit looks too tempting to ignore, as I am sure you will all agree.' Prosser stressed the word 'sure', just to emphasise that dissension would not be tolerated. 'Sally, pass the papers round, would you?'

Sitting to his left, Sally did as she was asked. She felt sorry for these once proud owners of their own companies, all of whom had been foolish enough to let them fall into the grubby hands of Prosser. All surely rued the day they allowed monetary considerations to sway their better judgement. She watched one or two doodling on the pads laid out in front of them. The poor fools probably had no idea that after they had gone their scribblings were taken away for examination by Marketing Intelligence which then sent reports of any disrespectful or disloyal comments or doodles to the chairman.

101

While the proposals were being studied, Prosser glanced around the boardroom, tastefully decorated to his own specifications with marbled walls, mock Grecian columns, a painting of clouds scudding across a blue sky on the ceiling and a few Reubenesque nudes dotted around the walls. His left hand wandered on to Sally's leg, only to be slapped away as he began feeling his way upwards. Out of the corner of his eye, Prosser noticed Peter Akenside becoming steadily redder as he read. At last the expected outburst materialised.

'As the director with immediate responsibility for British Iron Girders, surely I should have been consulted before a proposal like this was drawn up?'

'Ah, Peter, I am sorry about that,' said Prosser insincerely. 'But I was so sure you would agree, I didn't think it mattered.'

'Well it bloody well does matter! There are six hundred workers at that plant. Goodness knows how many at our suppliers and sub-contactors. You can't take such important decisions without reference to me.'

The other directors looked on in amazement, marvelling at Akenside's bravery. The last director to show any serious sign of independence had been Hindmarsh, who had once run a thriving package holiday company, and was now rumoured to be a nightwatchman for one of BIG's plants in South Wales.

'Oh dear, Peter. I had hoped for a more enlightened attitude from you. I appreciate your attachment to the old firm. After all, it's where I started out, too. But we can't stand in the way of progress, and it's not as if everybody will be out of work. When the park is completed in three years' time, there'll be plenty of jobs: taking money on the gate, driving the trains, cleaning the lavatories.' Prosser looked straight at Akenside as he mentioned this last activity, transforming it into a direct threat.

Akenside still had some wind left in his sails. 'They're skilled men, Alex, with expertise built up over generations. You can't make them into amusement park attendants.'

'Ah, but sadly their skills are the skills of yesteryear. Still, maybe we could have a mock foundry in the park where people could go to watch them at work. I'll suggest it to the planners.' Akenside clearly wasn't satisfied. 'I do hope you're not thinking of doing anything silly, Peter. It would be such a pity to jeopardise those share options you've got coming up on a point of silly principle. Of course if you want to throw a hundred and fifty thousands pounds away. . .'

'Will there be helter-skelters?' asked Brand abruptly. 'I used to like helter-skelters.' Half-deaf and practically gaga, he would have been retired from any other board years ago.

'You do realise,' said Akenside, 'that British Iron Girders is in the Prime Minister's constituency?'

Prosser feigned surprise. 'Now that you come to mention it, I think it is. Surely, though, you're not suggesting we would allow such a consideration to override our dedication to sound business principles?'

'And coconut shies,' burbled Brand, half to himself.

Prosser paused, but Akenside had slumped back into his seat. If the bastard was willing to take on the Prime Minister, who was he to stand in his way? He noticed his fellow directors looking intently at the papers in front of them, none willing to take the risk of catching the chairman's eye.

Prosser had noticed it too. Spineless fools, the lot of them. 'Right, let's get on with the rest of the business.'

'I think I liked the Gavioli steam roundabouts best of all,' warbled Brand.

The aesthetic attractions of the atrium had long since paled for Jeremy and the crowd of journalists, sadly concluding that nothing exciting was going to happen, at least during daylight hours, had drifted away. The terrible thought occurred to him that perhaps his stuff had not been stolen at all. Perhaps he had been dismissed. He wandered over to the reception desk.

'Remember me?' he asked.

Charmaine giggled. As if she could forget.

'Would it make any difference if I told you my name was Jeremy Seaman?'

'Seaman? Why didn't you say so before? They've been waiting for you for ever such a long time. I'll get someone to take you up.'

The house martin flew low over the entrance to BIG House, trying to make sense of what was happening. Everything about humans puzzled him. He'd tried explaining to his friends that these strange creatures kept trees inside their nests, but no one would believe

103

him, just as they refused to believe him about the giant worm he had seen.

He was too old to care what the others thought, but not too old to be curious. He flew on into the park, still trying to puzzle it out.

It took another hour for the directors to go through the motions of rubber-stamping Prosser's decisions.

His mind was only half on the meeting. He had other, more important things to do. When it finally trundled to a conclusion, he stayed for a few minutes chatting politely over sherry and canapés and smoothing down Akenside's ruffled feathers. Although this shower could not organise a gang-bang in a brothel, it would be a terrible faff to have to find similarly pliant replacements.

On the way back to his own office, he looked in on Roach.

'Just a second, Alex. . . No, Desirée, it is not reasonable to expect the man from British Gas to remove his shoes when he comes into the house just because it's raining. . . Well, let him read the meter and mop the hall up afterwards. . . . Got to go, darling. . . Sorry about that, Alex. How did the meeting go?'

'Waste of bloody time as always. Does the law specify that directors have to be human? Monkeys would be cheaper and more effective. I don't think we'll have any trouble from them, though. Akenside may bluster a bit once his options have been exercised, but that's all. Let's hope the news doesn't get picked up at the plant. We don't want to find the workers revolting.'

'I thought you always found the workers revolting, Alex.' Roach had an unfortunate fondness for old jokes.

As he entered his office, Prosser noticed the light flashing on the fax machine. He tapped in his code number and read the sheets as they emerged. All the share deals had been carried out, and at a very satisfactory price. He put the disc from round his neck into the computer, transferred the details into the machine and then shredded the fax. Number One had been well looked after. Now it was time to get British Industrial Group in on the action.

He picked up his cellular phone and punched out the number for Morrie Minchkin, the sharpest stockbroker Prosser knew.

'Morrie, it's Alex.'

'So, how's tricks? This is a business call, I hope?'

'Morrie, I need you to build up a couple of share stakes for the company. I don't want what we're doing to get out, so I'm keeping the blabbermouth merchant bankers out of it. Unless you hear from me to the contrary, keep going until we are just below the stage where we legally have to declare them.'

'Which shares?' Morrie was as economical with words as he was with his clients' money, which endeared him to Prosser. He hated the modern breed of stockbrokers. Giggling, callow, overpaid incompetents, the lot of them. You might as well take an advert in the *Evening Standard* classifieds saying what you were doing as get any of those yomping yuppies to buy shares on the quiet. Give him an old hand every time.

'Nostrum and Pardoe Trust. Try not to take the shares from anybody in sympathy with BIG if you can. Their shares might turn out to be useful to us later on.'

'Pardoe shouldn't be too much trouble,' said Morrie, after a moment's thought. 'Nostrum, though, is a thin market. It might be difficult to buy many without moving the price, but I'll do what I can.'

The line went dead. Prosser knew that the first thing Morrie would do was buy shares in both companies for himself. Only then would he start buying for British Industrial. The rogue regarded getting the first bit of the cherry as part of his fee.

Prosser leaned back in his chair, well content with the way things were going. He was looking forward to doing battle with Pardoe. 'You stab my back, Sir Jocelyn,' he said to no-one in particular, 'and I'll stab yours.'

'If you'd like to follow me please, Mr Seaman.' The girl who had been under Prosser's desk the day before materialised at Jeremy's elbow. Puzzled, he complied. Hips and pearls swinging, Lucinda led him towards the lifts, ignoring the continuous Paternoster and making instead for an unobtrusive door beyond it that Jeremy had not used before.

As a four-digit code was tapped in, the lift doors opened. Observant as ever Jeremy noticed the number was 1777. 'Brandywine. How are we supposed to know that, I ask you?' she said enigmatically. There was no easy answer to that so they travelled up in silence, each apparently transfixed by the passing figures on the floor indicator. When it read '13', the lift stopped.

Lucinda got out and walked briskly down the corridor, with Jeremy loping along in her wake. He was disappointed not to see Miss Fluke around.

'Here we are,' she said, smiling coolly, as she ushered him into an office.

There was no-one around, so Jeremy risked a tentative peek about him. Surely he wouldn't have been brought up to the thirteenth floor just to be sacked?

What a difference from his own office. Thick carpet, a magnificent view, proper lighting, a sophisticated phone system, two large new desks, delightful prints on the walls.

As he nosed around, he found a few surprisingly familiar things. In addition to a thriving Swiss cheese plant in the corner, there was also a very dead ivy similar to the one that had been in his room. The only book in the bookcase was the *A-Z of Business Terms*, just like his. He looked more closely. It *was* his. It had the same Marmite stain on the back. In fact, those were his papers on the desk. What on earth was going on?

As if in answer to his question, the door was flung open and Prosser strode in.

'Jeremy, my boy, how are you? Are they looking after you properly? How do you like your new office? Not bad, eh?'

Jeremy did an imitation of a goldfish waiting lazily with its mouth open for the food to arrive. Prosser simply ploughed on. 'I was very taken with you yesterday, Jeremy, very taken indeed. I'm sure you're going to do a grand job with that article. So much so that I've decided to have you near me all the time.'

He put his arm around Jeremy's shoulder and led him to the window. 'I'm worried that we aren't devoting enough of our attention to thinking, Jeremy. After all, where would this company be without new ideas? We need our own Think Tank. Governments have them. Why shouldn't we? Who are the best thinkers? Not old fogeys, but the young. Jeremy, we need some young blood at the top of British Industrial Group.

'That's where you come in. I've read your file. It's very impressive. You're my man, my new young blood. You are going to be my own personal Think Tank, my extra brain. I want you to sit here and to think. Think long, Jeremy, think hard. Give me new ideas. Tell me what we're doing right and what we're doing wrong.

You're young. You're talented. You're the new Director of British Industrial Group's Think Tank. Congratulations.

'I've had some business cards prepared for you,' he continued, ripping open the packet in his hand. 'Perhaps I'd better keep one or two, in case you become famous one day, eh?' He took a few and placed them carefully inside his wallet.

Prosser shook Jeremy by the hand. It was like shaking hands with a rag doll.

'I've got a bit of work to catch up on, so I'll give you a chance to get settled in. I'm expecting great things from you, Jeremy. Great things.'

Jeremy knew British Industrial Group had a reputation as a place where things happened quickly, but he had no idea they happened with quite this degree of rapidity. He looked at the cards. Jeremy Seaman, Director of the Think Tank, British Industrial Group. It had quite a ring to it. The cards had the triangular company logo at the top and his name, his proper name, in raised gold lettering. None of this Jeffrey Simpson rubbish.

It was all a little bewildering. It was true that he *was* young. There was no denying that. He supposed he was fairly talented, but original thought was not something he had ever excelled in. On the contrary, he had tried to rein in any such dangerous tendencies, preferring to stick to well-established facts conclusively proven by others. So why had Mr Prosser singled him out for the job?

Back in his own office, Prosser was giving Sally equal cause for mystification. 'You are no longer one of my personal assistants. From now on you will act as secretary to a promising young chap called Jeremy Seaman. I don't imagine it will be too strenuous.' Or too permanent either, he thought.

Prosser paced around the room. Parting with Sally was proving harder that he'd expected. True, she had been a bit of troublemaker, but she was undeniably gorgeous. Every time she switched on that wicked smile of hers he felt horny.

'I am taking a bit of a chance promoting this bloke,' he continued. 'He's new, still a bit wet behind the ears. I need somebody I can rely on to keep an eye on him. I want to know everything he does, everywhere he goes, everything he thinks. If he farts, I want to know what it smells like.'

'You put it so charmingly.' She was damned if she was going to act as his spy.

'Just so long as you understand me. He'll need a helping hand finding his way around. So stick close to him. Very close, if you have to.'

'What about your fraternisation rule?'

'Bugger the fraternisation rule,' said Prosser sharply. Why did he feel so jealous, all of a sudden? Hell, the guy was probably a fairy anyway.

Sally was overjoyed not to be working directly for Prosser any more although she tried not to let it show. The only thing she would miss was the considerable pleasure she got from teasing him where it hurt most.

The phone on Prosser's desk rang. One last time, then. Revolving her hips, Sally walked deliberately slowly over to the other side of the desk. Bending over to reach the phone, she purposefully presented Prosser with a splendid view of her rear.

No bull ever had such a flagrant red flag waved in front of it. Without wasting time pawing the ground and panting, this animal decided to charge and avail itself of the goodies on display. Coming up behind Sally, Prosser whipped her skirt up, opened his fly and had his member out in a flash.

She looked over her shoulder and fixed him with her sexiest smile. 'It's the Prime Minister's office,' she said sweetly, handing him the phone.

As she walked out of the room, smoothing down her skirt, Sally glanced back. Prosser still had it in his hand, but it was wilting rapidly. Game, set and match to her.

She went in search of Jeremy Seaman, whoever he was.

The Prime Minister was not in her sunniest mood. 'I expect to be presented with problems by my political opponents, Alexander. I do not expect to be let down in this way by one of my most loyal supporters.'

'You have me at a disadvantage, Prime Minister,' said Prosser. 'To what are you referring?'

'You know damn well what I'm talking about. This hare-brained plan of yours to close down British Iron Girders.'

Roach had certainly worked quickly. 'It's true we have had a feasibility study prepared along those lines, Prime Minister. But, as I'm sure you're aware, many discussion documents are prepared which are never put into practice.'

What a woman! Prosser found her domineering attitude arousing in the extreme. He had tamed her namesake, Maggie, upstairs. Why shouldn't he try to tame her too? What a challenge.

'How do you think it will look if one of the party's greatest friends and fund-raisers lays off six hundred people in my constituency? The press would have a field day. I give you fair warning, Alexander. If it goes, so does your chance of a knighthood.'

'We have discussed the possibility of a knighthood on several occasions, as you will recall. That prospect has had a lot to do with my company's considerable contribution to party funds. But it never seems to materialise.'

'I'll be frank. Your name *was* in the list about to go to the Queen. But in the light of the unfortunate publicity surrounding that awful word appearing on your building. I have had no choice but to withdraw it.'

'That *is* a pity, Prime Minister.' She was lying, just using it as an excuse, he was sure of it. Well, he had had enough excuses. 'I am quite taken with the plans for developing the British Iron Girders' site and I'm not sure it would be right for me to stand in the way of progress simply because of my allegiance to a political party. Perhaps the only answer is to stop our contributions to party funds.'

The line was silent for a moment. 'And if I were to promise that you'll receive a knighthood in the next New Year's Honours List when all this fuss has died down?'

'Then I imagine the proposal will be found wanting and you won't want for cash.'

'In that case you have my word on it.'

'Thank you Prime Minister. I am deeply honoured. You won't mind putting that in writing, I hope?'

The lady sighed. 'It will be done. You are, of course, a grade-one bastard, Alexander, as I am sure you are aware.'

'Thank you for calling, Prime Minister.' He replaced the phone on its rest.

Noticing what was still in his hand, he pressed the buzzer for one of his remaining personal assistants to come in and personally assist him.

When the door opened, Jeremy was prepared for the worst; Prosser saying it had all been a ghastly mistake or Nettle giving him his cards. He was both relieved and delighted when Sally entered. She had been in his thoughts a good deal since their last meeting. Suddenly recalling the rôle she had played in an unaccustomed dream just the night before, he blushed deeply.

'We meet again,' she said, shaking his hand. 'Is your name really Seaman?'

'Yes,' said Jeremy warily. Surely she wasn't going to descend to the gutter with a cheap jibe like all the rest of them?

'Your poor thing. I've had to put up with the name Fluke all my life which isn't much better. Apparently, I'm to be your secretary.'

'Why that's wonderful, Miss Fluke,' said Jeremy sincerely.

'For goodness' sake, call me Sally.'

'You'll never guess what has happened, Sally. Mr Prosser has put me in charge of the company's Think Tank.'

'Congratulations. I didn't even know we had a Think Tank. What have you been doing that has so impressed the great man?'

'Well, that's the puzzling thing. Apart from getting hold of that tramp's costume, nothing. I'm writing an article for him, but he hasn't even seen it yet.'

'How peculiar,' said Sally. What on earth was Prosser up to? There were managers of some of the group's biggest subsidiaries who had never been allowed up to the thirteenth floor. 'What *is* a Think Tank exactly?'

'Apparently I'm to be one of Mr Prosser's brains, coming up with new ideas for British Industrial.'

Sally giggled, then noticed how hurt he looked. 'I'm sorry. I shouldn't have laughed but it just seems so odd. You only started work a few days ago. Yet here you are on the thirteenth floor, bosom pals with Mr Prosser himself, possessor of a wonderful office, a grand title and the very best secretary in the whole of British Industrial Group.'

'It is all bit bewildering,' said Jeremy dreamily. 'I half expect to wake up at any moment. But ours not reason why. I've decided I must work hard to prove that Mr Prosser's faith in me is justified.'

'That's the ticket,' said Sally. 'So where do you want me to start?'

'I don't know. I've got this article to finish, but I haven't thought any further than that.'

'Isn't there anything you can give me to do?'

'If you could help me sort out a little problem with Mr Nettle, I would be very grateful. Then I might be in a position to pay you back the money you so kindly lent me.'

Jeremy explained the spot of bother he was having with Human Resources. 'Leave it to me,' said Sally. 'I'll do my best, although some of our best people have died fighting that bally computer.'

'Have they really?' asked Jeremy, horrified.

'It was just a figure of speech.' She watched him as he picked up his pen and went back to work drafting his article. He was so extraordinarily. . . keen. Yes, that was the word. Everything was so new and bright and wonderful to him. He had not yet had time to become disillusioned like everybody else in British Industrial Group.

He was so vulnerable, so helpless, so ignorant of the reality of office politics. Surely he realised that people like Prosser didn't just pluck unknown graduate trainees from nowhere? Such things didn't happen in the real word. And because it *had* happened, there had to be a very good reason for it. BIG had countless ideas people, but they were all stuck somewhere around the fourth or fifth floors, not up here. It was all very well his shrugging his shoulders and saying he would make the best of his good fortune, but she suspected that the well-being of Jeremy Seaman was not uppermost in the mind of Alexander Prosser.

She put down the phone. 'I can't get through to Nettle at the moment.' She walked across to Jeremy and looked over his shoulder. 'Perhaps I could help you instead? What exactly do you have to do?'

'Mr Prosser wants me to write about the books I'm currently reading, pretending to be him. Apparently he doesn't have much time for books.'

'I'll bet he hasn't.' Sally saw what Jeremy had written. 'Is that really what you're reading at the moment?' She asked.

'Yes.'

'Well, I'd better leave you to it.' She went back to her desk. She needn't have worried. Jeremy wouldn't be on the thirteenth floor for much longer.

After last night, the Major had expected that the purple light illuminating BIG House would be a thing of the past. He had reckoned without Alexander Charles Prosser. The light went on at its usual time.

111

The Major, cutting out the articles describing his triumph from that day's papers, ready to paste into his scrapbook, leapt up in fury and ran to the kitchen. He stood on the chair to get a proper view. Surely they couldn't have left it as it was? They hadn't. Prosser had ordered another cover to be cut and placed over the light.

Across the front of BIG House, in letters ninety feet high and visible to much of London, were the letters 'B-I-G'. The Major slunk back to his chair. His brainwave had been hijacked and twisted to create the biggest advertising sign in Britain.

He screwed up his cuttings and threw them on to the fire. It was as he stared unseeing into the flames that a new, rather more dramatic idea came to him.

∗ ∗ ∗ 13 ∗ ∗ ∗

NOW that Jeremy worked on the thirteenth floor, he assumed he was entitled to use the restricted lift. But when he tapped in 1777 to call it as he had seen Lucinda do, an ear-splitting alarm went off, bringing Mr Bennett and two of his militiamen at the run.

Had he been given a chance Jeremy could have explained everything. Instead he was frog-marched unceremoniously off to the security office and there frisked, unnecessarily roughly he thought, by the jubilant Bennett, convinced that the miscreant had been brought to book.

While two guards held Jeremy's arms, Bennett strutted up and down, hands behind his back, firing questions at him like a bad actor playing a Gestapo officer in an old B-movie.

'I don't understand,' said Jeremy. 'I thought the code was 1777.'

'Ha!' spat Bennett. 'You're out of date, son. Magersfontein you should have had, and the fact you didn't means I've got you bang to rights this time. What's your name, sonny?' As he spoke, he prodded Jeremy's chest with a truncheon.

'Jeremy Seaman.'

'I see. So why do you have in your possession an identity card claiming that your name is Jeffrey Simpson. Note that, lads. Suspect using an alias.'

'I can explain that,' said Jeremy, as Mr Bennett's truncheon was pushed hard into his stomach.

'Shut it, laddie,' ordered the security chief. He was enjoying showing off in front of his minions. 'What were you trying to do with that lift?'

'Trying to get to the thirteenth floor. I work there.'

'Oh, yes. Since when?'

113

'Since yesterday. I'm the director of the company's Think Tank,' said Jeremy indignantly. 'If you just let go of me for a minute, I can prove it. My business card's in my pocket.'

'It's obviously a trick, lads. Keep tight hold of him. He's very dangerous.'

Despite his predicament, the idea that he was considered in any way dangerous struck Jeremy as being extremely funny. His laughter merely infuriated Mr Bennett, who dug the truncheon in under Jeremy's chin, forcing his head back.

'You'll be laughing the other side of the face when the police cart you off, my lad.'

'The police? Oh, don't be ridiculous, you silly little man. Ever since I started work here, you've done nothing but harass me. If you don't believe that I work on the thirteenth floor, then why not ask Mr Prosser? He appointed me.'

Mr Bennett attempted to ram the truncheon up Jeremy's right nostril. 'Oh, yes. A right prat I'd look. "Tell me, guv'nor, did you employ a terrorist to run your Think Tank yesterday?"'

'Terrorist? What on earth are you talking about? Do I look like a terrorist?' exclaimed Jeremy. 'Look, this has gone far enough. If you won't ring Mr Prosser, then ring Miss Fluke. She'll confirm what I've told you.'

'All right, son, I'll call your bluff. Then we'll see where it gets you,' said Mr Bennett, winking at the guards holding Jeremy.

He picked up the phone and dialled. 'Miss Fluke? Mr Bennett here. Security. Do you know a Jeremy Seaman, alias Jeffrey Simpson? We have him in custody for attempting to use the restricted lift without permission.' Jeremy couldn't hear what Sally was saying, but whatever it was, it was having a splendid effect. Mr Bennett's face was turning grey.

'I see. . . Yes, Miss Fluke. . . At once, Miss Fluke.' He replaced the phone and said, with great reluctance, 'Let him go, boys. Apparently I owe you an apology,' he whispered, glowering at Jeremy. 'Miss Fluke informs me that you are indeed entitled to use the lift. I have been asked to escort you to the thirteenth floor myself. If you would follow me, Sir,' he said, the last word sticking in his throat.

As he marched towards the lift with parade-ground precision, Mr Bennett thought he could hear his two employees guffawing behind him. He'd show them. He'd show them all. This chap might

114

have pulled the wool over everyone else's eyes, but he hadn't fooled Gordon Bennett for one minute. Something fishy was going on, and he intended to get to the bottom of it.

'Things seem to be going our way, Joe. Look at this.' Prosser burst into Roach's room without knocking.

He was in a good mood. The same papers which had vilified him the day before for allowing the pollution of the minds of Londoners with ninety-foot high smut had this morning spoken of his genius in turning the act of vandals and hooligans to his considerable advantage. Most had carried photographs of the new-look night-time BIG House, giving the company a small fortune's worth of free publicity. Prosser was feeling very pleased with himself.

Roach was on the phone as usual. He held up his hand, indicating he would be with his boss in a moment. 'It's in the nature of little girls to want to dress the cat up in clothes, Desirée. . . Look at it this way. We've probably got the only cat in London that wears Roland Klein dresses and Chanel Number Five. I've got to go now. Speak to you later.' He rolled his eyes to the ceiling. 'I am going to have to get that phone number changed. What's up with you anyway, Alex? You look like you've just won the pools.'

'We run the pools, Joe. We don't *need* to win them. You've seen the papers, of course? What a triumph. And there's more good news, too.' He threw on to the desk the list of Nostrum shareholders Butterley had sent him. 'Cast your peepers at that and see if you spot anything.'

Roach ran his finger down the left hand column, letting out a whistle when he came to one name. 'Empire Assurance. Six per cent of Nostrum shares. Hot diggety dog.' He grinned at Prosser. 'It looks like your friend and mine, Bernie Korngold, has just struck lucky again.'

'That's not all,' said Prosser. 'Daniels says that Bernie's fund managers have got a four per cent stake in Pardoe Trust as well. With him on our side, I don't see how we can lose.'

'He *is* on our side, is he? Bernie's not renowned for his loyalty to anyone except Bernie.'

'We'd better make sure. See if he likes sailing. I'm sure we can arrange a week for him on the *BIG Princess*, cruising around the Mediterranean on a fact-finding expedition. We might also lay on a bit of company to help him coat his revolting body in sun-tan lotion.

'Morrie says he's nearly finished buying the shares for BIG, so we should encourage Bernie to get Empire to pick up a little more. The more in friendly hands, the better. It might be a good idea if we got our codewords sorted out now. I don't want those merchant banking pricks to pick them this time. What was it they chose last time to show off their fucking great education? Greek gods, wasn't it?'

'I've got an idea,' said Roach, reaching into his briefcase and withdrawing a small book. 'My kids are besotted with Noddy at the moment. What's wrong with using characters from Toytown?'

Prosser smiled. 'You mean Pardoe as Mr Plod?'

Roach took out a pen and began making notes. 'Why not? The company can simply be referred to as Mr Plod's house. Mickey Monkey would have to be David Westbury. Michael Westbury can be Bumpy Dog and Uncle Timothy is undoubtedly Bruiny Bear.'

'What other names are there?' asked Prosser.

Roach thumbed through the book. 'How about turning Seaman into Gilbert Golly?'

'That sounds about right. I've set Sally to watch over him.'

'She can be Miss Fluffy Cat. Who else have we got? How about Wobbly Man for Butterley?'

'That sounds right. He'll be wobbling like a jelly before we've finished this thing. And Lady Amanda. Don't forget the part she has to play.'

'She'll have to be Tessie Bear. Which just leaves us, Noddy and Big Ears.'

As Jeremy walked past Roach's open door on the way to his own office, he could not help hearing the raised voices. One he knew was Prosser's. He did not recognise the other.

'I'll be Noddy. You can be Big Ears.'

'You'll do as you're bloody well told! I'm Noddy and we're not having any arguments about it. *You're* Big Ears.'

'It's not fair. I thought of the idea, so I should be Noddy.'

'It's my company, so I decide who's who. I'm Noddy. So there, with bells on.'

'Look, I know how to settle this. We'll dip for it. Dip, doo, magazoo, Big Ears is You.'

'If we're going to dip, that's not the way to do it. It's One Potato,

Two Potato, Three Potato, Four, Five Potato, Six Potato, Seven Potato, Your. . . No, hang on a second, that can't be right. I'll try again. One Potato. . .'

'It was right first time, Big Ears.'

'I am not bloody Big Ears! I know, let's fight for it.'

'That's cheating. You used to fight professionally. I'm an accountant. What chance would I have?'

'Cowardy, cowardy custard. Do you want to fight or not?'

'All right, all right, you win. I'll be Big Ears. But I still think I ought to have been Noddy.'

'Sore loser,' said Prosser triumphantly, charging out of the office and bumping straight into Jeremy, standing transfixed outside the door. 'Oh look, Big Ears,' he shouted over his shoulder, 'it's Gilbert Golly.'

Things were getting to the stage at which nothing about British Industrial surprised Jeremy any more. Prosser hared off down the corridor. Jeremy ran after him.

'I've finished the article, Sir,' he said eagerly. 'Would you like to read it?'

'Don't bother me with trivia, Golly. Just send it off. I'm sure it will be fine.'

Jeremy was disappointed. He and Sally had worked hard to finish the article the night before. When they were done, she had suggested supper and suddenly the work he had been intending to do for the Think Tank lost its attraction.

They had talked for hours, although it was really Jeremy who had done most of the talking. Normally so shy, there was something about the way Sally looked at him that encouraged him to open up. She had such a wonderful smile and such friendly eyes. Above all, she didn't laugh at him in the same way everybody else did. Although he didn't yet realise it, Carole Lombard was being replaced in Jeremy's fickle affections by another. He was in the early stages of falling in love.

He had talked, and talked, and talked. After twenty-four years of loneliness, he had a lot of catching up to do. He poured out his life story, such as it was: the endless practical jokes and teasing he had suffered at school and college; the solace and comfort he found in hard work and the inspiration he derived from the example of Alex Prosser; his excitement at being asked to join the company and his interest in the business ethics course he had recently studied.

Sally was such a good listener, such a sympathetic audience, that Jeremy even found himself telling her about his greatest humiliation at Cambridge, his attempt to master the intricacies of riding a bicycle. Even though he avoided mechanical objects whenever possible, every other student in Cambridge, of whatever intellectual or physical ability, could ride one. Surely it couldn't be beyond him? But he had found the machine a monster, more interested in devouring his limbs than in transporting him from place to place. In the closed community, word of Jeremy's efforts soon got around. Watching him setting off for lectures in the morning became one of the "in" things to do. Determined not to give the assembled mob the satisfaction of seeing him defeated, each morning Jeremy would leave his rooms at the top of South Court, lead his bicycle through "Dustbin Court" and the Lodge into the street, mount it, wobble a few times and then fall off, to the delight of the onlookers.

'What I couldn't understand at the time was why I was getting invited to so many parties. Then I discovered that when I left everyone would crowd to the windows to watch me try to cycle away. I only found out when somebody asked me if I would like to reproduce my "act" on stage for that year's Footlights.'

He didn't object to Sally's laughter. On the contrary, it gave Jeremy a warm feeling inside. She didn't laugh *at* him like everyone else. She laughed *with* him. And she looked so terribly pretty when she did, with her eyes sparkling.

Towards the end of his story, when Jeremy was talking of his immense pride at working for a company like British Industrial Group and at having made such a big impression on Alexander Prosser so early on, she became rather serious.

'Jeremy,' she said, 'I've been here a lot longer than you. You shouldn't believe everything you read about BIG or about Prosser in the magazines and newspapers. A lot of it is simply what he and Roach want people to read. Prosser's a businessman, after all, and you need to be tough and sometimes ruthless to succeed in business. You wouldn't believe everything you read about a film star, would you?'

This flummoxed Jeremy, who obstinately believed every precious word he had been able to find on Carole Lombard, despite the contradictory nature of much of the more outrageous Hollywood publicity. He had always assumed that everything he came across in print was true.

Sally shook her head at him. His story had convinced her that he was even more in need of her care and attention than she had thought. He knew next to nothing about real life and his idolising of Prosser was positively unhealthy. It might hurt, but he was going have to be told some of the facts of life.

In fact the longer she listened, the more convinced Sally became that Jeremy would needed to be told *all* the facts of life. When she favoured him with the well-practised come-hither look which made most men turn weak at the knees, Jeremy just smiled broadly back at her and continued regardless. Had he, unlike all the thrusting, upwardly mobile young executives she usually dated, no experience of women at all? Sally was surprised to discover that she found the idea rather piquant . . .

The following morning she was in the office bright and early, and outraged to hear of his treatment at the hands of Mr Bennett. She made him a cup of tea and listened solicitously to his story.

'I feel awful,' she said when Jeremy had finished. 'I should have told you about the lift code. It changes every day. Prosser's so obsessed with security, though, that he won't allow the code number to appear on the notice board. Instead he gives us the name of a battle and we have to find out the date for ourselves. Yesterday was the Battle of Brandywine, 1777. Today is Magersfontein which was 1899.

'You'll need one of these,' she said, drawing a dictionary of dates from her desk. 'Be careful with it. They're like gold dust. You'll find the latest battle on the board outside Roach's office.'

The mention of Roach's office reminded Jeremy of the extraordinary conversation he had just overheard about Noddy and Big Ears which he now recounted to an attentive Sally. Codewords were usually used in takeovers. But if that was the case, why did Jeremy merit a codeword? She was sure it must all have something to do with Nostrum but couldn't work out where Jeremy fitted into the picture.

She put it to the back of her mind for the moment and returned to her task of persuading Human Resources that British Industrial Group *did* have such a post as Director of Think Tank and that Jeremy occupied it. Only when the computer recognised him as an employee would he be able to get his four hundred pounds back, and without it his financial position was precarious in the extreme. Sally had already had to lend him another fifty pounds.

Prosser was on the roof, talking to Fallas.

'I got your message. You're quite sure they're due to go to Barbados next week?'

'I do not make mistakes.'

'Do you think she would go on her own if he was unavoidably detained for some reason?'

'I should say that it was a possibility.'

'In that case, I think we should make it as difficult as possible for Mr Plod, as we must now call him, to tear himself away from his desk. I should be grateful for any suggestions.'

Fallas had already anticipated Prosser's request. He outlined a scheme to which Prosser readily agreed, despite the obvious expense involved. P C Plod was about to get a bit of trouble on his patch.

From the safety of his doorway, screened from the curiosity of casual passers-by by a Safeway's supermarket trolley full of carrier bags, Sebastian Embleton watched Alexander Prosser closely, putting down his binoculars only to glance at his watch and jot something in his notebook.

When the call was over Prosser walked over to a shed in one corner of the roof. He opened the door and adjusted his eyes to the darkness.

'Hello, Maggie. It's me.' His voice was soft and gentle, quite a different Prosser altogether from the Machiavellian tyrant of the thirteenth floor. 'I'm going to have to go away for a few days soon. So we'd better give you an outing before then, hadn't we?'

He reached up to a shelf and took from it a stout buckskin gauntlet which he pulled on to his left hand. Undoing the leash which bound her to the rail, he raised Maggie and carried her into the sunlight. She blinked and looked around with wide, bright orange eyes, her head bobbing up and down with anticipation. She flapped her wings, but Prosser held her tightly. She was his pride and joy, a beautiful one-year-old female Goshawk, two and a half pounds of ferocious fighting machine.

He took from his pocket a bloody piece of rabbit. The bird grabbed it, wolfing it down greedily. 'Hungry, are we?' he asked. 'Let's find you something a little more lively then, shall we?' He walked to the edge of the roof and loosened his grip on the bird. The hawk's neck swivelled as she searched for prey, chortling quietly to herself. A jet passed overhead, disturbing her. She flapped her wings and gripped the gauntlet tightly. Without its protection, the talons would have dug deep into Prosser's hand. He had heard tales of some birds having their feet cut off as the only way of freeing their agonised owners.

Maggie stiffened and became alert. She had spotted something. Prosser let go of the jesses holding her and she was off. He took up the binoculars and focussed them. She seemed to be after a common or garden pigeon. If Maggie had a fault, it was a lack of discernment when picking her prey, quite unlike her more discriminating owner.

He watched her getting into position above the bird, hovering until she was certain of her quarry and then dropping like a stone. Some premonition of what was about to happen made the pigeon put on a spurt of speed. But it was no match for Maggie, who swooped down upon it and dug her talons into its skull. It was dead in a trice.

The hawk turned back to the roof, carrying the corpse like a commuter would his briefcase.

Prosser let her have her fill before taking her on to his arm again. She was in fine form. She jumped on to his outstretched glove, burped, wiped her beak against his glove and went to sleep, content. Gently, Prosser carried her back to her perch, stroking her feathers and listening to her soft cooing.

The house martin, exhausted, regained the safety of his nest, tucked away behind an array of pipes just under the eaves of BIG House. For one horrible moment, he had thought that monstrous bird was chasing him. It came as a great relief when he saw it nab that dozy, fat pigeon. Town living was getting a little dangerous these days.

He didn't plan on leaving, though. This building was so much more interesting than the last one. There was always so much to see, particularly near the top.

He sidestepped along the pipes, looking through each window in turn until he found something worthy of his attention. Look, there he was again, that stubby little human who carried his own personal worm around with him. Look at the size of it! And so pink and juicy. He'd never seen one like that before.

He supposed he was witnessing some sort of human courting

display. This one was always giving his worm to various females. Presumably they didn't like him very much, because they always gave it back to him.

The house martin gazed through the window, fascinated. Humans were so screamingly funny.

* * * 14 * * *

THE NEW WEEK dawned peacefully at BIG House. The Major's campaign was temporarily put on the back burner while he was shown the ropes by Mr Bennett. His trepidation at venturing into the enemy's stronghold had evaporated. It was the first time in his life that he had been in uniform and, as he mentioned several times to Rommel as he dressed that morning, it did rather become him, even though he did say so himself. Standing to attention beside Mr Bennett as the crowds drifted lethargically into work on yet another Monday morning, the Major found himself intoxicated by the power wielded by the chief security officer. He had been particularly impressed when a secretary who had forgotten her identity pass was sent home in tears to fetch it even though, as Mr Bennett freely admitted to the Major, the girl had worked in the marketing department for at least three years.

'That's not the point, though, Major. These people must be made to realise the importance of constant vigilance. We've got that red-headed troublemaker to come. That should be fun. Let's see what name he's using today.'

But Mr Bennett and the Major were to be disappointed. Jeremy was already safely ensconced in his office. It had been Sally's idea for him to nip down into the basement car park and take the restricted lift from there straight to the thirteenth floor, avoiding the foyer altogether. He tapped in 1709, praying he had remembered the correct date for the Battle of Malplaquet. No bells rang. No security guards arrived to bundle him off and he reached his office safely.

It had been a disturbing weekend for Jeremy, whose mind had been increasingly occupied with unusual and distracting thoughts of Sally. He had tried to escape them by seeing a showing of Twentieth Century, but it was Sally's head that he saw on the body of Carole Lombard. She was still appearing in his dreams, too, and to Jeremy's

123

growing consternation and shame, wearing fewer and fewer clothes each night.

A dose of hard work was obviously what was needed, but it is difficult to conjure up original ideas when your mind is clogged with visions of your secretary. To be fair to Jeremy, his thoughts were remarkably chaste by present moral standards. They could hardly be otherwise as his knowledge of the opposite sex, and indeed of the more fiddly bits of his own sex, was remarkably limited. Much of what little he knew of the subject had been picked up from watching old Hollywood films of the thirties and forties where one moment a couple are kissing and the next they are smoking cigarettes. What happened in between was still something of a mystery. He had picked up a few of the schoolboy's notions about the act of procreation but his solitary habits in later life and his parents' evasions on the subject meant that these ludicrous misconceptions had never been dispelled. As far as he was aware, the mysterious act of 'screwing' meant lying on top of a woman at right angles and turning yourself through ninety degrees. Why else would it be called that?

Sally had arrived early at work that morning so that she could move a few pieces of furniture around undisturbed. With time on her hands, she went in search of company and found Jacqui having her breakfast.

'What's this? One of the hoi polloi secretaries mixing with the personal assistants?' said Jacqui, guffawing loudly.

'Shut up, and pass me the toast. At least I'm well rid of the wandering hands of Prosser.'

'He's not so bad. I've known far worse, believe me.'

'Oh, I do,' said Sally sweetly, buttering her toast.

'You can sneer, but I'm happy just as long as my men are well endowed,' said Jacqui. 'To please me, all they need to have is a nice, thick wallet. Prosser certainly fits the bill.'

'What's this?' asked Sally, picking up a piece of paper from the table.

'Expenses, ducky.'

'Expenses? Stockings, suspenders, basques, peek-a-boo bras, crotchless panties? You can't claim for those, surely?'

'I thought I'd try it. If Prosser insists on me prancing about in them, why shouldn't he be the one who pays for them, especially the way he mistreats them?'

'I'd like to see their faces in Human Resources when they get that little list. Nettle's eyes will jump right out of their podgy sockets,' said Sally.

'You won't be needing any gear like that any more, will you? Not with that chap you're working for now. What a drip, eh?'

Sally bit her tongue. 'Oh, he's all right,' she said.

'Must be. The boss seems to think highly of him. He made me take down the minutes of a meeting yesterday and the Emperor gave him all the credit for the good ideas. Not like Prosser at all. Seems your man was the one who came up with the wheeze of putting the company name all over the building at night. Seaman, that's his name, isn't it?'

'Mmm,' agreed Sally, her mouth full of toast and her mind full of questions. Jeremy hadn't come up with that idea, she was sure. What was Prosser playing at?

'Lor'. Look at the time,' said Jacqui. 'Better get ready for His Lordship's wake-up call. He hates it if I'm late.' She produced a bright crimson lipstick from her bag and began daubing it on her lips. 'I know,' she said, noticing Sally's stares. 'Terrible, isn't it? But you know how much he likes seeing lipstick all over his winkle. . .or then, perhaps you don't. That's probably why you were given the shove. You should try being a bit more accommodating love, and see where it gets you. Cheerio for now.'

Sally wandered back to the office to find Jeremy at his desk, staring into space. He started guiltily as she came in, trying to avoid her gaze. He couldn't understand what had come over him. It really was most unprofessional.

'I'll get that article typed up,' said Sally, 'and you can get on with your deep pondering or whatever it is you're supposed to do.'

Try as he might, Jeremy could keep neither his thoughts nor his gaze away from her for long. She sat directly in front of him, partially blocking the view through the window, but instead of facing Jeremy as before the weekend, her desk and chair had been moved so that she now sat at right angles to him.

This new position, which Sally had carefully arranged before Jeremy arrived for work that morning, enabled him to study her profile. He tried to do this surreptitiously, affecting to stare into space, pensively tapping his teeth with a pencil, and then catching a distracting glimpse of her as he moved the direction of his gaze to stare at a different bit of thin air. Her nose, he noticed after a sidelong glance or two, turned up a little at the end. It was very fetching. Not at all a run of the mill nose. Another glance and he realised that it had some very dainty freckles on it. Yet another and he got a glimpse of her mouth. Another, and he got a good look at her chin. Another, and her neck was stored for future memory retrieval. Another, and. . . oh. . . oh dear.

Jeremy looked quickly down at the desk. The light from the window was shining through Sally's blouse and you could see them. Not just the bumps they made, but actually *them*.

He became aware of an embarrassing bulge developing in his trousers. He drew shapes furiously on the pad in front of him, then had to scribble over the doodles because they looked slightly obscene and were just making things worse. He tried to think of nothing, but that didn't work. The more he willed the terrible impulse to disappear, the stronger it became.

He couldn't risk looking up. He'd be bound to look in Sally's direction and she might see him. He looked up. He couldn't stop himself. But he made sure he did not look at Sally, concentrating instead on the Centrepoint tower in the middle distance.

Maybe he hadn't seen what he had thought he had seen. Though he fought to keep them averted, his eyes were drawn irresistibly back towards Sally, first towards her nose, then her mouth, then her chin, then her neck, then her. . .

At that very moment she turned to him and asked, 'Why don't we take a break for lunch? There's a cosy Italian place round the corner that's reasonably cheap.'

Red-faced, Jeremy nodded eagerly. Anything to get her away from the window. But as he made to stand up, he realised he couldn't possibly do so while she was in the room. If she saw him in his current predicament, she would probably never talk to him again.

'Wouldn't you like to go and freshen up first?'

'No thanks, I'm fine.'

'Perhaps you ought to post that article if Mr Prosser doesn't want to read it?'

'I can pop it into the chute on the way out.'

'Oh. . . ah. . . Come to think of it, I'm not sure I'm all that hungry at the moment. Perhaps we should wait a bit?'

'It gets terribly crowded later on. We really should go now,' she said to the miserable Jeremy. 'Come on. I'll call the lift.'

His miscreant member hadn't quite returned to normal when he joined a puzzled Sally a few moments later, but thanks to his overcoat, at least he had his mobility back.

They passed through the reception area, greeting Mr Bennett in unison. At the sight of the chief security officer's bewilderment, they left BIG House giggling loudly.

Prosser and Roach were watching the BBC's lunchtime news with considerable interest. The reporter, Justin Ewer, was attempting to explain how such a minor industrial dispute had escalated so quickly at a plant with no record of industrial strife. His opening remarks made it clear that the fault lay firmly with the bosses. This was always Ewer's line. He hadn't survived twelve years of BBC politics by being objective about these things. Behind him, a score or so men in green anoraks were barring the entry to the factory gate, holding placards aloft and chanting slogans. Facing them were a handful of police. Ewer turned to one of the green anoraks standing beside him.

'Ben Lobb, you're the shop steward at this plant. Perhaps you can explain the background to this dispute?'

Lobb contorted his face into that sad, serious, nothing-at-all-to-do-with-me-mate look he had been taught at the "Handling the Media" course at Transport House – where his teacher had been a moonlighting Justin Ewer – and reminded himself to drop a few aitches. 'It stems from the blatant way in which the management of this appalling sweat-shop, this workhouse of the twentieth century, are refusing my members their basic rights as 'uman beings, rights which are inalienable.'

Behind Ewer several coaches were drawing up. Out of them spilled more green anoraks. 'Perhaps you could be more specific?' Ewer asked Lobb.

'One of my members wanted to go to the lavatory. Not an unreasonable request, you might think. But not here at Pardoe's. Here, the management think they have the right to tell men when they can and cannot 'ave a pee. It's outrageous. Diabolical even.'

More coaches arrived. This time, it was police reinforcements, already kitted out in riot gear, who poured out of the doors. 'What do you say, Mr Lobb, in response to the plant manager's statement that the man in question had already been to the lavatory seven times in the previous two hours?'

'A man's gotta do what a man's gotta do,' said Lobb, leering into the camera. 'Who are these people that they can decide for us whether we can spend a penny or not? Not that a penny is worth much in Thatcher's Britain. A man with a weak bladder ought to be pitied, not punished.'

The camera zoomed in on the men at the gates, panning across placards carrying slogans like 'Freedom To Pee Freely', 'Piss Off Pardoe', 'Pardoe – Our Bizness Is Our Bizness', 'Hands Off Our Leaks', 'Number Ones For Everyone', 'Pardoe Slashes Slashing Time' and 'Leave our Members' Members alone'.

At the end of the line, one picket decided to demonstrate his contempt for the management ban in the most practical way possible. Another joined him by lowering his fly, then another. Soon, there was a competition taking place to see who could urinate the furthest. The police began falling back discreetly.

The camera hurriedly panned back to Ewer. 'Do all these men work for Pardoe Trust?' he asked, indicating the stream of pickets arriving from the coaches.

'I can't say that I recognise every single face,' said Lobb truthfully, knowing that the vast majority were students supplementing their meagre grants by renting themselves out for the day, 'but if other workers or members of the great mass of Thatcher's unemployed choose to show their support for our plight, I am powerless to stand in their way.'

The cameraman panned back to the factory gates. He was trained to point his thing where the action was, and if the action was grown men pointing their things then so be it. One policeman's patience snapped after he had been splattered by urine for a second time. He was bursting anyway as they hadn't been allowed to leave their post since coming on duty. Such uncalled-for police provocation could not go unanswered and, all along the line, the zips of the pickets were lowered and weapons drawn out.

The voice of the Inspector in charge of the police could be heard through a loudhailer. 'Put that away at once, Jones. . . This has gone far enough.' But this affront to the dignity of the boys in blue could not be ignored. Throughout the ranks, police flies were undone. 'If those officers who are exposing themselves will put their willies away instantly, we'll say no more about it. Otherwise. . . ' But battle proper commenced. Spray arched through the air.

Events moved with bewildering speed. The riot police, grouping behind the lines of the uniformed boys, came to the relief of their colleagues. They began fumbling in their own outfits although, as these had been designed specifically to stop anybody getting to those regions of the body to which access was now sought, they had quite a job. Soon they too were advancing, riot shields in one hand, Jimmy Riddles in the other. It began to look as if the police were getting the upper hand. Arcs of yellow liquid showered onto the pickets.

But the police, whose weapons had been primed only with canteen tea, were no match for the new arrivals at the factory gates. Although lacking in basic facilities, each coach had been equipped with several cases of beer, not one bottle of which remained to be consumed by the time they had arrived at the Pardoe plant. Accompanied by the strains of the *Internationale,* the reinforcements began demonstrating just how mighty tools can be in the hands of the proletariat. The police began to fall back, their ammunition running out.

'Shit,' Ewer cried, a description that, as the viewers could plainly see for themselves, was not strictly apposite. But his concern was with a police horse which had wandered in front of the camera. 'Get that bloody camera back.'

The cameraman did as he was told, just in time to catch star BBC reporter Justin Ewer slipping up in the now unpleasantly wet grass. He fell on his back and, under the gaze of the TV audience, lay cowering and whimpering beneath the horse, terrified that the brute would step on him.

It didn't. Instead the well-trained animal decided to show solidarity with the police contingent. The hot, steaming, jet powered straight into the face of the BBC's Industrial Correspondent.

All over the country hundreds of businessmen who had, at one time or another, been on the receiving end of a grilling from Ewer, stood and cheered.

Prosser was a little more restrained. 'God knows what the bill for that little lot will be,' he said tetchily.

'You have to hand it to Fallas,' cried Roach, tears streaming down his cheeks. 'It worked. It's going to take Pardoe days to calm that little lot down. Look at the share price. Down ten pence already.

Prosser pressed a button on his control unit and said into thin air, 'Get me Morrie Minchkin, pronto.' He turned to Roach. 'I'll fly out as soon as I hear from Fallas. I don't want anybody to know where I am going. 'You'd better hold the fort while I'm away. Tell the press we see our holding in Pardoe in the nature of a long-term investment. The usual crap that means nothing and leaves us with all our options open. Oh, and have a few more meetings minuted at which Gilbert Golly comes up with some brainstorming ideas.'

'Alex.' Morrie's voice came over the speakerphone. 'I take it you've heard about Pardoe's little trouble. The shares are heading south quickly.'

'Excellent. It'll give us our chance to buy more. Do it now, and do it as clumsily as possible. This is not one of your softly-softly catchee-catchee operations. And don't hang about with the declaration, either. I want both the Stock Exchange and Sir High-and-Mighty Jocelyn to know this afternoon that British Industrial Group has a declarable stake in Pardoe Trust.'

∗ ∗ ∗ 15 ∗ ∗ ∗

THE SUNNY Caribbean skies were not mirrored by Alexander Prosser's foul mood. To conceal his movements from prying eyes he had been forced to make all the travel arrangements himself. Having been warned by Fallas not to use the company jet on the grounds that international movements were logged, he had had to slum it on an ageing British Airways Concorde.

Prosser was not accustomed to travelling by public transport. Not only had he had to turn up at Heathrow to check in hours before the flight, but the ticket booking staff had refused to take seriously his request for three seats so that he would not have to sit next to anybody. As a result, he had been sandwiched between a recently bereaved widow intoxicated by an enormous life insurance payout, and a travel writer for one of the Sunday newspapers intoxicated by the complimentary champagne. Prosser, who didn't hold with such poncey drinks, as he told everybody within earshot, balled out the stewardesses because the plane didn't carry Newcastle Brown Ale and then sulked because, wedged in as he was, there was no opportunity to suggest to them a different sort of balling.

Why had he listened to Fallas? On the company plane, he could have been looked after by one, or more, of the girls in the Jacuzzi. As it was, he felt unbearably horny throughout the long flight. Once on the ground at Grantley Adams Airport, he felt both unbearably horny and unbearably hot, aching not only for a chance to relieve the tension in his groin but also for a chance to get out of his thick flannel suit. But although he had arrived safely in Barbados, his luggage had not. Nor could anyone, despite Prosser's fulsome if unenforceable threats, enlighten him as to where it might be.

According to Fallas's man on the spot, comfortably attired in Hawaiian shirt and shorts, Amanda Pardoe was staying at the

Cobbler's Lane Hotel. He drove the heavily perspiring Prosser there in a battered Ford Cortina.

Prosser hated 'abroad'. It smelt different for one thing and this place, full of darkies and bloody palm trees, was worse than most. He strode straight up to the girl at the reception desk and snarled at her to give him the finest room in the hotel. Up since six o'clock that morning, travelling for seven hours in a hot suit that was now considerably rumpled, short, sweating, in need of a shave, with no reservation and no luggage, Prosser did not look the ideal five-star hotel guest.

She didn't even bother consulting the computer. 'I'm terribly sorry, Sir, but we're completely full at the moment. Perhaps I could suggest. . . '

'I am hot and I am tired. I do not intend staying in another hotel, so I suggest very strongly that you have a good look and find me a room before I lose my temper.'

'I'm afraid we are fully booked, Sir.'

'Really?' snarled Prosser. 'In that case, I'll buy the shitty place. How much?'

'I beg your pardon, Sir?' The girl began looking about her for assistance. This one was obviously completely coconuts.

'I said how much for the hotel? I'll buy it, lock, stock and barrel.'

'Perhaps I'd better get the manager?'

'Yes. Perhaps you *had* better go and get the bloody manager.'

The mere sight of the manager, towering above him in morning coat, cravat and striped trousers, infuriated Prosser. The supercilious French accent and habit of rubbing his hands together when he spoke didn't help. It had been a long time since he had been talked down to like this.

''ow do you do? I am Pierre Valeron, manager of the Cobbler's Lane. 'ow can I help you, Sir?' The 'Sir' was almost an insult.

'It's very simple really, chum. I want to buy this hotel, as it would seem to be the only way of getting myself a room. So if you would be so kind as to put me in touch with somebody capable of representing the owner.'

'And might I ask Monsieur's name?'

'Prosser. Alexander Prosser.'

The manager's manner changed abruptly. 'Of British Industrial Group?'

'That's right.' Prosser was slightly mollified to realise how far his fame had spread.

The manager pushed the receptionist out of the way and pressed a few buttons on the computer keyboard. 'Ah, the girl must have been mistaken, Sir,' he gabbled. 'You are in luck, Sir. A cancelled reservation. Our penthouse suite is free, Sir.'

'I don't give a toss. It's too late. I still want to buy the place.' Prosser had got the bit between his teeth and didn't intend giving in as easily as all that. 'If you're as full as this after the peak of the season, it must be a thriving business. I intend to have it.'

The manager nervously ran his finger around the inside of his collar. 'I'm afraid that won't be possible, Sir.'

'Who do you think you're talking to, Froggie? I can do whatever I fucking well want and I want to buy this hotel.'

'But you cannot, Mr Prosser. It is not feasible.'

'Oh, and why not? Just give me one good reason, chum.'

'Because you already own it, Sir.'

'Ah, there you are, my boy.' Jeremy had arrived at work early – the day's battle was Chatanooga, 1863 – to move Sally's desk to a less disturbing position. But Roach caught him in the corridor. 'In bright and early. That's what I like to see, someone who's really keen. I can see Mr Prosser's faith in you is going to be amply rewarded. We're pleased with you, Jeremy. Very pleased. Here are the keys to your car, a brand-new BMW 525i, currently waiting downstairs for you to fire up its ignition.'

'But. . . ' began Jeremy.

'No buts, Jeremy. It's only fitting for a chap in your position to have a decent company car. If you'd just sign here,' said Roach, pushing the keys under a dazed Jeremy's nose.

'You don't understand. I don't. . . '

'Please don't be awkward, Jeremy.'

He took the keys reluctantly. 'Mr Roach? I wondered if I could have a word with you about my salary.'

Roach looked disapproving. 'Now don't let's get greedy. Twenty thousand for a chap in your position, plus car, seems generous enough to me.'

'Twenty thousand pounds?' he said slowly. 'But it isn't the amount, it's. . . '

'I'm a little disappointed in you, Jeremy. You can't possibly expect a rise so soon. After all, you've only been here. . . excuse me.' He broke off to respond to a burbling noise from the inside pocket of his jacket. He drew out a cellular phone. 'Roach. . . Desirée. How nice of you to call.' He waved Jeremy away. 'Yes of course the plumber can use the inside lavatory if he needs to. . . If he doesn't have a leak, he won't fix *our* leak. . . Well, swamp it in disinfectant afterwards like you do when anybody else uses it.'

Jeremy wandered into his office in a daze. Twenty thousand pounds, a car, his own office on the thirteenth floor – it didn't make sense. How could Roach say they were pleased with him when he hadn't done anything yet?

He was still pondering this when Sally found him a few minutes later. He was standing with his mouth open, as was his habit when he was deep in thought. It was a habit she was going to have to break him of, along with a few others.

'It sounds as if they've flipped to me. But why should you care? Just take what's given,' she told him when he had recapped the conversation with Roach.

'But it hasn't been given. Unless you've sorted things out with Human Resources?'

'No,' she admitted, 'but I'm working on it.'

'I got this this morning, just before I left my flat.' Jeremy handed over a letter. It was from Nettle. Addressed to Jeffrey Simpson, it informed him that his unexplained absence from work was causing concern and that unless he was able to produce a doctor's certificate justifying this unwarranted dereliction of duty, it was Nettle's painful duty to inform him that his employment with British Industrial Group would be terminated.

'But this doesn't affect you.'

'Not if they think that Jeffrey Simpson is Jeffrey Simpson, no. But if they think Jeffrey Simpson is Jeremy Seaman or that Jeremy Seaman is Jeffrey Simpson, then they might mean me in the letter, and not Jeffrey Simpson at all. Do you see?'

'Not entirely, but I'll get on to Human Resources again for you.'

She sat down at her desk, still in the same position as the day before.

'Sally, I wonder. . . ' began Jeremy.

'Yes?'

'Oh, nothing.' If he asked her to move her desk, she might want

134

to know why. Perhaps if he just kept his head down for the day, he'd be all right.

Despite his exhaustion, Prosser gave up trying to get any sleep. With the windows open, the noise from the countless water-bikes ploughing up and down in the bay was unbearable. No wonder they were known locally as 'mosquitoes'. But with the windows shut, the hum of the air conditioning kept him awake. It had to be the noise. High-powered businessmen like him didn't get jet lag like ordinary mortals.

The girl was soundly asleep, an arm flung across him. He had opened the door several hours earlier to find her there, a card pinned to her breast bearing the words 'With the Compliments of the Management'. She didn't appear to speak any English, but that had not proved to be a problem. Prosser pushed her away roughly, but she did not wake. He yawned, scratched his crotch, dragged himself off the bed and dressed. His clothes had been laundered while the girl had been initiating him into a few local customs.

Prosser pulled a couple of notes out of his wallet and put them where, if the girl didn't find them, her next customer certainly would, then went downstairs. He called Fallas's man from a call box in the lobby and then wandered the grounds searching for Lady Pardoe.

He found her lounging under an umbrella by the side of the swimming pool, reading the latest Jackie Collins. She was in a one-piece bathing suit and hadn't aged too badly. Her face still had that vaguely oriental look to it, with that square jaw and those long, thin eyes. There was an elegance about her that he didn't recall from the old days. She still had a great pair of tits on her. He remembered that before she met Pardoe she had been a model, which probably meant she was now largely made out of plastic, like one of those old Airfix kits.

At that moment she looked up. Seeing someone standing in front of her, she slid her sunglasses down her nose to get a proper look. Not recognising him, she picked up a glass and took a swig. When she looked back, he was still there, blocking the sun.

'Do I know you?. . . Shit, I do. It's Prosser. Porker Prosser.'

'Shh,' hissed Prosser. 'Don't use that name, for God's sake.'

'Not ashamed of your past surely, Porker?' she said loudly.

Prosser slid on to the lounger next to hers. 'I'm not the only one to have wiped out part of my life history, Miss Ada Hawthornthwaite.'

'It's Amanda now, not Ada, and I dropped the Thwaite by deed poll a long time before I became Lady Amanda Pardoe,' she said icily, looking at him over the tops of her sunglasses. 'God, you've put on weight. Except on top. Where's all your hair gone?' Prosser curbed his natural aggression. He didn't want to antagonise the bitch. 'And what on earth are you doing in that ridiculous suit? It must be a hundred degrees in the shade.'

'You're wearing well, Ada. I mean, Amanda.'

'I keep myself fit, as does Jocelyn. You should try it,' she said, prodding his well-upholstered stomach. 'What the hell are you doing here anyway?'

'On a tour of inspection, I own this place. I'm surprised Jocelyn wanted to come here. Where is he?' said Prosser, looking about him.

'I picked the hotel. And Jocelyn is in London, thanks to you. Apparently British Industrial has just declared a stake in Pardoe Trust.'

'Really?' said Prosser, raising his eyebrows. 'I hadn't realised. I give my young turks a good deal of autonomy on the more trivial matters. I hope it isn't spoiling your holiday.'

'Well, things were a teensy bit dull. Now that you're here, though, we can have a good old chin-wag about the old times. Just let me mark the place in my book.' She opened it where she had left off, bent the spine sharply backwards and tore off the block of pages she had already read, throwing it to the ground. 'So, how long has it been?'

'It must be about twenty-six years. You were sixteen at the time and I was fourteen. What was your nickname, then? It's gone clean out of my mind.'

'I can't remember,' Amanda said frostily.

Prosser clicked his fingers. 'Ada, the Byker bike, that was it. Trust you to change your name by stuffing a 'man' into the middle of it! What a reputation. It was said that a threepenny bit was all it took to get you to spread your legs. I remember beating up a dozen kids at school to get hold of ready cash. When I'd got what I thought was a reasonable amount I skipped school and waylaid you in the street.'

Amanda laughed. 'I remember. A proper mess you were. One of your eyes closed up. Cuts and bruises everywhere. Showed me your grubby little fist full of coins and the odd IOU and asked me what you could get for that. I clouted you round the ear and told you not to be so cheeky.'

'You didn't send me away, though.'

'Mmm,' murmured Amanda dreamily. Her hand had moved on to Prosser's leg and was progressing upwards. 'You certainly were a willing pupil. Your nickname was well deserved, Porker. A proper little pig you made of yourself.' She leaned closer and began scratching at his trousers with her long fingernails. 'I bet you've learnt quite a few things since then,' she purred.

Prosser looked at his watch, feigning boredom. He didn't want to seem eager. 'Good God, is that the time? I've got a few things to attend to. Besides, I'm not sure your husband would be too keen on these reminiscences.'

Amanda's face darkened as she reached for her drink. 'He'd chew up the carpet if he knew I was even talking to you. He hates your guts. But it's his bloody fault he's not here, so bugger him.' Prosser fully intended to – metaphorically. 'Let's have dinner together, Alex.'

Prosser pretended to think about it. 'I'll try to get away,' he said reluctantly.

He stood up then bent to kiss Amanda, a moment captured for posterity by the photographer concealed on the other side of the pool.

The Major glanced at his watch. Just another few minutes until he was relieved. Only one day in the job and his feet were already sore. He stamped on the ground in an effort to get the circulation going again.

It was time to revive his campaign. The problem was that the Major's efforts had so far been mere pinpricks in the hide of the elephant. He could see that clearly now that he was on the inside. He was going to have to come up with something a little more disruptive, something that would really get under the skin of the beast and irritate it to distraction. Fortunately, now that he was employed by BIG there was no problem getting information about the enemy. Mr Bennett was a compulsive talker and the Major found himself being given all manner of valuable information, not only about the building but also about Mr Prosser himself. Mr Bennett had even revealed that the chairman of British Industrial Group kept a bird of prey on the roof of BIG House.

When his relief arrived the Major let himself into Mr Bennett's office. The head of security had given the Major his key together with permission to use it whenever he wanted. The Major locked the door behind him, sat himself down with the Yellow Pages, put his aching feet up on the desk and made his first phone call.

'Hello. Metro Office Supplies? Could I speak to somebody in sales?. . .My name is Nettle, Head of Human Resources at British Industrial Group.'

'So the manageress of the supermarket took her to one side and pointed out her appearance. The woman looked down, saw her tit was hanging out of her dress and screamed, "Oh God, I've left the bairn on the bus".' Prosser roared uproariously at his own joke and Amanda joined him.

They were in the hotel restaurant and having to talk loudly to compete with the noise of the steel band serenading the diners. Although he would have been happier with beer, Lady Pardoe had suggested champagne. After that had gone, they polished off a bottle of Brouilly and were now on to the liqueurs, regaling each other with Geordie jokes and stories from their other, earlier lives.

Prosser's speech was most definitely slurred. He looked across the table. Lady Amanda was dressed to the nines in a slinky low-cut black number, the jewels round her neck deliberately drawing attention to her deep cleavage. Prosser had been staring into it all evening. The leg playing footsie with him under the table implied he would soon be getting a lot closer to it. He topped up her glass.

'Why does your husband dislike me so much, Amanda?'

'I once made the mistake of telling him we had known each other in the old days back in Byker. I think he suspects that we might have known each other in the Biblical sense as well. Now he can't even hear your name mentioned without frothing at the mouth.'

'He's over sixty, for Christ's sake. You can only have married him for his money.'

'Of course I did, darling. But a girl's got to live. And you hadn't anything worth talking about when I was searching for a husband. I wanted a darn sight more than a grubby handful of coins by that stage.'

Prosser leant forward and whispered conspiratorially. 'And have you got all you need now?'

'Materially or physically?'

'Both.'

'I'm not complaining, but I can always do with a little bit more of one or the other.'

'I'm all for a bit of the other,' said Prosser, pulling out a hand which had been squirrelling about in his pocket. It held several coins which he fed, one by one, into Lady Amanda's cleavage. She did nothing to stop him. He was still the same coarse, ugly brute. But there was something fascinating about the aura of animal power and dangerous determination that oozed from him, such a change from the languid and sadly undemonstrative Jocelyn. 'Why don't we adjourn to my room for some bible study?' she purred.

Jeremy sat in the driver's seat of his new car, revelling in its luxury. Sally had sent him on first to get acquainted with its controls.

He looked around. There was nobody in sight. It couldn't hurt to turn on the ignition. The engine was so quiet, he had to press his foot on the accelerator a few times to convince himself it was working. The roar from the exhaust reverberated through the underground garage. He turned on the lights. The beam picked up his newly-painted name on the whitewashed wall, beside that of Prosser whose Rolls occupied the next space. He experimented with the windscreen wipers, with the steering wheel, with the radio cassette, with the heater and, unintentionally, with the horn, which was deafening in the enclosed space.

The BMW was an automatic. He had never driven an automatic before. In fact, he had never driven a car of any sort before. But he'd seen it done often enough. He moved the gearstick tentatively into reverse and, pressing lightly on the accelerator, looked over his shoulder. Nothing happened. He pressed a little harder. Still nothing. The car didn't budge. What was he doing wrong? Ah! The handbrake.

He took it off and the car, its engine racing, leapt back, hit a concrete column and stalled.

Shakily Jeremy got out and inspected the damage. It didn't look too bad. Just a slight dent in the bumper. If he put the car back into place, nobody would notice anything untoward. He tried pushing it, but it wouldn't budge. He started the ignition again and gingerly moved the gearstick into the drive position, leaving the accelerator well alone.

The car inched forward and Jeremy turned the wheel to manoeuvre it back into its space. He turned it too far and the car crawled slowly towards Prosser's Rolls-Royce. Jeremy was taking no chances this time. He stabbed his foot down on the brake before he could do any more damage.

But it landed on the accelerator. The car bounded forward.

The Major stared at his monitor in disbelief. Mr Bennett had obviously been right. The chap *was* a saboteur. Just look at the havoc he was wreaking. The Major wasn't upset to discover a competitor. Far from it. As far as he was concerned, the more the merrier. But it was a bit public. The chap risked discovery at any moment.

The Major loosened the plug at the back of the video recorder and the picture vanished. He rewound the recorder for a while, then set it going again. Now nobody would be any the wiser. You really couldn't trust modern technology. Terribly unreliable. He picked up the phone again.

'If you want to make a few bob, I've got just the thing for you, old girl. Cast-iron certainly.' Amanda poured out the rum, handed Prosser his glass and sat beside him on the bed.

'I'm all ears.' She hiccoughed, then laughed. 'Bit sozzled, I'm afraid.'

'Better not tell you. Not strictly kosher. Anyway, you're drunk. Might forget.'

'Aw, go on. I'll write it down. Promise. Scout's honour.'

'You were never a Scout.'

'Never had any honour either.' Amanda giggled, then turned her back to Prosser. 'Get the zip.'

Prosser obliged. She stood up and shook her dress to the floor, standing before him clad in black stockings, suspenders, knickers and a bra which had its work cut out keeping its charges under control. 'Tell you what,' she said, dragging him to his feet by his tie and nibbling his ear, 'I'll swop my body for your information.'

'I don't know. Shouldn't have said anything really. Sorry I spoke.'

'Just think how great it'd be to screw the wife of your biggest enemy. Just think how mad Jocelyn would be if he ever found out.' One hand had wormed its way inside his underpants and was doing an excellent job of persuasion. The other was

140

unbuttoning buttons and unzipping zips wherever it encountered them.

'Body first. Information afterwards.'

'Why don't you start by trying to get your coins back, Porker, without using your hands?'

'Like bobbing for apples?' he asked.

'Like bobbing for apples,' she agreed.

On the darkened balcony, Fallas's man put his camera to his eye again.

When Sally appeared in the car-park, Jeremy was still trying to get the BMW back into its parking place. For the umpteenth time he yanked the gear-stick into reverse and then slammed it into drive, then back into reverse, then forward into drive again, seemingly oblivious to the grinding, crunching and smashing noises accompanying his efforts. Sally stared at the carnage around her, appalled.

Prosser's Rolls, Roach's Mercedes, Godfrey Daniel's Porsche. . . none had escaped unscathed. There were smashed lights and dented bumpers everywhere. He had also fractured a pipe running up one of the columns from which steam was hissing out. Fortunately he seemed to have missed her car, tucked away in a corner. The front and rear of the BMW resembled a collapsed concertina. As she watched, it shot forward again, ramming the Rolls. The boot flew open. Then the BMW bounded backwards again, smashing into the Mercedes.

Sally ran over to the car and pulled the door open. 'What the hell are you doing?' she screamed.

'Nearly got it then,' mumbled Jeremy. 'Just one more go.'

'Can't you drive? Oh God, you can't, can you?'

'Couldn't before,' replied Jeremy proudly, 'but I reckon I've nearly got the hang of it now.'

'Move over, you idiot.' He shuffled across into the passenger seat and Sally leapt in, put the gearstick into the drive position and slammed her foot down on the accelerator. The BMW raced up the ramp and halted while Sally fed her card into the machine by the barrier. The grille rose and they shot out into the sunlight with a loud squeal as the dented metalwork scraped against one of the tyres. Sally turned left into the street, and the car was quickly swallowed up in the rush hour traffic.

She turned to Jeremy. 'With any luck, nobody at British Industrial will have seen us leave. Why didn't you say you couldn't drive, you imbecile?'

'It's no use blaming me,' said Jeremy huffily. 'I tried telling you and I tried telling Roach but you wouldn't listen. I reckoned it couldn't do any harm just to reverse it out. After all, any moron can drive, so it can't be that difficult.'

'It helps to have had a lesson or two, particularly if you *are* a moron. What is it with you and mechanical objects? Goodness knows how much damage you've done back there.' She pulled into the kerb, took an envelope and pencil from the glove compartment and began writing furiously. Damnation! Why couldn't she have fallen in love with a brainy, brawny hunk instead? Why Jeremy of all people? 'Listen carefully. I'm going to dump this car and go back and get mine. You take the Tube to my apartment and wait for me there. Take the key but don't you dare touch anything. Got it? This is the address, 85 Crown Reach.' She handed over the envelope and bundled him out of the car. 'You want Pimlico on the Victoria Line,' she screamed through the window as he walked away. 'You also want putting away,' she muttered as she steered the BMW back into the traffic.

Amanda Pardoe rummaged through her bag and pulled out a monogrammed leather diary. 'Fair's fair, Alex. I've kept my side of the bargain. Now you've got to keep yours. How am I going to make myself a little pocket money?'

Prosser raised himself on one elbow and ran his eyes over her naked body. No wonder she was in such good shape if she got this much exercise every day. Surely that fop Pardoe couldn't keep her satisfied?

'All right, Amanda, I'll tell you. But you must promise not to tell another soul.'

'Cross my heart and hope to die,' she said eagerly.

'There's a little drinks company we plan on taking over. The bloody pen-pushers have tied my hands and we can't move for at least three months – something to do with our tax position – so you'll have to tuck them away for a while.' Prosser giggled. 'It won't half put your husband's nose out of joint. Rumour has it he's interested in it too.'

'What's the name?' she asked, pen poised.

'Promise me that under no circumstances will you repeat this to Jocelyn,' said Prosser.

'Of course not. Come on. What is it?'

'It's called Nostrum.'

'Nostrum,' repeated Amanda, writing it down. She licked her lips. She loved the odd flutter on the market, especially when the outcome was certain. 'Alex, the thought of making money has made me horny again. Let's do it like we used to in the old days, standing up against the wall.'

There was a security guard on duty at Crown Reach, a newish brick block of flats right on the river hard by the north side of Vauxhall Bridge. The brightly-lit entrance lobby was full of prints, plants and comfortable but unused chairs. The only thing in the common hall-way of the house in which Jeremy lived was a pile of post, usually in brown envelopes, addressed to former residents of one or other of the flats.

The apartment took his breath away. The living room was vast, with extensive views over the river both upstream and down. Its opulent luxury made his own room in Paddington, with its peeling wallpaper and poky kitchenette, seem all the more dingy. He wandered about, looking at the framed posters and studying the books. Apart from a few novels, most of them were business books, on economics, finance and management. He thought they might just be for show but when he opened one or two at random they were heavily annotated and well-thumbed. Perhaps they weren't Sally's? Perhaps she shared the apartment with somebody else? Perhaps she had a boyfriend who lived here? Jeremy wished he knew a little more about her. He studied the notes carefully. Was there a way of telling if they were made by a man or a woman?

Taking one of the management books, he sank down on to the sofa with it. Sally's scent hung in the air. Jeremy slipped off his shoes, put up his feet and began to read.

Amanda Pardoe had become more sophisticated, not to say per-verted, in her sexual tastes since Prosser had last had the pleasure of her company. He gazed down at her sleeping, stretched out naked, each limb fastened, as she had insisted, to a post of the bed with curtain cords and belts from the towelling dressing gowns. He made a mental note to make sure they were put on the Pardoe's bill.

The pot of honey she had made him order from Room Service lay beside the bed, half empty. He swilled his mouth out with rum but couldn't get rid of the taste. He'd thought her a little bit cracked at first, wanting honey smeared all over her. But his licking it off had certainly had a powerful effect on her. The way she thrashed about, he had thought the bed would collapse.

'Ada?' he whispered. There was no response. She was dead to the world, snoring gently. Prosser moved stealthily over to the bedside table and picked up her handbag. He took it into the bathroom, closed the door, turned on the light, took a pair of surgical gloves from his pocket and put them on. Despite the bag's chaotic interior he found her credit card holder and took out her Visa and Access cards, laying them next to the sink, side by side. From his pocket he drew a miniature camera, supplied by Marketing Intelligence at BIG, made the adjustments as he had been taught and pressed the shutter. Turning the cards over, he took another. He opened her diary and saw her note: 'Buy Nostrum. Bid. Dead cert. Don't forget'. He put the small leather bound book in his pocket.

As he stuffed the cards back into her bag he noticed a packet of condoms nestling at the bottom. He tore the packet open and took three out, stuffing them in his pocket. Returning to the bedroom, he placed the rest conspicuously on the bedside table alongside her bag.

Prosser blew a kiss at the sleeping Amanda, took the 'Do Not Disturb' sign from the doorknob and hung it outside, pulling the door to quietly behind him.

He walked down to the lobby, chuckling. According to Fallas's man, Pardoe was already on the plane out to Barbados. How he would love to see Sir Jocelyn's face when he found his darling, devoted wife staked out like that.

Prosser hoped she woke up a long time before Pardoe arrived. Fancy suggesting he had put on weight. What a ludicrous idea!

*** 16 ***

'WAKE UP, Rambo.' Sally shook Jeremy awake. She had had to get the security guard to let her in. 'How you can sleep when you've just had the starring rôle in one of the most expensive demolition Derbys of all time is beyond me.'

'Was it really that bad?' He stretched his arms and sat up.

'Worse. I hope you like pizza.'

'Does it have onions in it?'

'I don't think so.'

'Then I like pizza.'

'Good. You may have to eat mine. I think I've lost my appetite.' She took some utensils from a kitchen drawer and began laying the table. 'I dumped the car in a multi-storey car park – one of BIG's as it happens – went back to BIG House, in through reception and straight up the stairs to the first floor. When there was no-one around I went down in the lift, emerging to find the car park looking as if a small earthquake had been getting in some practice before popping down to South America for the weekend. . . You can come and sit down now, Jeremy. . . Roach and Godfrey Daniels were screaming at each other and at half a dozen security guards, all claiming it had nothing to do with them. I had a job stopping myself laughing.

'When Roach saw me he asked – no, shrieked might be a better word – if I knew where you bloody well were. . . Tuck in. It seems to be mushroom with extra pineapple. Is that all right?. . . He wasn't awfully polite about you, I have to say. Used some very uncomplimentary words. When he claimed that you and your new car lay behind the scene of devastation, I was able to put him straight. . . Parmesan?. . . Not only did you not know how to drive, I enlightened him, a fact which you had been trying to communicate to him all day, but nobody had even thought fit to give you a car park pass, so you couldn't possibly have driven the car out. It must, I said truthfully, have been someone else who had access to the garage. In any case, I said, you had gone home feeling ill ages ago. So whoever had done this, it certainly wasn't you. . . Pepper?. . . That took the wind out of his sails.

'Then I said I was meeting you for supper and didn't want to be late. I waded through several inches of water coming from a pipe you had separated from its mounting, got in my car shaking like the proverbial leaf, and here I am. The odd thing was the way the new security man backed me up. He swore blind to Roach that he had been on duty at reception when you had gone past him an hour or so earlier. Then he winked at me. Drunk, I suppose.'

'It's awfully good of you to help out like this,' said Jeremy, in between mouthfuls of pizza. 'But don't you think it's a bit – well, unethical – for me not to own up?'

'If you keep quiet, it'll all be sorted out by the insurance company. If you don't, you'll probably end up on the street without a job and with the bill for the damage in your hand. It's not a question of ethics. It's one of survival.'

'I don't suppose I have any option, do I?' said Jeremy miserably, putting his knife and fork together. 'I should really thank you for all the trouble I've put you to.'

'Yes, you should,' said Sally, leaning across and grabbing a slab of unfinished pizza from his plate. 'Though I have to admit I did rather enjoy myself. Prosser will have a screaming meanie when he finds out what has happened to his precious car.'

'Why don't you like Mr Prosser?'

'Apart from the fact that he's boorish, lecherous, arrogant, bad-tempered, ruthless and a bully,' replied Sally, 'I also suspect him of being as bent as a nine-bob note, a crook of the first order.'

Jeremy was aghast. 'Surely not? He's one of the most respected businessmen in the country.'

'Respected? By whom? By the newspapers and magazines whose column inches pamper his giant ego? Big deal. What about all the companies he's bought up, bled dry and then thrown away? What about all the people he's thrown out of work? What about all the other businessmen whose careers he's destroyed? He has no conscience at all. Money and power are his motivating forces. If that makes him respected, then heaven help us. Oh, do close your mouth, Jeremy,' said Sally, losing patience.

'I agree he's tough, but that's. . .'

'Tough? Don't forget I've worked on the thirteenth floor for over six months. I've seen him at close quarters, closer than I might wish. He boasts about how he rules BIG through a blend of terror and greed. He enjoys frightening people. He gets a thrill out of sacking them. He even keeps a bird of prey on the roof as a pet. Jeremy, he is not a nice man.'

'That doesn't make him crooked,' he argued.

'No,' admitted Sally, 'it doesn't. But I'm convinced he is.'

'Pshaw,' said Jeremy dismissively. 'Not feminine intuition?'

'Don't you "pshaw" me. No, not *feminine* intuition. Just intuition, pure and simple. Its gender is unimportant.'

'Hah,' snorted Jeremy, as Sally picked up the plates and carried them through to the kitchen, banging them down loudly. 'I say, do you think I could use your, ah, little boys' room?'

'It's a little girls' room in this flat, Jeremy, and it's at the far end of the hallway.'

While he was gone, she opened a bottle of wine, taking it and two glasses over to the sofa. It was time to take him in hand.

Jeremy returned, somewhat agitated. 'That certificate hanging up in the little b. . . in the lavatory.'

'Yes?'

'Have you really got an MBA?'

'Yes,' said Sally, patting the place beside her.

'Golly,' said Jeremy, sitting down. A Master's degree in Business Administration. And from Harvard too. Then the books *were* hers. 'But I don't understand. What is somebody with your qualifications doing working as a secretary?'

'How many companies of any size do you know that are run by a woman? Having an MBA isn't enough, even these days. I thought that if I got close enough to study one of the best entrepreneurs in the country, it would be the quickest way to get on. If you're doing secretarial work, people behave as if you're not there at all. It's amazing what you can learn. When I started, I think I saw Prosser much as you do. I've had my eyes opened these past few months. The man is an abomination.'

This was all a bit much for Jeremy to take in at once. 'But having an MBA is wonderful. Why is it in the little boys'. . . where it is?'

'It's going to stay in the little boys' room for as long as the little boys won't let the girls come out to play. When I am a director of a decent-sized company, then it'll have pride of place here in the sitting room.'

'This place is amazing. You should see the dump I live in. How can you afford it on what you earn?'

'The company helps with the rent. Mr Prosser likes his personal assistants to be comfortable.' Perhaps it would be best not to tell him that Prosser's PAs got paid more than most of the company's board of directors. 'Drink?' she asked, moving closer to Jeremy as she handed him his glass.

'Do you have anything soft?' he asked.

'Why, Jeremy,' said Sally mischievously, 'what do you mean?'

He slid away, feeling increasingly uncomfortable. 'Do you have any soft drinks? I've never really got into the habit of drinking alcohol.'

'You don't drink, you don't smoke, you certainly don't drive. What else don't you do?' she asked slyly, looking deep into Jeremy's eyes as she nestled up to him.

He blushed deeply, edged away from her and took a sip from his glass to cover his embarrassment. 'It tastes quite pleasant. Is it very strong?'

'It shouldn't do you too much harm,' she said, inching further over. 'I've decided to fill in some of the areas of your education that you've missed out on.'

Jeremy tried to slide away again, but found himself up against the arm of the sofa. He was trying desperately to keep his mind firmly on mundane matters but, close to, Sally was proving even more distracting than at work. He took a gulp of wine. The top couple of buttons on her blouse were open and his eyes kept straying downwards. With a flash of inspiration, he pulled out his notebook and pen. 'You could start by telling me what this wine is,' he said, relieved.

She nestled up against him and put her arm along the back of the sofa, brushing her hand lightly against the hairs on the back of his neck. 'It's white Rioja. You spell that R-i-o-j-a. It's Spanish. But I wasn't only thinking of alcohol, Jeremy. There seem to be an awful lot of things you know nothing about.'

He jotted it down, trying to ignore Sally who had reached over and was kissing and licking his neck. 'I don't know very much yet about the organisational structure of BIG's head office. Perhaps you could talk me through it.'

'I wasn't thinking of organisational structure, either. If you want to grow up to be just like Prosser,' said Sally, nibbling gently on Jeremy's nearest earlobe, 'you've got to realise that there are other things than just work in which he is passionately interested.'

'I'd like to know more about his working practices. There is so much about them I don't yet understand.' Sally had now worked her way around to Jeremy's mouth. He was having to pull away to get his breath. This was all a bit bewildering. 'For instance,' he said desperately, recalling something else he didn't understand, 'the very first time I met Mr Prosser, one of his assistants, Lucinda, was hiding under his desk. She said she'd been looking for a contact lens but it's odd because I found out the other day she doesn't wear them. I've been puzzling ever since what she might have been doing.'

Sally looked hard at Jeremy. Could anybody really be as innocent as all that?

'You seem to have stumbled upon Prosser's favourite pastime. To be, frank, Jeremy, I hadn't intended broadening your horizons quite so widely so soon. But I suppose we can always go back and fill in some of the gaps later.'

'Oh,' he said, as she began the first lesson. 'Oh. . .oh. . .oooh.'

'And Prosser's personal assistants do that?' asked Jeremy afterwards.

'That and a lot more besides. They're his own little harem.'

'Gosh.' Jeremy's envy of Prosser moved up another notch. 'But you were one of them.'

'Don't get steamed up. I didn't see that sort of thing as part of my job description. I stuck strictly to secretarial duties. Why do you think Prosser handed me on to you?'

He gave Sally a chaste kiss, as he had seen countless actors do to countless actresses in old Hollywood films.

To Jeremy's surprise, she opened her mouth and began teaching him the rudiments of advanced osculation.

Sally, I've been wondering. This may sound like a stupid question, but am I. . .well, you know. . . am I still a virgin?'

'Actually that's quite an interesting question. I suppose technically you still are.'

149

'Oh.'

'I wouldn't worry too much about it. If you're amenable, we can soon do something about it.'

A few minutes later she asked crossly, 'Do you have to take notes about absolutely everything Jeremy?'

*** 17 ***

ROACH ENTERED Prosser's office to brief the great man on events while he had been away, to find him attacking three opened beer cans lined up on his desk.

Only when Prosser had downed the third did he speak. 'That's better. The beer out there was piss awful.'

Roach examined one of the cans. 'Why don't you ever drink BIG's beer?'

'You forget that I know what goes into it.'

'Did you have a good time?'

'I did, as a matter of a fact. But I'm not sure Mr Plod is going to enjoy his holiday.'

'He was hardly off the phone once we had declared our stake. Became quite officious when we told him you were unavailable. I put out some asinine statement through the Stock Exchange about it being a "trade investment". The usual guff. After you had rung to tell me where you were, I took the liberty of arranging for Ben Lobb, that union chappie at Pardoe's who did us such a good turn, to stay at the Cobbler's Lane during his "fact-finding mission" in Barbados. Ron arranged for a research assistant to accompany him. I thought Mr Plod might appreciate Lobb's company.'

'Brilliant. Let's hope we've done enough to goad him into action. My own bet is that the happy couple will be back within a day. There'll be one or two interesting photographs waiting for the master of the house on his return which should help to up his blood pressure.' Prosser took a swig of beer and pressed a button on his control unit. 'I see Pardoe's shares have taken quite a leap. Let's get Morrie to dump a few while we're sitting on a small profit. How's Gilbert Golly been getting on?'

'You'd better have a look at this,' said Roach, handing over a copy of *Business* magazine.

As Prosser read the article prepared by Jeremy, his hands began shaking. He tore the page from the magazine and screwed it up. Roach had rarely seen him so angry.

'What the hell is that moron trying to do? I'll be a laughing stock, an object of ridicule,' he screamed. '*Management Made Simple? The A–Z of Business Terms?* I might just about manage to live that down if he hadn't also told the readers of the biggest circulation business magazine on this side of the Atlantic that I am also an avid devotee of *Thomas the* fucking *Tank Engine*. I am going to tear that dickhead apart with my bare hands.'

'Hold on a second, Alex,' said Roach. 'You did tell him to write about what *he* was reading and that's just what he did. He seems to take instructions very literally.' Prosser was heading for the door. 'And before you rip his head from his shoulders, you ought to know that you've had fifteen calls of congratulations from various chairmen and chief executives, five invitations for after-dinner speaking and The Money Programme and Business Daily want to set up interviews with you.'

'What?'

'Everybody thinks it was intended as a joke. You're considered a great wit all of a sudden. It's done your image a power of good.'

'Fuck me. You don't think Seaman planned it like that, do you?'

'Not for a minute.'

'Thank goodness for that. I was worried he might be cleverer than we thought. Let's get him in here.' Prosser walked over to his desk and pressed a button on the speakerphone. 'Jeremy, could you come in here for a moment? . . . What did you say?'

Jeremy, who had been kissing Sally, broke off. 'Sorry, I was having a little nibble. Important to keep the brain cells fed. I'll be right with you.'

'Here. Something to give you courage,' said Sally, grabbing his tie to pull him towards her. 'Don't forget what I told you. You mustn't let him bully you. How's the head?'

'As long as I keep it perfectly still, there's no problem. It's only when I do something reckless like breathing that it gives me any trouble.'

'One glass of wine and you're anybody's! Go on, get off with you. And good luck.'

There appeared to be nobody at the reception desk.

'Hello?'

'Oh, hello,' said Charmaine, surfacing above the counter. 'I've lost me pen,' she explained. She had gone for blue today, with Turbulent Turquoise nails, Baby Blue eyeshadow and startling Incandescent Indigo lips. Her sudden appearance took the visitor aback for a moment.

'My name's Dipley. Felling Computers. I've an appointment with Mr Nettle in fifteen minutes. Bit early, I'm afraid. Still, early bird catches the worm, eh?'

'If you'd just take a seat,' said Charmaine, 'I'll tell Mr Nettle you're 'ere.' Where had that dratted pen gone?

Dipley forced his way through the jungle and balanced himself on one of the triangular stools, barely able to contain his excitement. Control yourself, Dipley, control yourself. This was the big one. The contract to re-equip BIG House. PCs on every desk. It had sounded almost in the bag on the phone. Get it right and the whole of British Industrial Group could be his for the asking.

'Can I help yer?' Charmaine asked the next visitor. Perhaps it had rolled under her chair. She tried feeling around with her foot.

'You certainly can, darling. Scholes of ZZZ Printers. I'm due to see Mr Nettle at half-past.'

'If you'd just take a seat, I'll tell him you're 'ere. Yes, can I help yer?' asked Charmaine, flustered. She hadn't even had a chance to pick up the phone yet. Dipley, Scholes. Dipley, Scholes, she repeated to herself over and over again.

'Mr Nettle is expecting me. Mr Bright of Metro Office Supplies.'

'Bright? Right. Take a seat,' said Charmaine. Dipley, Scholes, Bright. Dipley, Scholes, Bright.

The Major turned to the young security guard standing next to him. 'You'd better go and check out the car park. Don't want another catastrophe like yesterday's.'

The great man was seated behind his desk while Roach lounged on one of the settees.

'Jeremy, my dear boy,' said Prosser, 'I've just read your article. Very good. It struck just the right note. I'm impressed. So much so that I want you to do something else for me.' He patted a folder on the desk. 'My research boys have given me this bumf on some of the products they've been working on. I want you to take it away and have a look through it. I'd value your opinion. Let me know what

153

you think about each idea. A few hand written notes will be fine. Nothing too official. I'm sure I don't have to tell you how important secrecy is.'

Jeremy took the proffered file and then bent down, ostensibly to tie an errant shoelace. This gave him a chance to take a peek under the desk. Disappointingly, he could see nothing but Prosser's legs.

Dipley, Scholes, Bright, Pelham, Harbottle, Plush, Barrassford, Denham. She would scream if she didn't find that pen in a minute. And why didn't Nettle answer his phone?

At last. 'Mr Nettle,' blurted Charmaine, 'there's a Mr Dipley, a Mr Scholes, a Mr. . . ' Oh, damn. 'Those gentlemen you are expecting are waiting for you in reception.' She slammed the phone down. 'Yes?' She demanded.

'Good day to you, young miss. I wonder if you could tell Mr Nettle that I'm here? My name is Chewton.'

Charmaine buried her head in her arms and burst into tears.

Among the waiting salesmen, a certain restlessness was making itself felt. Pelham was sure he recognised Harbottle from somewhere. Barrassford, forced by the lack of chairs to stand, was convinced that Scholes had had a display at the recent Printers' and Typesetters' Fair at Olympia. Dipley, who felt superior to the others by virtue of having got there first, turned to his neighbour and asked, 'Salesman?'

Bright grunted in the affirmative.

'Ah,' said Dipley warily. 'I'm in computers,' he ventured.

'Office supplies,' admitted Bright. Both men breathed more easily. Not rivals at all.

'We're going to be given the contract to re-equip the whole of BIG House,' confided Dipley.

'Not if I've got anything to do with it,' said Pelham who, like all the others, had been eavesdropping. 'Mr Nettle is giving us the contract. Reliable Computers.'

'Reliable Computers? That's a joke. You should be prosecuted under the Trade Description Act for the name alone.'

'Stand up and say that,' dared Pelham. Dipley rose to his feet and repeated his aspersions. With an outraged roar, Pelham swung his briefcase into Dipley's midriff. Dipley, taken by surprise, managed to respond with a kick to Pelham's shin. Pelham dropped his briefcase, which landed on Harbottle's feet, and laid into

Dipley with his fists. His right felled the man from Felling Computers.

Harbottle tapped Pelham on the shoulder. 'That doesn't solve anything, my good man, because my firm, Computer Solutions, has already been told that *we* are to get the contract.' Harbottle ducked as Pelham swang. The punch connected with Chewton's jaw.

The violence escalated. Barrassford beat Scholes over the head with his briefcase. Harbottle poked his pen into Pelham's eye. Plush struggled to attach a bulldog clip to Harbottle's crotch. Chewton picked up a chair and threw it at Pelham. The chair hit Denton who retaliated by head-butting Chewton, getting his ear bitten in return.

Fresh arrivals, salesmen ready to offer BIG House the latest in telephones, filing systems, office furniture, photocopiers, computers, printing, stationery and vending machines were despatched by the weeping Charmaine through the jungle to the reception area where, with varying degrees of enthusiasm, they joined in the mêlée, assuming it to be some sort of initiative test.

Dipley had recovered from Pelham's blow and, stationing himself in the fountain, was hitting out at anyone who came within reach of his flailing fists. In front of him Scholes of ZZZ was having a zizz underneath a vending machine salesman whose soft drink samples had been thrown into the pool and were fizzing away merrily.

Only when he was sure that the blue touch paper was well alight did the Major call for reinforcements on his walkie-talkie. Mr Bennett dashed up the stairs from the canteen three steps at a time and, emerging in the foyer, instantly recognised the situation for what it was: a rugby game with none of those irritating rules to get in the way. Drawing upon his years of experience on the playing fields of South—east London he waded in, kicking, scratching, gouging, biting, spitting, hitting, butting and kneeing everyone who got in his way.

The Major picked up the phone and called the police. Thirty-five he made it. Five hadn't even turned up. It was disgraceful the cavalier manner some salesmen adopted towards potential clients.

Nettle stepped out of the lift, irritated at being called away from a heated meeting on the reclassification of Human Resources records. Although the distraught Charmaine's Turbulent Turquoise-tipped finger still pointed towards the waiting salesmen, Nettle could probably have found them without her help.

'What is going on?' he roared at the warring reps, stamping his foot futilely. The fracas continued unabated. The Major noted that a couple of motorbike messengers had, on their own initiative, decided to join the scrap. He felt their helmets gave them an unfair advantage.

'Stop it,' screamed the Head of Human Resources. And then he made a terrible mistake. 'My name is Nettle. I demand you stop it at once.'

Silence descended on the foyer of BIG House as abruptly as if somebody had pulled out the plug of a record player. For a moment, all that could be heard was the sobbing of Charmaine and the effervescing Cola-filled fountain. Then, with an almighty yell, the mob surged towards Nettle, each salesman vying for his undivided attention.

He turned and ran. The Major thought it wisest not to stand in his way. Nettle's fat little body came wobbling past, his clothes rippling as flab bounced in all directions. He threw himself at the Paternoster lift and landed in a cage, disappearing upwards. The howling pack thronged towards the lifts, pouring into the next compartment and the one after that and the one after that, wantonly disregarding the notice restricting passengers to six to a cage and kicking out at the hands of Mr Bennett and the other security guards trying to drag them back out.

The Major took advantage of the confusion to wander over to the nearest fire alarm. Unobserved, he smashed the glass.

The doors of offices were thrown open and, despite innumerable fire practices, the fleeing workers ignored the instructions not to use the lift and crammed into the Paternoster which duly gave up under the strain and juddered to a halt, its compartments stuck between floors.

As the fire alarm rang, the fountain fizzed, and those anguished souls stuck in the lift of what they believed to be a burning building screamed to the best of their lungs' ability, the might and majesty of the law arrived on the scene.

Entering through the revolving doors a solitary constable ambled over to the Major and Charmaine, removed his helmet and mopped his brow with his handkerchief. 'Been having a spot of bother, I understand?'

'WE'VE cracked it, Joe.' An excited Prosser came bustling into Roach's office.

'Then put a rubber glove on if you have to put your hand down it, Desirée. I can't unblock it from here, can I? Look, I have to go. Yes, yes. I love you too. Goodbye. . . Cracked what, Alex?'

'Fallas has just been on the phone. Pardoe's been seen coming out of Nostrum's head office.'

'Alex!' cautioned Roach, jumping up to close the door. 'Walls have ears and all that. Gilbert Golly and Miss Fluffy Cat are just next door, you know.'

'Oh, I am sorry, Big Ears,' said Prosser in a sing-song voice. 'Mr Plod has been to Mickey Monkey's house.'

'Good grief. You've done it, Alex.'

'Noddy, if you please. It certainly looks like it. Still, what else did Lady Amanda – sorry, Tessie Bear – have to bargain with but our desire to have Nostrum? She wouldn't have wanted to lose her husband, or at any rate his money.' Prosser sat down on the edge of the desk. 'You've got to hand it to old Plod. He really does believe in doing things the old-fashioned way. Who else these days bothers to see the head of a firm he wants to take over and asks politely if something amicable might not be arranged before the battle has even started?'

'Let's hope that Nostrum chooses to defend its honour, rather than give in gracefully.'

Lucinda's voice over the speakerphone on Roach's desk interrupted them. 'Is Mr Prosser with you?'

'Speak,' ordered Prosser.

'Mr Butterley is on the phone for you. He says he needs to speak to you urgently.'

157

'I'll bet he does. I'm on my way,' he said, winking at Roach as he made for the door. 'I'll just give him time to change into a new pair of underpants.'

Jeremy put down the glass and rubbed his ear.

'Anything?' asked Sally.

'Nothing I could make any sense of. I couldn't hear very clearly. Mr Plod came into it a few times and I heard mention of Gilbert Golly. Prosser mentioned something about a phallus . . . '

'That doesn't surprise me. He rarely thinks of anything else.'

'. . . and butter being needed urgently.'

'That sounds interesting.'

'Sally!' gasped Jeremy. 'Anyway, it hardly sounds like two master criminals plotting, does it?'

'What about these evaluations you've had to do for Prosser? New layouts for the petrol station forecourts, the children's building block, a computerised ticketing system for the multi-storey car parks, a new fizzy drink and all the rest?'

'Have you considered the possibility that he might genuinely want my opinion on these things?' asked Jeremy, indicating the file.

'Oh yes,' said Sally. 'I've considered and rejected it.'

'Thank you for your vote of confidence.'

'Jeremy, I think you're very sweet, but I can't believe that Prosser does too. There's got to be something here that explains it all.'

'We've been through it all time and time again. I can't hang on to it for much longer.'

Sally clicked her fingers. 'The drink. The fizzy drink. Of course, why didn't I think of it before? It's got to be something to do with that.'

'Why?'

'Because British Industrial Group doesn't make soft drinks, fizzy or otherwise. But Nostrum and Pardoe Trust both do. So why carry out an evaluation on a product your company is incapable of making?'

'That still doesn't imply anything illegal.'

'I've got an idea. Did you say you'd had a good scheme for the car parks.'

'Yes, but I'm not sure whether to add it to the report or not. It isn't terribly ethical, but it would boost revenues. You see, you begin paying from the moment you get your ticket and go through the barrier. As things are at the moment, the machines are arranged so that only those people who are going to be able to find spaces are let through. If, instead, you let more cars through, people would have to drive round for longer to find somewhere to park, and as the fee is computed from the moment they enter the place, revenue would go up considerably. Because the car parks would be more crowded, it would take longer for those on their way out to reach the exit so they would end up having to pay more, too. Across the whole group the gain could be significant.'

'That's quite ingenious,' said Sally. 'Prosser should definitely like that.'

'It isn't very nice, though.'

'Never mind. Put it down with all the others and then if Prosser doesn't get back to you about it, we'll see how interested he really is in your comments.' There was a knock on the door. 'Come in.'

Two trolley men stood there. 'Sorry, squire,' said one, 'didn't know there was anybody left in here. Won't be a moment.' The trolley men entered, positioned themselves at each end of Jeremy's desk, and lifted.

'What going on?' he demanded in alarm.

'This work station's got to go back to stores. Down your end, Jacko.'

'Why? What are you talking about? I need it. It can't go back to stores'.

'Our worksheet says it's got to go back to stores, so back to stores it's going. Over to your left, Jacko.' The Swiss cheese plant was knocked to the floor. 'No, sorry, your right.'

'On whose say so?' asked Jeremy.

'Mr Nettle's. That's it, Jacko. Now pull.'

'Right, I'll have a word with Mr Nettle,' retorted Jeremy, as officiously as he was able.

'He don't get out of the Middlesex Hospital for a few days yet. Close the door after us mate, would you?'

'I'll get on to Human Resources,' said Sally. 'You'd better get on with that report for Prosser. I shouldn't wait for them to get your desk back if I were you. You'd better use the floor.'

'Oh, well,' he said resignedly, 'at least I'll be able to get a better view of your legs from down there.'

'Jeremy! What has come over you?'

* * *

'But you've already done me once today,' the girl pleaded.

'I'm sorry, my dear,' lied Mr Bennett, running his hands over her body. 'But orders are orders. We're on maximum security alert until further notice, and that necessitates carrying out random body searches.'

'Why is it your so-called random searches concentrate on young female members of staff?'

'I really couldn't say, miss. What's that?' he asked, his stubby hands suddenly still.

'Well, if you don't know by now, I'm certainly not going to tell you. Now, if you don't mind, I've got work to do.'

Mr Bennett let her past. Getting Prosser to agree to random body searches had been an inspired idea. It was doing wonders for the morale of his staff, who embraced this extension of their duties heartily, not to say lustily. Finding volunteers for overtime was no longer a problem. What other job enabled you to fondle young ladies all over without fear of retribution? Only the Major, who although neither an officer nor a gentleman liked to pretend he was both, refused to enter wholeheartedly into what he saw as a rather distasteful activity.

Mr Bennett was in seventh heaven, transported back to his happy days at Gatwick with Customs and Excise. It was a little unfortunate for all concerned, but particularly for Tracey MacCullen, that things should have got so out of hand during a demonstration by him to his staff of the innumerable places on the female body where drugs or explosives could be concealed.

Mr Bennett still claimed that he did not know what all the fuss was about, maintaining proudly that he and his men were simply being thorough and that when they had finished with the girl there could be no question at all of her concealing anything upon her person. Human Resources did not take such a tolerant view. It had to cope not only with a sudden surge of resignations from female staff, but with threats of industrial action from the secretarial union.

This overreaction infuriated Mr Bennett. Every bloke in BIG House knew Tracey MacCullen was the office slag. What on earth was she complaining about?

He looked professionally at the pair of knockers that had just come through the revolving doors. They had to be false, he reasoned. Whatever she was harbouring under her sweater, it surely wasn't part of nature's bountiful treasures. He stepped forward. 'Excuse me, madam, but would you mind helping us with our security precautions? It won't take a minute.'

Prosser opened the door to the roof and stepped out into the sunlight. Butterley, along with the rest of the Nostrum board, had been told by chairman David Westbury of the merger offer from Pardoe, an offer which Westbury had peremptorily turned down without even bothering to consult his fellow directors. What, Butterley had demanded to know, did Prosser think he was playing at? Prosser's assurances that everything was going according to plan had done nothing to placate him.

Unaware that he was under close watch from Sebastian Embleton on the other side of the square, Prosser's podgy finger stabbed out Fallas's number. 'Noddy here.'

'I have been expecting your call. Do you wish to proceed?'

'I think the device should be procured in the manner discussed without delay. But you should wait until placing it. We don't want it discovered prematurely,' said Prosser.

'You can rely on me,' said Fallas. 'It will be done.'

For mine is the kingdom, the power and the glory, thought Prosser.

Time to give Maggie a little outing. It was a lovely day. The hunting should be good.

19

'NOSTRUM? They're 158–62,' said the market-maker still blurry-eyed into the phone, barely glancing at the screen in front of him. 'Make you that in a thousand, point out in five. . . Whaaat? Thanks, Jake. I owe you one.'

He snatched a microphone from the top of a nearby monitor and broadcast to the entire dealing room. 'Dawn raid. Bandits at eight o'clock. Cad's are bidding 185 for all the Nostrum stock they can lay their hands on.'

Among the salesmen seated behind their screen-bedecked desks, row upon row of them packed elbow to elbow in conditions that would cause battery hens to revolt, one or two broke off from their early morning calls and stabbed the button patching them straight through to their favourite institutional client. But if Cadwallader's were handling the business, any client who held the shares would know about the raid already.

'Shit,' said the market maker, as he adjusted upwards the price he displayed on the screen 'Shit, shit, shit, shit, shit.'

'What's the matter?' asked his neighbour.

'Fucking Nostrum is the matter, that's what. I'm short of two hundred thousand shares. Morrie Minchkin's bled me dry of the ruddy things. He's been picking them up for days. And I thought I was on to a nice little earner.' He hit his head against the screen.

'Has he now? Naughty Morrie.'

The market maker put his hands together. 'Please God, don't let there be a bid. If there isn't, I promise never to go over a hundred and twenty in the Porsche again.'

'Don't be a prat,' said his neighbour. 'You don't think Minchkin would be interested if there wasn't a bid on the cards, do you?'

* * *

'So how do I look?' asked Jeremy, giving Sally a twirl in his new suit as she prepared the breakfast.

'Not bad. Although considering that when I took you in you looked like someone who'd have been thrown off a Bulgarian trade delegation for insulting the country's sartorial reputation, it could hardly fail to be an improvement. I'm sorry it's only Marks & Sparks, but until we sort something out about your salary, Savile Row will have to hold its breath. Coffee?'

'Please.' Jeremy had moved in with Sally. There seemed little point in him spending money he hadn't got on a flat in which he spent no time.

'I can't thank you enough for all you've done, Sally.'

'It isn't charity. I expect to be paid. . . Shh!' she suddenly said, silencing him so that she could listen to the financial report on the Today programme.

'. . . were dull in Tokyo,' said the voice coming out of the radio, 'where the Nikkei average closed little changed. Here in London this morning, shares are similarly becalmed after Wall Street's lacklustre performance last night. The only company news of note is a dawn raid for the soft drinks firm Nostrum, whose shares have jumped twenty-five pence in response to an unknown buyer. Dealers say a full-scale bid is probably on the cards.'

'Did you hear that?' asked Sally triumphantly. 'What did I tell you? Come on, Jeremy. I want to get into the office to see what's happening.'

'Of course it's not BIG buying the shares, Morrie. Calm down, for goodness' sake. You'll give yourself another coronary. If they have to give you a transplant this time, you might get a gentile's heart by mistake. It would put you out of business.

'Anyway, you don't think we would use Cadwallader's, do you? Stuck-up blue-blooded twats who have to get their servants to wipe their bums for them? Much more likely to be somebody like Pardoe, if you ask me. Birds of a feather. Anyway, I don't want to buy Nostrum shares. I want to sell them.'

'Sell them? Alex, are you mad?' Prosser had to hold the handset away from his ear. 'There's bound to be a bid. You don't go around buying ten per cent of a company like Nostrum unless you intend to bid.'

'Morrie, I don't pay you to tell me how to run my business. I pay you to deal in shares. The market thinks there's going to be a bid. You think there's going to be a bid. I think there's going to be a bid. That's why I can now get forty pence more for Nostrum shares than BIG paid for them. That doesn't seem a bad turn to me.'

'But I thought you were going to bid for Nostrum.'

'Did you, Morrie? Did you really? I can't think what put that notion into your head. I'm sure I never said anything of the sort.'

'All right, all right, Alex. You're the client. So I'll sell the bloody things, but I. . . ah, it's just come up on the screen. You're right as usual. Pardoe Trust bidding for Nostrum. "One hundred and ninety-five pence, valuing the company at sixty-four million pounds". . . dee dum, dee dum, dee dum. . . "integral fit with Pardoe's existing drinks interests". . . dee dum, dee dum. . . "to be financed by the issue of shares". . . ah, here we are. . . "Together with existing holdings, after this morning's purchases Pardoe Trust now holds 14.9% of Nostrum plc." They certainly haven't wasted any time.'

'So much for the loyalty of the institutional shareholders.'

'I'd love to know how you knew Pardoe was going to bid.'

'Morrie, I'm surprised at you. It was just a hunch.'

'We should all have such hunches! I've obviously read the whole thing wrong. I thought *you* wanted Nostrum, but this way you'll just be helping Pardoe to get it.'

'Business before vendettas, Morrie, business before vendettas. Speak to you soon.'

Prosser tapped his fingers on the desk as he waited for the next call. It couldn't be long. The speaker buzzed.

'It's Mr Butterley for you, Mr Prosser.' He smiled. These people weren't businessmen. They were white mice being led round a maze by bits of cheese. And it was Prosser laying the trail.

'I'm not in, Jacqui. If you could manage to imply in your apology that I simply can't be bothered to talk to the likes of him, then so much the better.'

There was one more thing to be done before he could sit back and relax. Prosser climbed the circular stairs to the roof, tapping out the Cayman Islands number on his cellular phone. Through his secret dealings he owned over five per cent of Nostrum's shares. He had better get rid of them immediately. And if Pardoe ended up with them, so much the better.

* * *

164

'I don't understand it,' said Sally, shaking her head. 'I just don't understand it. I was convinced British Industrial was going to bid for Nostrum.'

'If you're wrong about that, couldn't you be wrong about everything else too?'

'Oh do shut up, Jeremy. I need to think. Why don't you do something useful?'

Exposed on his chair with no desk to protect him, Sally's attack stung all the more. Jeremy tried sulking, crossing his arms and scuffing the carpet with his feet, but she was engrossed in her thoughts and paid him no heed. He wandered out of the room and along to Prosser's office. Unusually, none of his personal assistants was on duty outside, so he knocked and entered.

Prosser and Lucinda were inside, on either side of the giant desk. It looked to Jeremy's eyes as if they were playing Tig, with Prosser, a banana in his hand, trying to catch Lucinda. He would feint first one way and then the other, while she kept as far from him as possible. As Jeremy entered she was screaming, 'No, Mr Prosser, not bananas. I'm sorry, but I absolutely draw the line at bananas.'

Prosser turned momentarily towards the door as Jeremy entered. Lucinda took advantage of the distraction and made a bolt for it.

'Thank you very much, Jeremy. Impeccable timing as usual. What do you want?'

'I'm sorry to interrupt, Sir. I just wanted to know if you had had a chance to look at my report yet.'

Prosser's mood changed abruptly from one of extreme irritation to fulsome admiration. 'Of course, of course. I'm most impressed with it, Jeremy, most impressed. The old brainbox is firing on all cylinders, I see. Particularly that stuff on the drink. It sounds fascinating. I think we might follow that one up,' he said, peeling the banana and stuffing it into his mouth.

'What did you think of my suggestion for the multi-storey car parks?' asked Jeremy.

Prosser looked blank. 'Car parks?' he muttered from behind a wall of banana.

Jeremy explained his idea to the tycoon.

'That's good, Jeremy my lad. That is very good. Why didn't my people. . . I mean, my other people. . . think of that? Tell you what, why don't you come and have lunch? Mr Roach and I like to invite a few people in from time to time, have a bit of a chin-wag, throw a few ideas into the air, bounce them around, see where they land, that sort of thing. You might enjoy yourself. Go and see Lucinda and tell her to put you on the list for the next lunch.'

Prosser noticed the light on his fax machine. His deals had already been carried out at very satisfactory prices. Morrie had dumped BIG's stake, too, so apart from one or two insignificant holdings, Prosser no longer had any Nostrum shares. Things were working out rather well. He transferred the information on to the computer disc around his neck, then fed the sheets into the shredder. Let the mice enjoy their cheese while they had the chance.

Mr Bennett was on duty in reception at BIG House, trying to ignore the infernal racket being made by the pneumatic drills right outside the door and to catch Charmaine's Happy Hyacinth-shaded eye. She had been very standoffish since that silly little episode with Tracey MacCullen. Lot of fuss about nothing. Wasn't even as if it was really his fault. The girl had led them on. Everybody knew she was always asking for it.

Mr Bennett's searches were having an even greater deterrent effect than he imagined. They were deterring most female members of staff from going anywhere near the security personnel. Unbeknown to the chief security officer, the ladies of BIG House were entering and exiting the building by clambering through a ground floor storeroom window, deeming the inconvenience preferable to running the gauntlet of Mr Bennett. As a result, his gauntlets had had very few female bodies to run over that morning. He passed up the opportunity presented by two spinsters in their fifties from the typing pool who had sauntered past him six times already in the hope that the Tracey MacCullen episode was not just an isolated incident.

The younger spirits, however, were still outraged at the treatment of poor Tracey. They had grown tired of the prevarications of Human Resources. No-one there seemed willing to take a decision in the absence of Nettle, whose stay in hospital showed no signs of coming to an end. So six of the girls decided to take the situation into their own hands. Bypassing Mr Bennett at reception Sharon, Elsie, Sandra, Barbara, Noreen and Tracey let themselves out of the storeroom window on to the pavement and headed off for Soho with a shopping list. The in-trays of the typing pool began to fill up.

* * *

'Mr Fallas, please.'

'Who shall I say is calling?'

'My name is Butterley.'

Fallas came on the line. 'How can I help you, Mr Butterley?'

'Your services have been highly recommended to me. Would any of your current cases prevent your taking on some work for my company, Nostrum, to keep a very close eye on both Sir Jocelyn Pardoe of Pardoe Trust and Alexander Prosser of British Industrial Group?'

'There is no conflict of interest that I am aware of.'

'In that case, Mr Fallas, consider yourself hired.'

Jeremy returned to his room and sat on the edge of the desk, blowing on his fingernails and rubbing them on his suit.

'That's a very smug expression. What's brought it on?' she asked.

'I've only been invited to lunch with Mr Prosser, that's all. To chew the fat, mull over my ideas with a few of his pals, that sort of thing.'

'In that case, I suggest you get in some drinking practice. Pretty rowdy affairs, Mr Prosser's power lunches.' Sour grapes, thought Jeremy. Pure sour grapes. 'Did he like your car park idea?'

'Once I'd explained it to him, he adored it.'

'Hadn't he read it?'

'He only seemed to have seen the stuff on the drink. Odd, that.'

'Or not so odd, depending on your point of view.'

'Don't keep going on about it, Sally. Just face up to the fact that you got it wrong.'

'If you say so. Full marks for wisdom. Zero for observation. Don't you notice anything different in here?'

'No.'

'Such as what you're sitting on.'

'My desk! Brilliant, Sally. How did you manage it?'

'The usual way anything gets done in this place. By bullying.'

There was a knock on the door. Jeremy opened it. Two trolley men stood there.

'Name of Seaman?'

'That depends,' said Jeremy warily, 'on whether you've come to take a desk away.'

'Not this time, squire.'

'In that case, yes, I'm Jeremy Seaman. How can I help you?'

'Don't need no help thanks, squire. Okay, Jacko. Lift.'

Jeremy was manhandled out of the way as the two men struggled to manoeuvre into the office another, significantly larger desk.

'I say,' protested Jeremy, 'you can't bring that in here. I don't need it. I've got my old desk back now. I'm quite happy. Just take it away.'

'Can't do that, squire. Worksheet says deliver executive work-station to this office, so that's what we've got to do. That's right innit, Jacko? Back a bit, then a push should do it.'

Behind him, Jeremy heard Sally sniggering.

'Stop it,' he turned and snapped, 'you never take anything seriously. Now look,' he said, 'I'm not going to let you bring that desk in here.'

'Too late for that, squire.' As he said it, Jacko gave a push and the enormous desk shot into the room. The trolleymen pushed it into the space between Jeremy and Sally's desk.

'This is silly,' said Jeremy exasperated. 'There's no room for the two of us and three desks. Surely you can see that? Oh, do be quiet, Sally. . . Won't you at least take this other one away?'

'Yes, we'll do that all right.'

'Thank goodness for that.'

'Just as soon as our worksheet says so.'

'Don't go. Please don't go,' pleaded Jeremy. The door closed behind them. 'Stop laughing, Sally. It isn't funny.'

'Of course it is, you clown. If your head hadn't swollen so much, you'd see that. Come on, let's go out and get some air. No, it's all right. I'll climb over.'

On the window ledge, the house martin, as curious as ever, shook his head in disbelief. He'd never seen such an uncomfortable nest in his life. Where were the young going to live? Had they thought about that?

Giggling hysterically, the girls climbed in through the storeroom window and spread their booty out on the floor. The natural indecision of six females on a shopping expedition had been exaggerated by the nature of their purchases. Noreen dare not admit that she still didn't understand what one or two of them were for.

Tracey, as the wronged party, had appointed herself leader of the group. 'Right, have we got everything? Lipstick, bag, superglue, bin-liner, ball, batteries? You did get alkaline, didn't you? We don't want them running out too quickly. Charmaine knows what she has to do, doesn't she?'

Sharon looked at her watch. 'She'll be moving about now.'

'All right girls,' said Tracey, 'let's go and strike a blow against sexual harassment in the workplace, particularly when it comes from fat, greasy, slobs.'

Charmaine left her desk and wandered over to Mr Bennett, who puffed up his chest as she approached. He'd known she wouldn't be able to keep up the cold shoulder stuff for long. Charmaine licked her Gorgeous Grape lips as she had seen it done umpteen times on Dallas and reached out towards Mr Bennett. She took his tie and began playing with it, diverting his attention from Sharon, Elsie, Sandra, Barbara, Noreen and Tracey creeping up behind him. As the bin-liner went over Mr Bennett's head, Charmaine pulled the tie sharply, so that the knot tightened around his neck.

'What's going on? Help. Terrorists. We're under attack,' yelled the blinded and choking Mr Bennett as, arms held firmly, he was propelled forwards by six pairs of hands. As they disappeared through the door of the ladies' lavatory, Charmaine hung up the 'Out of Order' sign, turned on her heel and returned to her duties.

Struggle as he might, the bewildered Mr Bennett could not prevent the removal of first his shoes and socks, then his jacket, tie, shirt and vest and finally his trousers and underpants. The echoing walls rang with coarse laughter as ribald comments were exchanged on the nature and proportions of Mr Bennett's tackle, remarks that would have been considered near the knuckle even in the changing room of the Lewisham Leopards. On the reception desk, Charmaine turned up the musak to drown out Mr Bennett's cries for help.

A rubber bodice was crammed down over his body, pinioning his arms to his sides.

'See, I told you it was the right size,' crowed Elsie.

Tracey reached up inside the bin-liner, fastened the blindfold in place and then ripped the plastic away. With the other girls holding his legs, Barbara and Noreen got first one, and then the other of

169

Mr Bennett's feet inside the legs of the crotchless panties and pulled them on. Stockings and suspenders followed.

'I still think it's a shame we couldn't find a pair of high-heel shoes in size eleven,' said Sharon.

Elsie took her parcel over to one of the lavatory seats, sat down and began blowing.

'It isn't going to work with his thingie limp like that and I'm certainly not going to touch it,' said Barbara.

'You won't have to,' said Tracey. 'Bend him over. Ready, Sandra? I'm going to enjoy this bit.'

Tracey MacCullen moved behind the security officer and, as the girls pushed his shoulders down, she switched on the vibrator and, with all the force she could muster, slammed it into Mr Bennett. As he opened his mouth, roaring with shock as much as with pain, Sandra popped the rubber ball inside, effectively preventing him from participating any further in the conversation.

'See? That's done the trick all right,' said Tracey gleefully. 'Just look at that.'

The girls did, marvelling at the extraordinary effect the vibrator was having. 'It seems a shame really,' said Sharon. 'Shouldn't we just. . . ?'

'No, we bloody well shouldn't!' said Tracey. 'This is supposed to be a punishment. Honestly, the minds of some people. Now, where's that spray?'

Noreen handed over the ozone-friendly can of *Stallion Delay*. Loud gurgling noises were heard from Mr Bennett as the contents of the entire can were sprayed over his tumescent member, anaesthetising it.

'Do you think it hurts?'

'Oh, I do hope so,' said Tracey, with feeling. 'Where's the superglue?'

'The condom's next, surely?' said Barbara.

'Let's just put the glue straight on.'

Barbara shuddered with horror at the thought. 'Ooh, you can't.'

The other girls, wincing, agreed. So did Mr Bennett, struggling violently, although his opinion was not sought in the matter.

'Oh, all right,' said Tracey sulkily. 'But I'm not putting the horrible thing on.'

'Give it to me.' Barbara took the rubber out of its packet.

'Go on,' ordered Tracey. 'Don't worry about him. He's not going to feel a bloody thing.'

Eyes averted, Barbara sheathed Mr Bennett.

'Done it,' said Elsie, triumphantly from her cubicle.

All eyes turned to the fully-inflated Wanda the Wonder-Doll, Servant of Your Desires.

'It's ghastly,' said Noreen, speaking for them all.

'Come on,' said Tracey. 'We've a job to do. Superglue first.'

Superglue was smeared over the condom and, with a cheer, Wanda was rammed into union with Mr Bennett.

'Not bad,' said Tracey, admiring their creation. 'Not bad at all. Just the lipstick and we're done.'

Mr Bennett was bewildered by the turn of events. One minute he had been standing calmly on duty. The next, he had been abducted by terrorists. Except they had not been terrorists, but Tracey MacCullen and her cronies. He almost wished they had been terrorists. Terrorists wouldn't have stripped him and shoved some buzzing thing up his rectum. Goodness knows what the bitches had done to his prick. He couldn't feel the thing at all. He shuddered at the thought of the damage they might have wrought with the superglue.

Mr Bennett could tell he was in the foyer. He could hear the fountain. If he kept that to his left and headed for the security office, the lads would help him. With luck nobody else would see him.

Charmaine, waiting behind the reception desk, had not known what to expect. The sight of a blindfolded Mr Bennett, a ball stuffed in his mouth, clad in rubber bodice, panties, stockings and suspenders, blundering out of the ladies' lavatory with the voluptuous Wanda the Wonder-Doll borne before him, was bad enough. But what was that terrible buzzing noise coming from him? Charmaine's was a delicate temperament. She ran screaming from her post.

Mr Bennett's hope of remaining unobserved faded with Charmaine's piercing scream. But he refused to be panicked. Remaining calm, he inched his way across the foyer, feeling where he was going with his feet.

It seemed a shame to Tracey MacCullen that their magnificent handiwork would be admired by so few. She smashed the glass of the fire alarm.

Now Mr Bennett panicked. He had no wish to be burnt alive. Terror-stricken, he ran forward at full tilt and, to his surprise, bounced off a wall. He ran in another direction only to find himself springing back again.

Quite an audience gathered to watch the spectacle. No-one rushing to the ground floor at the behest of the fire alarm seemed in a hurry to leave the building. But then, there wasn't actually any smoke and it isn't every day you see a fetishist security officer bearing a sex doll on his penis meandering blindfold around the foyer with 'rapist' scrawled in lipstick over his rubber bodice.

Mr Bennett moved forward gingerly. There had to be a simple explanation for his bouncing off walls. He kept coming up against something squishy. Those bloody women must have attached something to him. He had no idea what it was, nor for the life of him could he work out how it was fastened on.

A terrible thought occurred to Mr Bennett. Surely not. They couldn't have done. He blundered to the left, once again bouncing off something. His growing audience laughed, cheered, whistled and stamped its appreciation of his efforts. Mr Bennett was quite obviously no longer alone.

At this point, BIG's chief security officer went completely to pieces. He fled in the opposite direction to the noise.

It was a mistake. Mr Bennett ran straight towards the foliage lavishly strewn around the reception area.

The forest of yuccas, with their pointed leaves, lay in wait for him.

With the most dramatic bang of her short working life, Wanda the Wonder-Doll exploded.

* * * 20 * * *

WITH the dismissal of Mr Bennett from British Industrial for conduct exceedingly unbecoming, and the promotion of the Major to the post of chief security officer, the spate of disturbances inexplicably ceased.

The Major was a changed person. He found that he enjoyed being a cog in the British Industrial machine. He relished opening his paper in the morning and reading of yet another company which had been swallowed, slimmed, slaughtered or shut by BIG, in deals which he would explain to Rommel over breakfast. But relations between the two had grown more distant and the dachshund, becoming fat through lack of exercise, did not stir itself to reply.

Jeremy meanwhile blossomed under Sally's care and tutelage. It would be going too far to say that he was a new man, but he was certainly a less reticent and insecure one. Despite the assurance of Nettle, now returned from the Middlesex Hospital, that his salary would be sorted out any day now, Jeremy still depended on her financial support. Prosser consulted him frequently and although he and Sally still disagreed on the honesty or otherwise of the head of British Industrial Group, everything else in the garden was rosy.

Pardoe's bid for Nostrum rumbled along in the background. As many another takeover bid, it progressed like one of those cycle races in which the competitors dawdle around the track until somebody's nerve cracks, whereupon there is a sudden, mad dash for the finishing line. No-one would commit himself to either side until the very last moment. It was clear, however, even to David Westbury and Jack Butterley, that the bid was going Pardoe's way. Nostrum had shunned the City for too long to be able to rally support effectively, particularly as the other members of the Westbury clan were showing as much family loyalty as the Borgias. Pardoe Trust built up its stake in the company to nearly thirty per cent and, as the closing date for the bid approached, it was clear that Nostrum's days of independence were numbered.

David Westbury's spirit was broken. For weeks, the chairman of Nostrum had been woken in the early hours of the morning by mysterious callers; he appeared to be followed wherever he went; his house was burgled at least twice and, although his valuables were left untouched, assorted business papers disappeared. What other explanation could there be but that Pardoe was not the gentleman he appeared? Yet without proof, David Westbury could do nothing. The expensive services of Fallas's agency, brought in by Butterley, had turned up nothing that was even remotely of interest.

If David Westbury was distraught, Jack Butterley was beside himself with worry. When Pardoe succeeded in his bid then Butterley, the finance director, would no doubt be one of the first to get his P-45. Bang would go his chances of glory with Fizzical. Well, he had made up his mind. If Nostrum went, so did Prosser. Butterley had enough on him to blow him out of the water. But rather than drag them both down, it would be better to find some driftwood to cling to.

'Alex, you've got to do something to help.'

'Jack, I'd like to help you. Really I would,' lied Prosser, 'but Pardoe has got the whole thing sewn up as tight as a virgin's pussy.'

'You could lick him with one hand tied behind your back,' said Butterley.

Prefer to lick his wife with both hands tied to the bedposts, mused Prosser. 'I've run the numbers through time and time again,' he said wearily, 'and frankly the biggest stumbling block is this damned one per cent royalty you want on sales of Fizzical. Eats right into the profit margin.'

'All right, Alex. You win.' Butterley choked on the words. 'If you step in, I'll cut it to a half per cent.'

'Jack, if only I could,' said Prosser sympathetically. 'But things have changed a great deal since you first came to see me. Pardoe only needs a couple of big institutions to commit themselves irrevocably and he's won. It could be tough. A quarter of one per cent seems far more reasonable.'

'I suppose I don't have a choice. But can I have your word that that figure is final?' One day he would have the chance to get even with Prosser. He would look forward to that moment.

'Of course, Jack. A quarter per cent it is.'

With that remarkable degree of trust which characterises the dealings of two honest English businessmen, a pair of machines recorded every detail of the conversation.

It was the day of the great lunch. Jeremy, who had left the flat early to get into work, found as the morning wore on that he was becoming increasingly jittery. He remained in considerable awe of Prosser and knew that, in addition to him and Roach, an institutional fund manager and another industrialist would be lunching. As he told Sally, he was determined to make a good impression.

'In that case, you'd do best to keep quiet the whole time.'

'That isn't very nice.'

'I'm serious,' she said. 'If you sit still, smile, and say nothing the others will be left with the impression that you are terribly wise. Open your mouth and someone is almost certain to disagree with what you have to say. Don't forget how much experience there is around that table. Oh, and don't leave anything on your plate. Ron Niblo can get very grumpy with people who appear not to like his food. A journalist who didn't eat up his greens had to go straight from here to Casualty – and it wasn't food poisoning he was suffering from.'

Jeremy shuddered at the thought of the lumbering Niblo. It had been he whom Sally had persuaded to remove the superfluous desk, lifting it singlehanded as if it had been balsa wood. Jeremy was proud of the new one, which was identical to the desk Prosser had in his own office. Just sitting at it made coming to work each day a pleasure.

'Why doesn't Prosser have a proper cook?'

Sally stuffed a letter into an envelope before answering. 'The man's obsessed with security. He's terrified that somebody might try to kill him. There must be plenty of people who would like to see him dead. That's why he prefers flying to travelling by road. Can't be avoided altogether, of course. He bought a London taxi once so that he could pass through the London traffic unnoticed, but his ego couldn't stand the anonymity. Now he's got the bulletproof Rolls.'

She stuck down the flap of the envelope. 'Some time back he read of an Italian businessman being poisoned, so he won't let even his PAs touch his food. Niblo's the only person he trusts to prepare it.

175

Actually, his cooking's not all that bad. A bit institutional perhaps, but not bad. Prosser says he learnt it in Wormwood Scrubs.'

Sally threw the letter into the mail basket. 'Come on then, let's have a look at you. Get out from behind that desk.'

Jeremy did as he was told. 'Well, do I pass muster?'

She leant her head on her cupped hands. 'It really was terribly sweet of you to get dressed in the dark this morning, so that you didn't wake me. The jacket I chose for you looks good. The trousers I chose for you look good. Together, they look terrible. You're wearing two different suits, you noodle!'

On the roof, Prosser phoned Morrie Minchkin.

'Yes, Alex?'

'Morrie, I'm a little worried about Pardoe Trust. We still hold quite a few. I get the feeling they could go down at any moment. Begin unloading them as carefully as you can.'

'I'll give it my attention just as soon as I get back from lunch.'

'I'd rather you didn't go out to lunch.'

Morrie chuckled. 'I'll send for sandwiches. You know that with a bid in progress, you'll have to declare what you've done tomorrow? That could send the price down.'

'Grannie doesn't need you to teach her how to suck eggs, Morrie.'

'I thought Grannie was happier sucking blood.'

'Goodbye, Morrie.'

He cut the line and dialled Fallas.

'Noddy here. Is everything ready?'

'It is.'

'Fine. I'll inform Wobbly Man immediately, and let you know when the drop is to be.'

'As you wish.'

Prosser stared at the disconnected phone for a moment. This was it. He normally never felt nerves of any sort, but now he could feel his hands becoming clammy. He wiped them on his trousers then rang Nostrum. Unconsciously, he crossed the fingers of his left hand.

'Jack Butterley, please.'

'Who shall I say is calling?'

'His brother.'

'One moment please.' The operator's voice disappeared, to be replaced with an electronic rendering of 'Hail the Conquering Hero'.

'Hello?' Butterley sounded puzzled.

'Do you recognise my voice?'

'Yes of course, Al. . . I'm a little surprised to hear from you so soon, brother.'

'Is David Westbury in the building?'

'I think so.'

'Take him into the boardroom. You have something very important to talk to him about.'

'I have?'

'There is a glass ashtray on the boardroom table. While you are talking, knock it onto the floor, shattering it into little pieces.'

'What will that achieve?'

'Salvation, little brother, salvation. Now if you excuse me, I have a lunch to attend.'

'Mineral water!' exclaimed Prosser. 'Nonsense, my boy. You won't impress me by asking for a soft drink, Jeremy. Alcohol's good for the brain. Everyone knows that. Have a beer.'

Prosser gave the reluctant Jeremy a frothing pewter tankard and led him over to the others. 'Let me introduce you,' he said, breaking straight into the conversation. 'Gentlemen, this is Jeremy Seaman, Director of our Think Tank and one of the brightest of our bright young men. Jeremy, this is Max Milton. Max runs Argent. He's into lingerie in a big way. Max has had his hand in a substantial proportion of the knickers in the country, so to speak.' The others all chuckled dutifully at the joke. Jeremy shook hands with Milton, a red-faced man in his fifties sporting long sideburns and with heavily-lidded, very weary-looking eyes.

'And this is Bernie Korngold, head of fund management at Empire Assurance. One word from Bernie and millions of pounds can be added to or wiped off a share price. Empire's one of our biggest shareholders, so we have to be especially nice to Bernie.' Korngold was extremely sun-tanned. His freckled bald head shone under the lights of the room and gold chains on his wrist clanked as Jeremy shook his hand, trying to look as unobtrusive as possible in case anybody noticed that the pinstripes did not extend below his waist.

'Bernie's just come back from a little sailing holiday,' explained Prosser. 'How was it, Bernie?'

'Wonderful, but exhausting, Alex. One long round of bonking, for which many thanks.'

Prosser turned to Jeremy. 'A nautical term, I think.' The others laughed, to Jeremy's bewilderment. Prosser led Korngold over to the table. 'Pas devant les enfants, eh, Bernie?'

'You clumsy clod, Butterley. Now look what you've done.' David Westbury gave his finance director a withering glance. He was a tidy man and liked a tidy boardroom, at least while it was still his. He got to his knees to pick up the bits of broken glass.

Butterley stared at the floor. It was just an ashtray, a broken ashtray. Nothing more, nothing less. So much for Prosser. He got to his knees and helped his chairman gather up the bits.

'Careful, man. You've missed a bit.' Westbury really was tetchy these days. 'Over there, under the table.' Butterley scrambled after it.

'Bloody hell,' said Westbury. 'What on earth is that?'

Butterley followed his boss's gaze. 'That, David, if I am not very much mistaken, is our salvation.'

It was a boast of Prosser's that British Industrial Group ran like a well-oiled machine. By the time the pudding, spotted dick, arrived at the table, its boss was similarly well-oiled. His luncheon guests were also fairly merry. This was no Perrier and salad repast, but full blown three-course English stodge. Jeremy had been glad to sit down, hiding his trousers, and had followed Sally's advice, staying as quiet as a mouse throughout the entire meal. He had little option. There was no way he could have joined in the conversation, even if he had wanted to. Prosser, Korngold and Milton's chief topic was not business or politics but sex. They discussed women in a most ungentlemanly manner. They boasted of women they'd had, women they wished they'd had and women they were glad they hadn't had. Although Jeremy noticed that Roach didn't join in that part of the table talk he was perfectly happy to throw in the odd smutty joke along with the others. To Jeremy's dismay, Prosser was the worst, regaling the gathering with an endless stream of filthy stories.

Jeremy ate the food that was put before him, making sure he cleaned every scrap from his plate, and drank the drink that was poured into his glass. By the time the liqueurs came round, he was as sozzled as the rest. Unfortunately, the alcohol did nothing to alter the barrack-room flavour of the conversation. Only isolated snatches made their way through to Jeremy's subconscious.

'Oh, God, I've left the bairn on the bus!' roared Prosser at one point, and 'So I said, "Come and have a ride on my chopper" and the stupid bimbo thought I meant the helicopter!' Towards the end of the proceedings, Jeremy's head suddenly cleared.

'That was the condition, you see,' spluttered Prosser, as he poured some more Kümmel into his glass. 'Wendy would only sleep with him if he had her name tattooed on his prick. He agreed, only to discover that it only said "Wendy" when it was erect. When it was limp, you could just see "W" and "Y". Come on, Jeremy, drink up. You're falling behind. Then one day he was in the bog at a pub and this big black bloke comes in and stands next to him. Our man's peeing away happily when he looks across and sees that the coon's got "W" and "Y" tattooed on *his* prick. "Bloody hell," he says, "don't tell me you know Wendy?" "What you talking about, honky?" says the darkie. "You've got Wendy tattooed on your John Thomas," points out our chap. "That ain't no Wendy tattoo, honky," says the coon. "Watch." He has a quick wank, unveiling the full message: "Welcome to Jamaica. Have a nice day." Come on, Jeremy, loosen up. That's what's called a joke.'

Jeremy smiled weakly. Surely it couldn't be long until this ordeal was over and he was allowed to leave? He was desperate to go to the lavatory.

'Cigar, Jeremy?' A thick Havana was thrust into the mouth and a light applied to the other end. Jeremy had never smoked before but it didn't seem too difficult. Breathe through one end and the other end glows. Easy, peasy.

No reason, come to think of it, why jokes had to be dirty. Plenty of clean jokes. He had never really gone in for joke-telling in a big way but there flashed into his mind a long-forgotten riddle from childhood.

'I've got one,' mumbled Jeremy.

'Take the cigar out of your mouth first, kid,' advised Milton.

'I've got a joke for you.' Jeremy glared at Milton. Stupid man. Didn't he realise he looked like a Thunderbirds puppet?

'Come on, then,' said Prosser. 'This should be good, lads.'

Jeremy burped. 'Alright, answer me this. Why do elephants have big ears?'

Korngold leaned towards him. 'I don't know. Why *do* elephants have big ears?'

'Because,' said Jeremy, beaming, 'Noddy won't pay the ransom.'

Roach's glass shattered on the table top. He and Prosser stared at each other in alarm. Korngold and Milton merely groaned.

Jeremy noticed none of this. He got to his feet, steadying himself by holding on to the table. He hiccoughed. "scuse me. Got to see a man about a leak.'

A worried Roach turned to Prosser and asked quietly, 'What was all that stuff about Noddy and Big Ears. And what did he mean by a leak?'

'I don't know, but I think I'd better find out. Keep our friends happy while I'm gone.'

Even though Minchkin lived off his ability to find out anything and everything that was happening in the stock market, he had to hand it to Prosser. For an outsider, he had impeccable sources. Pardoe's shares were strong that morning, with several institutional buying orders outstanding. It wasn't too difficult to feed out BIG's stake to the waiting jaws of the fund managers. The exercise had gone off with hardly a ripple in the Pardoe share price.

But in the early part of the afternoon, shares in both Pardoe Trust and Nostrum began to fall back and, to his intense frustration and annoyance, Minchkin couldn't pin down the story that lay behind it. It was the stock market reporter of the *Evening Standard* who gave the first indication that a bugging device had been discovered in Nostrum's boardroom. This was confirmed by a statement put out by the company on the Stock Exchange's TOPIC news system. On the advice of Nostrum's lawyers, the message was bland, pinning the blame on an 'unknown party'. The Police were being called in to investigate.

City dealers may not be renowned for their original thinking, but it didn't need an Einstein to put two and two together and come up with the answer Pardoe Trust. Who else could possibly want to put a bug in the Nostrum boardroom? The shattering of the hitherto unblemished image of Pardoe sent the shares falling sharply, and with them Nostrum. The offer for Nostrum was in the form of the now rapidly devaluing Pardoe shares, and there were fears that the bid itself might be in jeopardy.

* * *

'Enjoy lunch, Jeremy?' Prosser unzipped himself at the next urinal. Jeremy, in the midst of ridding himself of some of the drink consumed over the past two hours, could only mumble in return. He still had the blasted cigar, and, even though it was making him feel more than a little queasy, with both hands occupied the only place he could find to put it was in his mouth.

'Mmm,' he answered, unwillingly. Every time he breathed, his lungs filled with more of that pungent smoke.

'I think it went off well, don't you?' asked Prosser.

'Mmm.' Would Prosser think it rude if he just threw the foul-smelling thing away?

'Interesting joke of yours. Did it, uh, have any other meaning that I didn't understand?'

'Mmm?' Jeremy groaned loudly.

'Is that a yes?' Alarmed, Prosser turned, forgetting where he was.

Jeremy jumped back sharply from the unexpected torrent assailing him. 'Look what you're doing,' he yelled instinctively, sending the cigar flying from his mouth. He didn't care where it landed.

Prosser did, though. Despite the anaesthetising effect of the alcohol, he could feel it. He could even smell burning flesh. He screamed loudly.

Jeremy took one look at Prosser's face, contorted in agony, risked a quick peek at the spot where the cigar had landed, and fled from the lavatory.

He tried explaining to the other luncheon guests what had happened, but they merely found the situation funny, collapsing in hysterics, particularly when Milton pointed out Jeremy's trendily uncoordinated line in suits.

He wandered off to tell Sally, only to have her react as if her premium bonds had come up trumps, running round the room, embracing him and screaming with laughter. 'You did what? Oh my God, that's brilliant! First-degree burns on his pecker. Oh, wait till I tell the girls. I can just see the headlines. "Seaman's Smoke Singes Tycoon's Schlong". Damn, I can't think of anything for Prosser beginning with an "s" sound. What about "Prosser's Pecker Parched by. . ." ? No, that doesn't work, either.'

'Sally, don't you dare tell anybody. It isn't funny. Mr Prosser is obviously in great pain. I have to find the First Aid kit quickly.'

'I'll get it. Putting iodine on that thing will give me great pleasure.'

Jeremy drew himself up. 'You most certainly will not.'

'Oh, all right,' she said huffily. 'I suppose I should be pleased you don't want me to go. I'll send Lucinda in. She'll no doubt kiss it better for him. Jeremy? Jeremy, are you all right? You don't look too good.'

The cigar had claimed another victim. Jeremy rushed to the windowsill and was sick into the Swiss cheese plant.

* * * 21 * * *

SIR JOCELYN PARDOE shaded his eyes from the glare of the television lights. Unseen behind him someone held a large golfing umbrella over his head to protect the papers in his hand from getting damp in the evening drizzle. His normally urbane manner was beginning to fray slightly under the onslaught of repetitive and asinine questions. 'Surely I have already answered that in my prepared statement? This board would never countenance or condone any such surreptitious operation. The bug, if it exists, has nothing to do with us at all.'

'Ewer, BBC,' shouted the infamous reporter, now known around the Corporation and in *Private Eye* as Urine Ewer. 'If the bug wasn't planted by Pardoe Trust, who did plant it?'

'I am not sure it would be right for me to speculate. However, I find it fortuitous that the device should be discovered at such a crucial stage of the takeover bid. So helpful and so convenient, don't you think?'

'Will Pardoe Trust withdraw its bid in the light of the discovery?' pressed Ewer.

'The rules governing takeovers are very strict and it would be quite wrong for me to say too much on that subject. But we see no reason not to proceed with the bid. Each and every board member has assured me that he has no connection with the incident. I am sure all our directors are gentlemen and their word is good enough for me.' Pardoe ignored the spate of questions which continued to be directed at him. 'You must all be getting very wet, ladies and gentlemen. I really have nothing more to add, so I had better say good night.' And with that he, and the other members of his entourage, turned back up the steps and disappeared into the head office of Pardoe Trust.

As Justin Ewer was summing up the situation as he saw it, Sally clicked the remote button to turn the television off and turned to

183

Jeremy, lying in bed beside her.

'Aren't you interested?'

'All I'm interested in,' groaned the ailing Jeremy, 'is trying to get some sleep. Please can we have the light out now? Anyway, I heard all about it at lunchtime. They were talking about it then.'

'Really?' asked Sally excitedly. 'What time would that have been?'

'Keep your voice down. Somewhere in the main course, I think. Probably just after the one about the Bishop and the cast of Macbeth. What does it matter what time?'

'Don't you see, birdbrain? Where's the *Standard*?' She reached across Jeremy, who moaned loudly as she leaned on him for support. 'Oh, you are a baby,' she said, rapidly turning the pages of the newspaper. 'Here we are. "The news, revealed to the market at two-thirty, caused a sharp reaction", et cetera, et cetera. You were being sick into the Swiss cheese plant then. Surely that proves it?'

'I've told you, something I ate disagreed with me. Proves what?'

'That either Prosser or Roach had prior knowledge of the bugging. Your main course must have been well before two o'clock.'

'Sally, Prosser probably has far better sources of information than the *Evening Standard*. Anyway, it's pretty obvious that Pardoe's lot had something to do with it. What possible reason could there be for Prosser to be involved?'

'I don't know yet. But I'll work it out.'

'Can you *please* work it out with the light off. . . Thank you and good night.'

'Good night,' came the grumpy reply from the darkness.

'Sally?'

'What?'

'Do you know anything about sailing?'

'A little. Why?'

'What's bonking?'

'You're kidding, aren't you? What makes you think it has anything to do with sailing?'

'Prosser told me it was a sailing term. Whatever it is, Korngold of Empire Assurance kept thanking Prosser for it. Strange, he didn't look the sporty type.'

'Korngold of Empire Assurance was thanking Prosser for fixing him up with some bonking?'

'Yes. It was something to do with a big princess.'

'Some research into Empire is called for. They're obviously involved in all this.'

'Stop talking in riddles. What is bonking?'

'Tell me, Jeremy. Does the bed feel as though it's whirling through space?'

'Yet it does. I feel ghastly.'

'In that case, I don't reckon your navigation skills would be up to it at the moment. I'll explain in the morning. Good night, Jeremy.'

* * * 22 * * *

'HOW ARE YOU feeling today?'

'I warn you, one giggle – just one giggle out of you, Big Ears – and I won't be held responsible for my actions.'

Roach tried to keep his eyes away from the bandaged bulge in Prosser's trousers. 'It still hurts, then?'

'Of course it bloody hurts! Wouldn't your plonker hurt if some half-witted cretin used your crotch as an ashtray?' Prosser's voice became soft and menacing. He picked up a pencil from his desk. 'I'll tell you one thing, though. Whatever happens, I am going to get even with that sod, one way or another.' The pencil snapped in two. 'The only thing cheering me up is reading about Sir Jocelyn's inquisition at the hands of the press. Poor man. So his board are all composed of gentlemen, eh? We'll see about that.'

He turned to the monitor displaying London share prices. 'I see the market still thinks a gentleman's word is his bond. Look at that. The shares are practically back to yesterday's level. Is that yours or mine?'

'Mine,' said Roach, picking up his ringing cellular phone from Prosser's desk. 'Roach here. Hello, Desirée. What a surprise.' He grimaced at Prosser. 'So the nanny's sick. What am I supposed to be able to do about it from five miles away?. . . No, of course I can't look after the ruddy children. . . A tennis lesson? Can't you cancel it?. . . Surely the only thing to do is take them along. . . Goodbye, Desirée. . . Desirée, I really have to go. . . Goodbye, Desirée.' He put the phone back on the desk. 'Women, eh?'

Prosser dialled Minchkin's number. 'Women are all right, Joe. It's wives that are the problem. . . Hello, Morrie?. . . Yes, I've seen the price. You can go ahead and announce British Industrial Group has sold those Pardoe shares whenever you want. . .I know we've got until twelve, but I want it done now.' He began punching

186

out numbers again. 'I'm going to ring Fallas. Time for the coup de grâce.'

'I'll see you later,' said Roach, getting up to leave the room. The less he knew about what was to follow the better. Prosser pursed his lips and was about to pass comment about Roach's yellow streak when Fallas came on the line.

'This is Noddy. . . Yes, as we agreed. . . Yes, the *Evening Standard* would be best. . . Let's just leave it like that for the moment. Let them do the detective work. If they need more help, we can always give it to them later. Goodbye.'

Prosser put down the phone and, wandering over to the window, began humming another of his beloved Sousa marches. 'Not long now. Not long at all. Goodbye, Sir Jocelyn. It's been nice knowing you.'

Peter Mottram signed for the envelope and took it from the messenger. He ripped it open. What was so important that only the eyes of the City editor could gaze upon it? Probably another PR stunt. He spilled the envelope's contents on to the desk. A funny sort of invitation, if that's what it was. He picked up the photograph. It was very grainy but the chap coming out of the building was definitely Jocelyn Pardoe. Mottram, investing surreptitiously on the market against house rules, was a shareholder of long standing in Pardoe Trust. He had just finished writing an editorial defending Sir Jocelyn and his board against the possibility of any wrongdoing and accusing Nostrum of indulging in a dirty tricks campaign to see off a perfectly well-grounded bid. Although David Westbury had regaled the press with stories of mysterious midnight phone calls, of having his footsteps dogged every moment of the day and of having his house burgled, in his column, Mottram vigorously expressed scepticism. They only had Westbury's word for any of it.

He looked at the photograph again, more carefully. There was a brass name plate to one side of the door behind Pardoe: 'Nostrum plc'. Mottram's interest was awakened. He looked at the diary which had also fallen out of the envelope. The initials ARP were on the front. Amanda Pardoe? It could be. He swivelled his chair round and yelled to a reporter picking his nose behind him, 'Quick, find out from News Inf. if Lady Amanda Pardoe has a middle name.'

187

He opened the diary and began flicking through its pages. Appointments with hairdressers, lunch with girlfriends and, possibly, boyfriends, arrangements for a holiday. Just what you'd expect in the diary of a rich, bored lady. Nothing here to interest him, though the gossip boys might think differently.

When he reached the last scribbled entry Mottram sat bolt upright. 'Buy Nostrum. Bid. Dead cert. Don't forget.' He checked the date. So her husband had been stupid enough to tell her he was going to bid for Nostrum? Surely she wouldn't have been daft enough to have bought any shares?

'Her middle name's Rowena,' said the reporter behind Mottram.

'Right. Find out what her maiden name was. Then get yourself round to Nostrum as quick as lightning and get a look at that share register. See if you can spot her buying any shares in either name before the bid was announced. Unlikely, I know, but it's worth a try. Considering what we're after, the company secretary ought to fall over himself to help you.'

Mottram was about to drop the envelope into the bin when he spotted something jammed at the bottom. He shook it and a photocopy of an Access card voucher fell out. From an electrical shop in Tottenham Court Road, it was made out to Lady Amanda Pardoe. Dated just a few days earlier, it showed that she had paid £112.50 for 'goods'.

An increasingly excited Mottram put a call through to his stockbroker, leaving an order to sell his Pardoe shares urgently. Only when he had confirmation of the deal did he dial an internal number. 'Ruth, could the editor spare me a moment? I think the best City story since Guinness may just have landed in our laps. Thanks, I'll be right over. It might be a good idea to drag along one of the lawyers too.' He looked around the City desk. He needed a woman.

'Pam, get your butt over here,' he called. 'Do whatever you have to to find out what was bought on this credit card receipt tootysweety. Whatever you do, do not lose it. I rather think our friend bought herself some sort of bugging device. They're pretty easy to get hold of. If so, get an identical one yourself and get it back here pronto. Check with Nostrum and see if it's the same type that was found under their boardroom table. Oh, and we'll need a picture of the shop, too. Take a photographer along. Well go on then, woman, what the hell are you hanging round here for?'

* * *

Sir Jocelyn Pardoe's secretary of twenty-three years was crying as she brought the newspaper in to him. 'How can they say those terrible things?'

Pardoe already knew the gist of the front page story. 'Don't fret, Miss Kemble,' he said as he skimmed through the article. 'Just think how well we'll do out of the libel action. Perhaps you'd better get my wife on the phone.'

'Yes, Sir Jocelyn,' she snivelled.

Pardoe picked up the phone when it rang a moment later. 'Amanda? Have you seen the *Evening Standard*?'

'Yes, I fucking well have,' screamed his wife.

'Bad language isn't going to help the situation.'

'What the hell have you been doing with my credit card, you devious shit?'

'Me?' Pardoe's cloak of unruffled calm slipped. 'Don't start trying to blame me. I may be capable of many things, but passing myself off as a woman when I go shopping is not one of them.'

'I hope,' said Lady Amanda slowly, 'that you are not suggesting I bought the fucking thing?'

'No, of course not,' he said hastily and unconvincingly, 'although after that Barbados episode, I'm not sure what to think about you any more. What about the shares? Did you buy them?'

'Of course I did. What was the harm in that? It was money in the bank.'

Until now, Pardoe had somehow believed the whole thing would all turn out to be a terrible mistake. 'Oh, you stupid bitch,' he snapped. 'Insider dealing's a criminal offence. Surely even you know that? You can be put in prison for it.'

'How did I know anybody would find out? Will you just get down off your high horse for a minute, Jocelyn, and tell me what we are going to do, for Chrissake?' Lady Amanda was now screaming at her husband.

'Calm down, Amanda. I'll think of something.'

'Well, it had better be bloody good.'

'Where did the paper get your diary from anyway?'

'I haven't the slightest idea. I lost it on holiday. I don't know who. . .oh my God, yes I do. Of all the filthy, rotten, underhand, contemptible, low-down, no-good scumbags, he is without doubt the vilest of all.'

'Who? What are you raving about, woman? Who?'

'Prosser, that's who. Alexander Charles Prosser!'

Now it was Pardoe's turn to scream. 'Prosser? Oh, wonderful. Thank you very much indeed, Amanda. First the little Napoleon gets to screw my wife. Now he gets to screw me as well.'

'Lorraine, will you lower your bloody hemline and cover up a bit of that bust of yours?'

She pouted sexily at her boss. 'I thought you liked seeing as much flesh as I can spare, Mr Prosser.'

'Thanks to that half-wit stubbing his cigar out on my prick, things are a little different today. I don't want my dressings subjected to undue stress. Surely even somebody with as few brains as you can realise the necessity of putting on something less revealing? Normal service will be resumed as soon as possible. You can rest assured that as soon as it is, you'll be the first to know.' He snatched at the ringing phone. 'Yes, what is it? Oh hello, Morrie.'

'Alex, I thought you should turn on the telly. There's someone you know on the news. Call me back afterwards.'

Prosser pressed one of the buttons on his remote control panel and the face of Sir Jocelyn Pardoe, standing once more on the steps of Pardoe Trust, filled the screen.

'. . . and the board and I agree that until this, uh, unfortunate incident is satisfactorily explained, it would be best for all concerned if I relinquish my executive duties with Pardoe Trust. My fellow board members have asked me to point out,' said Pardoe, gritting his teeth, 'that the decision to make a takeover bid for Nostrum was not a unanimous one and that the bid will accordingly be abandoned. My colleague Henry Garstang will assume my duties for the time being. Thank you, ladies and gentlemen.'

Pardoe tried to dodge through the throng, but was headed off by the euphoric Justin Ewer, who thrust a microphone in his face. There was nothing he liked better than finding creatures who were down and kicking them until they bled in front of millions of television viewers.

Roach came into Prosser's office and was motioned to sit down and keep quiet.

'Sir Jocelyn, was it you or your wife who was responsible for planting the bugging device in the Nostrum boardroom?'

'My lawyers have advised me to make no comment on that at the present time.'

'Sir Jocelyn, is it true that, in addition to the purchase of Nostrum shares made by your wife, a Cayman Islands' bank bought shares in the name of Jocelyn Nominees just before the bid?'

Pardoe was completely taken aback by the question. 'I have no idea,' he spluttered. 'If that is the case, it is certainly nothing to do with me. I have always conducted my affairs with the utmost propriety. You have to believe that. I am the victim of an outrageous smear campaign. You. . . you. . . you journalists are unwitting pawns in his evil game.'

Ewer pressed closer. 'Sir Jocelyn, in the light of events, would it not be sensible for Pardoe Trust to change its name to something less inflammatory?'

Ewer was balanced precariously on the steps. Pardoe's punch had little force behind it, but was enough to send the reporter flying backwards. It was the blow to the back of the head he received when he struck the ground that knocked him out, and not Pardoe's fist, but that was not how it looked to viewers, nor indeed to the other reporters present. Pardoe was booed and hissed as he forced his way through the throng.

'You shouldn't have done that, Sir Jocelyn,' admonished the grinning Prosser. 'You really are a silly bugger, you know. Get it?' he asked Roach. 'Silly bugger. Oh, I did enjoy that. The BBC is giving bloody good value these days.'

'What was all that about Jocelyn Nominees? He didn't really buy shares in his own name, did he?'

'I shouldn't think so. He's too honest for his own good. No, Jocelyn Nominees was a little idea of my own. I didn't realise it would take as long as this for Nostrum to uncover it on their share register. They really are a dozy bunch.'

'I've got to hand it to you. It's all working out the way you said it would.' Roach did not sound overjoyed.

'It's not over yet, Joe. We've still got to make sure that Pardoe Trust *does* change its name. . . to British Industrial Group. Time for another talk with Fallas, I think.'

191

* * * 23 * * *

THE NEW chairman of Nostrum rose, beaming, from behind his desk and walked forward to greet his visitor.

'Alex, I heard the chopper arrive. You look in a good mood.'

The two men shook hands. 'And why not, Jack? I'm eager to see how you're getting on with our wonder drink. After all, I've put a lot of effort into getting hold of the bloody thing.'

Butterley led Prosser out of his office. As they entered the lift, Butterley said, 'It's good to be working together again, but I don't mind telling you that you've given me a few sleepless nights over the past few months.'

'Surely you never doubted my word?'

Butterley's deep laugh reverberated in the confined space. 'Of course I bloody did! At first I thought you were going to let Pardoe have us. Then after the furore over that bug, which I assume some confederate of yours planted. . .' he hesitated for a moment, but Prosser said nothing, '. . . I thought you'd simply step into the breach so neatly vacated by Sir Jocelyn. It was obvious that the bunch of drongos left on the Pardoe board after he had gone would happily have sold their thirty per cent stake to you.'

He stopped talking as the lift doors opened and they walked through the lobby and into the bright sunshine. Butterley held the door open for Prosser and they turned right towards the factory. Neither man wore a coat and their breath hung in the crisp autumn air as they talked. They lowered their voices for a moment while Janice from Sterile Bottle Inspection passed by, hurrying to the canteen still puzzling over whether the father of her unborn child was a dead security guard or one of a pair of over-helpful policemen. She turned round to stare at Prosser's back. Surely she knew him from somewhere?

'I should have realised that a straight takeover would have been too simple for a devious mind like yours. I think I can see how you managed to destroy Pardoe's reputation. It's easy enough to set up a company and call it Jocelyn Nominees, especially in the Cayman Islands, and no trouble to knock up a phony credit card. The poor sod was far too straight to stand a chance once you'd got him in your sights.

'Presumably you also had something to do with those dirty pictures of Lady Amanda that so mysteriously dropped into the hands of the *News of the World, Men Only* and similar upright organs? It was only when you appeared to be the only ready buyer of the shares that the divorcing Pardoes dumped – everyone else treating them as if they were carrying some terrible disease – that I realised what you were up to. It can't have been too difficult for a man like you to bully the board of Pardoe Trust, running round like chickens with their heads cut off, into accepting an agreed takeover. And along with control of Pardoe Trust, of course, came its thirty per cent of Nostrum. Your existing shares made a full bid for Nostrum compulsory. You didn't need many friends to make the thing a foregone conclusion.'

'You always had a vivid imagination, Jack.'

'Still, at least you couldn't have picked a better person to run British Industrial's new soft beverage division! Though I wonder whether you'd have employed me if I hadn't had those photos of you rummaging about in our bins.'

'I confess for a while I thought you had gone soft. But I changed my mind when I discovered you were employing Fallas to spy on me. Not a bad idea of yours. The only problem was he was already working for me.'

'Shit!' said Butterley, letting out his breath noisily. 'You can't trust anybody these days. Whatever happened to client confidentiality? Here we are. The crock of gold at the end of the rainbow.' They had arrived at the entrance to the factory.

Butterley turned to Prosser and looked at him carefully. 'Even with hindsight your plan seems terribly risky. What would you have done if it had gone wrong?'

'You won't mind if I ask you to open your jacket, Jack?'

'Not at all,' replied Butterley. 'But why? . . . Ah, I understand,' he said as Prosser checked to see if his former colleague was wired for sound.

193

'No offence. Just an elementary precaution. As things stand, I'm only too happy to accept the adulation and admiration of City, press and shareholders. If they think the sun shines out of my arse, who am I to disillusion them? I'm the one who spotted that Pardoe Trust was a snip, I'm the one who was forced by circumstances and the stupid rules of the Takeover Code into making a bid for Nostrum, a company I'd never shown the slightest inkling of wanting, and I'm the lucky bastard who suddenly finds a few days after taking it over that the research department is sitting on a new product that's set to turn it into a goldmine.

'However, had, heaven forbid, things not turned out quite as smoothly as they did, it wouldn't have been me who carried the can. We set up someone to take the rap, if need be. The strange thing is, he was chosen because he seemed so naive and stupid and he's actually had one or two good ideas about marketing your drink.

'Now, shall we go inside and have a look round before our bollocks freeze off?'

'I still can't believe you're prepared to accept all these coincidences at face value,' said Sally, hanging up her coat.

'How many more times? They do happen.' Jeremy's coat joined hers. He sat behind his desk, running his hands lovingly along its edge as he did every morning.

'Coincidence one,' said Sally, counting them off on her fingers, 'British Industrial Group gains control of Pardoe Trust with the help of an insurance company whose head of investment just happens to have had lunch with BIG's senior management and would appear to have had sun, sex and sailing laid on by the company, too.'

'I probably misheard all that stuff about bonking.'

'Coincidence two, Empire Assurance turn out not only to have a stake in Pardoe Trust, but also a handy few shares in Nostrum.' Jeremy shrugged his shoulders. 'Coincidence three, Nostrum is now run by a man who used to be Prosser's close colleague and who apparently visited him here just before this whole business started.'

'So the business community is a small world. That doesn't prove anything.'

'Coincidence four, my own dear darling boy was asked to comment on a research report into a remarkable new type of drink at a time when the company in question didn't even have any soft beverage manufacturing facilities. Now, surprise, surprise, it *does* have that capacity, millions of gallons' worth of it, and what does it find locked away behind the cobwebs in the boffins' cupboard, but that very self-same hypothetical new drink?'

'Change the record, will you, Sally? It's stuck in a groove.' Jeremy looked disapproving. 'Why can't you just accept that Prosser is a business genius as everybody else does? Now will you please let me get on with some work. . .blast!'

'What's the matter?'

'I must have left the keys to my desk in my other jacket.'

'I don't know why you want to lock it in the first place.'

Jeremy looked offended. 'The work I am doing on marketing Fizzical is highly confidential.' He ignored Sally's raised eyebrows and got to his knees.

'What on earth are you doing now?' she asked.

'It isn't the first time I've forgotten them.' Jeremy's muffled voice floated up to her. 'I discovered that there's a gap underneath the desk. It's a bit tight but you can reach into the drawers. . . ah, there we are.' He emerged with a folder held aloft and was soon happily making notes.

'Jeremy?' she asked thoughtfully, 'is that a design fault in your desk or do all of them. . . ?'

'Post,' yelled a trolley man as the door shot open, a hand reached in with the mail, deposited it in the Mail In tray, grabbed everything in the Mail Out tray and disappeared again. Sally shuffled through the post and extracted her pay packet. 'Good grief. Look,' she said, holding up another long, thin envelope. 'Are you sitting comfortably? Can you stand the shock? I think it's your very first pay packet. It's even addressed to you. We've cracked it. Nettle certainly met his match when he took me on.'

Jeremy grabbed the envelope from Sally, ripped it open and fumbled with the computerised slip jammed inside.

'Well, how much is it?' asked Sally.

'It depends whether you look at the top left-hand corner, or the bottom right-hand corner. In the top left, we have one thousand six hundred and sixty-six pounds. In the bottom right, we have two pounds and fifty-three pee.'

'You've never had a salary slip before. There's an art to reading them,' said Sally, shouldering him out of the way. 'No, as you were. It *is* two pounds fifty-three. Those are some pretty hefty deductions. I'll try and sort it out for you while you run along to your meeting. You don't want to be late, do you?' she said, adjusting his tie and smoothing down an errant strand of hair.

Prosser watched Maggie devouring the bird. Although she seemed pleased with her catch, he was irritated at having been deprived of his sport. No sooner had the bird risen above him than she had spotted something and dived. But whatever it was she was after it had been out of sight of the roof. The next thing he knew, Maggie had reappeared above the parapet with a house martin and was now ripping it to pieces with her beak and claws. When she finished, her beak was covered with small scraps of guts and gore. There were feathers everywhere.

When Prosser failed to arrive at the meeting, Godfrey Daniels suggested that Jeremy be sent off to find him. If the thirteenth floor was grand, the fourteenth was positively sumptuous. Cautiously he stepped off the circular staircase. If Prosser was on the roof, surely he could risk a quick glance around. Most of the visible doors were shut, but ahead of him Jeremy could see a swimming pool. He moved towards it, calling 'Mr Prosser' as he went, just in case he came across the tycoon. He stopped at the entrance. The pool, brightly lit by the sunlight coming through its glass roof, was surrounded by elaborately-patterned pillars in mosaic. The walls of the poolroom, too, were mosaic. It looked like the sort of place Roman Emperors would have done their daily twenty lengths in.

Jeremy realised with a start that Lucinda was in the pool, treading water. She waved, then swam towards him. 'Hello, handsome,' she called, pulling herself out of the pool. Good grief! Jeremy stood staring, frozen to the spot for a moment, then turned tail and ran. She had no clothes on.

Sally had already torn a strip off him when he had gone out for an innocent drink with Lucinda shortly after the big lunch, claiming that she was 'chasing tail'. Although Jeremy had not come across the phrase before, he could guess its meaning. Sally had made abundantly clear her views on Jeremy's mixing with any of Prosser's personal assistants. He didn't think she would be too pleased if he was found with a naked specimen of the breed.

As he raced up the spiral staircase, he could hear Lucinda laughing at him, the sound amplified by the acoustics of the swimming pool. Jeremy opened the door to the roof and stepped on to it. 'Mr Prosser?' he shouted.

Prosser turned round sharply and put his finger to his lips to silence Jeremy. Even though Seamen had come up with some good ideas on marketing Fizzical, Prosser still hadn't forgiven him the episode with the cigar. It had had most unfortunate consequences. Prosser had been hors de combat for a week.

Holding Maggie on his fist, Prosser stroked her feathers, soothing the bird. Goshawks, like all trained birds of prey, are very nervous and suspicious of strangers. However, the chance to get a little of his own back was too good to miss. He signalled that Jeremy should approach quietly. 'Stay behind her, then she won't get frightened.' He held his fist as high as he could. A full meal like that ought to have the desired effect very quickly.

'Just there ought to be fine,' said Prosser, when Jeremy was about three feet behind him and the bird. Any moment now, with a bit of luck.

'I've come to remind you about the meeting, Mr Prosser,' said Jeremy.

He got no further. True to form, Maggie finished the digestion of her food. She squirted out a mute behind her, a creamy jet of droppings shooting out at high speed which slapped on to Jeremy's shirt and jacket like wet paper from a schoolboy's ruler. Prosser roared with laughter at the look of horror on Jeremy's face. The steaming shit dribbled down his front. 'Call of nature, Seaman, call of nature. Should have warned you. It packs in a pretty powerful punch, doesn't it? It does that so its nest doesn't get soiled. Shame about your shirt and jacket, though. Come on, we'd better go down to the meeting. You can get cleaned up later. Don't want to be late, do we?'

On the other side of Gilbert Square, Sebastian Embleton wiped tears of laughter from his eyes and put his binoculars away. He noted the time in his notebook and then picked up his small cassette recorder and began dictating.

The house martin took one last look around his nest and took off. He had been saying for days that they should have begun the flight south, but she always knew best. She had been enjoying the unseasonally pleasant weather and had refused to listen to him. If they had gone when he had said, she would still be alive, instead of ripped to pieces by that hawk.

Still, at least the young had all been hatched safely and had long since flown the nest. Now it was time for him to head off, not to return until next year.

'So far, everything seems to be going according to plan,' said Prosser. 'The test marketing carried out by Nostrum has been phenomenally successful. You've got the results in front of you. The plants at Luton and Reading are being turned over entirely to the production of Fizzical, ready for the launch proper. The factories we acquired with Pardoe in Belgium, Spain, Hong Kong and Australia will also be making the stuff, although not exclusively. We're working on a few licence arrangements in other countries. We'll leave the States for the time being. The initial marketing budget will be twenty million pounds for the UK and another fifty million for the overseas launch. We are not talking peanuts here, but the revolutionary nature of the product necessitates a blitz campaign. We're risking a lot. I will not be pleased if there are any hiccoughs.'

Jeremy sat in some discomfort as Prosser led them through the plans for Fizzical. Prosser had refused to let him get rid of the bird muck before the meeting and he was only too well aware of the pungent aroma it was giving off.

'I'm sorry?' said Jeremy, with a start.

'I said let's hear your bloody ideas, man,' snapped Prosser. 'Do try and pay attention, Seaman. I can't afford to carry any passengers.'

'Yes, Sir.' Jeremy opened a folder. Ever since the incident with the cigar, Prosser invariably called him by his surname. Would he never be forgiven? He stood up, cleared his throat and began. 'As you know, gentlemen. . . '

'Oh, sit down for God's sake, Seaman. This isn't a bloody public meeting.'

Jeremy sat down, blushing deeply. He kept his face lowered to his papers as he made his presentation. 'As you know, the drink is being launched internationally. So it makes sense to have a unified marketing campaign that can simply be adapted for each country in which the drink is available. We also want to increase the awareness, both here and abroad, of BIG and at the same time to stress the British nature of the product.' Jeremy took a sip of water and ploughed on.

'To that end, our advertising jingles will utilise the chimes of Big Ben. Not only are they famous here, but right around the world. They are probably the most well-known sound from Britain, broadcast as they are every hour on World Service. A few jingles are being run up at the moment which begin with the ponderous chimes and then go into a catchy disco number. Obviously, the drink is being aimed most closely at the young consumer and in the campaign we will be giving the impression that there is something just a little naughty about Fizzical. If we implant the idea that perhaps parents might not want them to drink the stuff, we ought to guarantee that most youngsters will go right out and buy it. Our market research already shows that there's an enormous anti-health-kick market out there just waiting to be tapped.

'The print campaign will feature the slogan "Fizzical's Fizz Fizzes Faster". Because the name is onomatopoeic, we'll have to make very little in the way of changes abroad.'

Daniels took over from Jeremy. 'In addition to the money we're spending on promoting it, we're anticipating an enormous amount of free coverage from the media. Mr Prosser's house and estate in Northumberland are being used for the weekend launch party, which is as lavish as we can make it, with all creature comforts – and I mean all – laid on for the journalists. There'll also be a substantial City contingent of analysts and fund managers. Within the month, Fizzical should be on everybody's lips.'

'And down their gullets as well, I hope,' interrupted Prosser, 'or heads will roll.' He turned to Jeremy with a look of intense disgust on his face. 'I think, Seaman, it would be a good idea if you got cleaned up. You ought to have more sense than to turn up for a meeting smelling like a dung-heap. Go on. Off you run.'

Prosser waved him away. As the door closed behind Jeremy, Daniels, sensing that his moment had come, said, 'I think I have an idea that will interest you.'

He explained what he had in mind to Prosser and Roach. 'Brilliant!' exclaimed Prosser. 'That's absolutely bloody brilliant. I take my hat off to you. It will be the advertising coup of all time.'

'So we'll do it?' Daniels was thrilled.

Prosser thought for a moment. 'Two problems. We'll have to hold it until after the turn of the year. I can't tell you why, but I daren't risk it until next February. In fact, that may help because we'll have had a couple of months for the initial campaign to sink into the public consciousness by then. My other concern is that we could be breaking the law. It will be worth it for the publicity, but we'll be doing so in such a public fashion that we need to have somebody to take the rap for it.'

Daniels turned to look at the chair just vacated by Jeremy. 'Yes, he would seem to be the most obvious candidate,' mused Prosser.

'So where's the problem?' asked Daniels.

'In order for it to be believable, I'm afraid he's going to have to be credited publicly as the architect of the whole thing.'

'If it's for the good of the company,' said Daniels reluctantly, 'then I'd better get to work on it at once.' He gathered up his papers and left the room.

'Hang on a moment, Joe,' said Prosser. 'I've got something to show you.' He drew from his inside pocket a long, white envelope marked 'Urgent. Personal and Confidential'.

Roach took out the letter and read aloud, 'Sir, The Prime Minister has asked me to inform you, in strict confidence, that she has it in mind, on the occasion of the forthcoming list of New Year Honours, to submit your name to The Queen with a recommendation that Her Majesty may be graciously pleased to approve that the honour of knighthood be conferred upon you.' Roach looked up to see, for what was probably the first time, a look of real happiness on Prosser's face.

'Congratulations. About time too, if I may say so.'

'You're absolutely right. Long overdue. I really ought not to have shown you, but I'd have burst trying to keep it to myself for the next six weeks. From January 1st, I shall be Sir Alexander Prosser.'

'Don't you have to wait until the sword actually descends on the shoulder?'

'That won't be until February, at the earliest. I can use the title from the moment it's announced. It may just be a coincidence, but I also got a snivelling letter of apology today from the secretary of Bart's Club, blaming Pardoe for my blackballing and saying that the committee was reconsidering its decision. They say things go in threes. Getting rid of that wally Seaman will complete the trio nicely.'

'A shame really. I know you can't stand him, but I was rather growing to like him,' said Roach as he made for the door. He stopped on the way out and turned round. 'Incidentally, what will you do with British Iron Girders?'

'Eh? Oh, I'll close it down and turn it into a theme park. I'm a business man. I can't have important business decisions decided by bloody politicians. The next thing you know, they'll be thinking they run the country.'

It was important for the busy businessman to find time in his hectic schedule to relax. So Prosser leaned back against the side of the pool, letting Lucinda, her legs wrapped around him, do all the work. The swimming pool was the one place, apart from the shower, where he could have sex with Lucinda without her bloody pearls getting in the way. He was surprised no budding entrepreneur had yet found a way of waterproofing the string so that Sloanes could keep them on twenty-four hours a day.

Ron Niblo entered the pool room and dropped a box on the pool side behind Prosser. 'I've got your shopping, boss,' he announced. Prosser fumbled around in the box behind him.

'I've got something here that I want you to try, Lucinda.'

She watched him warily, the incident with the banana still fresh in her mind. Despite her Convent upbringing, she was a conventional girl at heart and she found many of Prosser's ideas for introducing variety into their sexual sessions outrageous. But she kept her misgivings to herself, knowing that Prosser would only find forcing her to do something she found distasteful that much more exciting.

She was perplexed when Prosser finally retrieved what he was looking for, holding it aloft with that horrible lascivious grin of his.

'What do you say to a little gooseberry fool, eh?'

'Er. . . yes, fine,' stammered the perplexed Lucinda. Perhaps she had him wrong after all.

'When we've finished here, I want to show you a new way of eating it that I picked up on a recent trip abroad. Some people prefer honey, but I find it too sickly. Gooseberry fool is an infinitely better idea. You need your horizons expanded, my girl.'

* * * 24 * * *

'STOP LOOKING so smug. You really are repulsive when you're so full of yourself, Jeremy.'

'I thought you'd be pleased, Sally.'

'I am pleased. Even though it is well known that early January is traditionally a very quiet time for news,' she said cattily, 'I still think it's splendid that the *Sunday Times* Business Section should devote a whole page to the new marketing genius of British Industrial Group. But you read it to me three times yesterday and this would be the second time today. I know it off by heart. You can take it that I agree wholeheartedly with everything said by the sycophantic illiterate who wrote the article.

'If the fact that you've never met the journalist and that the entire story was concocted by Prosser doesn't bother you, why should it bother me? And if the fact that the press party at Prosser's mansion to launch the drink took place without the genius who supposedly made its global success possible doesn't bother you, then why should it bother me?'

'Sir Alexander wanted to shield me from the press,' said Jeremy sulkily. 'Journalists are always misinterpreting things, he said. I should leave it to someone who's had experience of them.'

'Since getting that knighthood, he's become almost as pompous as you. Sir Alexander indeed! Only somebody as egocentric as him would send a memo around the entire firm informing staff of the correct way to address him.'

'Proper etiquette is very important.'

'I'd hardly call it proper etiquette to have a giant oil painting of the man leering down at everybody in the lobby downstairs. It's horrible.'

'I think it's a very good likeness.'

'That's what I mean.'

'Sally!' said Jeremy, shocked at her blasphemy. 'Anyway, you've got to admit that the drink's doing brilliantly. We're exceeding our sales targets in every market.'

'I heard some jerk humming that awful jingle on the Tube into work again this morning. That's your fault.'

'It's supposed to be catchy.'

'So is bubonic plague. It's getting on my nerves. You can't escape Fizzical wherever you go these days. It's on the hoardings, on the TV, on the radio, in the papers. If it isn't an ad from the company, then it's yet another free plug of some sort. There was even something in the fashion pages of the *Telegraph* this morning. 'Fizzical clothes'. It's a drink, for heaven's sake. What's it got to do with clothes?'

'Blanket coverage,' said Jeremy, taking it all as a compliment. 'It's working very well. The Phil Collins' single of it will be out next week. It isn't only in Britain, you know. We're giving it this sort of treatment right around the world.'

'Then heaven help the world,' said Sally heavily. 'And are they all going in for this farcical competition you dreamt up? Are there children and grown-ups in places from Timbuktoo to Tibet repeating "Fizzical's Fizz Fizzes Faster" over and over again?'

Her constant carping irritated Jeremy. It was as if she resented his success. He stood up and walked over to the window to calm himself. He always found the view reassuring. It served to place everything in perspective. He tried to change the subject. 'Do you think the holes in the Swiss cheese plant are getting bigger?' Damn it. Why *should* he change the subject? He was very proud of his work on Fizzical.

'With adaptations for different languages, yes. It's proving terribly popular,' he persisted. 'That youngster who won last week was managing a rate of fifty to the minute. He got to over thirty-six thousand before stumbling. Won himself a lifetime's supply of Fizzical.'

'If twelve hours mumbling that inane phrase over and over again hasn't shortened his life considerably, the drink will. . . what's the matter?'

Jeremy was screwing up his eyes, trying to see something in the distance. 'You remember that posh tramp who lent me his clothes that time? Sebastian, that was his name. I'd forgotten all about him, but I think he's still there.'

'Where?' asked Sally.

'Down there,' said Jeremy, pointing. 'I saw a flash of light. Probably from his binoculars.'

'Binoculars? What would a tramp be doing with binoculars?'

'Oh, he was a very rum character. I saw inside his bags once. It wasn't just binoculars. There was also a very impressive camera, one of those little tape recorders you use for dictation and a cellular phone. Couldn't make him out at all. He must be freezing in this weather.'

Sally retrieved the pile of mail dumped in the tray and sorted through it, filtering out the probable junk and handing anything that looked as though it needed prompt attention to Jeremy.

'Now what?' she asked. He was staring with horror at a piece of paper held shakily in his hand.

'It's a telephone bill, made out in my name. Sally, it's for well over a thousand pounds.'

She took it from him. 'It's for a cellular phone. Don't look so glum. You haven't got one, so it must be a mistake. I'll get Roach to sort it out for you. You can hardly be made to pay for something you don't have, especially as you don't have any money of your own yet. Perhaps we should tell the reporter from the *Sunday Times* that BIG's marketing genius is owed nine months' pay by its hyper-inefficient Human Resources Department. . . Just joking, just joking.'

As she wandered down the corridor, Sally examined the bill. If it wasn't Jeremy's phone, whose was it? Every call was itemised. It might be worth studying later. She made a quick detour on the way to Roach's office, stopping off at the photocopier.

The Major handed his duty-sheet over to young Thomas, one of his new appointees, and set off to his flat for lunch. He usually ate in the canteen or the 'Mess' as he insisted on calling it. But he was concerned about Rommel. The dachshund had been off-colour recently and the Major didn't like to leave him for too long.

Besides, on a crisp, sunny day like this a walk through the park before lunch was just the ticket. The Major was a contented man. He had a purpose in life. His ideas for maintaining the security of BIG House were poles apart from Mr Bennett's policy of fear and intimidation. The Major insisted on politeness and cordiality from his guards at all times and set the example himself. He enjoyed nodding the employees through in the mornings and home at night and passing the time of day with them.

He let himself into his flat, calling out Rommel's name. The dog wasn't inside but, through the back door, he could see it at the bottom of the garden. The Major had installed a cat flap when he started work at British Industrial so that Rommel could have freedom of access. He unlocked the door to the garden, breathed deeply and stepped out.

That was peculiar. The dog was lying in a very odd position on its side. It didn't seem to be asleep. He could see movement. As he approached he realised, horrified, that it wasn't the dog he could see moving, but an enormous bird which was pecking and tearing at what was left of the dachshund's head.

Anger overwhelmed the Major. He rushed towards the corpse, shouting and flapping his arms wildly. The bird, more in surprise than fear, rose into the air and hovered above the garden.

The Major dropped to his knees. The body was still warm. He looked up. He didn't know much about birds, but that was definitely a bird of prey. There was only one place it could have come from. The Major rushed back to the house for his air rifle, but when he returned the bird had flown.

'I'm truly sorry, Rommel, old boy,' he said to the corpse. 'Don't you worry, though. I'll make the bastard pay for it or my name isn't Major Peregrine.'

Sally smiled her brightest, makes-men-go-weak-at-the-knees smile. 'Excuse me, but would your name be Sebastian by any chance?'

'Sandpits steaming with pink custard,' came the enigmatic reply.

'Jeremy said I might find you here.'

'Ah, did he now?' The tramp stood up, took Sally's hand and kissed it. 'In that case, yes. Sebastian Embleton at your service, good lady. Pull up a doorstep and tell me how I can help you.'

Prosser was in a foul mood. He had waited ages on the roof in the freezing cold for the bird to return. She had flown over the houses opposite, leaving him to kick his heels for half an hour. He had blown the whistle, which she had been trained to associate with food, but she had not responded. One of the disadvantages of falconry was that he couldn't bring one of the girls up onto the roof to while away the time. Hawks were nervous of strangers and particularly wary of women.

He had munched his way through a bag of extremely green apples. His stomach was already beginning to rebel. He just hoped the bird wouldn't be too long, or it would have been for nothing.

He felt a strange prickling sensation on his neck. If he didn't know better, he could swear somebody on the other side of the Square was watching him. The sun was glinting off something in one of the doorways. There was definitely somebody there. He raised his binoculars. Only a tramp. He must be getting paranoid. Why did they allow such derelicts to clutter up the place? He didn't pay his taxes to have eyesores like that living over the road from him. He made a mental note to have something done about it.

When Maggie returned, she was covered in blood. Whatever she had got into a tussle with, it had obviously put up a tremendous fight. One of the hawk's primary feathers had been wrenched out and another had been damaged. On top of it all, the damned bird was still hungry. He had to give her some rabbit. She greedily gobbled up a foreleg, hindleg, two kidneys and half the liver before she was satisfied. At least there was no waste. Even the bones disappeared down her gullet. The speed with which she had eaten gave the bird hiccoughs. Prosser flinched from her hot, putrid breath.

She obviously hadn't made a kill. That wasn't good for hawks. They quickly got out of the habit and became lazy. If things didn't pick up soon then he'd have to resort to the same tactics as last year, with Ron taking doped live prey into the park below and releasing it for Maggie to chase.

He glanced at his watch. Time to send Mr Seaman off on the little errand which ought to see an end to that particular nuisance. Was there ever a man who asked so many questions? With the takeover of Pardoe and Nostrum safely over and the drink successfully launched, his function within the organisation was at an end as far as Prosser was concerned. He removed one of Jeremy's business cards from his wallet and, chuckling as he looked at it, headed downstairs.

As Prosser passed the fourteenth floor, he saw Jacqui, clad only in one of his Hilditch & Key shirts. She lifted the shirt slowly, giving him a come-hither glance. 'I'll be back,' he called out, continuing down the stairs. 'Keep it hot for me.'

* * *

Sally sat on the edge of the desk, making small talk with Lucinda. Only part of her mind was concentrating on the conversation. The rest was mulling over what she had learnt from Sebastian, if that really was his name.

Her little tête-à-tête had proved to be quite enlightening. Jeremy had been right. Sebastian really did have all the wonders of modern technology at hand. He also had a perfectly satisfactory wristwatch.

Sally kept an ear cocked towards Prosser's office as she glanced at her own wrist. If only Lucinda would stop prattling on about her new recipe for baked avocados with stilton she'd be able to hear a little better. The second hand approached the vertical. Nothing happened. Damn. It began the downward tack again. Then Sally heard it. From Prosser's room came the distinct sound of a phone ringing. Bingo!

'Hello? Hello? . . . No, of course this isn't Madame Frigging Tussaud's! Well, dial more carefully in future, you stupid jerk,' said Prosser, putting the phone back in his pocket. Those apples were giving his stomach hell. Still, not long now. 'As I was saying, Jeremy my boy, it's just a small package. But I need someone I can trust to deliver it personally. Would you mind?'

'Not at all, Sir Alexander.' Back to first names, Jeremy was delighted to hear. He had obviously been forgiven.

'Excellent,' said Prosser, handing over a small box, measuring no more than six inches by three. 'It's actually a present for someone, a loyal British Industrial worker that I want to reward. But this way, his colleagues won't get jealous and all start demanding presents too.'

'I quite understand, Sir Alexander.'

'You do? Splendid. I'll come down in the lift with you. See you into the taxi.'

'A taxi?' spluttered Jeremy. 'But. . .'

'Charge it, of course, if you're worried about the cost.' Prosser looked at Jeremy severely. 'Though on the money we pay you young chaps, I'd have thought an occasional act of generosity in return wouldn't go amiss from time to time.'

'About my pay, Sir Alexander. . .'

Prosser stabbed a stubby finger at Jeremy. 'It's very handsome. I won't be bullied into paying any more. You can wait until your annual review. Now let's get going.'

In the lift, which opened on being told that the battle of Aspromonte took place in 1862, Prosser explained that Jeremy was to go to St Stephen's Tavern in Westminster, directly opposite the Houses of Parliament. 'Someone called Patrick Riordan will take it from you. He'll be waiting for you by the entrance to the pub. I've told him what you look like. All right? What's the matter? Cat got your tongue?'

It wasn't the cat that had got Jeremy's tongue, but something far worse. As soon as the lift doors had closed, Prosser reaped the benefit of the apples and loudly and quite unselfconsciously had broken wind. The sound took Jeremy aback while the smell – from which there was no escape – was quite over-powering, filling his nostrils with an aroma of a noxiousness and severity he could not recall encountering before. His business school lecturers had never thought to tell Jeremy the correct behaviour to adopt when your boss fills a lift with a record-breaking fart. He held his breath for as long as he could, watching the indicators flash the descending numbers of the floors with agonising slowness.

Throughout the descent, Prosser maliciously kept asking questions of Jeremy, relishing the young man's discomfort. He'd teach the whipper-snapper to go around stubbing out lighted cigars on peoples' pricks.

As the doors opened Jeremy threw courtesy to the wind, as it were, and threw himself into the foyer ahead of Prosser, gasping for fresh air.

'You ought to keep yourself fit, young man. The way you're breathing, anybody would think you'd just walked down the thirteen flights of stairs. Come on.'

Prosser stopped by the fountain. The coloured liquid in it was fizzing furiously. 'That was an excellent idea of mine, putting Fizzical concentrate in the water. Very impressive.'

'But. . . ' began Jeremy.

'Yes?'

'Nothing, Sir Alexander.' Surely he remembered that it had been Jeremy's idea?

As they continued their progress out of the building, the sea of staff passing through the foyer parted to give them a wide berth.

Cries of 'Good morning, Sir Alexander', 'Nice day, Sir Alexander' and 'Hello, Sir Alexander' assailed them from all sides. Each and every one made sure their voice could be heard good and strong, just in case it was thought that they were disobeying Prosser's memo.

The tycoon stepped smartly over to the reception desk, with Jeremy following in his wake, still panting.

'You,' he barked at Charmaine, who cowered away from his pointing finger as if it were a loaded gun. 'Get somebody to adjust the light shining on my picture. It doesn't catch the face properly. I won't put up with this slovenliness.'

'Yes, Sir Alexander. At once, Sir Alexander.'

'And get that disgusting muck off your face and fingernails. You look like a bloody traffic light.'

A taxi was waiting outside. 'Thought it would make it easier if I ordered one up,' explained Prosser. 'Do be careful with the package. It's quite delicate.'

'Yes, Sir Alexander. You can rely on me.'

Prosser smiled his broadest smile as Jeremy stepped into the taxi. This would be BIG's greatest triumph yet. Daniels really had got a fine head on his shoulders. Perhaps it was time he was brought up onto the thirteenth floor? He could have Seaman's office.

Sally took the International Telephone Guide down from the shelf and began flicking through the pages. Sebastian's call had proved that the bill was for Prosser's phone. She was looking for the country whose dialling code began with 010–180994. It appeared on the phone bill more regularly than any other overseas number. It wasn't Anguilla or Antigua or Barbados or Bermuda. She found it on the next page. The Cayman Islands.

Of course, the place famous as the international centre of insider trading. If she was right about Prosser, it would certainly make sense. She had a horrible feeling that she knew now why the bill was in Jeremy's name. What was simpler than putting the phone in someone else's name if it was being used for something shifty? If Jeremy was being made the scapegoat for some misdemeanour of Prosser's, it would explain his surprising presence on the thirteenth floor. If he was made to look important enough to the outside world he could take the rap instead of the chairman. That meeting minuted by Jacqui: what was it she had said? Jeremy was being given the credit for all the good ideas. And what about all those research reports he had had to comment on. Prosser was now in possession of a hand-written note from Jeremy about the merits of a drink just like Fizzical, dated before the takeover of Nostrum had even happened.

She had to warn him. She had seen him get in the lift with Prosser. Where had they gone? She hunted for Jeremy's diary, but he had locked everything away in his desk. He was as obsessed with locking things away as Prosser was.

She got to her knees, as Jeremy had done, and found that from underneath the desk, you could reach into the back of the drawers. She extracted the diary, but that day's page was blank.

What could she say to him anyway? He was so stubbornly loyal to Prosser that he wouldn't believe her suspicions for a moment. She needed proof.

The taxi pulled up just outside St Stephen's Tavern and Jeremy, ordering it to wait for him, stepped out. A burly man, wearing a donkey jacket and hard, scruffy work boots, moved away from the wall against which he had been leaning.

'Mr Seaman?' The voice was unmistakably Irish. 'I t'ink you have a package for me.'

Jeremy handed it over, whereupon the man grabbed him by the hand and, with an amazingly strong grip, shook it vigorously. Then, exceeding his brief slightly, he gave Jeremy a bearhug for good measure. He put the package in a pocket inside his jacket and without saying another word, turned and headed towards the Underground station, disappearing inside. He did not go through the ticket barriers, but turned right into the subway that led under Bridge Street. He walked past the stairs that led up to the other side of the road and, unseen by Jeremy, went through the gate leading to the Houses of Parliament, showing his pass to the policeman on duty.

Even if Jeremy had seen Fallas's man, he would have assumed he was just another tourist photographing the Mother of Parliaments.

The Major undid the last of the screws fastening the cover in place and removed it, placing it quietly on the ground. He waited, tense, listening in case anyone had heard him.

The Major reached inside the black rubbish sack and took out the dead dachshund, placing it inside the air conditioning duct. He paused, stroking the matted hair for a moment then, with all the strength he could muster, he gave the corpse a shove along the duct. He replaced the cover, doing up the four screws.

'Goodbye Rommel, old thing.'

* * * 25 * * *

'I GOT A phone call from Riordan at Westminster this morning. He's tried it out. Works fine. He's all set for tonight.' Daniels was having breakfast with Prosser and Roach in the boardroom. They had a big day ahead of them.

'You're sure he'll not muck it up?' asked Prosser. 'You know what the Micks are like.'

Daniels shook his head. 'The rewards we're offering him should help to concentrate his mind wonderfully, Irish or not. He'll practically be out of the country before anybody knows what's happening.'

'Joe,' said Prosser, 'You'd better handle the newspapers. I'm going to be out for much of the day. I've got to open that new supermarket in Newcastle.'

'Fine. But I don't understand why we have to let the Press know. Surely they'll find out soon enough.'

'This way it will be crystal clear that Seaman has planned it all. There'll be no witch-hunt. The culprit will simply be handed over, nicely bound and trussed. The photos came out beautifully, don't you think?'

The three men looked at the large black and white photographs on the desk showing Jeremy giving a package to Riordan.

There was a tap at the door. Lorraine stuck her head in and gesticulated, pointing upwards. 'I'd better go,' said Prosser. 'The helicopter's waiting. I'll be back later this afternoon. Remember, nothing must go wrong. I'm collecting my knighthood on Tuesday.'

'No. *The Anarchist's Cook Book*. It's American, don't yer know,' said the Major wearily. This was the third department he had been to in Foyles. There were books everywhere: books on shelves, books on the floor, books up the sides of the escalator. But the location of individual books within the store was a secret obviously kept well hidden from the sales assistants, all of whom appeared to have wandered in from their first lesson at a nearby English language school.

The assistant, obviously new, smiled broadly. 'You want the cooks' books. Down.'

'I don't want the bally cookery section. It's not for baking a cake. It's for making bom. . .' The Major, exasperated, lowered his voice. 'Bombs. Bang bang boom,' he added helpfully.

'Ah. Boom.'

'Yes, that's it. Boom.'

'You want music. Up,' said the assistant, pointing to the escalator.

'Jeremy,' said Sally suspiciously, 'are you wearing a vest?'

There was no answer.

'Jeremy, answer me, you're wearing a vest, aren't you?'

'Well, what if I am? My mother always told me that. . .'

'I don't care what your mother told you. Thrusting young executives do not wear vests, particularly string vests. Take it off.'

'What?'

'You heard me.'

'But it's cold outside.'

'Off.'

Jeremy knew when he was beaten. He removed his jacket, tie and shirt.

'Sally,' he said plaintively.

'If you won't, I will,' she said, striding across and pulling it over Jeremy's head, just as the door to the office was thrown open.

'Ooh. Sorry I'm sure,' said the bug-eyed trolley man as he deposited the post in the in-tray.

Jeremy, topless, retrieved it and riffled through the pile. He ripped open an envelope.

'I don't believe it,' said Jeremy, staring at the computer-printed pay slip in his hand. He tapped out some calculations on his calculator. 'I just don't believe it.'

'I'll get on to Nettle again,' said Sally wearily. 'Then I'll give the *Guinness Book of Records* a call. They'll probably be interested, even if Nettle isn't.'

'No, no,' said Jeremy, picking up the phone. 'They've got it right. Ten months' pay. The deductions look right, too. Perhaps before I start celebrating, I'd better just check the money's gone into my bank account. Sally, don't do that!' But it was too late. She had opened the window and through it she bundled his vest.

The Major had abandoned his policy of whispering and had reverted to the traditional English method of communicating with foreigners. 'Lookee here,' he screamed. '*Anarchist's Cook Book*. Bombs. Boom, boom, bang, bang.' He gesticulated wildly with his hands, imitating a mushroom cloud.

Comprehension dawned in the sales assistant's face. 'Ah. Not music?'

'No, not dashed music.'

'Want dance. Over there.'

Sally let herself into Prosser's office, her heart pounding. She waited inside the door for a moment in case there was anybody moving round upstairs. All she could hear was the blood pumping through her temples. She was far too jumpy for this sort of thing.

Oh well, it was now or never. She strode across to Prosser's desk, fearing every moment that somebody would call out and ask what she was doing. But there was no challenge.

She dived under the desk, and waited again, tense, listening. She felt underneath. It was just like Jeremy's. Slowly she reached inside the back of the bottom drawer and felt around.

She heard a click from somewhere in the room. She stopped breathing and hunched up, petrified. A clock struck the hour and she opened her mouth and gulped in air. Her probing hand came across something. Drawing it out, she retrieved a cassette. On the label was written 'Wobbly Man'.

There was another noise, but she couldn't place it at first. It got louder and louder. Damn! It was the helicopter, landing. Prosser was back early. She dashed to the door, stuffing her booty into her pocket, and opened it gently. The coast was clear. She slipped out and back to her own room.

Dance! Well he might as well try it. He'd been to every other damned department in the building.

214

'*Anarchist's Cook Book*. Bombs. Boom,' he shouted at the badge-bestrewn assistant who had hair reaching down to his shoulders.

'Hey, not so loud, man. You'll wake up the management. You got the name wrong anyway. You want the *Revolutionary's Recipe Book*.'

The Major was dumbfounded. 'You know it?'

'Of course, man. I went to Berkeley. Standard text book there.'

'Really?'

'A joke, man, a joke. Jeez, you Limeys.'

'How much is it?'

'Hey, you can't buy it over here. It's banned. Whatever happened to freedom of expression, eh? What do you want it for anyway?'

'Why should I tell you?'

'Look, man, I might know where to lay my hands on a copy. A lot depends on what you want to do with it.'

The Major, exhausted and at his wits' end, threw caution to the wind and sketchily explained his intended plan. He was desperate for that book.

'Hey, that's cool, man. I mean that really is cool. You don't need the book for that, though.'

'I don't, man?' said the Major. 'I mean, young man.'

'Shit, no. I can tell you how to make one of those. Practically graduated on the things. First off, you need to get yourself a rubber.'

'A rubber,' repeated the Major, taking out his notebook. 'Is there a stationery department here?'

'Hey, man, are you taking the piss?'

'No, I assure you. But where else would I get a rubber?'

'A chemist's, of course.'

'A chemist's? Oh, you mean a rubber Johnnie,' said the Major. 'How does that help?'

'If you goddam keep quiet, I'll tell you.'

At last Patrick Riordan reached the bottom of the stairs leading up the Clock Tower. He was glad he wouldn't be doing that climb again. He hauled his kit-bag on to his shoulders and headed out across New Palace Yard and into the street.

He'd set the device, just as he'd been told to do. No-one would find it, unless they knew where to look. He had made sure of that.

He had no qualms about what he'd done, not when he was being paid twenty thousand pounds and provided with first-class transportation to the Bahamas. He was only a temporary workman at Parliament anyway. What would he have done when the contract came to an end?

Now that he was a rich man, he toyed with the idea of hailing a cab. But at this time of day, the tube to Heathrow would be much quicker. They had stressed the importance of getting away as quickly as possible. Not that he was likely to hang about. The ruddy thing would go off in less than an hour and he didn't want to be here when it did.

The chap hadn't specified which sort of rubber to buy, so the Major had bought a packet of each of the major brands, an act which, as he was evidently of an age to be in possession of a free bus pass, obviously impressed the girl behind the counter at Boots. He'd have to experiment with each to see which worked best. He'd got the baby oil and battery there too.

A lightbulb, digital alarm clock and a tube of superglue from Woolies and he would practically be ready.

'The dummies that make up Nostrum's board won't touch Fizzical with a ten-foot bargepole. I don't give a bugger about them, but I'm damned if I'll let the opportunity of a lifetime slip through my fingers. The only way I can be certain it gets produced with the proper backing is if someone like you takes over the company and kicks out the existing board. . .with one exception, of course.'

'I see. And in addition to becoming chief executive of Nostrum, which I assume is your aim, what else are you after?'

'Complete operational and financial autonomy. No meddling from you. A five-year service contract at £150,000 a year. That's all. Oh, and an itsy-witsy royalty from the sales of Fizzical to see me through nicely to my old age. Say one per cent of turnover?'

'One per cent? What a good job you're not greedy, Jack.'

Sally turned off the tape and took it out of the machine. Jeremy's hangdog expression was so pitiful that she was almost sorry she had played it to him.

'And Jack presumably is Jack Butterley?' he asked.

Sally nodded. 'It looks as if Prosser planned the whole thing from beginning to end.'

'But that's absolutely amazing.'

'It's also absolutely illegal.'

Jeremy stared at the tape, trying to think of some other rational explanation for what he had heard.

Sally clicked her fingers. 'Come on, Jeremy. Snap out of it. So your idol wasn't all you cracked him up to be. So what? It's time to think of Number One. I'm convinced that he's set you up as the fall guy in case anything goes wrong. You can't spend the rest of your life wondering if your collar is about to be felt by the long arm of the law because of Prosser's misdemeanours.'

'It's all very well saying that, but what are we going to do?'

'Why don't we just take the tape to the Police?'

'I thought you were supposed to be the bright one. There's not enough evidence on that tape to bring a case, let alone a conviction, and just because I'm not one of the two conspirators doesn't mean that I'm off the hook. If you're right about him, then goodness knows what Prosser might have got stored against me. If the downfall of Sir Jocelyn Pardoe was his doing, then *I'm* hardly going to be a match for him, am I?'

'Perhaps we ought not to discuss this here. I'd better hang around until I get a chance to put the tape back. We certainly don't want Prosser to notice it's gone. He's having some sort of pow-wow in his office with Roach and Daniels at the moment. Why don't you go down to the pub and wait for me there?'

Sally suddenly sniffed the air. 'Is it my imagination, or is there rather an odd smell in here?'

The Major had to stand outside the school gates for a quarter of an hour before the lad returned. He was terrified somebody might challenge him, accuse him of being a pervert of some sort.

'Here you are, mister.' The Major looked down at the unkempt youngster holding out the bottle.

'A fiver, we said.' The Major opened his wallet and pulled out a note.

'Let's say a tenner, shall we?'

'You cheeky little monkey.'

'If you don't want it.'

'All right. A tenner it is.'

The Major handed over the money and carefully put the bottle of phosphorus, fresh from the chemistry lab, in his pocket. He now had all the ingredients he needed.

217

* * * 26 * * *

REGINALD ROYSTON, Speaker of Her Majesty's House of Commons, struggled to keep his eyelids from drooping. But he was fighting a losing battle against the soporific effects of the first reading of the Sewerage Maintenance and Improvements Bill. Despite the insistence of the Right Honourable Member for Ripon, presently on his feet, that the matter was one of the greatest urgency and importance to the nation, all but forty-six MPs had felt able to resist the attractions of the debate.

Through half-closed eyes, the Speaker glowered sourly about him. He glowered at the apologies for human beings who sat, wide-eyed, in the public gallery; he glowered at the digital clocks suspended underneath which desecrated the holy Chamber; he glowered at the backs of the heads of the clerks in front of him, wigged and gowned whippersnappers who delighted in telling him what he could and could not do; and he glowered at the sparse shower of humanity sprawled over the green leather in whose hands the fate of the country lay.

To think that this was the pinnacle of his career. Every since that first glorious moment when he had entered the House of Commons as an MP, his greatest ambition had been not to achieve Cabinet office, but to become the Speaker of the House of Commons. As each year passed, and he watched the standard of debate and behaviour in the House deteriorate, so the prize he cherished became ever more tarnished.

Now enthroned in the Speaker's chair, the third commoner in the land, togged up in knee breeches, black stockings, buckled shoes, a gown and full-bottomed wig, Reginald Royston was far from satisfied with his lot. He had spent years steeping himself in the traditions of the House, sitting up in bed each night avidly studying Erkine May's *Treatise on the Law, Privileges, Proceedings*

218

and Usage of Parliament, the MP's bible, until he had become as concerned with posterity as with the present. He desperately wanted to go down in history as one of the great Speakers of all time. But with the enormous majority this Government had, there was little chance of that. The Opposition was a demoralised shower, the party in power an arrogant leviathan. The heart had gone out of the debating. What point was there to vicious cut and thrust if the result was a foregone conclusion? The idea that this was Parliamentary democracy at its best was frequently ridiculed in the press. And presiding over this sorry state of affairs was Reginald Royston.

The power Royston had at his fingertips ought to have made grown men quake and tremble in their shoes, but he knew that was not the case. His charges refused to take seriously a Speaker who, when he was not half asleep, looked only half awake. Known in the House as the Slumbering Speaker, he was a martinet when it came to procedure. But he cautioned, suspended and named Members for infringements of the rules so often that the MPs now treated such disciplinary proceedings in the same way a schoolboy might a hundred lines.

Speaker Royston tilted his head back to get his ear closer to the loudspeaker located in the headrest of his chair. His hearing was not what it was and even with the volume turned right up he still found it hard to catch all of what was being said.

'. . . that the strain placed upon the nation's sewerage network by the modern population through, er, through, the substantial volume of waste matter. . .'

'Perhaps the honourable Gentleman will tell the House whether the problem is caused primarily by number ones or number twos?'

The Member for Leith sat down to laughter from both sides of the House, his reputation as one of the wits of the Commons intact. His intervention served only to increase the embarrassment of the right honourable Member for Ripon. 'I thank the Member opposite for his help, but I am quite capable . . . '

The Speaker's attention drifted. He took a pinch of snuff in the hope that it would keep him awake. It made him sneeze violently. He searched within the folds of his robe for a handkerchief but its presence eluded him. He wiped the half-fingered woollen gloves he habitually wore in the Chamber across his face, smearing the discharge over him and them.

Reginald Royston would have been happiest as a Speaker two hundred years or more ago, in the days when Speaker Cornwall staved off his boredom with copious draughts of porter. Nobody grumbled overmuch when *he* took the odd forty winks in the chair. When he needed the convenience of a convenience, curtains were drawn round and the seat lifted to reveal a commode. His favourite Speaker was Sir Richard Rich, who had helped bring about the downfall of Wolsley and the deaths of Sir Thomas More, Fisher, Thomas Cromwell, the Protector Somerset, Lord Seymour and the Duke of Northumbland. When Anne Askew was tortured in the Tower of London, Rich had turned the rack himself. That was power.

Speaker Royston grimaced at the buffoons puffing themselves up before him. What he wouldn't give to be able to put one or two of these windbags on the rack. There was nothing to them but hot air. Prick them and they would burst. His eyes wandered along the red lines woven into the carpet in front of Government and Opposition benches, two sword-lengths apart in case the arguments became so heated that Members were tempted to skewer one another. In his imagination he saw an MP leaping from his place and, rapier held aloft, jumping on to the Despatch Box and despatching a member of the opposing side.

'. . . of which the majority are Victorian and suffering badly from the ravages of age.' 'Like the Cabinet!' came a shout which was ignored. 'Repairs must be taken in hand or . . . yes, all right, I will give way.'

'I am sure honourable Members of this side of the House must be delighted that, after years in which we have warned of the dangers of a collapsing sewerage system, this Government has at last come out of the closet − or should I say out of the water closet? − and realised the importance of such environmental matters. One might say that they are not only embracing the green movement, but the brown movement, too; lots of little brown movements, in fact.'

'The honourable Member for Leith goes too far, surely, Mr Speaker? Mr Speaker?' But neither the right honourable Member for Ripon nor the rest of the House, frantically waving order papers, were able to catch Mr Speaker's eye. It was firmly closed, as was the other one.

* * *

220

Felix Mumbles shook off the last few drops and zipped up his fly. Taking deep breaths, he crossed to the washbasin and filled it with warm water. He plunged in his hands, then tipped up the soap dispenser. Nothing. He tried the one to his left. Nothing. Nor the one to his right. Bloody cheapskate BBC.

He pressed the button on the hot air dryer. It gave a wheeze and stopped. Mumbles pulled at the roller towel next to it, but it would not budge. By the look of it, that dirt had been there for weeks. Who was he to disturb it?

He opened the door and, still taking deep breaths, turned left into the radio newsroom, shaking the water off his hands. How the hell did they expect him to read the news with wet hands? Around him, journalists tapped stories into the computer.

Mumbles glanced at the clock. Ten minutes to go. Plenty of time. He picked up his script and headed off towards Studio 3E and the waiting millions. Flipping the pages as he went, he voiced out loud the words with which might give him difficulty. 'Merionnydd Nant Conwy... Ruddy stupid Welsh gits ... Zimbabwe ... What's wrong with good old Rhodesia ... Ploughkeepsie ... What the hell's one of those when it's at home, for Pete's sake?'

Mumbles pulled hard at the outer door of the studio. It opened slowly at first, hissing and then giving suddenly once the air seal was broken. As it shut behind him, he filled his lungs a few more times and opened another door to enter the studio itself, nodding at the studio manager sitting at his control panel behind the glass. He sat down and plugged in the black bakelite headphones.

'Izvestiya... must remember to pick some milk up on the way home ... Weigerstrofer ... Polly's birthday on Thursday, Polly's birthday on Thursday. More than my life's worth to forget ... Zivojinovic...how's that for level?'

The studio manager nodded to express satisfaction and returned to his study of *Personal Computing Weekly*. These old-timers were always the same. Sorry they weren't still wearing dinner jackets. Making the thing into a big production. As if it wasn't exactly the same every bloody day.

High above the Palace of Westminster, in the belfry of the Clock Tower, the apparatus secreted by Riordan nestled securely in its hiding place. It was taped to a rafter just behind the pair of BBC microphones which pointed permanently at the bell known as Big Ben.

Twelve miles away, Patrick Riordan got off the Tube at Heathrow and headed for the British Airways check-in desk.

'All the papers been informed?' asked Prosser.

'Don't fret, Alex,' said Daniels. 'It's all in hand. We can't be certain they'll listen, but they're certainly all in receipt of that teaser press pack sent out by BIG's ace marketeer Jeremy Seaman. If it doesn't mean anything to them now, it certainly will after six o'clock. They'll get the second pack then, which will include the photos.'

Prosser and Daniels chuckled at the thought of what lay ahead. Roach was silent. He didn't approve. But what could he do?

Daniels stood up. 'Perhaps we'd better turn on the news.'

Speaker Royston jerked awake with a start. Look at the time. Not yet six. As he half-heartedly stifled a yawn, several MPs turned in his direction. He heard a few sniggers from the Government side. Cheeky beggars. He had his eye on them. But only for a moment or two.

'. . . And so, Mr Speaker, I beg to move this motion. . .'

'Bearing in mind the nature of this debate, does the right honourable Gentleman not think he should use different phraseology? In the context of this Bill moving motions could be misinterpreted.'

'I thank the honourable Member of Leith for his renewed intervention. He himself appears to be inflicted with verbal diarrhoea, of a particularly virulent kind.'

'At least my faeces come out of the proper place, not like the pile of excrement shooting from the mouth of the right honourable Gentleman.'

'Mr Speaker, I appeal to you.'

Cries of 'Ohh, ducky, do you?' greeted this. But there was no response from the Speaker. He was dreaming of the days of the rack, thumbscrew and the other sort of iron maiden.

As the language in the Chamber sank lower, so the Chamber itself began filling up with those MPs who always hang around in the hope of a good scrap materialising.

'I imagine that the right honourable Gentleman's exalted position is why he was thought qualified to present this bill. Presumably the Government believe that, as a Privy Councillor, he knows all there

222

is to know about privies. If there were fewer privies about, the whole problem might disappear.'

'Potties.' This from the Member for Alnwick. 'Always been good enough for me. Don't hold with these new-fangled hoojahs.'

The right honourable Member for Ripon rounded on his back-bencher. 'Potties? You're the one who's potty. You've still got to put the, uh, the waste matter somewhere.'

Several MPs, touched by the Member for Ripon's difficulties in describing what was at the heart of the matter, were kind enough to assist him as he faltered.

'Stools,' cried one.

'Turds,' yelled another.

'Dung.'

'Cess.'

The majority of the House were now helpless with laughter at their brilliance, not only at daring to voice such words, but at getting away with it.

'Bearing in mind,' said the Member for Leith, 'the load of crap emanating from that orifice of the right honourable Gentleman from which the sun does not shine, I suggest that the House treat this Bill with the contempt it deserves, and flushes it down the bog.'

'I have always thought the Member opposite a little shit. Now I realise that I was considerably underestimating his odiousness.'

'I thank the right honourable Member for that. I will treasure his words. They will help my rhubarb along a treat.'

The barracking back-benchers chanted 'Rhubarb, rhubarb' just to help the proceedings along.

The Member for Ripon was not to be outdone by an Opposition backbencher. 'I would not stoop so low as to wipe my bottom with the notes used by the honourable Gentleman opposite for his ludicrous speech. Who knows what I might catch?'

'You'll catch my fist in your face if you don't withdraw that last remark.'

'Oh, yeah? You and whose army?'

'Right, you lump of steaming filth. You asked for it.' The Member for Leith leapt over the Opposition front bench and got his hands around the throat of the Member for Ripon, who retaliated by kneeing the honourable Gentleman opposite in the groin. Rather than drag the two men apart, honourable Members instead cheered on one or other of the antagonists. The public in the gallery divided themselves into cheerers or booers, depending upon their political complexion. On the floor, order papers were waved wildly in the air.

At this point the Speaker woke with a start. Half-deaf he might be, but with his eyes open even Speaker Royston noticed that things were not as they should be in the debating chamber. 'Order, order,' he screamed.

'On a point of order, Mr Speaker. Was that "order, order" or "ordure, ordure"?'

'I will not have this . . . this . . . this kerfuffle. Get back to your seats at once, I say. Honourable Members must learn how to behave themselves.'

The Speaker's words had little effect upon the brawling Parliamentarians. He pulled himself to his feet. 'May I remind Members that when the Speaker is standing, he must be heard in silence and all honourable Members must resume their seats.'

Gradually the hubbub subsided.

'This really is not good enough. Do my eyes deceive me?' asked the Speaker. 'Am I seeing things?'

'Pink elephants, probably,' shouted one backbencher out of the side of his mouth, but without the aid of the loudspeaker mounted in his chair the Speaker did not hear it.

'I am referring to the Member for Lytham St Annes,' thundered the Speaker. 'He would appear to be showing the utmost disrespect for the Chair and the House as a whole.'

A hundred pairs of eyes swivelled towards the honourable Member who, until now, had been resting peacefully at the rear of the Government benches and had taken no part either in the debate or in the rumpus that followed it.

'Me? What have I done, Mr Speaker?'

'Not only done, but still doing. Don't come the innocent with me. Answer me this if you dare. What have you got in your mouth?'

The Member for Lytham St Annes flushed and tried to get the rest of the muesli bar down his throat quickly. 'Nothing,' he said, choking.

'I distinctly saw you eating, in flagrant breach of the conventions of this House. You know as well as I do that no food or drink must be brought into the Chamber.'

224

'Why pick on me?' the bewildered MP asked. 'What about all the rest of them? Brawling. Bandying around words like "shit", "turd" and the like?'

'Unparliamentary language, too. And on top of everything else, trying to shift the blame to other Members. Really, sir, you should be ashamed of yourself. This is a matter of the utmost gravity, as I am sure the House agrees. I must ask the honourable Gentleman to leave the Chamber immediately, otherwise I shall be forced to name him.'

The dazed MP for Lytham St Annes made his way out, shaking his head as he went.

The Speaker called for the debate to continue. 'Sir John Boredom, I mean Boreham.'

Sir John Boreham, Member for Ripon, Privy Councillor and Leader of the House, got to his feet once more.

'As I was saying, Mr Speaker, before I was so rudely interrupted. . .'

The Studio Manager tweaked a knob here and twiddled a knob there. He faded up the channel connected to the microphones above Big Ben, satisfying himself that he could hear the atmosphere through the speaker. In the background, he could hear faintly the noise of the street two hundred feet below. He returned to his perusal of the small ads in his computer magazine.

Behind him, another SM was checking and sorting the tape reports, arranging them in the order in which they were to be played into the news.

At two minutes to six, the door to the control room was thrown open and the assistant editor bustled in. He took his seat without a word to either of the SMs.

In the studio the senior duty editor sat down to the left of Mumbles and donned his headphones. He riffled through the copy of the completed script. It was the SDE's role to feed the sheets to the newsreader as the news progressed, ensuring that the half-hour programme finished exactly on time.

With just a minute to go, Mumbles cast his eye down the opening headlines. Nothing that should cause a problem there, at any rate. He did some more deep breathing exercises, to the annoyance of the SDE whose nostrils got the full benefit of the mixture of beer and halitosis.

Forty-five seconds to go. The SM switched on the red light in the corridor outside the studio. Over the loudspeaker in the cubicle could be heard the voice of the continuity announcer, unveiling details of the thrilling programmes yet to come on Radio Four that evening.

She finished with just thirty seconds to go to the hour. The SM faded up the microphone at Westminster. Mumbles took a swig of water, swilled it round his throat and swallowed it. A couple of coughs to clear the throat, a shuffle in his chair to get comfortable, and he was ready.

Through his headphones, Mumbles heard the chimes of Big Ben begin at twenty seconds to the hour, the four quarter bells ringing out the famous tune penned by Doctors Jowett and Crotch. 'Ding, dong, ding, dong. . . ding, dong, ding, dong. . . ding, dong, ding, dong. . . ding, dong, ding, dong.'

'BBC News at six o'clock. Good evening, this is Felix Mumbles. . . What the fucking blue blazes is that?'

Through his headphones came not the familiar sonorous tones of Big Ben striking the hour, but the jingle that had insinuated itself into the nation's subconscious over the past few weeks. 'Fizzical, Fizzical, Fizzical,' sang the backing group, just in case anybody was in any doubt what product was being promoted.

Too late, it dawned on Mumbles that the BBC does not encourage its newsreaders to employ such language before a live microphone, no matter what the provocation. Certain that his job had just disappeared in a puff of smoke, he gave vent to his feelings. 'Fuck this for a game of soldiers,' he said bitterly, just as the horrified Studio Manager galvanised himself into action and slammed the fader shut, depriving the fascinated radio audience of the rest of the Fizzical jingle.

'We seem to be encountering slight technical problems with the news,' said the continuity announcer. 'So while we're trying to rectify the situation, here's some music. Some *proper* music, that is.'

Within moments, all the lights on the switchboard at Broadcasting House had come on. It took a little longer, but soon the telephonists at Bush House, home of the World Service, were under siege too.

'That was most entertaining,' said Prosser, turning off the radio. 'Well done, Godfrey. Worked a treat. Make sure the couriers drop off the second press pack as soon as possible. If Fizzical isn't on the front page of every newspaper in the land tomorrow, perhaps even the world, I'll eat my hat. Now, if you'll excuse me, I've a little work to do.'

After they had let themselves out, Prosser noticed a peculiar smell hanging in the air. He did hope it wasn't Daniels. He didn't want anyone with BO on the thirteenth floor.

There are three hundred and thirty-four stone steps from ground level to the belfry of the Clock Tower at the Houses of Parliament. Walking up it was bad enough. Running was sheer murder. Albert Todd leaned against the doorway at the entrance of the belfry and wheezed and coughed for a while.

He looked above his head. There was the grille, above which were secured the two microphones. He unlocked a pair of steps being used by the workmen doing restoration work and set them in place. The grille moved easily and Todd poked his head through the gap. The leads running to the pair of microphones had been disconnected. They ran to a personal stereo taped to the girder. There was a cassette inside it, and taped to the machine was somebody's business card. Todd decided he'd better leave it all for the Police.

* * * 27 * * *

'WELL, where is he? I need him,' said Prosser.

'I'm afraid I don't know, Sir Alexander,' lied Sally.

'Damn, damn, damn!'

'Yes, Sir Alexander.'

'Well when he gets back, tell him I want to see him immediately.'
Prosser slammed the door shut behind him. What should she do? If
she went downstairs to warn Jeremy that Prosser was looking for
him, she might miss the chance to put the cassette back. She decided
to hang on for a while.

The great sewer debate continued. The Speaker was in a furious
mood. Something was going on. There were murmurs going around
the Chamber. He couldn't so much hear them as sense them. There
was a sudden influx of MPs, too, which could hardly be accounted
for by the debate itself, with some Welsh Nationalist Member
droning on about the ecological benefits of cesspits.

The newcomers seemed highly excited. Several were consulting
the Clerks of the House. What was happening? He was the Speaker
of the House of Commons, the third commoner in the land. He did
not like being kept in the dark.

'Order. As I am sure Members will recall, it was resolved in 1641
"That if any man shall whisper or stir out of his place to the disturb-
ance of the House, Mr Speaker is ordered to present his name to
the House." I have already had necessity to send one Member from
the Chamber during the debate. Mr Gwilym Williams,' he called,
inviting the Plaid Cymru Member to resume his turgid speech.

But Edward Stickler, Member for Leatherhead, was on his feet.

The Speaker snapped at him. He disliked this sort of behaviour,
particularly when it came from one of his favourite MPs, a man who
knew more about the workings and traditions of the House than

228

any other, himself included. 'I would have expected rather better behaviour from the Member for Leatherhead. The Member for Llanfairpwll. . .for Llanfairpwllgwyng. . .the Member concerned is obviously not giving way.'

'Not to that pompous windbag I'm not,' muttered the MP.

Stickler remained on his feet. 'But Mr Speaker. . .'

'Surely I am not going to have to discipline so distinguished a Member of this House?'

'Mr Speaker, I am trying to raise a point of privilege which, I am sure you realise, takes precedence over all other matters.'

'Privilege, eh?' said the Speaker, sitting up in his chair. He adored matters of privilege, the more obscure and archaic the better. 'Well, why on earth didn't you say so before?'

Now that he had the attention of the whole House, Stickler made the most of it. He was not an MP content to give speeches in the Commons. He orated. Although no division bells had sounded the chamber, which only quarter an hour earlier had been well-nigh deserted, was now packed. With his sonorous voice and precise diction, Stickler sounded like an old repertory actor, trying to make himself heard up in the gods on a wet Wednesday matinée.

'I have, Mr Speaker, to report the most flagrant case of contempt of this House that has taken place for many a year. The whole House will no doubt be aware that the BBC has microphones installed in the belfry of the Clock Tower to pick up the chimes of Big Ben, which are broadcast not only on the domestic Radio Four but also on the World Service.'

'It would appear that before six of the clock this evening, these microphones were tampered with so that listeners across the nation and around the globe were regaled not with the sound of Big Ben but with an advertising jingle for a soft drink.'

The House made its displeasure at the news known in the habitual manner – by giving its impressions of assorted farmyard animals.

'As if this was not enough, it would appear that the perpetrator of this dastardly deed has actually boasted of his actions by sending press releases to all the national newspapers. I have one here. It is headed "First Ever Advert On BBC" and gloats openly about how the act was executed.

'Although this person may not have offended against any of the laws of the land, I would remind the House that contempt of Parliament is a very serious matter. If I may be permitted to quote from Erskine May for a moment: "Acts which though they do not tend directly to obstruct or impede either House in the performance of its functions, yet have a tendency to produce this result indirectly by bringing such House into odium, contempt or ridicule or by lowering its authority may constitute contempt". This could surely hardly be a clearer case of contempt. One and a half million people in Britain listen to Radio Four at this time and I am informed that over eight million people around the world tune in to World Service. It seems unlikely that word of this outrage will not spread further.'

One MP began chanting 'Privilege, privilege, privilege' and his chanting was taken up by other members, until the assembled Parliament resembled a particularly boisterous football crowd. It sounded as though the nation's elected representatives would burst any moment into a chorus of 'Here We Go, Here We Go, Here We Go.'

'Before discussing what action the House should take, Mr Speaker, perhaps I should remind honourable Members that this is the first serious issue of privilege that has arisen since the broadcasting of our business began. I believe it would be better if we were not over-heard.'

The House roared its approval. The Speaker, who had been listening to all this in rapture, called to the Serjeant at Arms, Major Godfrey Proudfoot. 'Please ensure that all recording equipment is turned off immediately and station your men to ensure compliance with this order.' What a day, oh, what a day. He turned back to the Member for Leatherhead. 'Mr Edward Stickler.'

'Thank you, Mr Speaker. Surely it is vital that the House acts, and acts immediately, to punish and expunge this gross offence against its dignity. This is not a case where the identity of the culprit is open to doubt. This person has openly boasted of his deed, and even had the audacity to attach his business card to the infernal device. I believe we should act immediately, before he has time to evade us.'

Cries of 'Who is it?' came from both sides of the Chamber.

'The name of this infamous brigand, an employee of British Indus-trial Group, is Jeremy Seaman. Although honourable Members use only rarely the powers that we have at our disposal to defend our privileges, I fear this must be one such occasion. The House must act, Mr Speaker, and must act swiftly to bring this hideous miscreant

230

within its jurisdiction. I beg to move that Jeremy Seaman be brought into the custody of this House.'

A roar of approval erupted from all sides. Members flung their order papers in the air and, for the first time since taking the Speaker's Chair of the House of Commons, Speaker Royston knew true happiness.

The Major had been expecting a quiet evening's turn of duty, largely spent nattering with young Thomas and watching the sport on the television. But within minutes of taking over, he was having to keep hordes of pressmen at bay.

Fortunately, as it was after six, the main doors of BIG House were locked. But it was still a struggle stopping the blighters getting in each time the side door had to be opened to let a late-leaver out of the building. What made it all the more infuriating was that the Major and young Thomas had not the slightest idea what all the fuss was about.

On the thirteenth floor, Roach and Daniels were fielding calls from the press. The door to Roach's office was slightly open and Sally, prowling the corridor, could hear them both on the telephone.

'. . . Oh, yes. He's an extremely bright young man. He's come up with some splendid ideas for marketing the drink over the past few months, but he is inclined to go a little over the top at times. In the ordinary run of things, BIG would naturally stand foursquare behind one of its employees. This sort of thing is, however, quite different. He has obviously considerably exceeded the bounds of his duty . . .'

'. . . Of course, he was given a great deal of autonomy. BIG is not a company to keep its brightest people on a short rein. It was never thought that he would do anything as rash as this. I can assure you that Sir Alexander is as outraged as everybody else at this disgraceful act of vandalism . . .'

Despite Sally's efforts at educating Jeremy into the delights of social drinking, he still had little head for alcohol. A small glass of wine would suffice him for a whole evening. On this occasion, however, he was drinking beer, trying to drown the sorrow of learning that the man whom he had idolised, the man whom he had trusted, the man for whom he had been working for almost a year, was nothing more than a common criminal.

Jeremy had by chance alighted upon a particularly expensive imported lager of quite extraordinary strength. Half way into his second bottle, he was already well into his cups.

A policewoman entered the pub and looked about her, searching for somebody. Her eye caught Jeremy's for a moment then passed on. She marched over to a group of office workers carousing on the other side of the bar and tapped one young chap on the shoulder. Jeremy couldn't hear what she was saying, but he could see the guilty expression on the man's face as he spun round and found himself face to face with the law.

The policewoman looked him full in the eye, removed her jacket and then began unbuttoning her blouse. The group around the chap burst first into laughter and then into a refrain of 'Happy Birthday, Kevin' as the garments fell one by one to the floor.

Lucky old Kevin. Where was Sally? An increasingly maudlin and inebriated Jeremy weaved his way to the bar to get himself a third bottle of extra-strength lager.

'Those in favour say "aye". . . . Those against say "nay". . . . Carried,' roared the Speaker, as the enthusiastic MPs cheered.

The Speaker got to his feet and waited for the noise to die down.

'Order. This is not a chimpanzees' tea party. The House has ordered Jeremy Seaman to be taken into custody forthwith. The Member for Leatherhead has pointed out the necessity for speed. The House must act quickly to repair its reputation and honour.

'I do not prepare to wait to have a formal warrant drawn up. The Serjeant at Arms will take as many men as he feels necessary and arrest Jeremy Seaman,' he said, consulting Erskine May, '"by warrant of the mace, and not by writ".'

'Without the presence of the mace, this House cannot, of course, continue in session. We will resume when Jeremy Seaman is brought to the Bar.'

Six or seven Members rose to their feet on points of order, but the Speaker ignored them, stood up, lifted his gown and descended the three steps to the floor of the House of Commons. He walked sedately the length of the chamber. As he passed Edward Stickler, he winked surreptitiously at the honourable Member.

Major Godfrey Proudfoot, Serjeant at Arms, summoned the Deputy Serjeant at Arms, the Assistant Sergeant at Arms and one of the Deputy Assistant Serjeants at Arms. He adjusted his sword and marched up to the mace resting on the Table of the House of Commons. Seventeenth-century silver-gilt, the mace was the symbol of Royal authority.

He hoped they knew what they were doing. Still, on their heads be it. He grasped the mace, rested it on his shoulder and strode out of the House and into New Palace Yard.

The Serjeant at Arms, Deputy Serjeant at Arms, Assistant Serjeant at Arms and Deputy Assistant Serjeant at Arms bundled themselves and the mace, all five feet of it, into the waiting taxi. The dangling sword forced Major Proudfoot to perch uncomfortably on one of the tip-up seats.

The cabbie turned round in his seat, looking them over with a jaundiced eye. 'Blimey O'Reilly,' he commented. 'That thing's extra, you know. Where you off to then? Fancy dress party?'

A former Major in the Marines, Major Proudfoot was not one of life's great conversationalists. 'Gilbert Square, and less of your lip,' he barked, slamming the dividing window shut. 'I say, you chaps, have any of you got any money on you?'

'What do you mean they won't let you into the building?' barked the *Daily Mail* editor into the phone. 'Don't they realise you are a gentleman of the press?. . . I don't want excuses from you, Miller. I want that interview with Seaman, no matter what it costs. We're going to run it under the headline: "A National Disgrace". So pull your bloody finger out.'

'Pull up here, my man, and wait,' ordered Major Proudfoot. 'We will be taking a prisoner back with us.' From the cab descended the Serjeant at Arms of the House of Commons, attired in black court suit with knee breeches and black buckle shoes, his sword in a white scabbard swinging at his left hip. He slung the mace over his right shoulder as the Deputy Serjeant at Arms, Assistant Serjeant at Arms and Deputy Assistant Serjeant at Arms, all in morning dress, emerged from the taxi.

'Huddle round me,' Proudfoot said. 'I'm not having this rabble damaging the mace.' The press were too busy trying to get into BIG House to notice the extraordinary quartet until they were in their midst. Major Proudfoot and his three staff pushed and shoved their way through to the entrance.

233

He rapped smartly on the door. But the Major, backed by young Thomas, merely shook his head.

'Open up in the name of Her Majesty's House of Commons.'

He was wasting his breath. The security guards could not hear a word he said through the glass. 'All right, break it down,' he ordered.

The Deputy Serjeant at Arms looked at the Assistant Serjeant at Arms. The Assistant Serjeant at Arms looked at the Deputy Serjeant at Arms. The Deputy Serjeant at Arms had nobody else to look at.

'I'll have a go,' he said pluckily. The sea of journalists parted as he moved away from the door and took a run at it. The glass, bomb-proof and bullet-proof, was also proof against the shoulder of the Deputy Assistant Serjeant at Arms, who retired with a severely bruised arm.

Major Proudfoot produced his House of Commons pass and held it to the glass. This seemed to do the trick. The door was opened just far enough to allow him through, although the mace got slightly dented as it was slammed shut after him.

'I am empowered by Her Majesty's House of Commons to arrest Jeremy Seaman,' said Major Proudfoot.

'He's not here,' said the Major.

'Well, where the hell is he?'

'I haven't the slightest idea.'

'I know where he is, Major,' said young Thomas.

'Where?' said both Majors as they turned to him.

'In the Hat and Stick, I mean the Crown and Sceptre. The pub on the corner.'

'Well, why didn't you say so?'

'Nobody told me we was looking for him, Major.'

'Major?' asked Major Proudfoot.

'Seventh Armoured Division, Special Operations.' The much-used reply was trotted out without thought.

'And I'm a Dutchman,' muttered Major Proudfoot, looking the security chief up and down. He turned to young Thomas. 'You! You'll show me where this public house is and point out our Mr Seaman.'

If getting in had been a problem, getting out was still more difficult. Once more the mace suffered a bash, when Major Proudfoot swung it too violently at a camera being thrust in his face.

Taxi after taxi was drawing up outside BIG House, each disgorging five or six MPs. Unable to carry on their business without the mace, they had joined in the chase. The reporters might not have the slightest idea who the Serjeant at Arms was, but they recognised many of the Parliamentarians emerging on to the pavement outside BIG House and crowded round them.

The Serjeant at Arms' party made its way along the pavement and into the Crown and Sceptre. The hubbub of Friday evening drinkers discussing, arguing and chatting up gradually subsided. It's not every day a man in knee breeches, wearing a sword and carrying the whopping great mace of the House of Commons, walks into a pub.

In the corner, Jeremy was now on his fifth beer. It took him a little while to realise that he was being spoken to and by a man in the oddest clothes imaginable, waving around a peculiar sort of stick pasted all over with costume jewels.

'What are you supposed to be?' he asked. 'Not a policewoman. 'S interesting. Give you that. Bit daft, but interesting.'

'Are you Jeremy Seaman?'

'Might be. Might not be. Look, no offence intended, but I don't really think I want you to see you with all your clothes off. If you were a policewoman, it would be another matter entirely. Pull up a chair. Join the party. Have you seen Sally?'

'Is this the man?' demanded Proudfoot, turning to young Thomas, who nodded.

'In the name of Her Majesty's House of Commons, I arrest you by warrant of the mace and not by writ.'

But Jeremy had had enough of stupid people playing stupid games. No time for it. Snatching up his half empty bottle he bolted into the lavatory. Couldn't wait for Sally any longer. Decided. Going to have it out with Prosser. Face him with it.

He climbed on to the toilet seat. But the seat was in the raised position.

He extricated his wet leg from the bowl, lowered the seat and, standing on it, forced open the window, wriggled through and leapt out into the alleyway.

As Jeremy emerged into Gilbert Square, there was a shout: 'There he is. After him.'

Drunk or sober, if a vast crowd of people suddenly surge in your direction, dormant primeval instincts for survival automatically take over. Jeremy turned to the right, away from BIG House, and began running. For a man with four and a half bottles of extra-strength Belgian lager inside him he did not do too badly. He turned right at the end of the block and kept running. The pack seemed to be no nearer. The life of the average reporter or MP does not befit him for a race any further than to the nearest bar.

Jeremy turned right again, risking a glance over his shoulder. The pack was thinning a little, but there were at least a dozen of them sticking tenaciously to the chase.

He turned right once more, feeling in his pocket with his free hand. Sally had been teaching him to drive. They had had a lesson on the way into work that morning. Please let him still have the car park pass. With relief his fingers found the oblong plastic card.

He stopped running as he turned the corner into Gilbert Square. Ahead of him, he could still see a knot of people by the entrance to BIG House. He strolled nonchalantly towards the gate of the underground car park.

Jeremy clung as close to the wall as he could. When he reached the gate, he pushed the pass into the slot. The grille began to climb upwards. He heard a shout behind him. He ducked under the gate and, inside, put his hand over the magic eye. It rolled downwards again.

The first runner to arrive rattled the gate furiously.

'Jeremy Seaman? Miller of the *Mail*. Was this Big Ben thing really your idea?'

Jeremy was still trying to catch his breath. His reply came in short, drunken, gasps. 'Miller of the *Mail*. That's good. . . Like that. Trips off the tongue. . . Big Ben? Oh, the jingle. . . Yes, that was my idea, all my idea. . . Didn't write the music, though. Someone else did that. . . Now, if you'll excuse me, I've got a few words to say to Mr Prosser. He's a crook, you know. Shh. Don't tell a soul,' said Jeremy, trying unsuccessfully to put the fingers of one hand to his lips, and the bottle with the other.

On the thirteenth floor, Prosser's shirt was unbuttoned and the disc he kept round his neck was whirring away inside the personal computer on his desk. Earlier in the day, he had arranged to buy a substantial quantity of British Industrial shares, hoping for a rise in the price in response to all the free publicity the company was about to get. This was the first chance he had had to input the record of the deal.

236

He removed the disc and replaced it on the chain around his neck. Buttoning his shirt, he made his way up the spiral staircase to his own floor. It had been a busy day and he had had no time at all for any relaxation. He needed to relieve the tension. Seven hours without a fuck was asking too much of a man. He went in search of Lorraine. Nothing was likely to happen for a while yet. Roach and Daniels were keeping the press at bay. He wondered if she would like gooseberry fool as much as Lucinda had seemed to.

'British Industrial,' said Roach wearily as he picked up his cellular phone. 'Oh, hello, Desirée, it's you. . . No, I don't know what time it is. . . Really, as late as that. . . Well, I'm sorry if you're stuck with the kids, darling, but I'm having to work late at the office. I should have told you, but you know what it's like. . . Isn't it a bit late to be having a tennis lesson? Your coach must be very keen. . . Hang on a second, will you?' He picked up another phone, buzzing persistently. 'Roach?. . . Good evening, Mr Junkin. . . I'm sorry, but the lines have been rather busy. . . Right, I'll tell him at once. Thank you. . . Got to go, Desirée. Something's cropped up. Bye.'

He slammed the phone down. 'Daniels, you'd better go and tell Prosser they're on their way.'

Sally put her head inside Prosser's office. Nobody. Thank goodness for that. She walked over to the desk on legs of jelly and ducked underneath it. Just as she was putting the cassette back into its drawer, the outer door opened. Sally hunched herself up and closed her eyes in the hope that, if she couldn't see whoever it was, they might not be able to see her.

She heard footsteps, and then Daniels' voice shouting: 'Alex, Alex.'

'What is it?' came Prosser's irascible tones from the top of the staircase.

'Your tame MP, Junkin, has just called. Apparently the House of Commons has decided to arrest Seaman.'

Prosser came down the stairs. 'The Commons? I didn't know they could do that. I thought it would be the Police. Does it make any difference as far as we are concerned?'

'I don't see how it can, as long as they get him out of our hair.'

'All right. Get Security to stall them as long as possible. Where the hell is Seaman?'

The door to the office was flung open, hitting the backstop so hard that it bounced back and slammed shut again. It was thrown open again, a little more gently this time, and Jeremy marched in.

'Prosser,' he shouted, drunk and out of breath, 'you. . . you. . . you cad! I know all about you. You're not as honest as the day is long. I know that now. Oh yes. Can't pull the wool over my eyes.'

'What are you babbling about, man?'

Jeremy hiccoughed loudly, waving his arms around wildly and spilling beer on Prosser's precious carpet. 'Deal between you and Butterley. Know everything.'

'My dear chap, you're overwrought. If I were you, I'd calm down and prepare myself to be arrested.'

'You're going to be arrested? That's good.' Jeremy hiccoughed again.

'Not me, no. It's you that's about to be arrested.'

'Me,' laughed Jeremy. 'What for? I did a course in business ethics. What could they want to arrest me for?'

Prosser took a photograph from a folder lying on his desk.

'Who do you see in that photograph?' he asked Jeremy.

'Hold this,' said Jeremy, handing Prosser the bottle and taking the photo. 'That's me. And the chap I gave your package to yesterday.'

'Well done. And do you know what was in the package? Will you stop that,' he snapped at Jeremy, who was playing with the Newton's cradle on Prosser's desk, fascinated by the clicking metal balls. One of them came off its string and rolled under the desk, ending up just beside Sally. 'It was a tape recording of the Fizzical jingle which was secreted in the Clock Tower at Westminster and played on the BBC at six o'clock instead of the chimes of Big Ben.'

'That's clever,' Jeremy conceded.

'It was very bright of you to think of it.'

'I didn't think of it.'

'You shouldn't be so modest, Jeremy. Your business card was attached to it. A good employee, wouldn't you say, Mr Daniels, if a little inclined toward excessive zeal at times? It would appear, Jeremy, that you were rash enough to send out press releases boasting of how you arranged to have the first ever ad played on the BBC. Accompanying them was this photograph, showing you handing over the package to Patrick Riordan, who has been working on restoration work at the Clock Tower for several months now.'

'This Riordan chappie will be able to tell them he doesn't know me.'

'Ah, well. That could be a problem,' said Prosser. 'Sadly Mr Riordan caught a flight to the Bahamas just a few hours ago. He has decided to emigrate, beyond the reach of the authorities.'

'But . . .' began Jeremy, his befuddled brain struggling to assimilate all he was being told.

'So I think the best thing for all concerned would be if you just took the medicine that's coming to you like a man. Under ordinary circumstances, I'd do all I could to help you but, with my investiture at the Palace on Tuesday, it might be better if I stayed aloof.

'I'm sure you'll face the music quietly, Jeremy. In fact, I know you will. Because if you don't, it might somehow come to light that the twenty thousand pounds paid to Patrick Riordan came from a Cayman Islands bank account in the name of Jeremy Seaman. That money in turn came from a company called Seaman Nominees, an enterprise which appears to have made a good deal of money out of dealing in Nostrum and Pardoe Trust shares. Considering that you were the one who was so keen on Fizzical before the rest of us even knew about it, as various meeting minutes will confirm, and that your cellular telephone bill confirms the extraordinary number of calls you have made to banks in the Cayman Islands, it might not be so wise if this information was made public. Do you get my drift?'

'Mum's the word and Bob's your uncle,' said Jeremy, who had taken in hardly a word of it and was beginning to feel rather sick.

There was a loud knock on the door. Daniels opened it to find Major Godfrey Proudfoot, Serjeant at Arms of the House of Commons, slightly dishevelled and winded by the thirteen flights of stairs, leaning against the doorway with the mace dragging on the carpet behind him.

'It's just as well that I know that the date of the Battle of Spion Kop was 1900 or I'd still be in that bloody reception area and you lot would all be under arrest for obstructing an officer of the House of Commons in his duty.'

'Oh look, it's that fancy dress chap back again,' said Jeremy. 'You like fancy dress, Prosser, don't you? Is he a friend of yours? What is that awful smell in here? Anybody else notice it. You, Daniels? Or you, you rotten rotter, Prosser? Maybe it's a rat. I can smell one of those all right.'

239

'Jeremy Seaman, I arrest you in the name of Her Majesty's House of Commons.' The words came out in breathless but stentorian tones. 'For high contempt of Parliament, by warrant of the mace and not by writ. And for anyone who is interested,' the Serjeant at Arms said viciously, hating them all for the indignities they had made him suffer that evening, 'the smell is Death. I've smelt it hundreds of times before in every major theatre of war. Always smells the same, Death.'

Jeremy's hand, leaning on the desk top, slipped. He fell to the floor, coming face to face with Sally, huddled on her hands and knees under the desk. He struggled to his feet again, helped by the Assistant Serjeant at Arms and the Deputy Assistant Serjeant at Arms.

As they led him away through the door, Sally plaintively cried out, 'Jeremy.'

He turned round. 'Your manners leave something to be desired, Sally,' he said. 'Didn't your mother ever teach you it was rude to talk with your mouth full?'

* * * 28 * * *

DANIELS saw them out. When they had gone, Sally emerged cautiously from underneath the desk.

'Er, hello, Sir Alexander.'

'What on earth are you doing under there?'

Sally thought quickly. 'I, um, I came to talk to you about the investiture. When I heard voices, I though it might have been one of the girls. So I hid. I thought it better if they didn't hear what I have to say.'

'What *do* you have to say?'

'I. . . . Have you thought who you'll be taking with you?'

'I wasn't planning on taking anybody.'

Sally sucked in breath sharply between her teeth. 'That's what I thought. Do you suppose that's wise? A leading businessman, attending his investiture unaccompanied by a woman? You know how quick people are to talk.'

Prosser exploded. 'You mean they'll think I'm a shirt-lifter?'

'It's possible, isn't it? They're not likely to know any differently.'

'Holy shit. I can't have that sort of rumour getting round. You're quite right. But I can't take Jacqui. She's an ex-hooker.' Ex? thought Sally. 'Lucinda will probably know half the people there and Lorraine is hardly presentable at Court. It will have to be you.'

'Me? Oh, I couldn't.'

'You'd enjoy it.'

'No, sorry.' She was playing hard to get, enjoying Prosser's discomfiture.

'Why not?'

'Well, for start, I don't have anything suitable to wear.'

'Buy whatever you want. The sky's the limit. But for God's sake, come to the Palace. I can't have people thinking I'm a ruddy poofter.'

'I don't suppose you'd consider saying please?'

'For crying out loud, I'm not asking you to open your legs for me! I'm only inviting you to fucking Buckingham Palace to see the bloody Queen.'

'What a charming invitation. I'll sleep on it and let you know in the morning. Good night, Sir Alexander.'

It was difficult to know at what stage Reginald Royston, Speaker of Her Majesty's House of Commons and third commoner in the land, ceased to be a harmless eccentric and became certifiably, barking mad. But it was almost certainly some time that evening. As he took his chair he was gratified to notice that the assembled MPs stopped their chatter, awed and cowed by the importance of the occasion. Their mood was just as he would have wished it to be. Honourable Members were out for blood. Nothing united them like being made to look collective fools. The Speaker was determined that this evening was to be the pinnacle of his career, the moment when he took his place in the history books alongside the great Parliamentary Speakers like Addington, Cornwall and Rich.

'Bring the prisoner to the bar,' he ordered. At the far end of the Chamber there was a white line woven into the carpet. Above it, two bronze railings at waist height were drawn out from the oak barriers to either side. The Serjeant at Arms, battered mace on his shoulder, marched slowly up to the bar with Jeremy, still befuddled by the four and a half extra-strength lagers, shuffling along by his side.

His clouded mind was in turmoil. Sally under Prosser's desk? He had been convinced that she hated the man and loved only him. How could she do it? And yet it was she who had warned him about Prosser's being a crook. Jeremy was confused. He tried to concentrate, but his head was hurting.

'Prisoner at the bar, kneel in obeisance to this House.'

'On a point of order, Mr Speaker.' The Member for Cowley, Ted Biles, got to his feet. A firebrand and the most irritating thorn in the Speaker's side, he was commonly known as the Creature from Cowley, largely because of his reptilian lisp. 'According to Erskine May, prisoners are no longer compelled to kneel at the bar.'

The Speaker was not in a mood for Bile's carping criticisms. 'The Member for Cowley would do well to remember that the precedents

242

in Erskine May were created by the Speaker. I am sure my successors will one day be glad of my guidance on this matter. The prisoner will kneel.'

Jeremy appeared not to have heard. He was very tired. The Serjeant at Arms pressed heavily on his shoulder and he fell to his knees, grasping hold of the Bar for support. That was much more comfortable. Now if only that silly buffer in the wig would shut up, he could get a bit of shut-eye.

'Jeremy Seaman, you stand accused of . . .'

'On a point of order, Mr Speaker. He's not standing. You made him kneel.' The Creature from Cowley was on his feet again. This time he was dragged down by the MPs on either side of him.

'Jeremy Seaman, you stand accused of a high contempt of this House, which is a breach of our privilege. By your own admission, you are guilty of this heinous offence, bringing this honourable House of Commons into ridicule and disrespect. It only remains for me to serve punishment upon you.'

'Mr Speaker,' yelled Biles, jumping up once more. 'This is nothing but a kangaroo court. Have we no respect for the concept of natural justice? Surely the prisoner should be entitled to some form of Counsel or at the very least to speak in his own defence.'

'The Member for Cowley is, as he has already told us tonight, a keen reader of Erskine May. He will therefore be well aware that persons accused of breaches of privilege or other contempts are not allowed to be defended by counsel. Nor, indeed, need the House even hear the accused speak in his own defence. The honourable Member is risking my wrath with these persistent interruptions which are, I am sure, very much against the feeling of the House.'

The House cackled and brayed its approval.

'Mr Speaker, these procedures are in flagrant breach of at least three articles of the European Convention of Human Rights.'

'I am not having the Member for Cowley pointing his finger at me. Unless he sits down now, I shall be forced to name him. Jeremy Seaman, the facts in this case could hardly be clearer. Although I do not need to let you speak, you may do so if you wish before the House passes sentence.'

The fog clouding Jeremy's brain came and went. Sometimes things were quite clear. At other times, he could hardly see or think at all. Before he could gather his thoughts together, the chap in the wig was off again. Jeremy hiccoughed loudly.

'In days gone by, it was within the power of this House to punish offenders by various means: to torture them, to hang, draw and quarter them, to imprison them and to fine them. It is a matter of considerable regret to me that we no longer have the use of stocks within the precincts of the Palace of Westminster. I am sure honourable Members would then be able to demonstrate their strength of feeling at your reprehensible behaviour.

'However, I do still have to power to commit you to the custody of the Serjeant at Arms during the pleasure of this House. I beg to move that the prisoner at the bar be so committed. Those in favour, say "aye". Those against, say "nay".'

Only a few MPs dared go against the mood of the majority of the House, which was baying for blood.

'The ayes have it.'

Jeremy's fog lifted momentarily. With horror, he saw the Speaker don a three-cornered black hat. Half way to the floor already, he slid from his knees to a totally prone position. Those some distance away maintained that he had fainted. Those a little nearer were convinced that he had passed out in a drunken stupor.

'Throw some water over him,' ordered the Speaker, continuing when Jeremy showed some signs of life again, 'Before I pass sentence, may I remind the members of the press in the gallery that although Parliament acts only rarely to protect its privileges, that in no way diminishes its inalienable right to do so. This is, after all, the highest court in the land. My rulings are based upon the precedents set by my predecessors over a seven hundred year period.

'I have been concerned recently about the increasingly irreverent tone shown by the press towards this House. Those members of the press in the gallery will know that this House only allows its proceedings to be reported under sufferance. I do not wish to see the contempt committed by the prisoner at the bar mirrored in the reports in the newspapers tomorrow. Slighting and contemning an order of this House is itself a breach of privilege and punishable as such.'

He turned back to the prisoner. 'Jeremy Seaman, you have been found guilty of high contempt against Her Majesty's House of Commons. In the name and by the authority of this House you will be given into the custody of the Serjeant at Arms during the pleasure of this House.

'I see no reason why the costs of your incarceration should be met from the public purse. It is evident from your position, or possibly your former position, with one of the leading companies of the land that you are a believer in market forces. You will no doubt be delighted to learn that I am reviving the custom whereby prisoners pay the cost of their upkeep whilst in the custody of the Serjeant at Arms. You will pay over the sum of one hundred pounds for every day you are held.

'Take him away.'

The *Daily Mail* editor was practically wetting himself with excitement. 'I don't care how short it is, Miller. We've got the one and only interview with him. We can easily pad it out to a full page, no trouble. Get back to the office, quick as you can.'

Jeremy was led from the Chamber to the base of the Clock Tower. Prodded and shoved from behind, he was forced up the stone steps. The constant turning to the right as he climbed was having a profoundly unpleasant effect upon his already suffering insides. He tried counting the stairs to sober himself up, but kept getting lost when he got to seventeen.

After what were, in fact, one hundred and fourteen of them a voice behind called: Halt, prisoner.'

An ordinary, brown wooden door was unlocked. Jeremy was shoved inside and the door closed and locked behind him.

For the first time in what seemed like hours, he was left in blissful peace. He curled up on the cold stone floor and was soon fast asleep.

The Major had now acquired the necessary ingredients for the recipe from the *Revolutionary's Recipe Book*. But before his final act, the immolation of Prosser and BIG House, he had one further task to undertake. He could not rest easy until the agent of Rommel's death was dead.

He took the service lift to the roof and, by the light of his flashlight, made his way across to Maggie's shed. He lifted the latch and entered.

* * *

Not even the full force of Sally's sweetest smile, which usually made even the mightiest of men tremble at the knees, could budge the policeman at the gates of New Palace Yard.

'I'm sorry, miss, but he's not to have any visitors. More than my job's worth to let you up there.'

She could only suppose that he was either short-sighted or queer. As she turned to walk home to Crown Reach, the policeman called after her: 'If you're friend of his, miss, you might bear in mind how cold it'll be up there. There's no heating and the room faces east. Brass monkeys wouldn't last a minute.'

* * * 29 * * *

THERE WAS a terrible ringing inside Jeremy's head. Never again. Not another touch of alcohol would ever pass his lips.

He levered his eyelids open a fraction. It looked as if he had woken in a station waiting room, with tedious brown walls and a cold stone floor.

The sound of twenty-one tons of bells just a few feet above him drove right into his skull like a pneumatic drill. The floor beneath him vibrated with the chimes.

Slowly the pieces began to drop into place. He remembered the pub. He remembered the arrest. He even remembered being brought up the stairs to this room. But he was still very unclear about what had happened in the House of Commons itself except that he had been found guilty. But of what? And what was his sentence? He had a dim recollection of hanging, drawing and quartering being mentioned at one point. It seemed almost appealing if the alternative was being cooped up below those damn bells for long. The noise was appalling.

So was the cold. Still on the floor, Jeremy sat up and pulled the duvet about him to keep the warm air in. Strange. He had a Thomas the Tank Engine duvet just like this one.

All the papers in the land had been preparing to run stories along the lines of the *Daily Mail's* 'National Disgrace' headline, sympathising with the plight of the BBC and its unfortunate newsreader, applauding Parliament's swift and decisive action, so much at odds with the plodding progress of the more usual channels of law. But the Speaker's ham-fisted warning to the press about its reporting of Jeremy's trial had the most extraordinary effect. His unwarranted interference with press freedom cast the story in a completely new light. Important principles, such as the integrity of the media, were at stake here. The front pages were hastily rewritten.

One moment Jeremy was about to be vilified as enemy number one; the next he was held aloft as the people's hero, a man whose cheeky audacity had, as the *Daily Telegraph* put it, served 'to puncture the pomposity of Parliament and crack the complacency of the Corporation.'

'Alex,' said Roach, bursting into Prosser's office, 'have you seen the *Daily Mail*? Right across the front page, "Parliament Gets Fizzical". Must be worth a fortune in free advertising.'

A bust of Napoleon smashed against the wall just to the right of his head.

'What on earth's the matter? You should be pleased.'

'If you'd read the frigging editorial or their "exclusive" interview,' snarled Prosser, 'you'd see that the paper lionises that imbecile Seaman. The cretin makes a fool out of the BBC and out of Parliament, the two greatest institutions in the land, and these stupid jerks make him out to be some sort of martyred hero. It isn't only the *Mail*, either. Look at this one, and this, and this.'

Prosser threw a handful of papers on to the desk one by one. 'All of them praise what the prat's done.'

'What's the problem? I thought the whole idea was to get free publicity for Fizzical. This will do wonders for sales. It isn't only the British papers, you know. There are stories like this right around the world.'

'There are times, Joe,' said Prosser despairingly, 'when I wonder where you keep your brain? Look at them all. Who is mentioned as the marketing genius? Who gets all the praise? Not yours truly. Not Sir Alexander Prosser, the man who has built this company up from nothing. No. Man of the hour is a snotty-nosed college kid with a passionate interest in business ethics who couldn't fight his way out of a paper bag. Do they honestly believe he's capable of something like this?'

'But we arranged it so that they would. Anyway, does it matter? He's been locked up. What harm can he do us now?'

'He has to be let out eventually. What's it going to look like if we give him the boot? We'd be crucified by the press. No, we're saddled with Mr Seaman now. I daren't even demote him. Daniels, however, is another matter entirely. . .

'You'd better get out. I've got some serious thinking to do. Do something useful. Find out why Maintenance still haven't done anything about that bloody awful pong.'

'I don't understand,' said Sally. 'Why can't I see him?'

'He's not to have any visitors. Orders.' The policeman was adamant.

'But I'm his. . . his secretary.'

'This chap Seaman must have a lot of secretaries. You're the fifth or sixth this morning. What's he got that I haven't, eh?'

'This is ridiculous. I'm going to see my MP about this.'

The policeman laughed a deep hearty laugh. 'Your MP? At this time of day? Oh, that is a good one, Miss, if you don't mind my saying so.'

Jeremy's headache would have been bad enough had he woken up in his own good time in bed. But with those bells chiming above him every quarter hour, the pain was obviously not going to go away.

He was also hungry and extremely bored. It was very cold up here too. There was no heating. At least he had the duvet to keep him warm. He might have caught his death without it. The only cheering thing was that, pinned to the cover, he had found a short note from Sally: 'Putting the tape back, you cretin. Love you.' How could he ever have doubted her?

He had to admit that the view was stupendous. Jeremy's cell, if such an ordinary room could be called that, was a third of the way up the clock tower and level with the main building's roof. Looking east, he could see right down the river, past the Shell building and the Savoy, as far as the grey towers of the Barbican. Upstream, the view was blocked by the Palace itself.

Down below was the road leading to Westminster Bridge, where there appeared to be a demonstration taking place.

It was impossible to relax, not only because there was no bed or chair or resting place of any sort, but because he found himself transfixed by his watch, waiting in trepidation for the next set of chimes. It was coming up to the hour now. That was the worst of all. He braced himself, wrapping the duvet round his head to muffle the din.

Sally wandered round the corner towards Westminster Tube station, but there was a demonstration of some sort blocking the pavement, and the going was slow. The Police were trying to clear the protesters away, but they kept spilling into the street, blocking the traffic and then reforming.

With the Londoner's usual interest in other people's causes, Sally put her head down and plunged into the crowd. It was only when she pushed past a group of giggling girls chanting 'We Love Jeremy, We Love Jeremy' that she stopped.

She grabbed one of them by the arm. 'Where is he?'

The girl was only too eager to confide. 'Look along the level of the roof. Then go to the far left of the clock tower. That's his cell. Isn't it romantic, being imprisoned by Parliament and all. Perhaps they'll chop off his head. Ooh, I'd just die if they did that, I know I would. It's so exciting.'

Sally looked around her. The crowd was a surprising mix of people, many, she supposed, merely stopping out of curiosity on their way to work. A few placards were being brandished in support of Jeremy. One enterprising entrepreneur was already doing a roaring trade in 'I've Seen Jeremy Seaman' T-shirts. Another was selling plastic opera glasses, a pair of which Sally bought for an exorbitant sum.

As the bells chimed nine, she focussed in the direction indicated by the girl. The blur at the window didn't look much like Jeremy. Then, as Big Ben chimed its ninth stroke, he unwrapped his sound-proofing and she saw his unmistakable red-headed mop.

She lost her customary cool-headedness and began waving and shouting his name. Why was this happening? It really wasn't fair. It should be Prosser in there, not Jeremy. Who had he ever hurt?

'Free Jeremy Seaman,' she suddenly screamed.

Sally's call was taken up by the girl beside her and then by her friends. Soon, the whole crowd, by now occupying the whole width of Bridge Street, blocking the approach to Westminster Bridge, was chanting: 'Free Jeremy Seaman. Free Jeremy Seaman.'

Those cars, buses and lorries blocked by the demonstration added to the noise with their horns, although whether in support or hostility it was impossible to say.

Pragmatically Sally realised she was achieving nothing just standing there. If they wouldn't let her see him, she had better go to BIG House and see if something couldn't be done about getting him out.

* * *

Prosser's moods changed more often than Danny La Rue's costumes. By the time Sally arrived on the thirteenth floor, he was positively boisterous and firing on all cylinders. Sacking Godfrey Daniels had done a lot to buoy him up. Prosser had watched it all with Roach on the closed-circuit TV in his office.

Daniels had arrived at work to find a security guard in reception holding a plastic bag, into which all his belongings had been dumped. The guard stood by him while he was made to turn out his pockets. His company credit card, identity card and car keys were taken from him. The guard accompanied him to the exit and pushed him into the revolving doors.

'How will he get home?' asked Roach.

'He can bloody well walk for all I care.' Prosser's eye left the monitor and alighted on the screen displaying stock market prices. 'Look at BIG, Joe. Up thirty pence this morning. The amount of money I've made today should just about compensate for having to take Seaman back. We have to drive home this advantage. I want the marketing boys to drum something up that will remind people of last night's events. Something along the lines of 'Big Ben says, "I drink Fizzical"' or 'Other drinks are beneath contempt', or 'It's a privilege to drink it'. They'll think up something good if they don't want to be joining Daniels on the pavement. Well, what are you waiting for? Piss off and do some work.'

Roach would have to go, decided Prosser. He was getting soft and flabby. Butterley, on the other hand, was proving himself to be as tough as old boots and would make a splendid Number Two. He enjoyed working with Butterley. They were birds of a feather. Roach had far too many principles and scruples.

On his own again, Prosser contemplated BIG's share price. Should he sell those shares he had bought last night? No. Hang on a while. Things were really on the up and up at the moment. He would ride the wave.

Sally spent over an hour sitting in Jeremy's office mulling things over. Her concentration was not helped by the disgusting stench which had now permeated all of BIG House.

Tough as she had always presumed herself to be, Sally had to face up to the fact that she missed Jeremy terribly. She would not be able to forgive herself if she did not try to plead with Prosser on Jeremy's behalf.

Fully expecting that the man would do nothing more than laugh in her face, she knocked on the door of Prosser's office and entered. He was spraying the room with air freshener and could hardly have been in a more jovial mood.

'Sally. Come in, come. Now lover boy's behind bars, you'll be coming back to work for me. I want a few improvements made in our working relationship. I think you can guess what I'm talking about. I've always had a soft spot for you.'

'It doesn't look soft from where I am standing.'

Lecherous neanderthal noises issued from Prosser's throat. 'What you need, my girl, is a real . . .'

The phone had rung and, through force of habit, Sally picked it up.

'Sir Alexander's office . . . Yes . . . yes. . . yes. . . Well, why isn't the Major handling it?. . . What do you mean he's missing?. . . Yes, I'll tell Sir Alexander. . . Stall them as long as you can.'

Of course. It was the Seventh. Sebastian. . . In all the excitement, it had completely slipped her mind.

'What is it?' demanded Prosser.

'It's security. Three officials, all suits and briefcases, have turned up at reception with the Police in tow. They're demanding to come up and see you. Apparently, they've got a search warrant.'

'Me. . . a search warrant?' Prosser had turned deathly pale. 'Oh my good God!'

Prosser stood frozen to the spot with fear. But it only lasted a moment. Then he swung into action, unlocked the drawers of his desk and began pulling out papers which he fed quickly into the shredder one by one. As he did so, he loosed off a volley of quick fire instructions at Sally.

'Go and see Roach. Tell him what's happened. Make sure he gets rid of anything incriminating. Then get on to Daniels in Marketing Intelligence. Shit, I sacked him. . . well tell whoever to make sure their hands are clean in case anybody goes snooping round.'

Sally watched the pages going through the shredder. The information on any one of those sheets might be enough to save Jeremy.

'Perhaps I should do that, Sir Alexander?' she suggested.

'Just do what I tell you. Go on, don't hang about. Christ almighty, women! Tell them to do something and they have to stand around and ask you a lot of damn fool questions first.'

As Sally reached the door, he called after her: 'Before you do anything else, tell that idiot pilot up on the roof to get the helicopter ready, just in case. Now, get out.'

But Prosser still wasn't done with her. Just as she was disappearing through the door, he yelled: 'Sally, get back in here.'

He undid the top buttons of his shirt, reached inside and lifted out the chain that hung there. Dangling on the end was a computer disc. He approached Sally and hung it around her neck. As he did so, he grasped her arm very tightly, hurting her.

'Take this. Keep it very, very safe, nestling in that warm spot where I intend to be myself before too long.'

'What is it?' asked Sally.

Prosser kept his grip on her arm. 'I call it Medusa. Anyone other than me looking at the contents of that disc is likely to be turned into stone – or, to be more accurate, into concrete. Do you understand me?'

'Yes, Sir Alexander.'

'Well, get on with it, sweetie,' he said, slapping her on the backside and returning to his shredding.

Roach took Sally's news surprisingly coolly. He almost looked relieved.

Letting herself back into Jeremy's office, she shut and locked the door and quickly made calls to Marketing Intelligence and the pilot. Then, using a tissue to keep her fingerprints off it, she lifted Prosser's disc from around her neck and inserted it into the computer. She set the copying program in motion, inserting first Prosser's disc and then a new one as the machine requested.

'Come on. Hurry, hurry,' she appealed to it.

The computer whirred away for what seemed like an eternity before the contents were copied across. Still holding it by the tissue, Sally unclipped Prosser's disc from the chain and examined it closely. Only when she was certain that there no distinguishing marks did she put the new, identical disc on to the chain and rehang it around her neck. Prosser's original disc she put in her handbag.

As she opened the door to the office, the lift at the end of the corridor opened and one of the security guards stepped out, followed by two policemen and three men in almost identical charcoal grey suits. One of them was Sebastian Embleton, no longer sporting a week's growth of hair on his face nor, judging by his immaculate turnout, sleeping in the doorway opposite BIG House.

253

As the guard led them down the corridor, Sally tried to keep the recognition out of her eyes. Sebastian ignored her as he passed.

Eager to see what happened, she followed the group at a discreet distance.

The guard knocked on Prosser's door. Sally could hear the shredder being turned off.

Sebastian, quite obviously the leader of the group, had already started the proceedings. '. . . Not obliged to say anything unless you wish to do so but what you say may be put in writing and may be given in evidence.'

Prosser was having trouble taking it all in. 'Could you tell me again what Act I am suspected of having committed offences under?'

'Don't play the innocent, Prosser. The Wildlife and Countryside Act, 1981. I have reason to believe you have in your possession a bird included in Schedule 4 of the Act which has not been registered and ringed or marked in accordance with regulations made by the Secretary of State. Failure to do so is an offence under the Act. There are other associated offences with which you may be charged, such as using live drugged bait, but this will do for now.'

'The frigging Wildlife and Countryside Act?' Prosser, incredulous, began to laugh, staring at the heap of unnecessarily shredded paper.

'You may not take the protection and preservation of wildlife seriously, Sir Alexander, but we do. Should you refuse to cooperate, I am empowered to search you and your entire premises.'

'You're not from the Department of Trade then?' spluttered Prosser between guffaws. 'No, obviously not. Well, search away, dear chap.'

'We'll start with the roof, I think.'

'Of course. I'll lead the way.'

The helicopter engine was at full power as the group emerged on to the roof, ready for a quick getaway. Prosser drew his hand across his throat and the pilot cut the power.

Despite his relief that the DTI had not arrived on his doorstep and that he wasn't going to have to flee the country, Prosser had no wish to be prosecuted under the Wildlife Act. The British might not give a bugger about financial fraud but they could be bloody touchy about anything to do with animals. He was terrified that, coming on top of the Big Ben scam, this development might somehow lead to problems with his investiture. He'd worked hard for that knighthood and he wanted it more than anything else in the world.

With Sebastian Embleton at his elbow, Prosser unlatched the door to Maggie's shed. There, blinking in the daylight like some gigantic owl, was the Major.

'Thank God for that,' he said, as he stumbled out into the open. 'I thought I was goin' to breathe my last in there.'

Prosser looked behind him into the shed, but there was no sign of Maggie. He turned to Sebastian. 'It looks as though the bird has flown, Mr Embleton. That's a crying shame. It was a prize homing pigeon if ever I saw one.'

'Pigeon?' exploded Sebastian. 'You're trying to tell me you kept a pigeon in there?'

'But of course. What did you think I had?'

'There was a female goshawk in here until the other day, I'd stake my life on it,' Sebastian said. 'You,' he barked at the Major, 'what sort of bird was in there?'

The Major, bewildered by the unexplained presence of the Police and three besuited men, didn't know what answer was for the best. 'I didn't see,' he answered truthfully. 'It was dark when I opened the door. Somethin' flew out at me and I fell. Next thing I know, I'm shut in. Whatever it was, it doesn't half pong.'

'Sally, perhaps you would escort these gentleman from the premises?' said Prosser.

'Goodbye, Sir Alexander,' said Embleton bitterly. 'I hope your bird returns soon.'

'Eh?' said Prosser.

'As a pigeon fancier, I'm sure you are aware that the whole point of homing pigeons is that they come home again.'

'Oh yes, of course. Yes, she'll be back.'

'And so will I. Good day.'

The cold had sharpened Jeremy's mind. Free from distraction for the first time in months, he found he was able to think clearly. He had become used to the chimes of the bells, even welcoming them as old friends.

He had filled several pages of his notebook. He couldn't wait to try out his new marketing ideas on Sally.

There was a knock on the door. It was unlocked and a tall and distinguished gentleman entered, stooping under the lintel as he did so. He offered Jeremy his hand.

'Sir John Boreham.'

255

'How do you do? I can't offer you a seat, I'm afraid. There aren't any.'

'Good gracious. It is a bit spartan in here, isn't it? I'll have somebody see to that.'

Sir John seemed a little uncomfortable. He wandered over to the window and peered out. 'A good view, at any rate.' He turned to face Jeremy. 'You've no doubt been wondering how long we intend keeping you here, Seaman – uh, Mister Seaman.'

'The thought had crossed my mind.'

'Well, we've had a word with the Opposition and they agree with us that there's really no need to keep you here much longer. In the cold light of day, we recognise that tempers were running a little high last night. It had been a long day and the House got a little over-excited. I should stress that this sentiment has nothing to do with the demonstration or the press coverage of your trial. Nothing at all. The House of Commons couldn't possibly bow to that sort of pressure. No, it's just that we recognise that you've probably learnt your lesson by now.'

'What demonstration? What press coverage?' asked Jeremy, but his question was drowned by the peals of the bells chiming the half-hour. Sir John covered his ears with his hands, aghast at Jeremy's indifference to the noise.

When they ended, Jeremy asked: 'Does that mean I can go now?'

'What?' yelled Sir John, his hearing still not back to normal. Jeremy repeated his question. 'Well, not quite yet. You see, the Speaker is unfortunately not of the same opinion. With what little mind he appears to have left he seems to be thinking less in terms of days, and more in terms of months, I'm afraid, or possibly even years. Now he's ranting on about bringing every newspaper proprietor and editor in the country before the House for contempt, which is obviously quite out of the question. We have to face up to the fact that the man has flipped his lid. It's tragic.

'So you see, to get *you* out, we've got to get *him* out first. The trouble is, deposing a Speaker isn't a terribly simple thing to do. It's going to take us until Monday, at the very earliest. The whole thing's bloody inconvenient, I don't mind telling you. Plays hell with the Parliamentary timetable. Do you think you could bear to stay here over the weekend?'

* * *

256

After handing the copy of Medusa to Prosser, Sally went home, claiming a stomach ache. In her handbag, she had the evidence that would ensure not only the release of Jeremy but also the downfall of Prosser.

In her study back at Crown Reach, she turned on the computer and, using a handkerchief to avoid adding her own fingerprints to those of Prosser, took the disc and inserted it in the machine. A message flashed on to the screen.

'Password 1?' It asked peremptorily.

Shit! A security disc. How the hell did she know what the password was? Presumably only Prosser knew. Damn it, she wasn't a hacker.

She typed in the word 'Prosser', only to receive the reply: 'Incorrect password. Please try again.'

'Alexander' didn't work, nor did 'Charles', his middle name.

Sally tried 'BIG', 'Pardoe' and 'Nostrum', with no more success.

Wearily, she took a pad of paper and began writing down the words as she tried them. This was likely to be a very long process. Still, she had all weekend.

Jeremy ripped open the envelope from British Industrial, hoping it was from Sally.

But it was a formal letter from Nettle, informing him that if he remained away from work beyond next Thursday, he would need to produce a medical certificate or face dismissal.

Jeremy screwed it up and threw it to the ground. They didn't waste any time, did they?

Sally wasn't wasting any time either. But nor was she getting anywhere. She tapped away at her keyboard until the early hours of Saturday morning, trying to break Prosser's code. At every attempt the screen flashed up the message: 'Incorrect password. Please try again.'

In the confusion on the roof, the Major had slipped away. He didn't want to have to explain to Prosser what he had been doing inside the shed. No doubt he would be summoned to see the man on Monday. But the Major had other plans for Monday.

257

Young Thomas had told him about the dismissal of Godfrey Daniels. It looked like the opportunity he had been waiting for. Daniels' office was directly underneath Prosser's.

It would very probably now be empty. If he set up the incendiary device there during Monday it was unlikely to be discovered in time. How satisfactory to burn down BIG House, together with its murdering tyrant, on the eve of his investiture at Buckingham Palace.

So, Monday evening it was. He would sit here in his kitchen watching as the purple light on his wall was overtaken by red and orange, as the flames devoured Prosser and his detested building.

The firebomb had already been prepared and was sitting in the corner of his living room, looking like something put together in an early edition of Blue Peter. But the Major wasn't concerned with aesthetics.

He set to work making a sign for Daniels' door.

In his garden, unseen by the Major, Maggie perched in the branches of a sycamore, preening herself.

Sally had intended to spend Saturday buying an outfit for the investiture on Tuesday. But it was already past noon when she woke, still in front of the computer, her head on the desk, and Prosser's disc had to come first. With luck, she might have cracked it before the shops shut.

But she was at it until dark. Around her the strewn plates and cups were evidence of hastily grabbed food and drink. The floor, covered with discarded pieces of paper, was ample proof of her lack of success. She'd tried every possible subsidiary of Prosser, every employee and every associate of his she could think of.

By about half-past eight, Sally was ready to give up. She was obviously never going to manage it.

'Damn,' she typed in frustration. It made her feel a little better.

'Incorrect password. Please try again,' was the inevitable reply.

'Shit,' she entered. It was quite theraputic.

'Incorrect password. Please try again.'

'Fuck,' she hammered on the keys.

'Thank you,' displayed the computer. 'Password 2?' it now asked.

Password 2? She had done it! She should have guessed. Just the sort of thing a foul-mouthed, foul-minded little creep like Prosser would use.

Now that she had latched on to the way his evil mind worked, it took Sally only ten minutes to find the next two passwords. Eschewing the clinical, polite words for the more intimate anatomical parts of the body, 'Cock' was the key that unlocked the second door.

'Thank you. Password 3?' prompted the computer.

'Fuck' and 'Cock'. If he was sticking to four-letter words, it was pretty obvious what the next one *ought* to be.

Sally typed: 'C-U-N-T'.

Bingo! She screamed with delight as the door to Aladdin's Cave opened and the screen filled up with characters.

As she explored the files on the disc, it quickly became clear why Prosser had been so keen for it not to fall into anyone else's hands. He had kept meticulously detailed records of his share dealings over a ten-year period, most of which had been conducted through various offshore banks. All the financial centres favoured by those anxious to avoid the attentions of the regulatory authorities were there: the Cayman Islands, Bermuda, The Turks and Caicos Islands, Netherlands Antilles, Liberia, Panama, the Cook Islands, Switzerland, Liechtenstein.

It wasn't only the shares of companies with which British Industrial Group had been involved that had attracted Prosser's attention, noticed Sally. His advance information about many of the takeover bids of the past few years appeared to be impeccable, judging by his success in buying shares just before the news became public. Sally whistled when she saw the size of his dealings in the shares of Nostrum and Pardoe Trust. The man must have made a fortune from that alone.

This information occupied only one of the files on the disc, however. The others contained details of the private lives, some scandalous, some merely unsavoury, of a variety of people, most of them in the business world. Roach was there, as was the entire BIG board. No wonder they all put up with Prosser's behaviour. They had to. He had each and every one of them in a painful half-Nelson from which there was no honourable escape.

To Sally's disgust, she came across the name of a businessman who had been vilified in the gutter press for his extra-marital sexual antics with a Page Three girl. The date of Prosser's computer entry pre-dated the scandal becoming public. Prosser's work, no doubt. It could hardly be a coincidence that his company had shortly afterwards been taken over by British Industrial.

Carefully, she went through every file on the original disc, weeding and sifting the information.

It was an arduous process. But it was a labour of love.

* * * 30 * * *

'JEREMY.'

'Sally.'

In the cell in the Clock Tower at Westminster, they hugged each other. Sally had had a phone call from Sir John Boreham just before lunch, telling her that Jeremy was to be freed.

'You've got terrible bags under your eyes, Sally. It ought to be me, the prisoner in the tower, who looks the wreck. In fact, it's not been too bad. I've been working jolly hard. I've had lots of good ideas. What do you think about luminous advertising billboards, for instance? Put them on corners and, as the car headlights sweep round, they pick out the luminous bubbles and the slogan "Fizzical's Fizz Fizzles Faster".'

'Jeremy,' interrupted Sally, but it was no use. The genius was in full flow.

'That's just one. I've had loads more. You know that in the cinema these days, placement is all the rage, companies paying to get their products on to the screen? Well, why don't we do it with books? BIG has got a publishing arm. We'll pay best-selling authors to pack their pages with British Industrial products. It'll be a great way of advertising our wares, particularly if we use the cover to good effect.'

'Jeremy, I have to tell you something . . .'

'Best of all though, Sally, is my idea for repackaging Fizzical. Prepare yourself for this one. What do we put the drink in at the moment? Ordinary cans, that's what, just like every other drink on the market.

'What do you immediately notice when you look at a whole load of cans from above? It's obvious, isn't it? No? Well I'll tell you. Lots of wasted space in between them. What's the radius of a can? Roughly one and a quarter inches, I reckon. Its area is pi r-squared, or about 4.9 square inches, right?'

261

'Jeremy, we have to talk . . .'

'Say you have sixty-four cans. That's a total area of 314 square inches. But – and here's the crucial thing – the floor area used is 400 square inches. Over twenty per cent of your floor space is nothing but air. So, instead of all this waste, why don't we take advantage of the BIG logo and make the cans triangular?

'Now, I know what you're going to say. You're going to tell me they'll be more expensive to produce. True, but they'll pack far more closely together, so we'll probably be using up ninety-six per cent or more of our storage space, and they won't have to be so high. That's an immense saving. In fact, because the cans will be such a novelty, we can probably put far less liquid in each can. Just think of the improvement we'll see in our margins.'

'Jeremy, I've got something far more important than. . . triangular? You know, that's not a bad idea. The cans would dovetail together.'

'Exactly.'

The Assistant Deputy at Arms, who had been waiting tactfully outside the door, nudged it open. He'd been told to treat Seaman with kid gloves, but she had been in there almost fifteen minutes.

'No, no, you noodle,' the girl was saying, 'that's not how you work out the area of a triangle. Don't you remember anything from your schooldays. It's. . . it's. . .'

'Ha, clever clogs. I'm not the only one who's forgotten elementary maths. Look, if you draw it, you can make a rough calculation. Suppose we keep the same amount per can. We can then get about eleven in a row of twenty inches. That's a hundred and thirty-two in all.'

'Oh, brilliant. That makes six hundred and sixty square inches of can in a floor space of four hundred square inches. It's not that revolutionary an idea. Oh, hello. Can we help?'

'Sorry, miss. I was just wondering if you'd be long, only it's nearly the hour and I would rather not be here when . . .'

'Too late,' crowed Jeremy, as the chimes began. He enjoyed watching the reactions of visitors as the bells did their stuff. Sally's face was a picture. He took her in his arms and kissed her hard, the reverberations of Big Ben echoing round the sound chamber created by their joined open mouths.

* * *

262

On the door of Godfrey Daniels' former office hung a sign: 'Absolutely no entry except by signed permission of Sir Alexander Prosser'.

Inside, the Major was at work, his progress hampered somewhat by the handkerchief held to his nose to stifle the smell of the decomposing Rommel. Inside the box he placed under the desk the highly inflammable phosphorus was safely wallowing in baby oil inside the condom. He had decided in the end on a French tickler.

The Major set the alarm clock for nine o'clock. He stood on the desk and, taking a screwdriver from his top pocket, disconnected the smoke detector and sprinkler.

Opening all the filing cabinets in the room, he piled every scrap of paper on to the desk.

Only when its top was submerged beneath the mound did the Major step back to admire his handiwork. That ought to do nicely.

He let himself out into the corridor and locked the door behind him.

Goodbye, Sir Alexander Prosser.

Sally unlocked the door to the flat. Jeremy was still sulking because she'd refused to allow him to talk to any of the reporters waiting outside Parliament or to sign any autographs.

'Wait till I explain what's going to happen tomorrow,' she had said. 'Then you'll see why it's wise to keep your head down today.'

She put Jeremy in front of the computer and sat in his lap. With one hand she tousled his hair. With the other, she inserted the disc and typed in the first of Prosser's passwords.

'Sally!' exclaimed Jeremy, when he saw what she had written.

Then the second password.

'Really, what has got into you?'

As she tapped in the third, Jeremy coloured. 'This really is too much, Sally. I had no idea you knew such language. . .what's that?'

'Less talking. More looking.'

'Good grief.'

'Good grief is right. The complete record of Sir Alexander Prosser's illegal share dealings, going back over an entire decade.'

'But this is just what we need, surely?'

'Give the man a telephone. He's got a whistle to blow.'

* * *

At that moment, Prosser was blowing his own whistle. On the roof of BIG House, he was trying to tempt Maggie back. But despite the familiar shrill noise and the lure of fresh rabbit, there was no sign of her. Damn the bird.

The longer a hawk was allowed to remain free, the harder it was to retrain them. Maggie had been away over the entire weekend and Prosser's hopes of getting her back were fading.

Behind him the door to the empty shed banged as it was blown to and fro in the breeze.

In a doorway on the other side of Gilbert Square, a cold and embittered Sebastian Embleton huddled, peering intently through a pair of binoculars.

'Hello. Fraud Squad, please. . . They're putting me through. . . Good afternoon. To whom am I speaking? Detective Constable Bosworth? Congratulations, Detective Constable Bosworth. It's your lucky day.

'If you check your records, I am sure they will confirm that the Stock Exchange investigations into the share dealings just before the takeover of Pilsbury Glass came to a dead end when they ran up against various Cayman Islands-based nominee companies. How would you like it if I gave you the name of the beneficial owner of those companies, a prominent British businessman, together with exact details of how the deals were done, bank accounts used, the stockbroker through whom the deals were routed, the lot?

'Go and get your file, Detective Constable Bosworth. You are about to be handed this nation's biggest insider dealer, all neatly tied up and gift-wrapped. Give me your direct number and I'll ring back in fifteen minutes.' He hung up.

'Really Jeremy! Try not to look as though you're enjoying it so much. Give me the phone. My turn now.'

Sally dialled the number of the first of BIG's directors. 'Mr Akenside? Sally Fluke here, Sir Alexander Prosser's personal assistant. I'm afraid that this week's board meeting has been brought forward to tomorrow afternoon at three. I know it's very short notice, but Sir Alexander asked me to stress how vital it is that you attend. . . You will? Splendid. I'll let him know.'

She went through the list. By the time Jeremy rang the Fraud Squad again, all but Bourne had been tracked down.

'Hello again. Surely it's not still Detective Constable Bosworth? I'm sorry to hear that. I'd have thought they'd have made you up to Detective Sergeant by now. It's only a matter of time, I'm sure. Got a pen?'

An excited Detective Constable Bosworth passed on what he had learnt to Detective Sergeant Davies. A cautious Detective Sergeant Davies thought that he ought to have a word with the Chief Inspector. The Chief Inspector thought that, all things considered, it might be best if he spoke to the Commander. The Commander, for his part, felt obliged to get on the phone to the Commissioner's Staff Officer who then had a word in the Commissioner's ear.

The Commissioner put in a call to 10 Downing Street and spoke to the Prime Minister's Parliamentary Private Secretary, who thanked the Commissioner, telling him that he knew the Prime Minister would take a very, very keen interest in this.

That, he thought as he put the phone down, was putting it mildly. The Prime Minister would be cock-a-bloody-hoop.

As nine o'clock approached, the Major sat in his kitchen, staring at BIG House. Not long now.

The building would be virtually deserted at this time of night, apart from Prosser's accommodation on the fourteenth floor. Just in case anybody should spot it too quickly, the Major had tampered with the building's fire detection system.

From Daniels' old room on the twelfth floor, the flames would spread upwards, forcing their way into Prosser's office and the surrounding rooms on the thirteenth floor. The circular staircase in Prosser's office would act like a chimney, sucking the heat and smoke up into the living quarters.

Would he die from the smoke or the fire? the Major wondered, as he tucked into his fish, chips and mushy peas. And why could you never get decent batter these days?

To get into BIG House, Jeremy and Sally had had to fight their way through a mob of waiting reporters.

Although Jeremy's return to the thirteenth floor had been welcomed by Roach, who had claimed truthfully that he had missed him, Prosser had been less gracious.

'If you're such a fucking genius, give me one good idea,' he had taunted Jeremy. 'You can't, can you, because you're just a nothing. I'm the one with the ideas here. And who gets the credit? A red-headed half-wit hardly out of nappies. Well, I'm warning you, Seaman. One foot wrong, just one foot wrong, and you're out.'

'Yes, Sir Alexander,' Jeremy had said humbly. The suggestions he had thought up during his incarceration could wait a day or two. The crucial thing was that he still had his job

'It looks as if the crowd has thinned out down there,' said Sally, just before nine o'clock. 'Shall we chance it?'

'Why not? I'm getting hungry. We have to go home sometime. Besides, I'm still hoping for the traditional welcome given to prisoners on their return home.'

'Why, Mr Seaman! What can you mean?'

'I'll explain later. Hadn't we better shut the windows? It's terribly cold in here.'

'We're lucky they open at all. Apart from those on the thirteenth and fourteenth floors all the other windows in Big House are sealed. The stench on the lower floors is just appalling. The air conditioning seems to make it worse. The Maintenance people have been trying to track down the source for days. If Prosser isn't careful, the building will be shut down as a health hazard.'

The phone rang just as they got to the door. Sally picked it up.

'Sally Fluke. . . Carol, how nice to hear from you. That's all right. I'm more often here than in the flat these days. Hold on a second, will you?' She put her hand over the phone. 'Jeremy, it's an old college friend. You don't mind hanging on a few minutes while we have a natter, do you?'

'Be my guest.'

Jeremy had had enough of being cold in the Clock Tower. He wanted to feel a bit of warmth. He closed the window, returned to his desk, and picked up the *Economist*.

The Major plucked a fishbone from between his teeth, staring intently at BIG House as he did so.

It was gone nine. Surely he should be able to see the flames by now?

* * *

266

Jeremy held his handkerchief against his nose. With the windows shut, the rancid, sickly smell was overpowering.

Sally was still talking. He looked pointedly at his watch. It was five past nine.

He ran his finger under his collar. With the windows shut it was getting awfully hot.

* * * 31 * * *

THE MAJOR's head was cradled in his folded arms. He was snoring loudly.

One of his arms slipped from the table, jerking him awake. He shivered as he emerged from the fog of sleep.

He glanced at his watch. Half-past seven! How could he have slept so long?

With a start, the Major remembered why he was sitting by the window. He looked out. BIG House was still standing, seemingly intact.

What on earth could have gone wrong?

He made his way sluggishly through to the bathroom and splashed his face awake. He'd have to get into his uniform one final time and find out for himself.

When Sally arrived at BIG House at about eight-thirty, Prosser's Rolls stood outside the entrance.

'Not due at the Palace till between ten and ten-thirty,' the disgruntled chauffeur told her, as she wound her window down. 'But His Nibs has had me up since six, cleaning his precious motor. I mean, it's not as if the Queen's going to come out and inspect it personally, is it?' He threw the sponge forcefully into the bucket.

Sally smiled and continued into the underground car park. She had persuaded Prosser that it was essential she get changed at BIG House and had insisted on the use of a room on the fourteenth floor.

Prosser had chosen 1815 – Waterloo – to mark the great day.

Stepping out of the lift, she found him already up and about, wandering round in a purple dressing gown throwing orders left, right and centre. Lucinda had been roped in and was pressing the pants of his morning dress. She looked daggers at the newcomer. It was bad enough Sally going to the Palace instead of her, without having to act as a skivvy too. Sally smiled sweetly at her.

All the windows were open, she noticed. The smell was obviously still as bad as ever.

'You,' snapped Prosser at Sally as soon as he saw her, a handkerchief soaked in cologne held to his nose. 'Is my car being washed?'

'It was sparkling when I passed it.'

'What about underneath?'

'What?'

'They look under cars with mirrors when you get to the Palace. What are they going to think if they look underneath my Roller and see it caked in dirt?' He turned to Niblo. 'Ron, go down and tell that bloody chauffeur I want it gleaming underneath. You look very pretty, my dear.'

'I haven't got changed yet, Sir Alexander.'

'No, of course you haven't. Of course you haven't.'

'The car's being got ready. Your suit's being pressed. You've got plenty of time. Why not go and relax with a bath or a shower while I get changed? You'll feel much better for it.'

'You're quite right,' he said, squeezing Sally's cheek. 'Come and have a shower with me and we can both relax.'

'Gosh, is that the time?' she said desperately. 'I really must go and get changed.' With a loud snort, Prosser turned on his heel and walked into his bedroom.

She waited a few minutes before following. This was the crucial bit. She opened his bedroom door an inch. She could hear the sounds of somebody taking a shower. She nipped inside. Prosser's clothes were lying all over the floor, but the computer disc and its chain were nowhere to be found.

Terrified that she would be discovered, Sally moved over to the bathroom door which stood ajar. Inside, Prosser was humming one of his beloved marches with a complete lack of either musical or military precision.

There was the disc, hanging on the corner of the shower cubicle. If he saw her now, everything would be ruined. She reached inside and unhooked it.

Nipping back into the bedroom, she unclipped the disc from its chain. Covering her hand with a tissue she clipped Prosser's original disc, which she and Jeremy had doctored heavily, on to the chain, putting the one she had just taken from the bathroom into her pocket.

Tip-toeing back to the bathroom, Sally was horrified to hear the water being turned off. Just as she was on the point of rehanging the chain, the cubicle door swung open.

She flung the disc on to the bathroom floor, hoping Prosser would think it had fallen off. She darted back into the bedroom and rushed through it into the corridor.

There she found Lucinda waiting for her, with arms folded.

'A very interesting performance. I don't suppose you want to tell me what all that was about?'

'All what?'

'Oh, don't play the innocent with me. I saw the whole thing.'

Sally toyed with the idea of hitting Lucinda and fleeing. But that would ruin everything.

'Oh, don't worry. If it's bad news for His Majesty, I won't snitch. The bastard gave me the sack this morning. Waited until he'd given me a good going over, of course, then told me I was getting too old. No bonuses for two months.'

'I am sorry, Lucinda. Look, I wouldn't worry too much. If things work out today. . .'

But Sally had no time to explain. Ron Niblo was running up the corridor, out of breath. 'Where's the boss?' he panted.

'In there,' said Lucinda, 'taking a shower. What on earth's the matter?'

Sally shushed her as Niblo barged into the bedroom, calling out. 'Boss, the Roller's been clamped.'

'Clamped. What do you mean clamped? Where was the fucking chauffeur?'

'He was underneath the car, cleaning it. He didn't see what was going on.' Outside the door, Sally and Lucinda struggled hard to suppress their giggles as Prosser's temper frayed. Somehow he looked less ferocious, wearing nothing but the chain round his neck, dripping water on to the carpet.

'The bastards! The stinking rotten bastards. How long will it take to remove it?'

'I've sent the chauffeur off to pay the fine. But it could take a couple of hours.'

'Hours? It can't be frigging hours. I'm due at the Palace in – oh my God – in just over an hour's time and I am damned if those little

Hitlers are going to stop me using my own car. Do something, Ron. Bloody well do something!'

'What do you suggest? These things take time. I can't whip up a miracle out of thin air?'

'Thin air. That's it. You're a bloody Einstein, Ron. Where's the chopper? Here or at the Battersea heliport?'

'It's up top.'

'Right. Dig out that pillock of a pilot. Get him to put the hoist on. We'll use it to whip the car on to the roof and away from those interfering busy-bodies. Maintenance can prise the clamp off up there. Go on, don't stand here like a dummy. Scram, vamoose, scat.'

Niblo bustled out in search of the pilot. Lucinda followed him down the corridor imitating his shambling gorilla-like walk. Smiling, Sally went off to get changed.

The warning sign still hung on the door to Daniels' old office. The Major unlocked it and let himself in. The air was no better in here than anywhere else in the building. Rommel was obviously rotting nicely. Unpleasant though his use of the dog's corpse might be, surely he would have approved of this method of hitting back at his killer.

Now to business. Whatever was wrong had to be something pretty simple. The apparatus wasn't all that complicated. It was designed to be used by thick left-wing hooligans, after all.

He began to pull the mounds of paper away from the desk.

Someone wandering down the corridor outside noticed the key in the door. Taking the stern warning notice to heart, they turned and removed it, planning to drop it in at security later.

Niblo found the pilot, Biddle – known to all and sundry as Biggles – in the canteen, wading through a hearty breakfast of cholesterol and chips.

When he explained what Prosser had in mind, the pilot demanded to know how much the car weighed.

'It's just a car. How much can it weigh, for God's sake?'

'It's completely illegal, you know.'

'Just a minor traffic offence.'

'Bringing a helicopter down to street level in the middle of London without permission is more than just a minor traffic offence, mate. Still, it might be fun. I can lift a ton and a half, so we should be all right.'

271

'Well, get a move on. His Lordship will fly off the handle completely if he doesn't get to the Palace in time. I'll go and rustle up someone from Maintenance.'

Jeremy arrived at work a little before nine, trying his hardest to pretend that this was just another working day like any other. But he found it almost impossible to sit still at his desk. He couldn't stop thinking the worst, wondering whether Sally was all right, worrying whether she had had a chance to swap discs. They had pinned an awful lot on this plan working just like clockwork.

It should have worked just like clockwork. The whole gizmo was so simple. It would probably turn out to be something daft like him setting the alarm on the clock wrongly. The Major had once had terrible problems with one of those new-fangled digital alarm clocks. Never could cope with the twenty-four hour business. Bloody foreign invention. Hitler, probably. The Major was much happier with hands. Knew where you were with hands. He pulled away more paper.

Biddle was a professional. His Almighty Highness Prosser might be in a hurry, but there was no way he was going to rush through the engine start procedures.

He ran through the check-list that was by now second nature. Contact breakers in. Rotor brake off. Fuel levers shut. Fuel sufficient. Booster pump on. Biddle pressed the starter and, as the engine turned, fed in fuel to light it.

Releasing the starter at forty per cent compressor speed, he advanced the fuel lever to the flight gate and the rotor span up. With the first of the two Turbomeca Arriel 1C1 turbine engines going, he ran through the same procedure with the other. Checking that pressure, temperature and voltages were normal, he flicked on the radios and navaids. Quickly glancing about him, first to see that the roof was clear, Biddle lifted the collective, applied forward cyclic and headed out over the lip of the roof and down to the street below.

Digital? Yes, by jingo, that was it. Twenty-four hour clock and all that rubbish. He had wanted to set the thing for nine o'clock. But he should have added twelve. 09:00 wasn't right at all.

What a mug he was.

'How do I look?' asked Prosser, parading about in his morning dress.

'Like a knight of the realm about to meet his Queen.'

Sally waited for the compliment to be returned, but Prosser was too busy admiring himself.

'I've got to pop down to my office for a moment,' she said.

'I'll come down with you. I've one or two things I want to check up on.'

Hovering just above the car, Biddle signalled for Niblo to attach the hoist to the cradle slung under the helicopter.

He revved the engines up to their maximum 705 horse-power and lifted the Rolls-Royce Silver Spur a few feet off the ground, holding it there while he made sure it was hanging properly.

Only then did he begin the climb back up to the roof. It was tougher than he had expected. It was certainly a substantial car.

The Major tutted at his own stupidity. As if to confirm it, the buzzer of the alarm clock went off. It was nine o'clock exactly.

It took the Major a crucial two seconds to remember that he had not disconnected the alarm from the battery, which in turn was still connected to the exposed filament of the light bulb. If that heated up before he could get to it, it would burn a hole in the condom, the baby oil would flow out and the unstable phosphorous would be exposed to the air.

In a panic, the Major began scrabbling away at the rest of the papers. But he was too late. The phosphorous flared up, catching those papers piled around it. Within seconds, the whole mound was alight, forcing the Major back.

There was a fire distinguisher in the corridor. He pulled at the door handle, but it would not budge. In terror, he banged heavily on the door, screaming for help as the bonfire of papers behind him caught hold. He could expect no help from the sprinkler or smoke detector. He had disconnected them himself.

The Major caught sight of the helicopter struggling upwards outside BIG House. He edged around the wall, keeping clear of the fire, and tried to open the triangular window to attract attention. But he was on the twelfth floor and the windows were not designed to open.

* * *

273

'Absolutely gorgeous,' said Jeremy.

'Quite right,' said Sally. 'Anything less enthusiastic and you'd have been pushing up daisies. Do you like the hat?'

'Mmm,' murmured Jeremy, trying to kiss her.

'Not on the lips, not on the lips,' she cried. 'I've just done them. And not there either, you filthy beast. I sometimes wonder if I was wise unleashing your animal instincts. Here's the disc. The full, unexpurgated version. Prosser's now wearing the one we've edited. Let's just pray he doesn't try to use it before we set off for the Palace.'

It was as he breasted the roof that Biddle encountered problems. The weight was proving too much, bugger it!

He'd had to force the engines to their limit just to keep the helicopter climbing, ignoring the needles of the rev counter and temperature gauge as they moved well into the danger area.

Biddle had been piloting the Dauphin 2 for two years now and was familiar with every sound it made. He felt, as much as heard, the ominous whining noise coming from one of the engines.

In desperation, the Major threw a chair through the window. But the helicopter had disappeared from sight.

The draught from the hole merely fanned the flames. He could feel the heat on the back of his neck. Terrified, he looked around for somewhere to hide.

He pulled at the doors of a metal cupboard on the far side of the room from the desk. The flames were kissing the ceiling and creating a foully pungent stench as they lapped away at the polystyrene roof tiles. The Major stepped into the cupboard and pulled the doors shut, praying that it was fireproof.

It was not.

In his office Prosser struggled with the studs on the unfamiliar dress shirt. Reaching inside, he pulled out the computer disc dangling on its chain.

This was serious. If he didn't do something, he would crash. Damn Prosser and his bloody car.

There was nothing for it. It would have to go, and quickly. Bugger finesse.

If he flew low enough over the roof and released the sling above the landing zone, the car shouldn't suffer too much damage. Compensating for the sudden weight loss would be tricky, but he should be able to manage it.

Biddle brought the helicopter in fast with the wheels of the Rolls only inches off the ground. He was just about to pull the lever to let the limousine go when he saw a pair of maintenance men ambling lazily across the roof ahead of him.

With the razor-sharp reactions of the good pilot, he banked steeply to one side. But he was not quick enough to stop his hand pulling the release lever. He struggled to control the helicopter as the car fell away, succeeding through skill and experience in righting it.

The designers at the famous Crewe factory had intended the Rolls-Royce Silver Spur to be the sleekest and most graceful motor car of its kind in the world. But no car looks at its best crashing through a glass roof, particularly if just beneath that roof is a swimming pool containing 25,000 gallons of water.

It was Archimedes who proved that when he got into his bath, the same volume of water got out. However, Archimedes was not dropped into his bath from a great height by a helicopter. The two-and-a-half tons of metal and machinery slammed into the middle of the pool, displacing, it was reckoned afterwards, around two and a half thousand gallons of heavily chlorinated water.

Having played around with Archimedes' Principle, the water which had escaped from the pool, over ten tons of it, now demonstrated the truth of Newton's Law of Gravity.

One moment a perfectly dry Sir Alexander Charles Prosser was sitting at the desk in his office. The next he was thrown from his chair by the torrent and swept, up to his neck in water, past one of Canaletto's finest Venetian scenes.

The water did not stop there. It found its way through to the twelfth floor. Unseen by the Major in his baking hot cupboard, it flooded through the ceiling of Daniels' former office and extinguished the inferno blazing there.

By the time it had reached the eleventh floor, the water had dwindled to the size of a small, but vertical, river. It was a mere stream at the tenth floor, a brook at the ninth and a trickle at the eighth. The few drops that came through the ceilings of one or two offices on the seventh floor were hardly worth putting up an umbrella for.

The water's effects were felt all over the building. Lights fused, computers exploded, the air conditioning flooded – washing away the remains of poor Rommel – and all the lifts stopped dead.

'Look on the bright side,' said Sally cheerfully as she, Prosser, Lucinda and Niblo stood on the side of the depleted swimming pool, staring at the bright yellow Rolls bobbing on the surface. 'If it hadn't been for the water, the car would have gone straight through and crushed you.' She and Lucinda chuckled. Prosser didn't seem to find it so amusing.

'Thank you for that, Sally. That makes everything all right, I suppose. I'm due at Buckingham Palace in less than three-quarters of an hour to receive my knighthood from the Queen, I'm soaking wet and I don't have any transport.'

'What has happened to your famous sense of humour?' asked Sally. 'Transport's no problem. We can go in my car. Lucinda and I will get your clothes dry if Mr Niblo would be so good as to try to round up as many heaters as he can. I've got a hair dryer in my bag. It shouldn't take too long.'

The temperature in the Major's cupboard had definitely fallen. Perhaps the sprinklers had worked after all.

He pushed on the door, but it would not give. For the second time in a week, he was locked in.

He hammered on the door but, if anybody heard him, they were dissuaded from coming to his assistance by the draconian warning notice hanging on the office door.

'You didn't tell me you had a Mini,' said a subdued Prosser.

'You didn't ask.'

'What's it going to look like? A man of my standing arriving at Buckingham Palace in a Mini. I am also sitting in a puddle.'

'What a shame,' said Sally, with conspicuous lack of sympathy.

'I still can't understand why they wouldn't let us land the helicopter in the grounds. We'd be there by now.'

'Strange that. Very unfriendly of them.'

'Sally?' said Prosser, as they drove around Trafalgar Square. 'I'm feeling terribly horny. Couldn't we pull over somewhere?'

'What on earth would the Queen think?'

'What will she think if I stand before her with a throbbing erection?'

She sneezed violently as she felt Prosser's stubby hand on her thigh.

'Probably drop the sword,' said Sally slapping it away as she changed gears, 'thus ending all our problems.'

'It's not a laughing matter,' said Prosser, as the Mini turned into the Mall and joined the line of cars queueing to enter the gates of Buckingham Palace.

'An amazing building,' he continued, slumped in his seat so that no one would recognise him. 'What a location. The Royal Family are supposed to hate it. It would make a wonderful hotel. You could charge the highest prices in London, make a fortune.'

'Perhaps you should mention it to Her Majesty when you're being dubbed? Put in an offer on the spot.'

'I don't know that that would be appropriate,' he said pompously. 'There's a time and a place, you know.'

His musings were interrupted by the intrusion of a policeman's head through the open window. Prosser pulled out the soggy letter from the Secretary of the Central Chancery of the Orders of Knighthood, giving them permission to park in the inner quadrangle. Sally was made to open the boot while mirrors were wheeled under the car.

Only then were they allowed to drive through the arch and into the quadrangle.

Standing in St James's Park, Jeremy and Detective Constable Bosworth watched the Mini passing through the gates.

'You do realise that if it doesn't go strictly according to plan,' said Jeremy, 'all the national papers will be sent the full details.'

'You've made that abundantly clear. Do you have the stuff with you?'

Jeremy reached into his briefcase and pulled out a bulky envelope. 'The printout of everything that's on the disc. The computer disc itself you'll find around his neck. The passwords for it are in the envelope.'

DC Bosworth took it and ripped it open. 'Don't mind if I check, do you?' He glanced through the first page of computer paper. 'Bloody hell, if you'll pardon my French. You weren't joking, were you?'

He reached into his pocket and withdrew a walkie-talkie. 'Pixie, this is Dixie. Over.'

'Reading you, Pixie.'

'Jinx is on his way. Repeat. Jinx is on his way.'

'You don't think the suit has shrunk, do you?' asked Prosser, as they got out of the Mini.

The sleeves of the jacket were at least an inch shorter than before and the trousers hung almost two inches above the shoes. 'Hardly at all,' said Sally. 'You look quite staggering. All eyes will be on you, I'm certain of that.' All noses as well, she thought, with that powerful whiff of chlorine hanging over him.

They walked through the Grand Entrance on the far side of the Quadrangle, hidden from the view of the public on the other side of the Palace gates, and across the red carpet in the Grand Hall. Sally marvelled at the gorgeous Carrara marble columns as they climbed up the Grand Staircase, troopers from the Household Cavalry standing to attention on each side.

Prosser, for his part, was wondering whether the soldiers and footmen could be thrown in as part of any deal to turn the place into a hotel.

The Ballroom was magnificent. The ceiling, with its pink chandeliers, stretched out far above their heads. The massive room itself was all cream and gold. At the far end, under a canopy, were two thrones standing on a dais.

Above them a band in the gallery tinkered about with some Gershwin melodies.

The Americans would go just wild for this sort of tradition and ceremony, thought Prosser, as he was separated from Sally and instructed on how to behave when he was summoned before the Queen.

Just before eleven o'clock five Yeomen of the Guard, in almost identical dress to the Beefeaters of the Tower of London, marched into the ballroom and took up position behind the throne. They were supposed to be the monarch's bodyguard. In their scarlet Tudor tunics, with red, white and blue ribbons around their hats, red and white rosettes on their shoes, sporting garters and white ruffs around their necks and carrying pikes, their deterrent effect was presumably to render any would-be assassin helpless with laughter. These were the brilliant guys, recalled Prosser, who searched the cellars of the Houses of Parliament each year on the eve of the State Opening looking for gunpowder with open paraffin lamps.

Everyone stood up as the drumroll announced the National Anthem and the arrival of the Queen. As the music drew to a close, the pings of Prosser's two wristwatches chiming the hour could clearly be heard throughout the Ballroom.

The ceremony began, with Her Majesty pinning on gongs, shaking hands and murmuring a few words before the next person was wheeled in front of her. She got through the punters at the rate of two a minute, Prosser noticed approvingly. A time and motion man would find no flies on her.

Prosser could see Fatty Fenwick of Fast and Easy Furnishing a few rows in front of him. How on earth had he qualified for a knighthood? All that poncey charity work he did, Prosser supposed. Bloody cheek! It was no better than buying a knighthood. Debased the whole system.

He watched Fenwick kneel on the red stool. The Queen brought the sword down on each shoulder. Fenwick stood up – none of that 'Arise, Sir Fatty' nonsense like in the films – and shook hands with her before stepping backwards. Ha! The man moved with all the grace and agility of a dead haddock.

In his mind's eye, Prosser ran over the coming moment again and again as it came closer to his turn. In his mind's eye, he could practically feel the sword touching him. . .

Prosser felt a pressure on his shoulder. He turned in irritation to find a footman in black tailcoat, trousers and red waistcoat, standing at his side.

'Mr Prosser?' he asked quietly.

'Sir Alexander,' corrected Prosser, whispering.

'Something has come up unexpectedly, Sir. I wonder if you could please accompany me?'

'But what about the . . .'

'Don't worry, Sir. There's plenty of time.'

Prosser, perplexed, followed the footman out of the Ballroom. Behind him the Lord Chamberlain whispered something near Her Majesty's ear. Sally thought she saw the Queen raise a quizzical eyebrow and wrinkle her nose, as if she had detected a bad smell.

The Lord Chamberlain read out the next name on the list and Her Majesty was back to pinning on medals, shaking hands, smiling and thanking people too dumfounded to do anything but gape.

'Now, what is all this?' blustered Prosser as soon as they were out of the Ballroom.

'Alexander Charles Prosser?'

Prosser turned. 'Yes. What's going on? I must get back inside as soon as possible.'

'Alexander Charles Prosser, my name is Detective Inspector Rowan. I am arresting you on suspicion of offences against the Companies Act. You are not obliged to say anything unless you wish to do so but what you say may be put in writing and may be given in evidence.'

Prosser sighed deeply. 'I don't suppose there's the slightest chance that you're from the Royal Society for the Protection of Birds?'

* * * 32 * * *

SALLY, her Palace wear now abandoned in favour of business attire, swept into the boardroom of British Industrial Group.

The whole board was there, seated in their allotted places: Collingwood, Armstrong, Eldon and Bourne, Akenside, Stowell and Brand. Lucinda, ready to take notes, winked surreptitiously at Sally as she took Prosser's place at the head of the table, to the consternation of the assembled directors.

She held up her hand to still their chattering. 'Gentlemen, I have to tell you that *Mr* Prosser will not be attending this board meeting. In fact, he does not even know that it is taking place. He is at this moment, as they say in all the best B-pictures, helping police with their enquiries.'

In place of the hubbub she had anticipated, there was absolute silence as the seven men around the table digested the news and tried to assess what it might mean for them.

'Might one ask the nature of these enquiries?' ventured one.

'Certainly, Mr Akenside. The Police believe they have evidence that Mr Prosser was involved in insider dealing on a massive scale stretching back over ten years.'

'Doesn't surprise me in the least. The man is a bounder, rotten to the core.' There was a murmur of approval round the table as the serfs scented the first sweet whiff of liberty.

'I am sure,' said Sally pointedly, 'that most of us have at least one skeleton in our closet.'

Akenside harrumphed and looked down at the table.

'The question is,' said Sally, 'what is to happen now? It can't be long before news of the arrest gets out.'

Eldon piped up: 'Ought to have a new chief executive in place before it happens. Show positive action.' It was the first time Sally could recall him speaking at a board meeting.

281

'Yes, but who?' asked Stowell.

'It ought to be Akenside,' said Eldon, the newfound deliverance from Prosser's tyranny rushing to his head. 'If any of us stood up to the man, he did.' There were grunts of agreement from each of the directors except Brand, who was having trouble with his hearing aid.

It was Jeremy's task to keep Roach occupied. As finance director and the person closest to Prosser, there was always a risk that he could manoeuvre himself into the driving seat if he got to hear of the board meeting going on just yards away.

It could be tricky. Prosser and Roach had worked together for years.

'Come in, my boy, come in,' said an exuberant Roach. 'Have a cigar,' he said, thrusting a box in front of Jeremy.

'No, thank you. I didn't exactly enjoy the last one, if you recall.' Jeremy sat down. 'You seem in a very good mood.'

'I am. I am. My wife has just rung. She is leaving me. She's running off with her tennis coach.'

'Oh, I am sorry.'

'I'm not. It's absolutely wonderful news. She's even taken those bloody precocious little children with her.' Roach stood up and began taking the photographs from the myriad of frames scattered around his office. He turned on the shredder and began feeding them in, one by one, giggling as he did so. 'I can't tell you the feeling of freedom this has given me. Don't ever get married, Jeremy.'

'Er, no, I won't. Look, I'm afraid I've got some bad news . . .'

'You know,' said Roach, appearing not to hear Jeremy as he watched a picture of Desirée, Jocasta and Jemima disintegrating into hundreds of little pieces, 'it only needs one other thing to make my happiness complete.'

'. . . I'm not quite sure how to tell you this, but Mr Prosser has been arrested.'

Roach's mouth dropped open. Then it closed and turned up at the sides, engulfing the finance director's entire face in one enormous smile. 'You don't mean it?'

'I'm afraid so. At the investiture ceremony.'

'Before he got knighted?'

Jeremy nodded.

Roach was lost in thought for a moment. 'Isn't the world a wonderful place, Jeremy?' he said dreamily. 'Are you sure you won't have a cigar?'

Exhausted after his flight from Africa, the house martin finally reached BIG House. To his surprise, last year's nest was still intact. A little bit of touching up was all it needed.

Before settling in, he decided to explore a little, just in case that bloody big bird was still around. But he was also curious to get another close-up glimpse of those hilarious humans.

Sally had to talk loudly to make herself heard. 'With his long and varied experience, Mr Akenside would be an invaluable chairman. But surely the pressures on his diary would make it impossible for him to carry out such exacting duties?'

'Oh, I don't know,' said Akenside, puffing himself up.

'Who did *you* have in mind?' asked Stowell of Sally.

'What about Jeremy Seaman?' she suggested quietly.

The response was unanimous, although their reasons were varied.

'Don't approve of what he did. Not at all,' blustered Akenside.

'Good God. Far too young,' said Bourne.

'No experience,' wailed Stowell.

'Would look like we were bowing to the wishes of the goddam press,' declared Eldon.

'When did you last see a chairman with red hair?' asked Armstrong.

'What did she say?' asked Brand, his hand cupped to his ear.

Sally nodded to Lucinda who stood up and placed a folder marked "Private and Confidential" in front of each director.

'I think before you make your decision, you ought to have a look at these, gentlemen. They were discovered amongst Mr Prosser's papers, papers which the Police may well wish to examine in their investigations.'

Silence descended on the room as each director opened the file containing the information Prosser had collected on their past misdemeanours. As they read, one or other glanced up from time to time and, catching another's guilty eye, would hurriedly look away. A couple cupped their hands around their folders, like schoolboys frightened their neighbours might cheat.

'Having given it a little thought, I am not sure I could find the time to take on such a senior post,' said Akenside, with ponderous gravity. 'Perhaps this Seaman chap would be the right man for the job. Obviously bursting with good ideas. Not many would have thought of that trick with Big Ben.'

'Young blood,' suggested Bourne.

'Show we mean to make a fresh start,' said Stowell.

'Very popular with the public and shareholders,' chipped in Eldon.

'Make a difference having a chairman with red hair,' reasoned Armstrong.

'I'm not sure I'm capable of donating semen at my age,' said Brand.

'So,' said Sally, 'I take it that it's unanimous, then? Jeremy Seaman is to be the new chairman of British Industrial Group and joint chief executive.'

'Joint?' queried Collingwood. 'Jointly with whom?'

Sally looked directly into his eyes, turning on the full force of her sweet, conquering smile.

'Right. Yes. Absolutely,' said Collingwood, raising his hand. Anything to stop that file falling into the wrong hands. 'I'm in favour.'

One by one, the others' hands went up, even Brand's, although in truth that was because he wanted to be excused.

Sally stood. 'I'd better find your new chairman and introduce him to you, gentlemen. He has some very interesting ideas to put to you. Perhaps you'd like to take those folders home. I can't possibly see how their contents could be relevant to the Police enquiries. Once the appointments have been announced to the Stock Exchange, all copies will be destroyed.'

'The triangular tin idea sounds as if it is definitely along the right tack,' said Roach. 'But there's something screwy about your figures. According to your calculations, you're packing 660 square inches of cans into a floor space of just 400 square inches.'

'No. You must be reading my notes wrongly,' protested Jeremy. 'Let's start from basic principles. The area of a triangle is . . .'

Sally poked her head around the door. 'I wonder if I might borrow Mr Seaman for a moment.'

She put her arm through his and led Jeremy along the corridor. 'Roach seems very keen on my ideas,' said Jeremy breathlessly. 'I've had another good one. You know the problem we've been having with corporate identity, nobody knowing that the different companies within the group belong to us. How about if we put, after the name of each of them the slogan, "It's a BIG business"? Neat don't you think? It's a play on words,' he added helpfully.

Sally ushered him into Prosser's office. The carpet squished and squelched as they walked into the room which only that morning had played host to 2,500 gallons of water from the swimming pool. It looked as though a minor explosion had gone off.

'Well, you can try it out soon enough. You're the new chairman and joint chief executive of British Industrial Group.'

'Wow,' was Jeremy's loquacious response. He wandered slowly round the room, touching everything as he went, the desk, the monitors, the pictures, the sofa, the table, the heads of Napoleon, Alexander and Churchill. 'I can hardly believe it. This, my office . . . Hang on a second. *Joint* chief executive. What went wrong? Jointly with whom?'

Sally stood in front of him, her hands on her hips, looking straight into his eyes. 'You don't honestly think I'd leave a poor, weak, defenceless man like you on your own in here, do you? You can have that side of the room. I'll have this. Of course, a few things are going to change. Some of the extravagant perks, such as the helicopter and the Roller, will have to go. A few of those pictures will have to be sold to pay for the damage. And no more dishy personal assistants. From now on, I'm to be the only good-looker in this office. And I don't want any of your bright ideas going to your head, either. All important decisions will be joint, and I mean joint. Every executive move must be made through me. Understand? No more unchecked managerial excesses.'

'I see. I'm to be the boss on the notepaper, but you're to be the boss in reality. I've got the picture. Pretty much like being married.'

'Oh, Jeremy,' said Sally, flinging her arms around his neck and kissing him. 'I thought you'd never ask.'

'Eh? I didn't mean . . . oh well, why not?'

'That's what I like about you. So romantic.'

'Do you ever get the feeling that you aren't the master of your own destiny?' asked Jeremy.

'Never,' she said firmly.

'Sally?' asked Jeremy when he surfaced for breath a couple of minutes later. 'Would a minor personnel matter have to be a joint decision?'

'No, I don't suppose so. Why?'

'In that case, perhaps you'll excuse me. As my first act as chairman and chief executive. . . as chairman and *joint* chief executive of British Industrial Group, I am going to grab hold of Nettle and give him his marching orders.'

'I do hope you're not going to turn out like Prosser, forever sacking people who irritate you. What happened to those all important ethics of yours?'

'I've learnt a lot from this whole affair,' said Jeremy, turning back to face his fiancée as he reached the door. 'As far as I am concerned, from now on ethics is just the county next to Hertfordshire.'

He ducked just in time. A bust of Winston Churchill slammed into the wall beside his head, shattering into a thousand pieces.

It was not long afterwards that the house martin landed on the window ledge outside Prosser's former office and looked through the window at the two people inside.

Huh! Yet another of those worms, he thought to himself disgustedly, as he viewed the scene in front of him.

Did humans never think of anything but food?